Seattle Lost Lovers #1

RAINY DAY

Rescue

JOSIE MALONE

Rainy Day Rescue is dedicated to my sister, Tamera who helped with the real-estate background for this series. Any mistakes are mine.

Chapter One

November 2022

The crash of thunder drowned out the classic rock station. Lightning flashed. High winds howled and the powerlines swayed. Torrential rain pounded the pavement. The drive from the Washington Coast to her Magnolia area penthouse in Seattle had been treacherous, making the typical four-hour trip take twice as long. Even in western Washington state, which was famous for its rainfall, this storm called an 'atmospheric river' was one for the record books. The news anchor on the radio warned flooding and power outages might last for days.

Lights from the apartment house windows greeted her. Thankfully, her building still had electricity. Claire Rocklin breathed a sigh of relief as she guided her Lincoln Navigator through one last huge puddle before pulling into the safety and security of the underground garage. Bang!

Outside, another electrical transformer burst into a shower of white and blue light. She shuddered.

Pulling into the reserved parking space, she grimaced when she noticed the distinctive, dark blue, late-model Hummer in the spot next to hers. It belonged to her business partner, Tony Baldusi. During her time away, she'd ignored his barrage of texts and voicemails. When she heard about a winter storm to end all storms, she opted to speak directly to their office managers, instructing them to close the real estate brokerages and send everyone home.

Closing her eyes, she took a moment to center herself before wearily unloading the SUV. Somehow, she — suitcase, laptop bag, briefcase, and the pizza she'd picked up on her last potty stop at her favorite Italian restaurant made it to the elevator. She'd sold one of her houses on the Washington Coast for an optimum price, reason for any realtor to celebrate. She'd planned on a quiet evening at home so she could focus on the paperwork, although if her twin brother Connor hadn't been pulling extra shifts at the cop shop, she might have made an exception for him.

She'd spent the past three days doing his ex-girlfriend's emotional laundry while the younger woman updated Claire's apartment. Fancy Flannagan was a total sweetheart who didn't deserve the cavalier treatment Connor had apparently handed out. He didn't have any business acting like a total slut-puppy. Clearly, they needed to have another of their *conversations* about his behavior.

Riding up in the elevator, Claire caught a glimpse of herself in the mirrored wall. Jeans, a white sweater, and low-heeled boots. At least she didn't look as haggard as she felt even if her shoulder-length black hair was a tangled mess. A heavy layer of makeup hid the dark circles under her eyes.

She'd need all her skills at subterfuge to avoid tipping her hand since she didn't want Tony to know what she'd been doing. Once on the sixth floor, she glanced up and down the hall, but he was nowhere in sight. Thankful for the reprieve, her thoughts turned to the bottle of wine chilling in the special fridge in her chef's kitchen. Once inside, she'd pour herself a glass or three, warm up her pizza and turn on the TV to stream one of her favorite crime dramas. And under no circumstances would she answer the door!

Rude? Maybe. But she didn't have the bandwidth to deal with Tony or his habit of ignoring boundaries tonight. Most of her real estate properties were hers alone, even if he was under the misapprehension that his investment in her company granted him special personal and professional rights.

Not hardly, she thought. As she'd said more than once, if she intended to be controlled, she'd have come with a remote.

Her two-bedroom apartment took up half the top floor while Connor's used the rest. She slid the key into the lock and stepped into the stark white foyer, towing her suitcase into the hall, and closing the door behind her. Unexpected light from the living room spilled through the arched doorway and she frowned.

Hadn't she decided it was enough to leave on the overhead hallway and kitchen lights? Did she forget to turn off the oversized floor lamps three days ago when they left town? Had Fancy?

Pizza box in hand, Claire entered the front room. And froze. A tall, brown-haired man stood watching her. Behind him the storm raged, captured in the picture windows like a movie. In the gray pinstriped suit that matched his eyes, he still reminded her of the combat soldier who marched back into her life three years before when he was thirty-six, saying he'd taken early retirement from the U.S. Army. He was home to stay and wanted to see *his* office.

His face had never been handsome. It was too weathered, too rawboned, each harsh plane fitting into the other. The shadow of dark beard stubble on his strong jaw made his rugged features even more attractive, not that she'd tell him so. Ignoring the silver threads in his dark brown hair, he kept it short in what he referred to as a 'high and tight' style similar to the way he wore it when he was in uniform.

For a moment, she wished she wore one of her favorite pairs of stilettos, so they'd be eye-level, rather than giving him those extra three inches over her. At five feet, eight, she wasn't a short woman, but at six feet, two, he wasn't as big as some of the men she'd dated in the past. He could be intimidating, but he'd never scared her. How had he managed to enter the apartment? Well...she wasn't about to give him the satisfaction of asking if he used his military training to break in or swiped her brother's key.

Placing the pizza carton on the tiled vintage table, she paused to remove her boots so she wouldn't track dirt on the new, white wall-to-wall carpet. "Hello, Tony. Did you get lost on the way home?"

"Did you get lost on the way to work?" He strode toward her. "Where the hell have you been?"

Claire shrugged out of her classic, gold bomber jacket and crossed to the black recliner, dropping the leather coat on the seat. "I told you I had plans."

"And I said we had too many closings on the calendar for you to run off to Mexico for two weeks."

She didn't bother to answer. She didn't do holidays, so she'd already booked tickets to go to Cancun at Thanksgiving for the holiday weekend, not two weeks. That happened at Christmas.

His tone took on an edge. "I'm waiting, Claire."

"I guess you didn't check your messages. I told you I needed a mini-vacay." She looked out the window at the storm before she closed the white drapes. Another flash of lightning. Another transformer exploded in a shower of blue and white sparks. And another section of the city went dark. She shivered, feeling her anxiety mount.

Turning, Claire faced him again. She'd allow him to distract her from the weather which set her nerves on edge. "If you bothered to check in with the office managers, they could have shared my itinerary."

"Would they have been able to tell me where the Designated Broker was hiding? Nobody at the Seattle realty can do your job, Claire. Did you actually expect those ten associates to stop selling houses for three days? They needed you to review their sales contracts before those go to the title company as you well know."

"I told you when you joined us that I run the Seattle brokerage, but I'm not going to be more than the head broker for the satellite offices. Step up, Tony. You're licensed. There's no reason you can't approve any potential sales contracts."

"Bullshit. I'm already up to my ass in alligators and I don't have time to drain the swamp. You draw the most we can afford in addition to your commissions. It means you make more than the brokers in the Everett, Eastside and Lake Maynard offices." His voice lowered. "You do less than half the work. Step up. You already know what needs to be done."

"And Seattle still makes more money than the rest of them. Without it, we'll never recover after the pandemic. If you kicked ass on the Eastside associates, they'd do better. All those tech employees living in Bellevue and Issaquah want multi-million-dollar homes. But Perry can't handle that much pressure. He should have thought of that before he convinced *you* he could be Designated Broker when Ryan left."

"Perry did fine until you messed with his head." Tony scowled, narrowing his steel gray eyes. "You know better than to crap where you eat. After you finished toying with Ryan, he couldn't run fast enough to Eastern Washington. Are you trying to bankrupt us? Or just drive me crazy?"

Claire swept him with a dispassionate gaze, telling herself she was only interested in learning how riled up she could make him. It was a lie. Even though he'd just turned thirty-nine, he was still extremely hot. It was impossible not to notice how his jacket emphasized his broad shoulders and muscular arms. Narrow hips and long legs – she shook her head. *Focus,* she told herself sternly. *Quit leering and pretend you're listening to his temper tantrum.*

She tilted her head to one side and decided to play her hole card. They both knew she wasn't serious, but it generally worked as a temporary truce. "You can always buy me out and I'll walk away."

"We both know that will never happen. We have a non-compete clause, remember? You can't work anywhere else in Washington State and I'm not going anywhere either." He took a step closer. "What's the game, Claire?"

"So, what if I enjoy dating a lot of men, Tony? They amuse me. Perry chased me for two months before I went out with him. I dumped him weeks ago. I'm tired of his drama."

"Right. And if I believe that, you'll sell me a bridge in Arizona." He folded his arms, his jaw tightening. "Do you know how many calls I've answered from your *boys* in the last couple of days?"

Rainy Day Rescue

Claire adopted a cool tone. "If they actually were important, one of the receptionists would have contacted me."

"Ryan left messages and wants you to call him in Spokane. Perry whined. Even Mike Flannagan wants to talk to you and he's one of our competitors. What's that about?"

"Poor baby," Claire cooed. "Do what I do. Ignore them."

"You've been engaged three times since last August," Tony continued. "I know because I've talked to all three of the poor slobs this past week."

Shaking her head, Claire gaped at him. "Now, that's sheer bullshit! I'm never getting married. *And you know why!*"

Chapter Two

Tony Baldusi glared at his once upon a time step-sister. Okay, she'd only been that when he was nine and she was five. Their parents divorced two years later, because his mother wouldn't tolerate a serial cheater like Claire's dad, Lee Rocklin. And it was the end of their blended family. Almost thirty years later, she still played the part of a spoiled princess to irritate him.

All right, time to take a giant breather.

He wouldn't get anywhere chewing her out as if she were a recalcitrant private who couldn't and wouldn't follow his orders. She'd continue being adversarial and he'd end up acting like the macho jackass she often called him.

Her white sweater clung in all the right places and so did the tight-fitting jeans glued to her slender waist, rounded hips, sassy backside, and seemingly endless legs. As always, her makeup was perfect, emphasizing the deep blue eyes, dark lashes, high cheekbones. For once her black hair was a tangled, tousled mess. It reminded him of when she was a kid who preferred climbing trees and riding her bike to hanging out at a shopping mall.

He glanced around the room. She'd said she arranged for the apartment to be redecorated, but he hadn't anticipated the black and white décor with a few red accents. That included the framed photographs arranged on an antique plant stand in one corner of the room. Some of him growing up, later in various military uniforms, her twin brother in his dress blues as an Army lieutenant, old ones of their mother holding them as babies, then as toddlers, and Claire's grandparents. Since she went no-contact with her father several years before, of course there weren't any of him and none of her stepmother or step-siblings. Claire never had liked indoor greenery. A large flatscreen hung above the black fireplace mantel. A large white vase filled with artificial sunflowers sat in the middle of the hearth, so she obviously intended to keep the fireplace as a decoration.

"What did you do with the *real* furniture?" Tony eyed her again. "I preferred the country look you had before."

"It got boring, and Fancy needed a pick-me-up after Connor dumped her for the latest flavor of the month." Claire crossed to the catch-all table by the entry, picked up the pizza box. "Come on. I'll let you open a bottle of wine and bitch some more."

"Why did they split up? He told me she was a one-of-a-kind woman."

"How do I know?" Claire tossed her head. "Next time I see him, I'll tell him not to follow in Lee's footsteps. We don't need more pond scum in the world."

Tony felt sudden amusement replace his initial irritation. She was the first to admit she had issues with her immediate family, and he didn't blame her. Claire's mother died when the twins were barely three and their dad remarried right away. The marriage didn't last. He'd married four more times in the next nine years until he ended up with his latest wife, Barbara, who managed to stick around for more than twenty-two years. The last thing she wanted was to raise his children. She barely had time for her own.

She sent Connor off to military school when he was twelve and Claire ran away to live with her maternal grandparents. They passed in a car accident while she was a senior in high school, leaving her everything they owned. She was set for life, but they always encouraged her to work for what she wanted, and Claire definitely did. He'd always admired her work ethic. If he hadn't, he'd have stayed in touch over the years, but he wouldn't have invested the money he earned in her business.

He followed her from the living-room down the hall with its black and white tiled floor. They passed what would have been a dining room for most people, but Claire used the room as a study. More photographs were arranged on the white walls, not of family, but of their five real estate offices and the first houses she'd sold in Rocklin, Washington. The kitchen was all white and black too—white walls, checked subway tiles, black appliances and a black table surrounded by four black chairs that looked surprisingly comfortable.

He shook his head. "Wow, kid. When does the coven arrive?"

She laughed. "I'm the head witch except I spell it with a 'B' and not until the full moon."

"Well don't forget to call me to watch if you gals do *magick* in the buff."

"In your dreams." She pulled a baking sheet out of a cupboard and proceeded to tuck the large combination pizza in one of the ovens to warm. She went to the windows and closed the blinds, pausing long enough to watch the next lightning strike hit another transformer. She opened the wine cabinet, checked vintages, and drew out a bottle of red wine.

"I prefer beer."

"Then, get one from the fridge. I don't wait on grown men."

"Watch it, kid. I told all three of your wanta-be ex-fiancés to bug off, that I was the current man in your life, and I don't share."

"And they believed you? Well, I wasn't dating them for their brains." She opened a cupboard and removed two white stoneware plates, putting them on the table along with napkins and silverware. She swung around and slowly scanned him, blue eyes mocking. "Let's see how you measure up, big bro."

"Better than any of those *boys* you've been dating." He stalked toward her, snagged the pointed chin between his thumb and first finger. "I'm not your brother! We're partners, remember?"

"Only in business, not in private."

"I'm changing that rule too." He lowered his head, his mouth a breath away from hers. "It's time we grew up, Claire. After listening to those whiners, I'm not waiting on the sidelines any longer."

"Want to bet?" She narrowed her eyes but didn't pull free. "I'm not dating you, Anthony Marco Baldusi."

"Good. I didn't have dating in mind. We've known each other too long." He brushed his lips over hers in a light, tasting kiss. "Pay attention. If you prefer, we'll take a fast trip to Vegas or Coeur d'Alene, Idaho and get married."

———

Wow, he was a temptation.

She pulled free. "Sorry, Tony. I'm not wrecking a perfect professional partnership by having a personal relationship with you. It'd take forever to find someone else to do everything you do so well. I don't want to handle advertisements, hiring staff, teaching new associates, training the existing ones, arranging security classes for them, and the promotion of our business. Now, get your beer and let's have dinner."

"I'm serious, Claire."

"So am I. You're worth more to me with your clothes on." The buzzer sounded and she went to remove the pizza from the oven. "Harassing you is too much fun, and the company is turning a larger profit now that you're home to help. I can't afford to lose you."

"I appreciate the honesty." He chuckled and went to the fridge. "Do you have any Parmesan cheese?"

"Damned if I know." Using a set of potholders, she eased the hot pizza out of the oven and carried it over to the table. "If you find some, I do."

"What was this before it died?" Tony demanded.

Claire looked over her shoulder at the moldy green object in his hand. "How should I know? If you want that instead of supreme pizza from Petrocelli's, help yourself."

The mysterious object landed in the garbage along with a box of sunken, black-spotted tomatoes and a collapsed cucumber. "I don't believe this, Claire."

"Normally, I have a cleaning service, but Mrs. Nayaka went on vacation three weeks ago. She'll be back soon. Do what I do. Leave the messes for her."

"How can you afford a service with the pittance you draw?"

"It's difficult, but somehow I manage."

"You probably subsidize the wages from your savings."

"Wash up and stop your belly-aching." Claire didn't tell him the East Indian woman owned the cleaning company that looked after the twelve apartments in the building. Most of the employees were related to her and took very good care of the senior tenants. Duties ranged from daily housework to bringing in groceries to driving people to do errands. As a bonus, one of them would zip through Claire's apartment and give it the proverbial lick and a promise. It didn't take much because Claire lived alone and usually spent most of her time at one of the brokerages.

The caregivers had really stepped up during the pandemic to the point where all the tenants survived despite being in a high-risk group and Claire was still over-whelmingly grateful. When Mrs. Nayaka's team wanted to go to their first family reunion in three years, Claire made it happen. As an early holiday bonus, she provided the round-trip airline tickets for the trip to California and passes to Disneyland.

Tony wiped out the refrigerator with a damp paper towel, tossed it and washed his hands before bringing over his favorite shredded cheese, a bottle of imported beer and her glass of wine. "I don't know why you're such a fasci-nating woman, Claire Erica Rocklin, but I'm not living without you."

She smiled and drew out a chair. "You don't have to, Tony." She clinked her glass against the beer bottle. "Part-ners, forever."

"You got it, sweetheart."

In spite of the earlier tension between them and their squabbling, the meal was peaceful. Claire ignored the rain pounding on the balcony and slashing against the windows while he reviewed the various pending deals and his solu-tions to personnel issues. In turn, she updated him on her latest sales. This last one in Ocean Shores would provide a large commission even after she divided it with the realty. It meant she could put more money aside for the renovations of the dilapidated apartment house she'd just bought.

She deliberately refused to discuss the trip she'd made to Grays Harbor County and the business that took her out of town for three days. He helped her tidy the kitchen after they finished eating. She escorted him to the front door. "You'll be at the Everett office tomorrow, so I'll see you on Monday."

"You usually work weekends, but do you want to take a break on Sunday? Come with me to Rocklin and have dinner at Mom's. She always asks about you. We could discuss which places to include on the sales preview tour next week."

"Not my thing, Tony. I love your mother. She's amazing. Why not invite her to the big city and then I'll join you?"

"Because she feels about Seattle like you feel about Rocklin." He chuckled. "Why are the women in my life so stubborn?"

"Just lucky I guess."

Suddenly, she heard a loud bang. The lights went out! Claire screamed.

A moment later, he pulled her into his arms. She felt the warmth of his strong body against hers.

"Take it easy." His deep voice held a note of tenderness that soothed her jangled nerves. "It's all right. I'm here."

She trembled. Tremors of terror shook her. It felt like an eternity before she managed to speak. "I'm okay. Let go of me."

He kissed her forehead. "Not yet, babe."

"You should leave before the storm gets worse." She

might be grateful he continued to hold and rock her against him, but she wasn't ready to confess that. *Not to him!*

"I'll stay until the power's on again. You may need me."

"I don't need anyone. Never have, never will." She pretended not to notice when he smoothed her hair and didn't admit she appreciated the comfort of his touch. "Why don't you go home?"

"I have a higher priority. I'm waiting until you admit you really do need me."

Chapter Three

If he'd been asked before tonight, Tony would have sworn Claire Rocklin wasn't afraid of anyone or anything and nothing she did could surprise him. Yet the frightened woman shaking in his arms had done both. What happened to her? He remembered thinking she'd be afraid of the fierce electrical storms around Rocklin when she was a little girl. She'd quickly corrected that assumption. She told him to comfort her five-year-old twin brother. She wanted to watch the lightning bolts strike the mountain peaks near their home without interruption and definitely without entertaining two, smelly icky boys.

"Where's your flashlight?" Tony held her tighter. "Or candles?"

"Why would I have candles?" Claire demanded. "I live in a real city, not a small town where the power's out for days on end."

"A flashlight?" Tony stroked her hair. "You must have one. How else do you inspect basements or dark closets or garages or outbuildings when you're listing properties?"

"I keep my flashlight in the car where it belongs."

"What about candles? You've got to have those when you serve a romantic dinner."

Claire sniffed. "There's nothing romantic about the smell of burning wax and not being able to see your food."

Tony grinned appreciatively. When he couldn't see the condescension on her lovely features, it was easier to keep his sense of humor intact. He was able to imagine laughing blue eyes and a warm smile that curved her mouth which was a shade too wide for pure beauty. "Since you're not prepared for this emergency, let's go visit Connor's place."

"How? I don't have a key to his apartment."

"I do. I stopped in to get the key to your place earlier." Tony wrapped an arm around her slender waist and guided her toward the door. He paused long enough to pull out his cell phone and click on the flashlight app. Granted, the black and white color scheme did make it easier to see where they were going. "Why does Connor have one?"

"He claims it's the cop in him and he likes to check my apartment if I'm out of town." She shrugged. "And he prefers my state-of-the-art kitchen to his spartan one. I don't cook. It's a waste of time."

Tony tugged gently on a strand of black hair that teased his arm. "Is this the girl who packed picnic lunches for us when she lived in the same neighborhood as my mom?"

Claire tossed her head and pulled away. "I didn't say I couldn't. I said I don't. And I'm not willing to discuss the past."

"Too bad. We might come up with better things to do than hunt for candles." She stumbled and he snagged her elbow, preventing her from falling. "Slow down, sweetheart. You never were able to see in the dark."

"That's Ms. Sweetheart to you. I suppose you're not having any difficulties at all."

"After almost twenty years in the Army?" He laughed. "I learned how to navigate across rough terrain on too many night missions and back then I didn't have my cell for light, although we did use goggles." He gestured further down the hallway. "We're halfway to Conn's. Why don't you get out your phone and be part of the solution?"

She gasped, dug into the pocket of her jeans, and pulled out her cell. "Now, I feel really stupid for not thinking of it."

"You're scared. Tell me why. You weren't as a kid."

"How would you know? You and your mom only lived with us for two years. Why should I share my secrets with you? I hate defending myself."

"Fair enough." He hadn't heard the pain underneath the defiance before. What was wrong with him? "What if I tell you something that bothers me even now? Then, you'll have something on me."

"You first."

"You really don't trust anyone, do you?" He didn't wait for an answer. "Okay, but don't let my mother know I still remember. She thinks I've forgotten."

"I only talk to Maria on holidays. No problem. Now, what is it?"

Tony smiled, hearing curiosity replace fear. "My old man was an alcoholic. When there wasn't any money for booze, he sold the food in the house to neighbors to buy it or traded groceries for whisky. Going hungry scares me. Even now, I keep the fridge, the pantry, and my cupboards full."

"You never told me that before." Claire heaved a sigh. "My turn. I wasn't scared of the dark until Lee's second wife locked me and Connor in the walk-in closet in our nursery. Then, she'd leave to hang out with friends. One day the light bulb burned out. I was so scared I wet my pants, and she made fun of me."

"Why on earth did she do that to little kids? It's abuse."

"She was pissed because she didn't understand Lee married her to take care of us. It was cheaper to have a wife than to hire a decent nanny. When Conn ratted her out, Lee divorced her, and we were in the church day-care until he met your mom."

They stopped outside Connor's apartment and Tony unlocked the door. He drew her closer. "Claire, that was nearly thirty years ago. I've got to buy you a flashlight to keep in your place."

"Oh, I was pretty much past that until James, Barbara's son decided it was fun to hide in dark corners in the house and around the estate. He thought it was fun to jump out of nowhere and terrify me."

"What did your dad say about that?"

"He laughed and told me not to be such a 'fraidy cat'. Things changed when Connor kicked the crap out of James."

"What? The guy's only a year younger than I am. He was a big brute even before he joined the high school football team back in the day." Tony guided her into the apartment which was a mirror image of hers. "How old was Connor?"

"Twelve. James was fifteen and Connor put him in the hospital. After that, Lee and Barbara sent Connor off to military school. I took my Shih-Tzu, Fonzie and ran away to live with my maternal grandparents. Lee got tired of dragging me back and Barb told him to let me go when I kept leaving. My grandparents wouldn't demand child support. If the state stepped in, she'd risk losing James and his sister, Kymm."

"What did Lee expect you to do?" Tony led her into the living-room. Unlike hers, it had a working fireplace and comfortable, overstuffed furniture. Once she was sitting on the couch, he crossed to the sideboard and lit the tapers in the waiting hurricane lamps. "You and Conn are closer than most twins. My mother thinks it's because your dad ignored you most of the time. She says he doesn't have much in the way of fatherly qualities."

"He really doesn't, does he?" Surprise filled Claire's voice. "I always figured it had to be our fault. If we'd been good kids, Lee would have loved us."

"Well, don't waste your time analyzing him now." Tony headed toward the fireplace. "We have a power outage to deal with, doll. Don't you need to check in with your maintenance guy? I thought you told me you'd installed a generator last summer. Shouldn't it be working by now? Why don't we have back-up lights yet?"

"Good point." Claire fussed with her smart phone. "Two of our tenants rely on oxygen machines and those need power twenty-four, seven. We had the new generator hooked up to natural gas and it's supposed to come on right away when we lose electricity." A moment later, she sounded perfectly calm and professional when she spoke to someone else. "Bonnie, it's Claire. How are you? How is everyone doing?"

While Claire chatted, Tony started a fire. They wouldn't need it for heat yet. He left her talking and went into the kitchen where he found a six-pack of imported Mexican colas in the fridge and a bag of chips. He headed into the main bedroom and snagged a patchwork quilt off a cedar chest. When he returned to the living-room, she'd just ended the call.

Tony handed her a soda, took one for himself and put the remainder of the six-pack on the coffee table. "What's the word on the generator?"

"It's still a work in progress." Claire put her phone on the end table. "They didn't have the one we ordered so the company downsized temporarily. It only lights the first five floors, which is okay. That means everyone else has limited power for tonight. Bonnie says meals will be served in the community room tomorrow."

"A community room. What's that?" Tony sat down beside Claire. He drew the blanket over them and wrapped an arm around her shoulders. "I don't remember you mentioning it before."

"When I bought the place, I had it remodeled into twelve decently sized apartments for rent, two to each floor, including mine and Conn's," Claire opened her cola. "Jerry and Bonnie Chambers have the super's place on the first floor. He does maintenance and she's a nurse. Across from their flat is what we call the 'community room.'"

"How can all the tenants use one large room?"

Claire laughed. "Get serious, Tony. Instead of being a three-bedroom rental, it has a commercial kitchen, a dining room with a gaming area where Conn and Jerry host their poker games, handicap accessible bathrooms, a media room, and a guestroom for a nurse's aide. Some of the folks play darts and we have a pool table too. The smallest bedroom is my management office."

"I didn't hear you say you had a cook on staff. How do you know she or he can get here tomorrow?"

"Oh no way, Tony." Still smiling, Claire shook her head. "Why would I hire a cook when I have so many people who have years of experience preparing meals?"

"I don't get it. What people?"

"The ones who live here, silly."

"Tell me more."

During the next few hours while they cuddled in the

dark, he continued asking questions. He kept her talking about the social structure she'd initiated at the apartment house as well as the renters. The various activities, from gardening to looking after the private dog-park to cooking to helping Jerry with maintenance ensured all the tenants felt as if they belonged here. It was truly their home.

Claire described some of the different pets at the apartment house. They ranged from dogs to cats to birds to fish and an iguana named Bite. It surprised him when she admitted she enjoyed helping the dogs exercise during inclement weather when their senior owners couldn't take them outside. She also looked after the cats, birds, and fish if their people were away for family visits or short hospital stays but dumped caring for the snakes and lizards on her brother.

Tony wouldn't have expected her to step up that much. Finally, her voice faded, and she drifted off to sleep. He continued to hold her. He could have covered her with the quilt and left, but it didn't seem like the right thing to do, not when she was so afraid of the dark. No wonder she refused to visit Rocklin or her immediate family.

He recalled his mother telling him that Lee's current wife, Barbara, happened to be smarter than her predecessors. She'd insisted on an ironclad prenup and didn't care when Lee strayed. The sound of a key turning in the lock and footsteps on the tile floor woke Tony. Daylight crept around the edges of the drapes on the picture windows. The rest of the apartment remained dark. Obviously, the power hadn't been restored yet.

Connor, a tall, dark-haired, muscular man in blue sweats paused in the doorway and smiled a greeting. "I wasn't expecting company."

"You should have." Tony eased off the couch, leaving

Claire to lie sleeping on the cushions. He covered her with the blanket and gestured for Connor to precede him to the kitchen. "She doesn't have any candles, so we came here. I knew you wouldn't mind."

"I ended up working a double shift." Connor strode to the counter and poured coffee from a large thermos into two mugs. "Glad you were here to look after her. She still freaks when the power goes out."

"Hey, it's my job."

"Sure, it is." Connor chuckled. "One of these days, you two will learn there's more to it than that."

"I did years ago," Tony said. "But your sister—"

"Cut her some slack." Connor shrugged. "She'll figure out sooner or later she measures every guy she dates against you. It's why she's still single."

Chapter Four

S he woke up to sunlight streaming through the picture windows and glimpsed blue skies. Hurray, the storm was over! Claire slowly sat up, pushing the quilt aside. She switched on the lamp next to the couch, but nothing happened. There still wasn't electricity. She stood, walked over to the window. Someone had opened the drapes. Tony? Where was he?

She gazed outside. She spotted a huge maple tree lying across a neighbor's lawn, one giant branch crushing the roof of his car. She was surprised she hadn't heard it fall, but the winds had been so loud last night. Luckily, it'd missed the house, but other branches lay scattered like giant toothpicks across the lawn. She heard footsteps and turned to see her twin brother.

Connor wore sweats, so he must not be ready to hit the sack yet. Although tact wasn't her strong suit, she decided to err on the side of courtesy and not mention her opinion that he prepped for romantic evenings with an overload of candles, firewood, and plenty of wine.

She thought of them as one-night stands, but Fancy had

said they were more properly called, 'coyote dates'. When Claire wanted a definition, Fancy said it was because some guys would chew off their arms rather than wake up the various flavors of the night on the following mornings.

Claire yawned and stretched. "Sorry to impose but Tony thought you might be prepared for the electricity going out when I wasn't. I don't do the homestead routine because we live in the big city now."

"No worries, little sis. I've got your back." He grinned at her. "Ready for coffee? I'll get you a cup. Mrs. DiFalco sent Jerry up with breakfast. We have frittata, fruit salad and muffins."

"Sounds good. I intended to go downstairs." Claire tilted her head to one side and studied him. Black hair and deep blue eyes like hers, but he topped six feet while she was only five feet, eight inches. "What's the special occasion? Usually, we eat in the community room with everybody else."

"We're the only place with power in a three-block radius, thanks to your generator, so the tenants are serving coffee, tea or hot chocolate and breakfast to the neighbors. Good thing Bonnie hit Costco last week before the storm. We should have electricity back tonight because we're in the big city, but that doesn't go for the rest of the region. The power's knocked out from south of Tacoma, north to the Canadian border and all along the coast."

"Where's Tony? Did he go to Rocklin to check on his mother?"

"Not yet. Most of the roads up north are impassable. He keeps a go-bag in his rig, so he went to change clothes and grab his chain-saw. He, Jerry, and some of the local guys are going to cut up a few of the fallen trees. I reminded them to take pictures for the various insurance adjusters."

Claire headed for the kitchen, followed by her twin brother who was only thirty minutes older despite his claims. "Is he still carrying around a full toolbox in that Hummer?"

"You know it." Connor refilled his cup and another for her. "You can take the guy out of the backwoods in Rocklin, but you can't take them out of him. And he's too much of a former soldier to give up that monster rig. He says it always takes him where he wants to go."

"Well, if you want to get some sleep, I'll clean up after I eat," Claire said. "Then, I'll go downstairs and see if Isabella DiFalco will let me wash the dishes for her."

"Good luck with that." Connor laughed. "Jerry claims her granddaughter, Sofia came to check on the old folks and is now on KP because her grandma says she has a sassy mouth."

"Why am I not surprised?" Smiling, Claire began to fill a plate with a helping of the baked egg, meat and cheese casserole, fresh fruit salad and a mini blueberry muffin. "Sofia's a sophomore in college. You'd think the girl would have learned not to harass her granny by now."

"Not yet." Connor snagged a muffin and followed her over to the table where the two of them sat down. "Tony said you were out of town for a few days. Where did you go?"

Claire shrugged and pretended buttering the muffin took her full attention, silently debating whether she should mention his former girlfriend or not. "Grays Harbor County. We still have those investment properties I've been trying to sell forever, but I'm not willing to give them away and the economy is so depressed on the Washington coast."

"I thought you'd pretty much sold off all the ones Grandma and Gramps left us."

"Not the big-ticket ones. Not yet anyway. We've kept them in good condition, and we want top dollar for them. We aren't desperate to sell, and the property management company handles it when we rent them to tourists. They called me because a group of them had a wild beach party, and the house needs a serious clean-up and redo. I've approved the work, and the party animals will pay for it."

"Makes sense to me. You invested the money I sent from my Army days in more real estate and Tony's contributions went into the brokerages. We depend on your expertise." Connor reached for the butter. "I saw Fancy's van in the garage but she's not around. I figured she'd be back once she got over being mad at me. Where is she?"

Claire eyed him. She thought they'd split up. At least, it was Fancy's story. Sounds like there was more detective work to be done. "She went with me to Ocean Shores, and I arranged a rental car for her when she's ready to return. You know she handles all the interior design. As for the van, it needs a tune-up, and the mechanic is picking it up on Monday. I said you wouldn't care if she left it in your extra parking spot. It's not a problem, is it? If you need the space, I have the keys and I can move it to one of my slots as soon as Tony leaves."

"It's fine."

They ate in shared silence for a few minutes, but she knew Connor was upset by the way he occasionally stared off into the distance. She'd wait for him to confide in her. While he kept what he considered minor issues private, Connor always shared important things with her. Eventually. But this morning didn't appear to be one of those times. He finished off the muffin, washed it down with the last of his coffee, put the cup in the dishwasher and headed to his room to catch some sleep before he returned to the precinct for his regular swing shift.

Claire wiped down the counters and put the leftover food in the refrigerator. After a quick stop at her place to change into comfortable black slacks and a pink sweatshirt over a matching blouse, she went downstairs. No power meant no elevator, but hopefully, there'd be electricity tonight. She didn't want to climb flights of stairs when she was ready to return home. Of course, she could always tell herself it made up for missing her daily workout at the local gym which was undoubtedly closed due to the power outage.

———

After breakfast with Connor, Tony went to the garage and grabbed the duffel he kept in his Hummer. When he returned to the apartment that Jerry referred to as the community room, Tony changed to jeans, a comfortable button-up, long-sleeved t-shirt under a flannel work shirt and his old, battered combat boots. By then, Jerry had rounded up a half-dozen younger men who lived in the neighborhood, leaving the seniors who lived at the apartment house to look after the rest of their guests.

Accompanied by Jerry and the volunteers, they spent most of the morning cutting fallen trees into firewood at three of the houses in the neighborhood. Now, they headed for the next one, a contemporary, large three-story that belonged to Ross Gamack, a sandy-haired thirty-something who talked endlessly about stocks and bonds. Still, he was a harder worker than his younger brother, Kevin, a blond, surfer type in long board shorts, a Hawaiian shirt, and flip-flops.

"I saw there's an apartment available at your place," Ross said. "How much is the rent?"

"You'd have to talk to my partner about that." Tony scanned the yard and the cluster of three fallen maples. "Claire runs the building, not me. She's fussy about references. She'll want a recent credit history and to talk to your brother's employer. Where does Kevin work?"

"He graduated last June from the University of Washington. He's been looking but hasn't found a position he likes yet and he's not settling for a minimum wage job."

Tony didn't say he'd been raised by a single mother in a small town. She'd counted on him to step up and help since his deadbeat dad wasn't in the picture and they didn't have a claim on Lee Rocklin's money after she divorced him. *So, I made Mom proud when I brought home my wages*, Tony thought. He'd mowed lawns, done errands, delivered newspapers, helped Claire's grandparents rehab distressed properties when they played a real-life game of Monopoly and bought an assortment of single-family dwellings. She was a chip off their block, as the saying went.

He focused on the tangle of thick maple and alder branches lying in the front yard. "Let's get started. After this, we'll head back for lunch."

When they started toward the apartment house two hours later, Jerry Chambers, a big, African-American in his sixties walked beside Tony. "If I were you, I wouldn't tell Claire that boy wants a rental."

Tony glanced at the tall, wide-shouldered, retired Marine, still all muscle after ten years as a civilian, but he'd served almost thirty years in uniform. "Why? Because he thinks he'll be able to throw all sorts of college parties even if he's not in a dorm or frat house?"

"There you go." Jerry ran a hand over close-cropped,

gray-black hair. "Not my circus or flying monkeys, man. You won't have to go to the *sandbox* again to be back in a shit-storm if you suggest it to Claire."

Tony grinned, shifting the chainsaw to his other hand. "Yeah, well how about if I don't? I prefer sleeping indoors, not bivouacking in my rig."

After putting away the tools, they followed the others into the community room. Tony glanced around the dining room but didn't see Claire. Granted, she didn't show up at any of the offices until noon and then worked until nine or ten at night, several times a week. However, he'd expected her to be downstairs by now. Was she still asleep?

Jerry's wife, Bonnie, a woman about his age, approached. Golden skin, regal, queenly even in the blue scrubs she wore to her job as a nurse, her long black hair in beaded braids, she flashed a warm smile. "Wash up and hit the buffet, guys. We have sub sandwiches, chips, and salads. Fill your plates and find a table."

"Where's Claire? Upstairs at Connor's place?" Tony let Jerry walk in front of them toward the long stainless steel, cold-food table on the far side of the room. "I'll go get her."

"No need. She'll be back soon. She's showing the vacant apartment."

"Really?" Jerry paused and glanced toward Rory and his younger brother who sat with a lovely blonde and three youngsters. "He wants it for his bro."

"They'll have to return in thirty or forty years." Bonnie shrugged, obviously dismissing the family. "Harry Gamack completed a rental application for our latest opening between breakfast and lunch."

"Who is he?" Tony studied the older couple. "I've never met him."

"He was visiting his grandson's family after a long road

trip across the country. He came here with them." Bonnie tucked her hand in the crook of her husband's arm and propelled him in the direction of the buffet. "Let's eat. Harry jumped in to help with the breakfast dishes today and then with prepping lunch. He's a widower. The gals are drooling over the new silver fox."

Jerry laughed. "Well, that's not going to make him popular with the men around here."

"He won't have a problem. When he met them, they all told war stories. He was a Marine in Vietnam. Retired cop. Plays a mean game of pool and offered to walk dogs with Fletcher. Harry asked Claire about his border collie mix coming here too. Admits she's a real diva and the grandson's wife doesn't like her."

"Probably jealous of the competition." Jerry passed a tray to Tony. "Sounds like he'll fit right in with the rest of us. Wonder if he plays poker."

"He's a Marine." Bonnie gestured to the sandwiches. "Load up. Remember, you have a budget, old man. Don't lose every cent to him. It's all right if you take *his* pocket money."

Tony grinned appreciatively and picked up a roast beef, ham, and turkey combo. "When is poker night? I'll come join you sometimes."

"Ask Claire," Bonnie said. "She has it marked on the calendar in her office. When she plays, she doesn't cut anybody slack and kicks butt."

"Why aren't I surprised?" Tony snagged a serving of fruit salad. "Her grandma used to clean our clocks on Friday nights when we played cards with her."

Chapter Five

The power wasn't on yet, but thanks to the generator, Claire had enough electricity to use the computer in her office. Thankfully, the Internet hadn't failed today, and the telephone system still worked. Most of the senior tenants who lived here preferred to use a landline although she'd arranged for a wireless service provider to offer tech classes, so her folks learned to use smart phones, tablets, and laptops.

No point in acting like they still lived in the Dark Ages when the medical establishment preferred emails, texting, and video conferences. Claire sent emails off to the various references Harry Gamack provided, knowing she probably wouldn't have answers before Sunday or Monday, but she had a good feeling about the potential tenant.

The office door opened, and Tony came inside, looking around the small room. "I thought I might have to track you down at Connor's, but Bonnie said you were working." He pointed over his shoulder. "You're making me feel like a moron, kid."

"Why? You're such a rocket scientist." She pushed back

from the oak rolltop desk inherited from her grandfather, spinning slightly in the wheeled chair. "What happened?"

"Over the last three years, you've never shown up at the brokerages until after lunch." He shrugged a broad shoulder. "Thought you didn't do mornings and then I saw the hours sign. You're here three days a week. What about the other four? Where do you go then?"

"I could be obnoxious and refuse to share, but why bother? I need some help with the new apartment house in the north end. I'm there two mornings and usually visit the 'tiny home' complex in Edmonds on the other two to handle their day-to-day concerns."

She beckoned for him to join her behind the desk and pulled up pictures on the monitor. "I thought Logan Turner did good work when we converted this place. He's been obstructive about what I want this time."

Tony rested his hand on the back of the chair, almost touching her shoulder. Amusement warmed his gray eyes. "What do you want, sweetheart? And how do I make it happen for you?"

"The new complex is a little smaller than this building. I think we can create eight decent one-bedroom places for tenants and still have a community room, my office and living quarters for the maintenance person on the first floor. Rents will be a bit lower and that will work for folks on reduced incomes."

Since she needed his input, she opted to ignore the endearment. Instead, she described her vision for the remodeling, trying not to breathe in the spicy scent of Tony's aftershave. He was so close, she felt the warmth of his breath on her cheek.

He was even sexier in work clothes than he'd been in his suit last night. She reminded herself he'd been her stepbrother for two years and she couldn't afford to lose him. *I'm just like my father and Connor. I suck at relationships. And if Tony walks out on me—No, I can't afford to lose him.*

"What's Turner's issue? This looks reasonable to me."

"Damned if I know." She paused, then tilted her head back so their gazes met. "Oh crap, Tony. He's gotten a divorce. Do you think—?"

"That he has the hots for you?" Tony chuckled. "You bet. Did you turn him down nicely?"

"Of course. Good contractors are hard to find and I'm sure as hell not wasting any time or energy trying to get into Hawke Construction's schedule. They're the best in the state, but they have a waiting list a mile long and I want this place done ASAP. We can't afford to sit around for a year or two until they have time for us. We need the building filled with tenants."

"Give me the address and I'll do a walk-through on my way back from Mom's on Monday. Text Turner and tell him to meet me at 1500 hours, 3PM, civilian time."

"You're a lifesaver." Claire shifted in her seat and returned her attention to the computer. It only took a few minutes to print the address and directions to the new apartment building since she wasn't sure when they'd have power and didn't want him to depend on a faulty app. "I emailed your mother, but I haven't heard back. Rocklin got thumped pretty hard by the storm. No power and the phone lines are down too. Have you been able to reach her?"

"Not yet. She gets crappy reception on her cell phone because they don't have enough towers up there, thanks to your Rocklin grandfather. He's too old school to see the necessity to upgrade the community. I may have to stay over tomorrow night if there's a lot of damage in Mom's neighborhood or near her house."

"Not a problem. I'll start in the Seattle office tomorrow and work my way north to the rest of the brokerages on Monday. When I called, the receptionists said they'd already heard from you about not opening until then."

"It was a management decision and that's my job."

"Nobody does it better." Claire slid the chair away from him and stood. She crossed to the short, wooden filing cabinet in the corner and the printer on top of it, bypassing the long worktable on one wall. She tried to pass the papers to him. He didn't take them. Instead, he caught her hand and drew her close. "What are you doing?"

"Something I've wanted to do a long time." He lowered his head, his breath warm on her lips. "Kissing you." And his mouth claimed hers!

———

The first kiss was only a taste, a whisper soft touch. She didn't resist or push him away. He lifted his head, trailed a line of kisses along her jaw. She sighed and her lashes drifted closed. He kissed her the way he'd wanted to for years, as if she'd always belonged to him. His tongue swept into her mouth and explored the depths. Her arms laced around his neck, body pressed tight against him, she returned the favor, her tongue teasing his into a longer duel.

Suddenly, she pulled back from him, opening her eyes. Her palms pressed against his chest. "We can't do this."

"It seems to be working just fine." He threaded his hands into her black hair, gazed down into the brilliant blue eyes, darker with passion. "I'm happy taking it slow."

She shook her head. "Not slow enough. I'm going to have to think about this."

"Think while I kiss you." He nipped her ear, worked his

way down her neck, one kiss following another. "And I'll wait for the rest."

"You'll wait all right." She pushed harder on his chest. "Give me space and time."

"You win, Claire." He kissed her again, quickly, and softly. "Now, let's talk about the next poker night. When is it?"

"Check it out for yourself." She stepped away from him and pointed to the wall calendar, with a picture of two lovely, long-haired kittens basking together on a chair. "Be ready for me to take all your money if you decide to join us."

"We can start there, but sooner or later, I'll convince you to play strip poker with me."

She laughed. "Such a dreamer. You'll be the one arrested for indecent exposure, not me."

"Oh, I wasn't planning on leaving your place before breakfast when we finally get down and dirty."

"Promises, promises."

In one corner of the room was her grandfather's antique wooden rocking chair. When Tony sat down, he saw the assortment of vintage Louis L'Amour paperback novels in the old bookcase. He remembered comforting Claire when she bought a copy of the latest release at the Rocklin grocery store shortly after she'd lost her grandparents. She'd forgotten her grandfather was dead. Tony had encouraged her to keep the collection as a way to remember them.

Since he didn't feel the need to spend the next hour or two before supper on his smart phone, he reached for a book instead. He paused and glanced at her, admiring the picture she made in a pink sweatshirt and black slacks. He nearly told her how cute she looked with a bright pink headband holding back her curly hair and opted to keep that to himself.

He held up the classic western copy of *Hondo*. "Okay, if I read this?"

"It's fine as long as you realize it doesn't leave the room. I don't loan Gramps' books, Anthony Marco Baldusi."

He chuckled. "When I marry you, am I allowed to take it upstairs?"

"Don't be silly." She rolled her eyes, pointedly ignoring his reference to his future plans. "I already cut the legs off that book. It doesn't go anywhere and if you try stealing it, your life will end, and no one will miss you."

"Okay, good to know." He switched on the pole lamp and opened the novel.

———

It was the beginning of the month. Claire pulled up her accounting spreadsheet and began reviewing the rents she'd already received from the tenants. She moistened suddenly dry lips and glanced across the room at the tall, dark-haired hunk apparently ignoring her while he read one of her grandfather's well-loved books.

Tony's mouth had been warm on hers. He'd started a storm within her, and she prayed it hadn't shown. Her heart still thudded when she recalled the way he held her. His body was so strong and hard, his arms muscled. She trembled, her nipples tightening against her bra. She forced herself to remain in her own chair, not rise and cross to him. What if she went over there, joined him in the big rocking chair and set his pulses skyrocketing like he had hers?

Damn it! The last thing I want is Tony rocking my world. If I lose him—

She shook her head, forced her gaze to return to the

numbers on the monitor. She had bills to pay before she joined everyone in the community room for supper. Her tenants would want to share the myriad details of their lives and part of her job was listening to them. Of course, the fact that she enjoyed the conversations was neither here nor there.

A tap on the partially open door an hour later interrupted her. Claire signaled for the visitor to enter and recognized the petite, curvy brunette as Isabella DiFalco's granddaughter. "Hi, Sofia. Are we late for supper?"

"Not yet." The twenty-something in jeans, a University of Washington sweatshirt and running shoes strolled inside, carrying a small, screened cloth bag, escorted by a little brown and white spaniel in a pink harness. "I need to talk to you."

"Great. Tell me about your friends." Claire waved to the comfy chair near hers. "Why did they come with you?"

Tears shimmered in the big, dark brown eyes and Sofia gulped back a sob. "My landlord found out about the pets and is evicting me from the house I share with three other girls because all of them said they're mine. And I brought them because I thought they could stay here with Nonna until I figure out what to do only her evil cat hates them and—"

"Don't cry." Claire pushed forward a box of tissues. "Sit down and talk to me. How do you know Isabella's cat hates company?"

"When I went to check on them, she'd driven them in the bedroom closet, and she wouldn't let them out. So, I rescued them again and brought them downstairs with me."

Claire nodded. "That makes perfect sense. Now, why does your landlord think you have pets and you're violating the lease?"

"Because my roommate, Jill Myers lied. She's the one who brought them home and then she started staying over with her boyfriend, so I took care of them. And now she's moved him into the house, and my landlord says I have to go, but all of them can stay."

"Why would you want to live with a bunch of liars?" Tony asked. "They're not your friends. I'd drop-kick them through the goalposts of life."

Sofia blew her nose. "I tried texting my landlord about the animals leaving and asked her to reconsider and she refused. I have to be out today. I already paid this month's rent, and I don't have any extra money. Where am I supposed to go?"

Claire watched a tiny black and white paw poke at the netting on the front of the carrier. "What does the kitten look like?"

Another sniffle. "Felix is a long-haired tuxedo. Black and white. He's three months old, housebroke and he's had his shots, and I wanted to get him fixed, but my roommate wouldn't agree."

"Is he micro-chipped?" Claire asked.

"Yes, and that's part of the problem. I had to take him to the vet. I had to and she wouldn't pay so I did, and he has my name as his owner, and the landlord says that makes him mine and—"

"Breathe, Sofia. Calm down and breathe." Claire rose, walked around the desk to the other chair and unzipped the carrier. She lifted out the furry guest. He was lovely with a distinctive black coat, a white chest, white around his nose and on his chin, plus four white-tipped paws. He did look as if he wore a formal, dark suit, befitting his color. "He's adorable."

"And he matches your updated apartment," Tony teased.

"If you take him, what will you do when you redecorate? Dye his fur?"

"Don't be silly. I'll tell Fancy to use his coat for an accent." Claire cuddled the kitten close. "Time for you to go shopping, Tony. He'll need some kitty supplies. Sofia will go with you and the two of you can pick up her belongings. I need an assistant here and she knows how I do things, so it will be a perfect fit."

Tony chuckled again. "And what about the dog? What are you doing with her?"

"My assistant definitely requires one of those so she can accompany Fletcher on his rounds. Pause by his place and ask him to doggy-sit while you're gone." Claire gestured toward the door. "You two better hustle or you'll be late for supper and I'm not getting on Isabella's bad side especially since I don't know what we're having."

"Lasagna," Sofia said. "Nonna says it's easy to make enough for a crowd." She drew a ragged breath. "Claire, I thought this was senior housing."

"It is, dear heart. It is." Claire carried the kitten back to her chair. "And how do you think I manage to look after everyone who lives here? Believe me, I'll work you half to death just like Tony, but hopefully you won't snivel as much as he does. Now, scat!"

Chapter Six

Tony started the Hummer SUV but waited until Sofia buckled her seatbelt before he drove toward the underground garage exit. "Okay, give me directions to your old place. We'll start there. Afterwards, we'll get pet supplies."

"I never thought you and Claire would help me." Sofia relaxed in the heated seat. "I just hoped you'd let Oscar and Felix stay a few days and I could couch surf with friends or Nonna while I figured out what to do."

"Claire survived her share of hard times." After crossing the Ballard Bridge, Tony drove toward Fifteenth Street. The arterial would take him to the University District and from there Sofia could direct him to her former residence. He saw a few crew members still working on the electricity but some of the buildings had lights shining in the windows. "Are you okay with her taking the kitten? If not, I'll ask her to return him."

"Please don't. I want her to have him. It's the right thing to do. He's a good kitty who deserves a *real* home."

"As long as you're fine with it."

A few minutes later, she began providing directions to the house a few blocks from what was more commonly known as the U-Dub not only the University of Washington. Tony pulled into the driveway, parking beside a well-cared-for single family home. Native plants, including a few dwarf maples and cedars in the landscaped yard framed the small two-story house.

"Any furniture that needs to go? I should have told Jerry we might need his pickup."

"No. All I have are my clothes, computer and books." Sofia led the way up the sidewalk to the front door and the formal entry. "I already packed those."

Tony followed her inside, admiring the hardwood floors. He'd been in the real estate business long enough to appreciate the double-paned, efficient windows, the fresh paint, and the updated flooring in the living room, hallway, and Sofia's bedroom. He wheeled the two suitcases back out to his rig. When he returned, he found her in the galley kitchen with new stainless-steel appliances including a gas stove. She piled a small assortment of dishes and coffee mugs in a box. He looked through the glass patio door to the covered deck and saw a custom garden with stone pathways.

"Little wonder your landlord is so fussy," Tony said. "Someone put a lot of time, effort, and money into this place. It's amazing she rents it to university students."

"She lives down the street and it belonged to her parents. They sold it to her when they retired to Arizona." Sofia passed him the box. "I want to check the bathroom and bedroom again to be sure I have everything. Then, I need to go to her house and give her my keys."

"Sounds like a winner." Pulling out his phone, Tony began taking pictures while he did his own walk-through and waited for Sofia. Once she locked the doors, he escorted her back to his vehicle. Then, it was a fast trip to a two-story Craftsman on the corner. Like the rental, this one had a fabulous yard and showed obvious pride of ownership. He stopped in front of it, this time on the street.

"I'll be right back." Sofia popped out of her door. She lifted her chin and took a deep breath. "Thanks again for everything."

"We've got this." Tony switched off the engine, ready to provide system support. A plump, gray-haired woman in casual clothes came out on the porch and watched them approach. When they were close enough, he held out his hand. "Hi, I'm Tony Baldusi."

"I'm Linda Marshall." She blinked, looking slightly shocked. "Are you from Rocklin Realties?"

"That's right. You have a wonderful, rental property. Have you ever considered selling it?"

More bewilderment as Linda goggled at him. "I didn't know Sofia knew you."

"Oh, it's more a case of she knows my partner." Tony smiled, giving Linda one of his business cards. "Her grandmother rents one of Claire's apartments and Sofia visits frequently in case her gramma needs anything."

"I didn't know that." Linda turned toward Sofia. "The girls told me you're barely there most of the time because you party so much."

"I do not! I'm doing a double major, English, and History plus my classes in Secondary Education." Sofia gasped, then planted her fists on her hips. "Are they crazy? I take more classes than the three of them and I study at the library on campus most days. I work part-time at a tutoring center for tweens, plus going to Nonna's two nights a week —."

"So, you don't have time for pets, and I've never allowed them in the house," Linda interrupted. "Read your lease."

"Felix and Oscar weren't mine," Sofia flashed again, temper rising in her face. "I told you that again and again. I just took care of them because Jill kept staying over with her boyfriend and she wasn't there to look after the animals when she brought them home. And I said I was trying to find them places to live, but you weren't listening."

"I've rented to college students for three years and I don't accept excuses or tolerate lies."

"Well, here are your keys." Sofia passed them to the older woman. "And I'm done living in your house."

It was his turn to talk. Tony pointed to the Hummer. "Go wait for me while Linda and I discuss business, Sofia."

The girl tossed her head, black hair flying before she spun and stomped to his rig. He ignored it when she slammed the passenger door. Once she was gone, he brought up the subject of the November rent. He began the discussion by agreeing with Linda that the smaller house was in fantastic shape. Of course, she shouldn't allow pets in it. Once she knew she was absolutely right in everything she did and he thought she provided a beautiful place for the college students to live, then it was time to convince her to give Sofia a partial refund.

As their conversation concluded, he asked when he could send Claire over to look at the rental. Tony tucked the check into his shirt pocket. "She'll be able to give you an accurate assessment of what she thinks the house will bring if you decide to sell."

"Won't it being a rental create issues?" Linda turned his card over in her hand. "The girls have leases until the end of December. Granted, they'll probably leave a week or two before on Christmas break."

"It depends on the buyer and what they want to do with it," Tony said. "Personally, I'd find a family for it and let the college kids live in dorms. But that's just me. I enlisted as soon as I graduated from high school and we had to toe the line when it came to the barracks, not only in boot camp or advanced training."

"Thank you for your service." Linda looked at the card again. "I'll consider selling. I can't believe you think my house is good enough for Claire Rocklin to market. I've heard she only accepts the best listings."

"We work on commission so if we want top-dollar for properties, we can't list everything people try to sell." A few more pleasantries and he had her contact information. Now, Claire could call or email to make an appointment for the following week. He headed for the Hummer.

Sofia sat sulking in the passenger seat. "She's such a witch."

"No, she's not. She got scammed." Tony slid the key into the ignition. "Kiddo, you've got to learn some life lessons."

"Like what?"

"Like she busted her ass putting together a lovely place for students to live and she's upset about being dissed by her tenants. If you ask Claire, she'll tell you that pets and children are rough on houses and often it affects property values." Tony started the engine. "I suggested Linda let us list the place and sell it for her."

"But that means Jill, her boyfriend and the other girls will be out on the street when they come back for classes in January." Sofia's eyes widened. "That's so mean."

"Wasn't what they did to you just as mean?" Tony pulled out the check and passed it to her. "Linda decided to refund your rent because you moved out today without creating a big fuss. She can either rent the room to someone else for a few weeks or let one of our associates sell the house."

"This is the same one I gave her three days ago for November. She's so old-school she doesn't take electronic payments, so I always had to drop off my rent." Sofia gaped at the check. "And she didn't cash it yet?"

"She hadn't made it to the bank." Tony pulled out on the street. "She'd have deposited it on Monday. Now, where is the closest grocery? If I don't bring kitty supplies to Claire, I'll be eating dinner with your puppy, Oscar."

Sofia managed a weak giggle, still staring at the check. "I know she's letting me keep Oscar, but to be honest, I'm okay taking her for walks. I want to find someone who will love and brush and cuddle her. I'm up to my eyeballs with classes and work, Tony. It's not fair to Oscar to be all alone for hours when I'm gone."

"We'll talk to Claire about a perfect owner when we get back. She'll help you and the dog."

———

The electricity still wasn't restored when Claire left her office to go to the dining room for supper. Felix snoozed on the visitor's chair, so she didn't bother putting him in the cat-tainer. She'd let the little guy sleep until Tony returned with the supplies. Then, she'd need to create an appropriate cat-space up in her apartment for a new roommate. She reminded herself she'd rather have a four-legged companion than a two-legged one, even if Tony stirred more feelings than he knew.

Halfway through the meal, the overhead lights brightened the large room. A round of applause ensued.

"We have real power again." Bonnie's words sparked more clapping and cheering.

Claire glanced at the doorway in time to see Tony enter, relieved to see him. After he left, she felt slightly guilty for dumping the conflama with Sofia on him, not guilty enough to change anything, but still—. She waved to him to join her. "Where's Sofia?"

"We dropped off her belongings in the guestroom. She'll be along in a few minutes." He squeezed her shoulder, leaned down to brush her forehead with a kiss. "Keep eating. Don't let your supper get cold. I left the cat stuff in your office. Thought I'd take it upstairs for you after dinner. Then, I have something to show you."

"Sounds good. I can't wait."

He returned to the table a few minutes later, his tray laden with a plate of lasagna, a bowl of salad and garlic bread neatly on the side near a cup of coffee. He sat down and drew out his cell phone. "I have some pictures you should see."

"Of what?" She took the phone and started to scroll through the gallery. He had several photos of her in various places, including when she wore a sexy cat costume to the company Halloween Party two weeks ago. "What is this? Do I need to tell Connor you're stalking me?"

"He already knows." Tony leaned across the table and kissed her, a quick, soft touch of his mouth on hers. Then, he took away the cell for a moment. "Can't keep secrets from your brother."

When he returned the phone, it revealed a series of pictures of a lovely house. "I like this. Where is it?"

"The U-District. It's where Sofia lived. I told the owner you'd call about listing it. Thought you might run some comps first."

"You know it. Got to see what other houses like it are bringing on today's market." Claire slowly skimmed through the various shots, stopping to assess the chef's kitchen and butler's pantry. "Wow, Connor would love this. Two ovens and a huge dishwasher. He'd be cooking up a storm."

"I thought you were happy having him live here."

"I am," Claire said. "He keeps bitching about the fact I can't find him a decent place to live so I'm stuck with him for the duration."

Tony forked up more lasagna. "Want me to tell him he has a credibility gap, or will you?"

Chapter Seven

In her apartment, Claire cranked up the electric heat to dispel the chill after being without power for almost twenty-four hours. It didn't take long to set up Felix's new litter-box in the butler's pantry adjacent to the laundry area. After she fed him and filled a water bowl, he took off on a kitten exploration of his new home.

She left him to it and found Tony in the living room tuning in the news on the flatscreen. "You have a long drive in the morning. Shouldn't you call it a night and head downtown to your condo?"

"Thought I'd hang out a while. The lights have been flickering for the last hour and a half. I know how you feel about sitting in the dark."

"I'll be fine. If the power goes out again, Felix and I will go to Connor's place." She lifted her chin and met his amused gaze. "Damn it, Tony. Will you just listen to me?"

"You bet. When you say something that makes sense, I will." He sauntered across the room and caught her hand. "Come watch TV with me for a while."

"All right, but only if you agree this doesn't mean anything."

He chuckled. "If you talk like that, I'm introducing you to an Army recruiter. It was our favorite saying when I was in combat."

Sighing, she shook her head and let him guide her to the couch where they sat down together. He wrapped an arm around her shoulders, drew her close and passed her the remote. "Choose something for us to watch, sweetheart, but please don't pick a chick-flick."

"You asked for it, darling." She pressed against him and switched over to a saccharine holiday movie. When he groaned, she laughed and changed channels to one of her favorite crime dramas. "Okay, but once we know 'whodun-nit', you're hitting the road."

"Only if you still have electricity." He dropped a kiss on her forehead.

Three episodes later, she led him to the front door. She tiptoed up and brushed her lips over his beard-stubbled cheek. "Thanks, Tony. I appreciate you being such a hero."

"I'd believe it if you really kissed me."

"You're such a whiner." She rested her hands on his shoulders. Their lips met. She didn't deepen the kiss, kept it sweet, soft, and far too innocent, telling herself it was a sign of sisterly affection, nothing more. Surprisingly, he followed her lead.

She closed the door behind him, locked it and went to check on the kitten. Felix had claimed her recliner, so she left him to sleep while she showered and got ready for bed. It wasn't her usual practice. Normally, she hit the shower in the morning, but that was when she had electricity, not when she'd been living without it.

Okay, so she was grateful to Tony for staying around and

being system support. That was all it was. *I'm not getting involved with him. I can't. It was terrifying when he was in Iraq and Afghanistan. If he left me now—*

———

Early the next morning after kitty breakfast, Claire headed to the Seattle office. Thankfully, her favorite espresso stand had electricity. That meant she could get a daily dose of caffeine, a triple-shot skinny orange mocha and a lemon-poppyseed muffin top. Surprisingly, she wasn't the first one at the realty. She recognized the office manager, Eileen Carpenter's older Jeep.

Claire parked next to it and went inside. "Good morning. How are you? Did you lose power?"

"We still don't have it, and I wasn't going another day without coffee. I picked up fresh doughnuts when I stopped at the espresso stand at the grocery. They're in the breakroom." Despite it being Sunday, Eileen dressed for professional success in a navy blue and white striped shirt along with a white skirt. She'd added a blue blazer and topped off the outfit with a beaded necklace. As usual, she preferred open-toe pumps because she said they didn't hurt her hammer toes.

She walked across the room to her L-shaped desk in the reception area and plopped down in her swivel chair. She gestured toward a blue mug that proclaimed, 'She who must be obeyed'. "I put your messages in your office. Your toy boys started calling me when your voicemail was full."

"And Tony." Claire heaved a sigh. "I already heard from him about Perry's whining and whinging. What's up with that?"

"The usual." Eileen ran a hand through her short silver

hair, scowling at the desktop computer. "I told Zelda, the head Eastside associate broker to email you the recent contracts. We have to demote that guy, Claire. Of course, I'd rather you fired his sorry backside. I thought you drop-kicking him out of your personal life would make him leave."

"Me too." Claire pulled a chair close enough to sit down on the opposite side of the desk. "At least, I never slept with him. Can you imagine what that would be like?"

"Awful." Eileen shuddered, shaking her head. Amusement trickled into her dark eyes. "He'd probably be complaining about how long it took to satisfy you."

"More than five minutes." Claire sipped her coffee. "Okay, what else is new? Tony said everyone here needed my input. How is George Delaney doing?"

"Too damned honest for this biz. He can't list anything, Claire. And when he shows houses, he tells the buyers everything that's wrong with the places. He's been here two months and hasn't brought in a cent. It'd be fine if we were like other brokerages and only paid commissions to our associates, but you insist on salaries for them. The accountant is screaming her head off."

"George is a credit to us, and he'll develop a following of clients who prefer honesty to the hard sell. It's why he's my kind of associate broker." Claire smiled. "Call him and tell him I have a prospective house for him. He needs to come in this morning and research comps. Then, he can contact the seller and set up an appointment for us to view the place. I'd like to do it this afternoon, but it may take a few days because she'll have to arrange it with the tenants."

"What's the rush?"

"Tony found it and I'm trying to get back on his good

side since he's still bitching about Ryan leaving us in the lurch. When he talked to Tony while I was out of town, Ryan insisted it was all my fault he left. I don't see why."

"Because you wouldn't let him bail on his 'daddy' and 'husband' responsibilities after his wife got that promotion in Spokane. You lectured him six ways from Sunday about what a 'real man' does and abandoning his family was utterly inappropriate. Then, you found him a high-paying position over there with Natasha Hollister."

"Well, yeah that's true. My sorority sisters come in handy when I need them."

"It's reciprocal. You're always there for them too, Claire." Eileen picked up her cup. "Remember you and the rest of the girls are doing your big three-day shopping extravaganza at the end of the month."

"Thanks for the reminder. I don't know what I'd do without you." Carrying her coffee, Claire walked through the large room with its long tables and the team-work complexes. The associates shared it, but she preferred the privacy of her own office next door to Tony's. She glanced in the open doorway. His desk was clear, and the blinds were closed. Across from their work-areas was the break-room which also included a comfy couch and a recliner for when somebody needed a power nap.

She missed him already but certainly wouldn't admit it aloud. Instead, she walked into her sanctuary, closing the door behind her. Eileen liked doing things the old-school way and Claire spotted a stack of pink message slips in the center of the blotter. Sighing, she went to sit behind the desk and skimmed through them.

She arranged them in various piles, noticing there were several from Mike Flannagan, Fancy's older brother. *Weird*,

Claire thought. If he was looking for his sister, he'd call her direct, not go through an intermediary. The messages increased in urgency. Time to solve the mystery, so she picked up the landline and pressed buttons. When he answered, she said, "Okay, Mike. It's Claire Rocklin. What's on fire? Why are you having a fit and falling in it?"

"It's about time. I've been trying to get you for days."

"Save the drama for someone who cares." Claire picked up a pen off the desk, rolling it in her fingers. "We barely talk at regional Chamber of Commerce meetings because you're always having conniptions about me making more money than you do."

"Only because you sell the high-price spreads and I stick to fixer-upper homes for real people out in the boonies." He paused. "When was the last time you talked to Lee?"

"Lee who?"

"Your father, Lee Rocklin."

"I don't." Claire shifted in her chair, frowning thoughtfully. "Let me see. I think my office manager, Eileen, sent him a card last Christmas. We're no contact, Mike. Why? What's the bastard done now?"

A short laugh. "Well, you certainly have him pegged. Okay, this may just be fresh news from the rumor mill, but I keep hearing he's in cahoots with Mailer Logging and they're going to clearcut the old-growth forests around Rocklin—."

"No way!" Claire gasped. "My grandfather, Lee's dad owns all those parcels. He'd never allow it."

"Yeah, right. He's not getting any younger, Claire. He must be in his eighties. When he checks out, who inherits? Your dad, that's who. Once the trees are gone, flooding and landslides will increase. Homes will be destroyed, and people will—"

"Die," Claire said, struggling to keep her tone even. She took a deep breath, recalling the way torrential winter rainstorms caused mudslides. One of the worst disasters a few years ago, near a small town in the Cascades, wiped out an entire neighborhood. Forty-three people died in the catastrophe. "Thanks for the heads-up, Mike. Tony's going to Rocklin today to visit his mother. I'll text and tell him to see what's up."

"All right. Let me know how I can help."

"No worries. I will." Fury rocketed through her. Claire replaced the receiver harder than she intended. *Damn Lee.* Wasn't it enough when he abandoned her and Conn? How could her father turn his back on an entire town, one established by his family back in the 19th century? She didn't doubt for a moment the rumors were true.

Mike Flannagan was a hard as nails realtor, with a core of unshakeable integrity. If he hadn't believed she needed to know her one-time hometown was at risk, he wouldn't have spent his time or energy sharing the news. This was serious. He hadn't even asked after his younger sister, and he knew Fancy handled all the upgrades on Claire's apartment houses and investment properties.

———

He'd left Seattle at oh-dark-thirty and headed north to Rocklin, a small mountain town in the Cascades. Tony always enjoyed leaving the huge buildings and highways behind. An hour out of the big city and the evergreen trees that gave Washington State its nickname began to dot the landscape. The further he traveled, the more rural the surroundings and he relished the sight of cedars, pines, and hemlocks.

He took the exit for Rocklin and followed the secondary highway east. He wouldn't end up on the other side of the mountains, but it didn't mean he couldn't continue to enjoy the scenery. Shortly before lunchtime, he drove into Rocklin. The storm had definitely caused its share of damage but at least lights shone in the windows of some of the stores, restaurants, and other businesses.

It was a typical hardscrabble one-time logging town with several cedar-shingled buildings that looked like they'd been built in the last century. Tony pulled into the first gas station to top off the Hummer's tank. He wasn't the only one with that idea. He spotted an older man at the next pump and recognized Claire's paternal grandfather, a former logger who still sported a flannel shirt, orange suspenders to hold up his whacked off jeans above laced-up boots. His wife, Agnes obviously, hadn't been able to dress him up for church. Tony glimpsed her sitting in the passenger seat of the old Cadillac, a flower-covered hat on a cap of her silver hair.

Tony nodded a greeting. "Morning, Beckett. How'd you survive the storm?"

"We're okay. Got a couple trees down in the side yard, but Lee and James are going to come by in a week or two and take care of them."

"I need to check in on my mother," Tony said. "After that, I'll swing by in an hour and deal with your business unless you prefer to wait."

"Bring Maria with you and we'll have lunch," Beckett said. "You can tell us what Claire and Connor are doing."

"Sounds like a plan." When Tony slid behind the wheel, he felt his phone vibrate and pulled it out to see a text from Claire. *'Mike Flannagan says Lee's raising hell and putting props under it. Talk to his dad while you're there.'*

Not a 'please' or 'thank-you' from that woman. Just another order and the sight amused him. They were two of a kind. He didn't waste a lot of time on polite platitudes either. *'I'm on it, sweetheart. Get those contracts in order and sent to escrow.'*

Chapter Eight

When she called the Eastside office, it came as no surprise that Perry Holmes wasn't there. He didn't work weekends, although it was peak time for potential buyers to look at houses or businesses. Rapidly tapping her pen on the desk, Claire waited for Zelda Torres, the top-selling associate, to answer the phone when the receptionist transferred the call.

After listening to the update on recent sales, Claire promised to review the contracts the other woman had already sent. It undoubtedly meant a discussion with Tony about Perry's position, Claire thought, but she told the other woman to email a current resume to the Seattle office.

Like Eileen said, Perry was in over his head with all the responsibilities of his promotion, and it was time to find someone who could actually handle the duties of a Designated Broker. Zelda could be the answer to the increasing problems at the other office. Of course, it depended upon whether her references, experience, and training checked all the required boxes for such an advanced position.

Next, came the call to Spokane and Ryan Walters who

was between the traditional rock and a hard place. He couldn't wait until the rest of his commissions were received by the brokerage. Everything was going well with the new job, but he wouldn't have any income for a couple months until the deals he'd made before his departure went through escrow and closed.

He needed an advance on his final check to make a downpayment on the house he was buying in Eastern Washington. Claire agreed to contact the accountant the next day, provided Ryan stopped hassling Tony.

"Are you serious?" Ryan laughed, his big, bass voice rumbling like a mountain. "Doesn't the guy have a sense of humor? Or was it removed during boot camp? Then, again he might have lost it in combat."

Claire shook her head, watching Ryan's dark face fill with mirth on the computer screen. "I think it's gone down the swirly ever since Perry took over your job."

"No way. Come on, Claire. The guy's a decent enough associate if somebody holds his hand and pats him on the po-po, but he can barely sell homes to first-time buyers."

"You're preaching to the choir." Claire leaned back in her chair. "I told Tony we shouldn't promote him, but he thought I was being too harsh."

"So, what's your plan to flush him? I know you have one."

"Between you and me, I'm thinking about asking Mike Flannagan to take him on—"

"No way! Why?" Ryan rested his chin on massive fists. "What's Mike ever done to you?"

"Perry would be a perfect fit for the kind of property Mike prefers to sell. Rocklin's is too high pressure for Perry and if I finesse this correctly, I think Mike will see it as a win-win."

"And Tony?"

"Oh, once I send Perry down the road, Tony will be happy enough to have less alligators chomping his butt. He's whining about all the ones he has to deal with when he's draining the proverbial swamp."

Another big laugh. "Claire, get real. Master Sergeants don't whine. They bitch a lot, and everyone ends up doing pushups or hunting snipe–cigarette butts on the parade ground."

"Well, then I'll be sure to remind the landscapers to clean the entire parking lot before he gets back from Rocklin. I don't want to wreck my manicure out there."

More laughter and their conversation ended on a good note. Claire sent off a quick email to the accounting firm before she headed to the break-room for a refill on her coffee. She paused when she saw George Delaney, a small, scrawny man in his late twenties ahead of her at the counter. He wore a crisply ironed white shirt tucked into pressed dark slacks and his recently polished black shoes gleamed.

She smiled at him. "Good morning, George. Glad you could make it in today."

"Like I had a choice when Eileen called and said you wanted me in the office ASAP." He scowled at Claire, anger rising on his thin face and landing in the icy-blue eyes. "I didn't have to be here for you to fire me. I know I'm not pulling my weight."

"So, are you always an asshat on Sundays?" Claire adopted one of Tony's favorite words and sauntered across the room to brew a fresh cup. "Or is this a special occasion? Do you have power at your apartment?"

"Not yet." He eyed her warily. "That electrical storm made it sound like I was back in the *sandbox* last night."

"I'm sorry." Claire gestured toward the couch. "There's blankets in the storage closet. Grab a couple tonight and stay here. Let Eileen know so she can show you how to set the security system if you go out to snag dinner."

"Really?"

Claire nodded. "I'd offer to loan you Tony to kick tails, but he kept me safe during the storm Friday night. He stuck around all day yesterday with me. I was scared half to death, and I never served in the military."

"Then, it was good you had Top to watch your six." George shifted slightly, steadied himself before limping over to the table and the box of doughnuts. "I got those comps for you. Eileen said to tell you that the owner is willing to see you this afternoon."

"Us." When the machine finished making her coffee, Claire joined him. "We'll go check out the place and see if it's as good as Tony claims. If it is, you list it and start showing it."

George stared at her. "I thought you'd be pissed because I refused to list those other houses. They were perfect shit-storms, Claire."

"Then, we don't want them." She selected one of the smaller apple fritters. "Rocklins' has a rep, George. We don't sell crap. We're honest with all our clientele. If you don't believe in what you're showing, you can't make your buyer happy."

"Top said he figured I'd do well here. I don't want to disappoint him."

"You won't." Claire bit into the pastry, chewed and swallowed. "We're not looking for lawsuits. I don't like going to court although my lawyer is one of my sorority sisters and a real shark. But she'd be the first to pitch a fit if we're not reputable."

While she finished the fritter, she looked at the places he showed her on his computer. He'd chosen a decent assortment of comparative properties that were similar to the house in the University district. He had a good eye for what worked and could explain his reasoning. She didn't tell him she'd speak to Eileen about letting him think he was in trouble.

The older woman was an excellent office manager, but she did enjoy 'stirring the pot to make it boil' upon occasion. Manipulating George so he'd worry about his job was inappropriate and Claire needed to handle it before Tony did. He had a soft spot for prior service soldiers, especially those who still needed him to look after them. Since he'd brought George on board here, Eileen would find herself looking for a job and Claire didn't want to lose the best supervisor she'd ever had.

———

After a hearty lunch of clam chowder, roasted vegetables, and slabs of cornbread topped with butter and homemade strawberry jam, Tony happily headed outdoors to assess the two big windblown maples lying in the side yard. Luckily, they'd missed the outbuildings. Beckett wanted the trees cut into two-foot pieces. After they seasoned for a year, he'd be able to burn them in the wood-stove he used to heat the older split-level home.

Halfway through the first log, a dark-haired teen, Jimmy Rocklin arrived, brandishing a splitting maul on his shoulder. He was accompanied by his cousin, Peyton, a smaller blonde girl. Tony recognized the pair as Lee's grandkids and shut off the saw for a moment, before nodding a greeting. "Hi there. Are your dad and grandpa here to help?"

"Nope." Jimmy walked to the other end of the log. "I'll split these rounds. Peyton, get the wheelbarrow out of the toolshed."

"Great-Gramma called and asked us to come help. She said she'd pay us, but Jimmy told her, no way. We don't want Great-Grampa back in the hospital." Peyton started toward the small red and white shed. "Besides, they already do lots for us."

"Like what?" Tony asked, waiting to fire up his chainsaw again.

"Oh, they pay for my sports gear at school. I do football, basketball, and baseball," Jimmy said. "And Peyton has riding lessons twice a week. We visit every weekend and they like that."

Peyton returned in time to hear him. "So do we. Great-Gramma says there's vanilla ice-cream and she'll have fresh brownies by the time we finish, so let's get started."

Tony chuckled. "You sound like Claire. She's a great recreational director too."

That earned him a long look before Peyton heaved a sigh. "I wish I could meet her and Uncle Connor, but Great-Gramma says they think nobody wants them here."

"Yeah, well when I go to college next year, I'm going to reach out to them," Jimmy said. "I remember Aunt Claire used to take me pony riding when I was little, and Uncle Connor always met us at the ice-cream parlor for sundaes. I don't care what my dad says. His war with them isn't mine."

"Good to know." Tony started his saw and moved down the log, cutting the next section into pieces. Behind him, he heard the solid thump of the maul hitting rounds while Jimmy split wood and his young cousin began loading the pieces into the wheelbarrow. The pair were always friendly when Tony ran into them during his visits to Rocklin.

He wondered if Claire reached out to them and how often she touched base with her paternal grandparents. He smiled. Inquiring minds wanted to know these things, and he wasn't afraid to bring up the subject. Perhaps, his mother might be aware of the answer. She certainly seemed comfortable visiting Agnes and Beckett Rocklin.

That evening, they had the warmed-up soup and corn-bread Agnes sent for supper. While they lingered over apple pie and coffee, Tony glanced at his pleasantly plump mother. She wasn't as tall as Claire, but both had clouds of black hair although streaks of gray accented Maria Baldusi's. "I didn't realize you and the older Rocklins still saw each other."

Maria shrugged, her dark brown eyes amused. "I divorced their son, not them. We're still friendly at church, but I wouldn't say I'm a hundred-percent in the loop. When Beckett came home from the hospital last spring, the pastor said Aggie needed help looking after him. Lee and Barb were nowhere to be found. And Barb's kids have busy lives. The only ones who showed up on a regular basis were Jimmy Junior and Peyton."

"They're hard workers." Tony swallowed more coffee. "Without them, I'd never have finished cutting up, splitting, and stacking that firewood in the shed. I don't think Beckett should be doing it."

"He'd have tried." Maria shook her head ruefully. "And I'd have been calling the EMTs to haul him back to the hospital. I'm glad Aggie phoned the kids."

Tony nodded, rubbing his jaw, feeling stubble against his fingers. "Claire texted me, concerned Lee is making trouble. Have you heard anything?"

"Hmm, that's an interesting question." Maria folded her arms and contemplated the idea. "I haven't, but that doesn't mean much because a lot of people aren't comfortable sharing items about my ex-husband with me. However, I do know one of the file clerks at the town hall left in a hurry. Rumor had it she and Barb got in a cat-fight."

"Sounds like Lee hasn't changed his spots, Mom. He's still cheating on his wives."

"Nothing new there, son. And if he doesn't have any morality where we're concerned, I'd be willing to bet he's just as crooked with the rest of his business dealings. Now, what are you going to do about the twins? Agnes wants them here for the holidays, but she's afraid to reach out to them. Claire sends cards from both of them on holidays but doesn't call or email or write or even visit. I don't know if Beckett will be around much longer and neither does he."

"Claire has 'daddy' issues and Connor supports her a hundred-plus percent."

"I understand perfectly, but I'm not talking about their father. They need to visit their grandparents. Make it happen, Anthony Marco Baldusi."

Chapter Nine

O n Monday morning, Claire met Sofia in the management office. Since the college student had afternoon classes, she'd catch up on the administrative tasks before going to the university. She agreed to text Claire the results of the reference checks on Harry Gamack, so he'd be able to move into the vacant apartment sooner rather than later. When she left for the Everett brokerage, Sofia had started filing correspondence.

Claire carefully timed the trip, so she'd miss rush hour traffic and reach the realty in an upscale strip mall near an exclusive waterfront neighborhood. Collecting her laptop bag and purse, she stood in the well-landscaped parking lot and scanned the after-effects of Friday's rainstorm.

Piles of gold, red and brown leaves filled the gutters by the street and covered the storm drains. She stepped around the deepening puddles to avoid soaking her new suede ankle boots. A few windblown branches still lay in the flowerbeds. Garbage from overturned cans littered the pavement, debris from the other businesses in the mall.

Frowning, Claire headed toward the front door of the building. When she stepped inside, she found a casually dressed young man behind the reception desk. Not recognizing him, she glanced at the nametag, Scott Jenkins. She waited for him to end his private conversation and put away his cell phone.

When she didn't move away, he finally asked. "Can I help you?"

"Do you know who I am?" Claire asked in her sweetest voice.

He shook his head, long hair flopping around his shoulders. "Should I?"

She pointed to one of the three portraits on the wall behind him. "I'm Claire Rocklin. I own this establishment. The guy in the other picture is my partner, Tony. And the last one is my brother, Conn who is a silent investor in the business."

"I thought Tony— I mean I was told it was Mr. Baldusi's place."

She let the silence continue too long. "No. He works with me and believe me when he arrives, we will discuss your presence." Claire adjusted the shoulder strap of her laptop. She pointed out the window toward the messy parking lot. "What time will the landscapers be here?"

"Next week."

"That won't do." She deliberately scanned his jeans, sweatshirt, and sandals. "You're dressed for it. Either you clean up out there or you get them here to do it." Turning, she eyed the coffee cups and leftover newspapers scattered around the room on the long tables where the associates worked. "Apparently, the cleaning service couldn't get here Friday night because of the weather. After you finish outside, you can take care of the inside. The same rule applies. Arrange for the people who are supposed to do the job to do it, or you take care of it."

"Yes, ma'am. I mean, of course, Ms. Rocklin." Scott hastily looked at the list of numbers beside the desk phone. "I'm on it."

"Good. I'll be in Mr. Baldusi's office. I want the latest contracts there." She ostentatiously looked at her gold, designer watch. "Tell David Badgley, the Designated Broker I'm waiting for him when he arrives."

"He's on the afternoon shift," Scott squawked. "He won't be here until two."

"I'm not waiting more than three hours for him. Call him. Tell him to be here by noon. I'm due in Bellevue by three and I'm never late."

"Yes, Ms. Rocklin."

Claire started away, then spun around. "One more thing. Does Mr. Baldusi allow casual clothes on Mondays?"

No answer and she swept Scott with a calm gaze. "I didn't think so. Pass the word to the associates that I expect professional attire at all times. At Rocklin, we sell the most elite properties and to make the kind of money I expect, we have to look not only like we're worth it but also like we don't need it."

"Yes, ma'am."

She heard him on the phone issuing orders as she strolled through the room. The cleaning service had a great deal of work to do, not only taking care of the clutter, but also wiping the blinds. The windows needed washing, and the decorator plants required care. She took time to check the breakroom while she headed for the coffee machine. More cups all over the place and stale doughnuts on the table. She avoided the refrigerator where the staff kept their lunches, concluding it was too big a risk to glance inside.

She debated silently whether she wanted to look at the restrooms and then decided against it. She'd wait until after the cleaning service arrived.

She turned on the lights in Tony's office. The desk was immaculate, not a speck of dust. Paperwork was stacked neatly in the basket on the corner. When she opened the blinds, sunlight shone through gleaming windows. It showed today's untidiness was an aberration, not a usual custom. *Good*, she thought. She hated firing people and clearing out and replacing all the staff would be a major headache. She set her laptop on the desk and opened the programs she needed to review the recent contracts.

Less than an hour later, someone tapped on the door. Claire looked toward it. "Come in."

David Badgley, a tall, graying man in a blue suit hurried inside. "I didn't expect you, Claire. If I'd known—"

Claire gestured to the door, opting for one of Tony's business maxims, 'Praise in public. Punish in private.' "Close it, David. We need to talk."

He did and she waved toward the visitor's chair on the other side of the desk. "Talk to me. Normally, you're the best in this business. I couldn't believe it when I walked in here today. What's going on, David? Why is this place such a disaster? And who the hell hired that kid to be the first person clients see?"

"It's my fault." David sank into the opposite chair. "My son-in-law called last Tuesday, and my daughter was in the hospital having the baby three weeks early. And my wife and I caught the first plane to Chicago, and everything went to hell while I was gone. I thought between Virginia, the senior associate, and Ingrid the office manager, the brokerage would be fine. Only—"

"Okay." Claire leaned back and smiled at him, opting for

charm. "I knew there was a good reason for the office to look like it'd been through one of Tony's shitstorms. Now, let's do the important stuff first. I've got to see a picture of the baby. Boy or girl?"

David relaxed and reached for his phone. "A girl. She's healthy and so is her mama. My wife is staying for a couple weeks to help, and I'll fly back for Thanksgiving."

"Good. That's great news. I'll work from here in December so you can stay a little longer." Claire oohed and aahed over the photos of a lovely newborn and an obviously exhausted, excited mother while listening to all the details David provided.

Baby first, Claire thought. *It's time to make all the right noises and I will.*

She quickly decided to remain in this office for the remainder of the day and help David get everything back on track. They'd set up an online conference for the two of them to connect with the Designated Brokers in the other Rocklin realties.

———

He was early for his appointment with the contractor to preview the new apartment house in north Seattle, so Tony stopped by the Everett brokerage on the way back from Rocklin. He spotted Claire's ruby-red Lincoln Navigator parked in his reserved spot and pulled in beside it. She'd undoubtedly tease him about showing up in the outdoor clothes he'd worn at his mom's rather than going straight to his condo and changing into a business suit. He glanced around the parking lot and saw two of the landscapers cleaning up branches and bagging leaves. A third person trimmed the ornamental rhododendrons.

Tony waved at the people from the teriyaki restaurant from the other end of the strip mall who cleaned their share of the parking lot. Obviously, everyone had the same thing in mind that he did when he was in Rocklin. After Friday night's storm, there was plenty of work to do. When he walked inside, he nodded to a young man sitting at the receptionist's desk instead of the woman who usually handled visitors and phone calls. "Where's Ingrid?"

"She and Virginia are having a meeting with the owner." The twenty-something eyed him warily. "Are you—?"

"Tony Baldusi." He frowned at the younger man who wore an oversized shirt and tie. "I didn't hire you."

"No, sir. My sister, Robyn, arranged for me to be here. I'm Scott Jenkins."

"Really?" Tony walked toward the far end of the room where the dark-haired associate broker made a show of scanning properties on her computer. "Why is your brother at Ingrid's desk?"

"She quit last week," Robyn said hastily. "And I knew we needed someone to do her job. I was just trying to help."

"And yet she's here talking to Claire?" Tony gazed at the woman and watched embarrassment creep in red patches across her face. "We'll discuss this later."

He strode down the hall and paused outside his closed office door. Shaking his head, he paused, then turned the knob and walked inside, past David Badgley, the Designated Broker. Claire sat behind the desk, her attention apparently on the other two women about his age who'd bypassed the couch on the inside wall for visitor chairs in front of her. "Hello, Tony. How was your trip?"

"Fine." He walked past Virginia Ryerson and Ingrid Swensen, both of whom looked upset. The receptionist, a petite brunette hunched in a chair, tears trickling down her face. "What's going on?"

"Drama City." Claire heaved a sigh and pushed a box of tissues toward Ingrid. "While David was away being a grandpa, these two abandoned the realty when he was counting on them. So, now I have to decide what to do with them." She tipped back her head when Tony walked over to stand beside her and looked up at him. "I hate histrionics. Isn't dealing with them your job?"

"Yes, it is, sweetness." He chuckled, leaned down to kiss her forehead. "Now, why don't you get your cute butt out of my chair, go to lunch with David and let me handle it?"

"Works for me." Claire pushed back the wheeled chair, rose to her feet. She smiled at him. "Stop sexually harassing me or I'll complain to your boss."

"Since that's you, I think I'm pretty safe." He kissed her quickly, his lips brushing hers.

In one of her pairs of red-soled, expensive high-heeled ankle boots, they were almost the same height. She was a fashion diva in a red, button-up tunic style top over black leggings. She'd French braided her black hair and as usual had perfect makeup.

He kissed her again. "Got room for another associate in the Seattle office if David can spare her?"

"Who are you thinking?" Claire lingered in the circle of his arm for a moment. "These two aren't going anywhere. David needs them when he has to return to Chicago to 'grandpa' up at Thanksgiving."

"Good to know. How about Robyn Jenkins and her brother?"

"David and I will talk about it." Claire eased around the contemporary wooden desk, narrowing her gaze on

Virginia. "Next time, somebody gives you crap, call for rein-forcements, damn it. Don't let her mess with my business."

"I've got this." Tony urged Claire in the direction of the door. "Bring me back one of their chicken teriyaki lunch specials and some eggrolls. Don't forget the sweet and sour sauce." He waited until she and the head broker left the room before he focused on the two older women. "Okay, let's see what we can work out. How long has Robyn Jenkins been sabotaging the place? Why didn't you bring me into the loop before?"

"Because I've been selling property for years." Virginia Ryerson ran a hand through her silvery auburn hair. "I was one of the first brokers Claire hired when she opened her own brokerage. How was I supposed to say I couldn't handle the little twit's manipulating? I've met all sorts of people. I got played."

"It wasn't all your fault." Ingrid Swensen wiped her small face with a tissue. "I got snookered too. She'd tell the other associates I misplaced their messages, didn't make appointments for them when I did. And I just lost it last week when three of them yelled at me. I'd already been hammered by the agent at the escrow office and the para-legal at the lawyer's pitched a fit about the closings this month. So, I stormed out. It was stupid."

"We should have called Claire, but she was dealing with the emergency in Ocean Shores when those tourists trashed that weekend rental and we knew she was up to her eyeballs already," Virginia went on. "And then the storm hit. I figured on handling this today when you were here, but I didn't expect Claire to get here first."

"Makes sense." Tony rubbed his jaw thoughtfully. "Now, after Robyn goes to the Seattle office, what happens with the rest of the associates? Will they continue to harass Ingrid?"

"Not when David and I get done reorganizing the shifts," Virginia said firmly. "We'll break up the cliques. It's all going to be okay, Tony. Rocklin's comes first."

Tony nodded. "That's what I want to see, everyone working out their issues. Ingrid, what do you say? Shall we go bounce that boy out from behind your desk while Ginny starts work on the new schedule? I need you out there keeping everything on the straight and narrow."

A faint smile slipped across her face, and she stood. "You're going to show everyone you have my back, aren't you?"

"Well, I can't let Ginny and Dave have all the fun." Tony agreed. "And if you try to leave us, Claire will have my guts for garters."

Ingrid led the way to the office door. She barely suppressed a giggle more suitable for a woman half her age and gestured to the sofa. "And you don't want to end up sleeping on that couch when she's mad."

Tony opened the door, cupped her elbow, and guided Ingrid in the direction of the reception area. "Please don't give Claire any ideas about how to torture me. She has plenty of her own."

Chapter Ten

C laire heaved a sigh of relief when she unlocked the door and escaped into the sanctuary of her apartment. She slipped off her shoes and dropped her laptop bag and purse on the chair in the hallway. She scooped up Felix, snuggling the tuxedo kitten. "It was a day. Let's go find a glass of wine for me and a dish of kitty meat for you."

A mew and a sandpaper tongue licked her chin. She continued to describe the drama at the brokerage in Everett. "Then, Robyn Jenkins pitched a fit when we told her about the transfer. She either works in Seattle or goes down the road. Making trouble with other staff puts her in violation of her employment contract. I told her younger brother that he has to dress and act appropriately. Eileen will train him to be the kind of receptionist I want."

More meowing as the young cat commented on the subject. Claire stroked soft fur. "So, then I had to call Eileen and give her a heads-up, or she'll be in a butt-kicking mood when I get there on Thursday. I definitely can't deal with her snarkiness too."

Once Felix had a spoonful of cat meat on his saucer and

she filled a glass with Riesling, she arranged assorted crackers, sharp cheddar cheese, and deli meat on a small plate of her own. She rinsed off a handful of grapes, adding them to her appetizers. Then, she headed into the living-room. She contemplated turning on the news and gave up the idea. After dealing with a daily dose of drama at work, she didn't want to listen to the local or national woes.

Instead, she curled up on the black couch and opened the latest magazine featuring local houses for sale. As always, Tony had done a great job of choosing potential Rocklin properties to advertise. A short time later, Felix joined her. He jumped up beside her and proceeded to lie down, washing his white-tipped paws.

Once she skimmed through their listings, Claire moved onto those of their competitors. Her gaze narrowed on a brick two-story with a widow's walk overlooking the bay in Everett. Oh yes, that definitely deserved a physical inspection, not merely a 'look-see' on the Internet. Since she'd be at that brokerage tomorrow, she could take George Delaney with her.

She'd already talked to him about transferring out to the other office, telling him she wanted Virginia Ryerson to train him to be her assistant. He was excited about the possibility of a promotion. It meant higher commissions and a larger salary. An added bonus would be giving the older woman somebody loyal to her who'd watch what Tony called, her 'six'. Claire marked the advertisement with a pen and then turned the page.

She sipped wine and ate munchies while she skimmed the rest of the brochure. She debated a second glass and decided she'd earned it. A knock on the front door interrupted her on the way to the kitchen. In her stocking feet, she padded to the door and peered through the peephole. Recognizing Tony, she unlocked and opened up. He always looked so handsome in one of his three-piece business suits. Still, he was super sexy in the flannel shirt, jeans and boots he wore when he visited the small town of Rocklin and was roughing it. He obviously hadn't gone home to his condo and changed yet.

She smiled up at him. "What's going on?"

"Dinner." Smiling at her, he stepped inside, carrying a box. "Bonnie said it was Pedro Ramirez's turn to cook. He sent up chicken-cheese enchiladas and salad. She added dark chocolate cheesecake bites for dessert. I'm ready to move in here."

"You're not old enough." Claire held the door for him and closed it quickly, so Felix didn't escape into the hall. They followed Tony to the eat-in kitchen. "Besides, nobody cooks supper again until Thursday. Tomorrow is breakfast and Wednesday is lunch."

"I'll have to write down that schedule." He put the box on the counter. "Are you ready to hear all about the renovations on the new apartment house?"

"Yes, tell me about it." She opened the cupboard and removed two plates, and two bowls for the salads. "What did you and Logan Turner work out for the duration?"

"First, you were right about his motivation. He hadn't realized you were involved with anyone. He wanted you, but that's over now. He took it fine when I introduced myself as your partner and you still have a contractor."

"Thanks. So glad you two managed to do the male bonding thing." Claire heaved a sigh. "And everybody thinks women are too emotional."

"Hey, doesn't matter the gender. When people are left in the lurch and have their hearts broke, they have issues."

Tony dished up the entrée, placing a serving on each plate. Green salad followed. "Got dressing?"

"In the fridge. You have a choice. Ranch or ranch."

"Guess we'll have ranch."

He nodded when she held up the wine bottle and she refilled her glass, plus one for him. When they sat at the table, Felix climbed up her leg to land in her lap. She petted him, then gently lowered him to the floor. She didn't want cat hair in her supper. "Tell me more."

"Only if you bring me up to speed on what you worked out with George Delaney."

"Sounds like a deal."

They discussed business over the meal. While she took the last serving of enchiladas and salad to Connor's so he could eat after his shift, Tony cleaned the kitchen. When she returned, she found him in the living-room, the tuxedo kitten curled up behind him on the back of the couch.

He was looking through the magazine of newly listed houses. He glanced up from the page she'd marked. "I like this place. I think I'll buy it and sell my condo."

"Why would you do something so quintessentially stupid? Your condo is perfect." She walked across the room, pulling out her phone to bring up the listing. She sat next to him and started scrolling through the pictures of the property. "The price is too high for this dump. No curb appeal. Blackberry bushes, scrub alder and nettles have overgrown the entire yard. The wrought iron decorator fence is more rust than metal in the front and you can't even see the back one."

"And the inside?"

"All four bedrooms are on the second floor. I'm not counting the main or primary bedroom which is way too close to the smallest. The ensuite is old. It only has one sink, no shower and a clawfoot bathtub." She wrinkled her nose in disgust. "Not a walk-in closet in the place. Don't get me started on the downstairs. Whoever designed it never heard of 'open-concept.'"

"Show me the kitchen." He leaned closer. "Does it have a butler's pantry for Felix?"

"No way, Anthony Marco Baldusi. You're not stealing my cat."

"I figure both of you will move in with me after the wedding."

"Typical male. You never listen. I told you before. I'm not the marrying kind." She went to the next set of photos, and they viewed the other two bathrooms, before she brought up the kitchen with its wooden cupboards and countertops. "It's a total gut-job, Tony."

"I like old-fashioned." He tugged gently on her braid. "Show me more. Where's the laundry?"

"In the basement." She shuddered and narrowed her eyes. "You're teasing me, right? Nobody sane would want to go down there. Would you believe they have one of those old-time laundry chutes like my grandmother's house did?"

"So, we move the washer and dryer up to the pantry and convert the basement into a media and game room." He trailed a finger over her lips. "We need somewhere to hold our poker games."

"Bah, humbug. Who'd show up? The demons will eat them."

"They're only invited if they bring enough money to ante up. Keep going. I want to see the rest."

"No." She tilted her chin, surprised to discover he'd drawn so close. "You're not buying a wreck like this, Tony. It's a waste of money."

"You're only saying that because you saw it first and you want it. If you didn't, you wouldn't have marked it."

She gasped. "How did you know?"

"Because I'm smarter than you think." His mouth was a breath away. "It's mine. Just like you."

"In your dreams. I'm keeping it."

He took the phone from her and put it on the coffee table. "And I'm keeping you." His mouth claimed hers.

She knew better but she couldn't resist. She surrendered to the kiss, her lips parting, her tongue inviting his to play. He accepted the invitation, and she laced her arms around his neck. A second kiss followed the first. She sighed when he turned his head, and his mouth slowly explored her neck to the hollow of her throat. "You should go home."

"I am home." He unfastened the buttons of her red tunic blouse. "Whenever I'm with you, I'm home."

"Seriously?" She moaned when the material parted to reveal her breasts. He cupped one and her nipple tightened against his thumb. His mouth captured hers again. He nipped at her lips. When they opened, his tongue swept inside. This time neither of them were playing. She kissed him back, hands tangling in his short hair. She pressed nearer, her body melting into his. He deepened the kiss, encouraging her tongue to duel with his.

He kept kissing her while he unhooked the front closure of her bra. She pulled back a little. She had to call a stop to it, but she enjoyed his touch far too much. He pushed the bra out of the way and freed her breasts. He slowly teased the first nipple with his tongue before he sucked on it. She groaned, dug her nails into his shoulders. He found her second nipple with his thumb and first finger, gently rubbing. He rolled the other nipple against his tongue, then sucked again.

She clutched his hair, sighed and whispered his name. She arched closer to him. "We shouldn't."

He smiled and raised his head a little. "We are."

He returned to her breasts. He drew the nipple back into his warm mouth and sucked again.

Turnabout was fair play. She unbuttoned his plaid shirt. She spread her fingers on his wide chest, wishing he hadn't worn a T-shirt, and she could feel the warmth of his skin. She nipped his ear before kissing the strong line of his neck.

One of his hands found the waist of her black jean leggings and he unfastened the top button. She trembled when he reached for the second one. She caught his wrist. "No more."

He paused, slowly lifted his head until their gazes met and clashed. "Are you sure about that? Let's go to bed."

"Not tonight." She shook her head, eased away from him. "You won't be satisfied with a one-night hook-up, Tony and I don't have any more to give than that."

"Oh yes, you do." He leaned over, brushed her mouth with his. "I can wait until you're ready to admit it."

"Never."

He winked at her. "Don't make me prove you're lying."

"I'm not." She fumbled with her bra and hastily clipped the front closure before she shrugged back into her blouse. "Let's call it a night."

"If you insist." He stood. "I'll have you one night soon, and you'll like it, Claire Rocklin."

"I'm sure I would. You're hard to resist." She rose to her feet, took his hand, and led him to the front door. "But I'm going to keep things the way they are a while longer. I need you in the business, more than I need to get laid."

———

Tony waited until she closed the door behind him before he buttoned his shirt. Damn, she was stubborn. God, he wanted her. He felt it everywhere, through every inch of his body. He'd warned her. Sooner or later, he'd have all of her and no, he wouldn't be satisfied with one night. He'd keep her for the rest of his life.

He headed for the elevator. The doors opened, revealing Connor coming home from his shift at the cop shop. Tony eyed the younger man's amused, dark blue gaze. "Don't say it."

"Somebody has to." Connor laughed. "Man, it's going to take forever before she admits what she feels for you."

"Nobody likes a smartass who says, 'I told you so.' Tony eyed the younger man. "When is your next night off? I need to talk to you and Claire about family stuff."

"Wednesday." The humor faded and Connor frowned, putting on an impassive cop face. Obviously, he'd learned to compartmentalize his emotions when he was a kid at military school. "The only family I have is my sister."

"You've got more than that and I'm not talking about Lee or Barb and the grown stepkids from hell. Wednesday night. We'll go to dinner and talk."

"I can cook for us."

"No. If we go to a restaurant, Claire won't have a temper tantrum."

"Wow, Tony. You really need to take some time to know my sister."

Chapter Eleven

B etween hitting the gym in the morning, returning to the office at the apartment building to train Sofia and then driving out to the Everett brokerage, Tuesday rushed by. Early that afternoon, Claire and George toured the brick two-story house. It was in worse condition than the pictures revealed, and she happily made a low-ball offer. She gave the owners two days to consider it but figured it was a done deal because she'd be paying cash for the place, and most people wouldn't turn down that kind of money.

Reshuffling the associates in the Everett brokerage had worked wonders. Nobody seemed upset or concerned Robyn Jenkins was reassigned to the Seattle one. George, her favorite spy, promised to keep Claire in the loop. Business-wise, everything was great. Now, all she had to deal with was nearly jumping Tony's bones on Monday night. He hadn't said anything about it when they saw one another at the office during the past two days.

He'd invited her out for dinner at one of the restaurants on the Everett waterfront when they finished work on Wednesday. It offered wonderful selections of Pacific North-west seafood, fancy beef steaks, and had a great wine selection so she was guaranteed a good meal. Plus, she had the added benefit of teasing him if she had the new house. She'd texted Logan Turner and let him know there'd be another project when he finished the apartment building in the north end of Seattle.

However, every once in a while, she caught Tony staring at her in a new way. She hoped he didn't realize it made her breath catch in her throat and her nipples tighten against her bra. And never mind what it did to her knees. Of course, she rarely slept with men she dated, but she didn't do well with ongoing personal commitments, and it was more fun finding perfect housing for senior citizens, her favorite project. As she'd warned him more than once, she wasn't risking their partnership for a roll in the sack. Then again, if he agreed to a 'no strings attached' booty call, they could 'hook up' occasionally.

Early Wednesday afternoon, Claire glared at the laptop screen. Why did she think he wouldn't go for that idea?

Because he's been talking about marriage and I'm not stupid. Still whenever I see the rain clouds outside the office window, they remind me of his eyes. Soft, gray and oh so tender. Nope, not going there. Stop this, Claire Erica Rocklin!

She stood and went to the window, adjusting the blinds so she wouldn't watch the November drizzle instead of her waiting work on the laptop screen. It wasn't a fierce storm, more the kind the locals referred to as 'Oregon mist' because it missed the neighboring state and landed here. The newscasters promised it'd clear off for the afternoon and they'd have occasional sunbursts. When she turned, she saw Tony, a tall hunk of masculinity in one of his black suits, standing in the doorway.

She took a deep breath, refusing to admit she felt a sudden surge of excitement. "What's going on?"

"Not much. Ingrid brought fresh doughnuts from the bakery when she came back from lunch. I thought you'd be ready for a break."

"I don't know." She glanced at her watch. "I have an online meeting with the Designated Brokers for the other offices in twenty minutes."

"David told me about it. He's setting up in the conference room." Tony walked toward her, holding out his hand. "Come on, sweetheart. You know how grumpy you get when you're dealing with stupid questions, and you can't tear people apart in one of the 'distance' rather than 'in-person' meetings. I'll run some interference for you if you join me for doughnut time."

"All right. You win, darling." She went to meet him, and his fingers closed over hers. "You've got a deal but be prepared for some fireworks. I'm promoting Zelda Torres to Designated Co-Broker over at the Eastside office and that should take some of the pressure off Perry's shoulders."

"Why would that be a problem?"

"Because it means he has to take a pay cut. She'll earn more money after the promotion."

"That's fair since she'll have more responsibility."

"Yeah, I'll let you point that out to Perry when he starts whining and whinging, Tony. I can't stand grown men who act like crybabies especially when I can't smack them because it's politically incorrect."

"It's all going to be okay."

"I'll hold you to that."

A sugar encrusted doughnut and cup of coffee later, Claire was ready for the meeting. She stopped back by her office to snag a copy of the agenda she'd emailed to the brokers earlier. She drew on her black jacket over a pin-striped blouse, her feminine version of what Tony wore. The blazer matched her ankle-length black slacks. Most realtors dressed much more casually than she or her staff did, but she always remembered what her maternal grand-father had said about 'selling the sizzle, not the steak.'

Rocklin's was a step-up from other brokerages, and she made sure everyone knew it from their clientele to their competition. David had set up the large wall-screen so they could see one another. It was the same one they used when Tony wanted to teach a class. Claire pulled up the chair at the end of the table. It meant everyone could see her and of course, she could see them too. Tony and David hadn't joined her, but she expected them any minute.

One of the first virtual arrivals was her one-time sorority sister, Dominique MacGillicudy from Baker City, the town in the Cascade foothills she was determined to restore. Claire waved at her. "Hey, Dominique. Are you coming to the big city for our shopping getaway in three weeks?"

"Wouldn't miss it for the world. You know I love hitting the holiday sales with you."

"Me too. What do you want?"

"Does that matter?" The tall, classy blonde raised an eyebrow. "Of course, I need a new pair of *Louboutin* shoes."

"Only one?" Claire lifted her leg so her former university roommate could see the bottom of her black stiletto with the distinctive red sole. "How can you get by with only a single pair?"

"Okay, I'll check the budget and go for broke. Maybe, I'll buy two or three pairs, but I can't go hog-wild if I want to load up with gifts for my niece and nephew."

"Perfect. I'll help with that, so Lilly and Nick don't rain on your parade."

"Oh, it's okay. I'll throw Jimmy under that particular bus and say he told me to do it."

Claire grinned appreciatively. "Are you ever making an honest man out of him?"

"When I'm ready. For now, we enjoy living in sin and irritating the entire MacGillicudy clan."

Tony entered and nodded a greeting at Dominique. "Hello, there. How's business up north?"

"Better than last year." She smiled at him and then greeted David. "Claire told me the good news about the baby. How's it feel to be a grandpa?"

While the two of them chatted, Tony leaned close to Claire. "Why did you invite one of our competitors to a staff meeting?"

"Dom isn't a competitor. She's a good friend and we work together on a lot of our sales. When she lists something one of our clients might like, she texts or emails me." Claire didn't mention the fact that she'd invested in the other woman's realty three years before, prior to Tony starting work with her. He didn't need to know about the MacGillicudy family *conflama*, a cross between the conflicts and drama that Dominique went through with her father. He always had a plan that included wiping out the natural resources of Washington State.

Worse than that, he thought he was irresistible to all women and constantly pursued Claire when she visited her friend. *Okay, so I bust my butt to look good because every salesperson realizes the first thing to do is sell herself in order to sell real estate, but that lecher knows I'm more than financially secure and he wants my money. He's not getting one red cent.*

Tony skimmed through the agenda one last time before the meeting began. After the introductions, they listened to the latest sales projections from each brokerage and Claire made notes. She went over the changes in the Everett office and told Zelda to cross-train the associates in the Eastside branch. Everyone needed to be able to work together.

Tony took over after that and brought up the new training schedule. If any broker hadn't completed the necessary professional hours, those needed to be done by the end of the year. Granted, most realties wouldn't make it a requirement, but Claire insisted Rocklin's be the pinnacle in their business. It was only one of the many reasons why they always turned a large profit and had managed to survive the pandemic better than some of their rivals.

Luckily, she'd had sense enough to follow her grandparents' advice and sell the properties she flipped rather than attempting to rent them. They'd discussed it several times when he was active duty and decided expanding into the other realm of the business didn't work for them. They didn't need to deal with the day-to-day responsibilities of handling tenants, which wasn't merely collecting rents but also maintaining the properties. Claire had enough issues with the vacation houses on the Washington coast.

That worked in their favor during the various shutdowns and eviction moratoriums during the last two years. She had something more going on with Dominique MacGillicudy but since it actually didn't affect their partnership, Tony opted for discretion. Sooner or later, Claire would confide in him. Meanwhile, he had other things in mind, like convincing her to take the risk of letting him into her life as more than a business partner.

After the meeting, he started for his office. His phone vibrated and he removed it from his jacket pocket, pausing in the hallway. He frowned when he recognized the caller, Mike Flannagan. What did the other realtor need? Well, only one way to find out. "Hello, Mike. How are you?"

"Doing great. Better than you." Mike sounded more amused than anything else. "So, I have good news and bad news. Which do you want first?"

"It's the sergeant in me. Tell me the bad first."

"Well, Claire's going to kick your ass from here to Tacoma. It's been nice knowing you, soldier boy."

"Really?" Tony chuckled. "What have I done to piss her off that I don't know about?"

"You offered full-price on that place she wanted to flip in Everett. One of my fellows was the listing agent and he didn't have the guts to call and say the owners accepted your deal."

"I'm guessing that's the good news." Tony glanced over his shoulder at the conference room. "I already have enough in the bank to pay for the house, so I don't have to wait until I sell my condo. I talked to the building manager a couple days ago, and he has three buyers waiting in the wings for a vacancy."

"Then, you're in luck. You're offering cash and they inherited the place during the pandemic and refused to invest any money in it. They'd be happy to go for an early closing."

"I'd like to start work on it before Christmas if that's possible."

"Let me see what I can do. Congratulations, Tony. It's a nice place with plenty of potential."

"That's what I thought, Mike. I've been looking for a home ever since I retired from the Army and this one is a keeper."

"I'm glad you got it. I like Claire, but she'd have turned

around and sold it after she rehabbed it. Fancy says everything goes toward Claire's apartment houses for senior citizens."

"Your little sis is right." Tony walked into his office. "Don't think I'm going to spare you. You're on your own, Flannagan. You have to call Claire yourself and tell her."

"I was afraid you'd say that." Mike laughed. "Okay but be prepared for the ship to hit the sand."

"Always!" He ended the call and put away his phone.

The quick tapping of heels on the tile floor a few minutes later warned Tony of her approach before she stormed into his office, slamming the door behind her. "You bastard!"

He swung around, eyeing her. Lord, she was a beauty especially in the middle of a raging fit. An ebony blazer clung to her breasts and slender waist. Matching slacks outlined her hips and long legs. Black hair swung around her shoulders, despite the blue decorator combs pinning back the sides. Fury lit the navy-blue eyes. Fists clenched, she advanced on him.

He grinned at her. "What's wrong, sweetheart?"

"You stole my house! Don't 'sweetheart' me, you son of a—"

"Now, Claire. You know you love my mother."

Tony couldn't resist. He caught her arm and pulled her against him. He kissed her. The fierce pressure of his mouth on hers bent back her head. He tangled his hands in her hair and heard the clatter of the combs hitting the floor. His tongue swept into her mouth as he staked a sensual, passionate claim. Regardless of how long it took her to admit it, she was his!

Chapter Twelve

Tony's lean, hard body pressed against hers and she gripped his arms, her hands sliding up to his broad shoulders. She tried to remind herself that she intended to keep her distance from him, but that was impossible. His mouth was on hers. The kiss was different than the ones a few nights before. Now, he kissed her as if he owned her. She liked it, wanted it more than she'd ever believed she could. Her head spun with a whirlwind of emotions.

Her pulses pounded and her excitement built. Sensations rocketed through her. He lifted his lips a scant inch from hers. Opening her eyes, she stared up into his rugged features. Their gazes met, clashed and she trembled when his mouth teased hers again.

Dimly, she was aware he'd unbuttoned her jacket. She gasped as he cupped her breast. Her nipples tightened even before his thumb found and tormented one. "Stop. We can't. Not here."

"Are you sure? I think we're doing just fine." He trailed a line of kisses along the side of her neck. "And you did close the door."

"It's not locked—"

"I can change that in a heartbeat."

She shook her head and managed to step back. "I need time to think about us."

His head lowered, his lips a breath away. "Thinking is over-rated."

"Not for me." She took another step and edged toward the door. "I have work to do and you're on my shit list. You knew I wanted that house for an investment. I could have made a million bucks on it and used the money for another apartment building."

"And I wanted it for a home." He shrugged a broad shoulder. "I win. You lose. I'll let you help rev it up before the wedding."

"What wedding?"

"Ours."

"In your dreams, Anthony Marco." She spun and stalked toward the door. "Payback is hard, and you'll get yours."

"As long as it means I'll have you in my bed, I'm good with it."

"Never happening."

"Oh, I'll change your mind sooner than you think, Claire Rocklin."

She tossed her head and realized the plastic combs she'd worn earlier were on the floor. She hastily scooped them up and left his office. She stopped by the restroom to straighten her appearance. At least, her blouse was still buttoned, and she left her jacket open. Her knees wobbled and she drew a ragged breath. Wow, she really wanted him. She'd known it before he kissed her, touched her and now, her damp panties really proved the point.

It doesn't matter, she told herself again. *I'm a grownup and there's been a lot of things I've wanted and haven't had, starting when my mother died, and Conner and I were alone in Lee's house. I can deal with what is and not bitch because life sucks sometimes.*

She worked the rest of the day, still annoyed about losing the house in Everett. But there would be other places, and she'd find a better one to flip. Then, she'd rub Tony's nose in his loss. Vengeance would be hers. Despite being irritated with him, she walked out of the building in time to join him for dinner.

He came over to the Lincoln Navigator when she opened the driver's door. "Give me a ride to the restaurant?" His tone made it a question.

"If you annoy me there, I'll leave you behind."

He feathered a thumb over her lips, lowering his voice to a bass rumble. "And then I'll show up at your door and we'll fight it out in your bedroom. I'll send you screaming to the moon and back. Don't be a brat."

She shivered at his touch. "Promises, promises."

"And one I'll keep someday." He kissed her quickly. "Let's go have supper and I'll wait on the multiple orgasms."

"Those are total fantasies." She pushed the button on the key-fob to unlock the passenger door. "You've been reading too much porn."

He laughed appreciatively. "Want to bet? You just shared that you've never made love with a *real* man."

On the way to the restaurant, they discussed the potential sale of his condo, and she agreed to handle it for him, so he'd get top dollar. Otherwise, he admitted he'd take the first offer just to get out from under and be able to move into the Everett house right away. She didn't admit his sexy threats thrilled her all the way to her stilettos. It was growing increasingly difficult to remind herself she wanted space, not to surrender to him. When they arrived at the waterfront, Tony pointed out a parking space next to Connor's pickup.

"I thought we were the only ones having dinner." Claire flicked Tony a sideways glance. "What's going on, Baldusi? Why is my brother here?"

"It's family business." He opened the door. "And at least if you ditch me, I'll be able to count on Conn giving me a ride back to the realty to get my Hummer."

"And you already had that in reserve." She sniffed and slid out from behind the wheel. She closed the door and hit the locks on the key-fob. "So much for the sex-talk. You're like the rest of the guys I've dated. As Blanche, one of my sorority sisters says, 'all mouth and nothing in the pants.' And she would know."

He grinned. "Okay, sweetheart. I'll show you what's in my pants soon."

Heat swamped her cheeks, and she stomped toward the main door of the restaurant where her twin waited. He greeted her with a quick kiss on the cheek. "What's happening? You look pissed."

"Tony's being a jerk." Claire waited while her brother escorted her inside the beautifully decorated entry. "I'm seriously considering shoving him in the bay when we go for a walk after dinner."

"Who said anything about a walk?" Tony caught up with them. "It looks like rain."

"Summer's over and it always rains here in November. If you're not man enough to take me out to look at the boats, then Connor will."

"Not if it's raining." Connor smiled at the waiting hostess. "I had enough shifts out in the weather this week."

"Then, I'll leave you wimps behind and go by myself." She ignored the glance they shared. Both of them were overprotective and they'd decided a long time ago she needed to be shielded from adversity. She often wondered what they thought she'd done when they were away on one of their combat tours in the military. She always managed to look after herself just fine.

During the meal, they talked about a variety of subjects ranging from Connor's work at the precinct to what was happening at the brokerages. He always turned down promotions, saying he preferred being a street cop to a desk jockey. Tony shared the news about his new house and Connor offered to help move what little furniture he had, a king-size bed, a dresser and a living-room set from the condo out to Everett.

"Sounds like we need to go shopping." Claire nodded at the waiter who offered to box up the remains of her 'surf and turf'dinner. She'd enjoy the leftover lobster and steak the next night. And now she could have cheesecake for dessert. "Make a list of what you want for the house, and we'll hit a few places when I get back from Cancun."

That earned a nod of approval from her twin. "Do you want me to drive you to the airport? Let me know when and I'll clear my schedule."

"Works for me." Claire saw concern mounting on Tony's rugged features and landing in the smoke-gray eyes. "Okay, what's on your mind? You know we don't do holidays. We haven't since Grandma and Gramps died right after my eighteenth birthday. I go to Mexico and Connor volunteers for extra shifts."

"Not this year." Tony looked at her and then at Connor. "You two need to change your plans and come with me to Rocklin."

"Why would I do anything so stupid?" Claire picked up her wineglass. "I'm buying two new bikinis when I go shopping with Dominique, Natasha, and some of the other 'sisters' before Thanksgiving. I can't wear those in the snow capital of the Cascades."

"And I've already told the desk sergeant he can rely on me for the entire holiday weekend." Connor folded his arms, leaning back in the booth. "I haven't been there in twelve years, not since Claire's cancelled wedding."

"You could have gone all night without bringing up that subject." Claire narrowed her eyes and glared at her twin. "It was over even before our stepsister, Kymm, the slut from hell ran off with my fiancé."

"Dex Yarbro only dumped you because he didn't want to sign the pre-nup that Gramps' lawyer insisted upon," Connor retorted. "He was dumb enough to believe Lee's stories about having more money than a tech mogul. He thought he'd have it all when he married Kymm."

"Well, it doesn't matter." Tony held up his hand to stop the argument. "She divorced him when she caught him cheating with the nanny. Anyway, I'm not talking about them. Your paternal grandpa, Beckett. Neither of you contacted him or his wife when he was in the hospital last spring, but he's not—"

"Hold up." Claire turned her head and glowered at Tony sitting next to her in the booth. "Why was he there? When? Did he have Covid? How is he? Is that why Grandmother Agnes didn't send a Valentines' Day card when I had Eileen send ours?"

"I don't know about that, but it sounds right." Tony drew out his phone and sent a quick text to his mother who responded quickly. "Okay, Mom says he had a combo of viral and bacterial pneumonia."

"That sounds bad." A frown creased Connor's face, wrinkling his forehead. "How long was he sick?"

Another text and Tony had the answer. "It was touch and go for a few days. He made it through because of the heavy-duty antibiotic cocktail the doctor prescribed."

"What else?" Claire demanded. "Why didn't they tell us?"

More detective work and Tony kept texting. It didn't take long to hear from Maria. "She says Lee and Barb agreed to contact you because Aggie was overwhelmed at the hospital and then the rehab center with Beckett. And Mom didn't find out until the minister put your grandpa on the prayer list."

Connor and Claire shared a look before she said. "They didn't call or email either of us. If they had, we'd have visited him in the hospital. Aggie must think we're the worst people in the world. We never even sent a card or a basket of fruit or anything. I can't believe she actually wants us to come to Rocklin for the holidays."

"My mother is the one who suggested it. I don't think she's brought up the subject with your grandparents either." Tony slipped an arm around Claire's shoulders. "I never got the word either. If I had, I'd have dragged the pair of you up north, kicking and screaming."

"You could have tried." She leaned against his side, welcoming the comfort he offered. Even if she claimed to be a total bitch, she was always happy he was one of the few people who didn't take her at face value. He accepted her as a complete individual. "I know I'm being a total wuss, but I really dread going to Rocklin and seeing Lee and his family."

"Tell them to go to hell," Connor said.

"I can't." Claire heaved a sigh. "I wish I could, but I keep remembering Grandma's lectures on etiquette. She always said to 'take the high road' and to treat everyone with kindness and courtesy."

"Okay, you do that, and I'll tell them to go to hell," Connor promised. "It will be okay, twin. We'll analyze the situation and figure out how to do what's best for us."

"I wish it was so easy, but it isn't. I may have more money than they'll ever see unless they win the lottery, but they always ask the most impertinent questions. They want to know if I'm married, where my husband or wife is, and if I'll have a kid soon."

"Piece of cake," Tony said.

His hand closed over hers and gripped her fingers. "We'll tell them I'm your partner in more than one way. And Connor doesn't need to tell them to go to hell. I will."

Chapter Thirteen

Tony's offer to rescue her from the Rocklin family still warmed Claire's heart the next morning. She debated using his strategy while she went through her usual routine of going to the gym, stopping by her favorite espresso stand on the way back to the apartment house and then reviewing daily tasks with Sofia. They'd heard from the last of Harry Gamack's references. He'd received another glowing review, and it meant he could move in immediately.

Claire called him and shared the good news. He promised to stop in soon to pick up the keys. She told him if she'd already left for Lynnwood, Sofia would be in the office until she left for class. He reminded Claire that he'd met the university student the previous weekend. They'd also run into each other during their daily doggie walks. He said everything was good to go and he'd be ready to join his new neighbors for supper in the community room that night. Claire promised to meet him there.

Most Thursday and Friday mornings, she went to the tiny house village outside Seattle. It was a different option for senior tenants who wanted more independence. The fifteen small homes were scattered around two large, carefully landscaped lots in a quiet neighborhood next to an old-fashioned church. Each place had its own garden spot and there was even a mini-dog park in one corner. A black wrought-iron fence on the perimeter provided security. Blanche LeVoie, Claire's former sorority sister, dealt with any daily issues.

When she arrived, Claire parked near the community center where the tenants gathered for events. She spotted her friend walking over from the church next door. Instead of her normal jeans and a sweatshirt, Blanche wore black slacks and a dark blouse that showed off her white, clerical collar with its rainbow flag pin, setting off her brilliant red hair.

Claire waited for her. "Looks like you were doing your day job today."

"Had to counsel a new parishioner and her daughter." Blanche greeted Claire with a quick sideways hug. "Seems like the girl is being bullied at school and other churches because she's gay. It's easier for people to share their problems when they see me as their minister and realize I'm not going to judge them. How are you?"

"Do you want the truth or shall I just b.s. you?"

"We've been too close, too long." Concern filtered across Blanche's face and her jaw tightened. She narrowed green eyes. "Talk to me. I have on my collar so I'm ready to do preacher stuff."

That made Claire laugh. She eyed the curvaceous redhead. "You asked for it, but it could take a while."

"Then, let's go to my place and have coffee." Blanche gestured toward the tiny house near the center. "I made brownies the other day and there's vanilla ice-cream in the freezer."

"Sounds like a winner." Once they were settled at the kitchen table a short time later, Claire dug into the treat, normally reserved for dessert. It was a good prelude to lunch.

"Talk." Blanche waved her spoon. "I'm waiting."

Claire heaved a sigh. "Tony, Conn and I went out for dinner last night."

"That's nice. You were out with the two guys you love the most in the world. So, what happened? I know them and they're totally decent. They wouldn't have deliberately said or done anything to hurt you."

"Tony was up in Rocklin last weekend after the storm." Between bites of brownie and ice-cream, Claire described the situation. Tears stung and she blinked hard. "I feel like such a horrible person. Why didn't I know my own grandfather was in the hospital?"

"Because you're a human being who wasn't notified." Blanche stood and went after the coffee pot, bringing back the carafe to top their cups. "Why have you gone no contact with your paternal grandparents?"

Claire took a swallow of coffee to wash down the last of her brownie sundae. "You were one of my bridesmaids twelve years ago and saw part of the debacle after Dex eloped with my stepsister, Kymm."

"Sure. We helped clean up the mess. We contacted guests, returned presents, and helped cancel the arrangements. What does that have to do with your grandparents?"

"The family chose up sides and it wasn't mine." Claire stared into the dark depths of her mug. "Conn and Tony's mom, Maria, were the only ones to support me. Beckett Rocklin, my paternal grandfather told me it was my fault because a real woman wouldn't make her fiancé sign a pre-nup to protect her assets."

"Seriously? Wow, what part of the Dark Ages was he from? Did he think you should give Dex a dowry?" Blanche shook her head. "Whoops, my bad. I'm not here to judge, merely listen and offer advice."

"Thanks." Claire reached across the table and took her friend's hand. "I always enjoy your words of wisdom."

"So, what changed things?" Blanche squeezed her fingers. "Something did or you wouldn't be carrying so much guilt."

"Beckett was in the hospital last spring and almost died. Apparently, my father was supposed to let me know and he didn't." Claire winced, then continued sharing the information she'd learned the previous evening. "My grandmother, Agnes wants us to come for Thanksgiving, and I feel stuck between a rock and a hard place as Gramps used to say."

"Why? You've gone no or low contact with people who've done absolutely nothing for you during the past twelve years. It's perfectly understandable. There isn't anything wrong with that, Claire. You're a harsh critic of yourself, especially when you do so much good for others. Now, what's your plan?"

"If I go—"

"Look, we know you're going. You wouldn't be the woman you are if you didn't reach out to an old couple who need you. That's your specialty, isn't it? You take care of the dispossessed and disposable elderly people that our society and their relatives throw away. Of course, you'll be there for family."

Claire glared at her friend and minister. "What if I want to do the selfish thing and walk away? A lot of women would after the crapfest at my wedding."

"Hold up." Blanche raised her free hand. "There wasn't a ceremony. So, no wedding. You'd paid for it along with the reception and the honeymoon. Discovering Dex used the airline tickets *you* purchased to take Kymm to Hawaii and intended to stay at the hotel where *you* had paid a deposit when *you* made a reservation for the honeymoon suite would have devastated anyone —."

"True, but I did cancel my credit cards and left the two of them holding the bag," Claire pointed out. "Grandmother Aggie said my maternal grandma would have been disappointed in me since I didn't 'take the high road' the way she taught me."

"Didn't your mom's parents arrange for you to have a kick-ass lawyer to protect you from your father who is Agnes', and Beckett's son? What do you think they'd have said and done if they'd been alive? Would they have supported you at the wedding? And wasn't that lawyer acting as your trustee? He's the one who drew up the prenuptial agreement Dex didn't sign."

"You're right." Claire relaxed her grip on Blanche's hand. "They always had my back and so did Maria. We had to talk Conn out of tracking down Dex and beating the crap out of him. And Maria called Kymm the slut princess of Rocklin, Washington. When Tony heard about it, he was furious too. He told me it was fine if I chose not to marry a jerk, but that same jerk had no business breaking my heart."

"Got to admit Tony does have a way with words nearly as well as I do." Blanche finished her coffee. "Okay, you've vented and now we know what you're doing for Thanksgiving. What else is on your mind?"

Claire hesitated. "Tony says we can let everyone think we're partners so they don't ask inappropriate questions about my personal life."

"You are partners."

"He means romantic partners."

"Okay, does that mean you finally get to be *partners* with fringe benefits?" Blanche giggled. "Oh, girlfriend. You should see the look on your face. How stupid do you think I am? You've had the hots for him forever. Jump the guy and get it out of your system."

"Some minister you are." Claire lifted her chin, refusing to admit that her friend had a valid point. "Aren't you supposed to preach at me about chastity?"

"That never was my thing. He's not attached to anyone else, and neither are you. I think you should go for being happy with each other."

"And on that note, let's go take care of the village." Claire rose to her feet, collected the dishes, and carried them to the counter a few feet away. "I'll consider it. When I attack his body, I'll tell him I have your permission."

"Works for me as long as you share all the deets with me next week."

———

Tony arrived at the Seattle office in the late afternoon. When he walked in the door, he glimpsed Eileen at the reception desk updating something on the computer. He saw Scott Jenkins in the adjacent file room, putting away paperwork. Three associate brokers, one of whom was his sister, Robyn, were at various stations around the room.

"I saw Claire's car." Tony glanced at Eileen. "Where is she?"

"In her office. She's putting together a poster for a contest she wants to have for the brokers this month."

"Talk to me. What contest?"

"Well, since her plans have changed for Thanksgiving, she needs to do something about the airline tickets and hotel reservation in Cancun," Eileen explained. "You know Claire. She cleans her nails over the proverbial flowerpot, and always buys non-refundable, first-class plane tickets. She says she's not willing to lose her 'hard-earned' money so someone has to use them, and the top-selling broker is winning an all-expense paid trip."

"Why am I not surprised?" Tony shook his head, chuckling. "Anything else?"

"I haven't been able to make a reservation at the Rocklin Hotel for Thanksgiving weekend. They're fully booked for the holiday," Eileen said. "So, I'm checking into the nearby towns. I haven't given up yet. As soon as I find a place for her and Connor, I'll email the details."

"All right. I'll see what I can do too." Tony walked through the large room, down the hallway and into Claire's office. He really didn't care for contemporary furniture but knew better than to share his opinion. Of course, the simplistic lift-top desk in front of her didn't hide anything. He admired her long legs in dark blue tights since she wore a knee-length, navy pencil skirt. She'd kicked off her shoes and the blue stilettos stood neatly nearby.

"Stop leering, Baldusi and tell me what you want." Claire pushed away from the desk. "Did Eileen find a hotel for the holiday weekend yet?"

"No, but she's still looking." He walked over, glancing at the light blue top that clung to every curve and emphasized the full breasts. "You're always a dream come true."

"And you're a total horndog." She smiled and leaned back into the office chair. "Tell me about Eastside. I'd like to get there tomorrow, but I don't know if it's going to happen or not."

He chuckled and dropped a kiss on her forehead.

"Would a horndog be happy staying at a respectful distance?"

"Undoubtedly not." She stood and stepped closer, pressing her hands onto his chest. "I've been talking to Blanche today and she says—"

"Something totally inappropriate if I know and love her."

"Yes, you certainly do." Claire tiptoed up and teased his mouth with hers. "She says I should jump you."

He slipped his hand into the black hair she'd left loose to frame her face. "Are you tempting me for a reason?"

"Definitely." She nipped his ear. "What happens if I invite you over for a night of hot, wild sex? Or do you already have plans?"

He gazed into her mischievous dark blue eyes. "Oh, I'd be there in a heartbeat, but I want more than a one-night stand."

"Friends or should I say, *partners* with benefits?"

He feathered her lips with his thumb, then bent his head and his mouth claimed hers for a moment. "Not until you let me put a ring on your finger, sweetheart."

"Been there and didn't do that." She laced her arms around his neck. "I'm not the marrying type, darling. I already told you how important you are to me. Sex, yes. A lifetime commitment, no."

"Then, I'll hold off on the sex for a while." He drew her closer and held her tight. "I'll go with you to church next time Blanche is preaching. While we're there, we can ask her to preside over the ceremony when I convince you to marry me."

Chapter Fourteen

F riday, Tony headed north toward Lake Maynard. It was a healthy drive to the furthest Rocklin office, but he hadn't been there since last week, and Claire wouldn't make it to what she referred to as 'the boonies' for a while. She'd insisted on buying the brokerage from one of her sorority sisters two years ago despite the fact that the realty was on a downhill slide after the pandemic and it was a very poor investment. Once they owned it, half the agents left to work for different real estate companies because they didn't want to take additional classes and become associate brokers, a requirement to remain at Rocklin's.

The others were happy to have guaranteed salaries in addition to their commissions. Some of them whined about the need to dress professionally when they showed up to complete their scheduled office hours or adhering to the security rules Tony insisted upon from screening potential buyers to not meeting new clients alone. However, once their income rose, the complaints stopped. While this brokerage didn't make as much as the other three branches, it made a small profit last year and would have a larger one this year.

When he stopped for breakfast at his favorite diner in Lake Maynard, he seized the opportunity to call his mother and let her know the twins would be joining them for Thanksgiving weekend. "Claire is trying to find hotel rooms, but she hasn't had a lot of luck. Everything in Rocklin and the surrounding towns is full."

"That makes sense, son. The ski resorts are already open, and we have lots of snow so they're anticipating a big weekend and that always fills the hotels and motels. Why don't you stay with me?"

"Because you only have one guestroom, Mom and I know how you feel about unmarried couples sharing it."

"Grow up, Anthony Marco. You'll be forty next year and Claire's almost thirty-five. You're not teenagers or college students who need one of my lectures. How stupid do you think I am? I know you're a couple even if you've never admitted it."

"How could I when we're not engaged yet? After the shitstorm with Dex—"

"Watch your potty mouth." Maria sighed. "Do you really think I'll lecture the two of you about morality now? I'll change the sheets on the bed, vacuum, and dust before you get here. Connor can have the sleeper sofa in the living-room."

"Claire will feel like she's imposing."

"Nonsense. The three of you will take me out for a few meals over the weekend and tidy the rooms before you leave for Seattle. Claire and I will go shopping with Aggie while you and Connor help Beckett with whatever chores he tries to do. Everything will be wonderful."

"I hope you're right, Mom."

"I know I am. Now, get off my phone so I can call Aggie and let her know to set three more places for Thanksgiving dinner for you and the twins. I'm already expected."

"Ask her what we can bring. Connor will need a 'heads-up' so he can cook something special."

"You've brought his pies a few times when you visited. Tell him to bake an assortment of apple, pumpkin, and pecan. Two of each because Aggie always has a houseful when Lee and his contingent arrive."

"Okay. Claire and I will bring wine and sparkling cider. See you in two weeks, Mom."

"All right, but you better call before then, Tony."

"You know I will." His order arrived and he ended the call so his omelet wouldn't get cold. He wondered how Claire would feel about staying at his mother's house and decided to wait to share the invitation.

———

Friday morning, when she returned from the gym and espresso stand, Claire found Sofia in the office. Lying beside the desk, Oscar chewed on an organic beef stick. Claire passed a double-shot, raspberry mocha to her new assistant. Sofia made a habit of dressing in appropriate office attire in the mornings, but Claire knew she changed to her favorite jeans, sweatshirt and running shoes before catching a bus to the university.

"What do you think of the job?" Claire asked. "You've been here a week. How's it going?"

"I'm liking it." Sofia smiled her thanks for the coffee. "I told Tony I wanted the two of you to find a new owner for Oscar, but I've decided to keep her. I hope that's okay."

"No worries." Claire looked at the happy brown and

white spaniel. "He didn't say a word to me about it, so I'd assume he wanted to give you time to reconsider. Now, why did you give her what a lot of people would call a 'guy's' name?"

"It's rather silly," Sofia admitted, stirring her drink with the straws. "I was watching an old comedy on TV when Jill brought them home. You hardly ever see a puppy and kitten who are totally inseparable, so I named them after the characters on the show."

It took a moment and then Claire caught the reference. "I get it. *The Odd Couple*! Oh, that's so cute. If Oscar wants to visit Felix some night, I'm good with it."

"Thank you." Sofia gestured toward the computer on the oak rolltop desk. "You have an email from the heating company about the generator. Do you want to deal with it before you leave for the tiny house village?"

"You know it." Claire headed toward her desk. "What time do you get home from college tonight? Do you want to join us for the poker game?"

"Cards really aren't my thing. I told Nonna I'd help make popcorn for movie night and Oscar and I are joining them for the *Homeward Bound* double feature. They're classics."

Claire laughed. "You can't get past 'cats rule and dogs drool'. Who wouldn't agree with that?"

"Exactly!" Sofia collected a few papers and went toward the filing cabinet. "I'll take care of this and then we're joining Fletcher for the morning doggie walk."

"Sounds good. If you're not back by the time I leave, I'll lock up."

On her way to the tiny house village a short time later, Claire stopped by the new apartment building. She found Logan Turner hanging drywall in one of the fourth-floor bedrooms. A construction helmet protected his sandy blond hair, and she had to admit he looked good in the rough clothes he wore, but she still preferred Tony's rugged features to Logan's pretty boy face.

She glanced around the room. The ceiling and three walls were finished while he was working on the last one. She heard the steady thumping of a nail-gun in the adjacent apartment and figured another member of the crew must be hard at work. "It's coming together. What's the timeframe? When should I tell Fancy's crew to start painting?"

"After Thanksgiving for sure. Possibly before." Logan paused to consider the question. His sky-blue eyes scanned the ongoing project. "I'll have my guys start taping and mudding in here next week after they finish the top floor. By then, we'll be on the third floor. Did you want me to arrange to have the parking lot re-paved and the stripes repainted?"

Claire nodded. "The weather's supposed to warm up the first week of December so let's have the custom paving done then. Once it's set up, I'll have the landscapers redo the grounds."

"Then, we have a plan. Ready for a walk-through?"

"Sure," Claire said. "Do you have a hard hat I can borrow?"

"You bet." Logan led the way to a nearby tool cabinet.

While they inspected the progress on the various floors, they discussed improvements to the kitchens and bathrooms. After he brought her up to date on the status of the apartment building, Logan shared what he'd heard from Tony about the house in Everett. "Closing is set for December and Rocklin's is one of my best clients, so I've rearranged my schedule to start the remodeling in January."

"That's good of you." Claire didn't mention how she felt

about being squeezed out of the place she'd intended to flip. "Thanks for helping him with it."

"From the pictures he emailed, it looks structurally sound. Since we won't be making any alterations to the existing building, or doing any new construction, that means I won't have to file for building permits. It will speed up the repairs and remodeling, so I'll be ready for your next project by March."

"That works, Logan. And it gives me time to find another multi-plex."

In an hour, Claire headed to her next stop. She found Blanche blowing fallen leaves into the flowerbeds for mulch. Despite the cool November breeze, it wasn't raining so they picnicked in the gazebo near the rose garden, enjoying the sub sandwiches Claire brought with her. It gave them time to talk about the Thanksgiving meal the tenants had volunteered to help with at the church.

By early afternoon, Claire was on the main highway to the Eastside brokerage. It didn't take long to reach the office in a Bellevue strip mall. She parked and walked inside, her stilettos tapping a new rhythm. Because this branch tended to have high traffic flow, there were usually six or seven associates working at the various stations in the large room.

Clusters of plants separated the three long tables providing an aura of privacy. A comfortable conversation area took up the center of the room. Claire paused to speak to Vincent Wong, the office manager, a tall, skinny Asian-American who opted for a casual look with a blazer over his button-down shirt and khakis. "Is Perry here?"

"He took a late lunch. He'll be back for the evening shift." Vincent lowered his voice, glancing cautiously around the room so they wouldn't be overheard. "He didn't tell me, but he's been getting calls from Mike Flannagan. I think the guy's head-hunting."

"Really?" Claire folded her arms, eyeing the manager and murmured. "If we lose Perry, how will we handle this office without him?"

Amusement flickered in Vincent's dark eyes, and he rubbed his jaw. "Oh, I think we'll cope just fine."

"My thoughts exactly." Laughing, Claire headed for the hallway that led to the Designated Broker's office. She saw Zelda Torres at the desk, focused on the computer screen in front of her. Black slacks, a red silk blouse and low-heeled shoes made for walking, recently colored blonde hair with mahogany streaks—the fifty-year-old woman was definitely stylin' after her promotion.

Claire smiled at her. "Hey there. How's it going? I think you're a proverbial shoo-in for the contest this month. What's your plan to win?"

———

It was almost seven that night when he reached his condo. Tony saw Claire standing in the hallway when he stepped out of the elevator. "I wasn't expecting you. What's happening?"

"Supper." She held up two large white bags. "I stopped for Chinese food. Thought we'd eat. You could bring me up to speed on the Lake Maynard branch. I'll tell you about the updates on the apartment building, the tiny house compound and Eastside before I abandon you to go play poker."

"Really?" He walked toward her, pulling out his keys. "And what would it take for me to convince you to spend the evening here?"

She shrugged. "I might be persuaded if we get to 'knock shoes' but other than that, I'm going home once we eat."

"You already know my conditions. If you're not wearing my ring, we'll remain celibate."

She laughed. "Oh, like you've even had time to buy one. I keep you too busy for that nonsense."

He grinned at her and reached in his pocket, drawing out a small, velvet-covered jewelry box. "I've been packing this around for three-plus years. Let me know when you're ready to wear it."

Chapter Fifteen

laire gaped at him and the jewelry box in his hand, slightly shocked and definitely bewildered. Yes, she'd been glad to see him when he returned three years ago, and she'd be the first to admit she cared about him. *Of course, I love him, but I'm not in love with him.* Still, she couldn't quite believe he'd been carrying a ring in his pocket for her.

"Are you serious, Tony?"

"I've never been more so." He opened the small box.

She stared at the ring. It was beautiful. He had amazing taste. Two halos of diamonds and sapphires framed a round diamond center stone, set on a diamond accented band. "Wow, it's lovely."

"Want to try it on?"

Claire hastily put her left hand behind her back and opted for one of Blanche's favorite quotes. "Get thee behind me, Satan!"

"Guess you're not ready yet." He chuckled, closed the box, and replaced it in his pocket before he unlocked the door and ushered her inside. "Let's eat instead. What did you bring?"

"I'm starving so I bought out the restaurant. Chicken fried rice, spring rolls, Lo Mein, broccoli with beef, sweet and sour pork, egg flower soup, and almond fried chicken." She led the way toward the kitchen and put the large bags on the table.

While she lifted out small cartons, he opened the cupboard door, removing two plates. "Silverware or chopsticks?"

"Silverware," Claire answered. "I'm too hungry to deal with chopsticks tonight. Wine or tea?"

He opened the refrigerator. "I have your favorite *Pinot Noir* chilling and I'm ready for a beer."

"Sounds good." In a few minutes, they were sitting at the table and enjoying their soup. "Tell me about Lake Maynard. How is Svetlana doing? She said at the meeting that she had a few issues with a couple of her recent sales and her cousin, Natasha was too busy to help."

"I told her again that we don't want Natasha Hollister poking her nose in at the brokerage. It's a Rocklin enterprise, not your sorority sister's any longer." Tony pushed Claire's favorite almond fried chicken toward her and then forked a healthy portion of the beef-broccoli onto his plate. "And since Natasha won't be making any money from the deals, it isn't fair to ask her to intercede."

"Good job." Claire snagged a spring roll and then added one to his plate. "Svetlana is a Designated Broker, and we need to build her confidence. She can do the job, can't she? Or should we be looking for another broker to help her?"

"Oh, she was right on it." Tony scooped fried rice onto her dish and took the remainder for his portion. "She just has to learn to trust her judgement. What about Eastside? How are Zelda and Perry getting along?"

"He was out to lunch when I arrived. Then, he called

and told her that he wouldn't be back today." Claire sipped her wine. "We reviewed the current contracts. They were more than ready to go to the escrow company, but I think she wanted me to feel important."

They continued discussing business while they ate. Afterwards, she helped tidy the kitchen, storing the leftovers in the fridge. She hastily slipped out the front door before he kissed her, still wondering about the ring. She'd never expected that, never thought he was serious about her. Why not? He'd always meant what he said and said what he meant.

I'm losing it. Time to wake up and smell the proverbial coffee, Claire Rocklin. He really does want me. Now, what am I going to do?

No answers came by the time she arrived home and headed for the game room. She found her brother and several of the usual suspects gathered around the poker table. She joined them and Jerry proceeded to deal her into the round.

"You're late," Connor said. "Where were you? Stuck at the offices?"

"I took dinner to Tony so he wouldn't microwave one of his favorite pot-pies." Claire collected the cards in front of her. "We talked business."

"Fair enough." Connor frowned thoughtfully at his hand. "He texted me earlier, said you couldn't get us a hotel reservation, so he arranged for us to stay with his mom."

Claire's mouth dropped open and she shook her head. "No way!"

"Yes, way. I'm supposed to bake pies."

"What kind?" Harry Gamack glanced across the table at them. "Need help?"

"Always," Connor said. "Bonnie already put in her order

Josie Malone

because I usually supply the ones we have here at Thanksgiving."

While they played five-card-stud, the talk was all about favorite kinds of pie and what would be served at the community meal. Very few of the residents had family to visit over the holiday so most would be here on that Thursday. Claire agreed to arrange for a couple of Mrs. Nayaka's crew to prepare the mini-bus and take people who wanted to hit the holiday sales to area malls on Black Friday.

They never made a late night of it at their poker games so by eleven, she and Connor headed for the elevator. "You were pretty quiet tonight, little sister. What's on your mind?"

She flicked a quick glance up at her dark-haired brother in one of his favorite flannel shirts and faded jeans. "Tony."

"What did he do? Kiss you goodnight?"

"No."

"Then, he's slipping. Want me to talk to him?"

"Hell, no!" She tossed her head and glared at her twin. "He's packing around an engagement ring. Did you know?"

"Nope." Connor grinned, amusement sliding across his handsome features and landing in the dark-blue eyes. "Tell me more. What does it look like? Why aren't you wearing it?"

"Because I'm not marrying him." She elbowed Connor when he laughed. "Damn it. Listen to me for once, you baboon. I suck at relationships. When I screw it up, he'll leave me."

"You've screwed things up before and he's still here."

The doors whooshed open, and she stormed out to the hallway. "I don't know why I bother talking to you."

"Especially since you're not real fond of my answers."

He caught up with her and hugged her quickly. "It's going to be fine, Claire. Trust yourself."

"That's why I'm keeping my distance." She lifted her chin. "I know me. And I also know him. He's too good a guy for a loser."

"Don't put yourself down." Connor kissed her forehead. "Be nice to my little sister. Okay?"

"I'll try, but I'm not promising a damn thing."

———

On Saturday mornings when Connor didn't work, the two of them met at a local golf course to have breakfast at the clubhouse and play eighteen holes. The sky was a surprising blue with only a few puffy clouds although rain was forecast for the late afternoon and into the night. Tony spotted the younger man parking his pickup when he arrived. He pulled into the adjacent spot and climbed from the Hummer. "Ready to eat?"

"You know it." Connor locked his rig and waited. "I hear you have a ring for my sister. Do I get to see it? Or do I have to wait until you manage to put it on her finger?"

"I'll show you." Tony reached into his pocket. "She's a stubborn woman."

"Don't tell me you're finally learning that."

When they walked toward the restaurant, Tony tucked away the jewelry box. "I'm going to marry her, Conn."

"I've always known that. You have too. It's going to take a while for her to get there." Connor gestured toward Tony's pocket. "Dex Yarbro really did a number on her and the rest of the Rocklins totally kicked her in the guts. She spends too much time working so she doesn't have to think about them."

"Is returning home a good idea?"

"It's not our home, Tony. It hasn't been for more than twelve years." Connor reached for the heavily carved wooden door. He waited until they'd been seated at a booth and the waiter departed to bring them coffee. "Truthfully, it wasn't mine after Barb sent me to military school and my father did nothing to protect me back in the day. He wanted Claire to move back to his house after Gramps and Grandma died, but—"

"Why didn't she?"

"It was a money issue. Claire was barely eighteen when she inherited everything our grandparents owned. They'd asked her to split it with me but didn't put that in writing because they were afraid Lee would come after it since he could claim to be my legal guardian until I graduated from military school."

"Makes sense. So, what happened? I thought she stayed in your grandparents' house until she graduated from high school."

"She did. The trustee told Lee that he could support Claire if she lived with him because he hadn't paid child support for six years."

"I'll bet Lee refused."

"Got that right, Tony. He and Barb didn't even buy us Christmas or birthday presents after they got together. The last thing they'd do was spend a dime on Claire." Connor stopped talking when the waiter returned with two cups of coffee. "Let's order."

Once they were alone, Tony continued the conversation. "So, Claire ended up staying at your grandparents' house for the next six months. My mother said she checked on her regularly."

"Exactly. Their lawyer, Wendell Frobisher was the

trustee. He helped Claire arrange to sell the various houses and businesses Gramps and Grandma owned in Rocklin. The deals went through because she'd turned eighteen and was a legal adult. Between Claire and Wendell, Lee didn't see a cent. He was still pissed when I came home that summer before boot camp."

"Why did you?"

"I wanted to be sure Claire got off to college okay."

"You're a good brother."

"Yup, I know." Their food arrived and Connor proceeded to drown his pancakes in maple syrup. "Lee was even angrier when he discovered I had scholarships from the military school for college and intended to accept a commission as an Army officer."

"What was his issue with that?"

"He wanted me to work for his dad, Beckett. My grandfather had offered to pay me a decent salary and provide an apartment while I was working in the family corporation. I refused and told them, my country came first."

Tony grinned appreciatively, cutting into his western omelet. "Having served in Vietnam, Beckett was thrilled to pieces at that idea."

"Exactly. He told me he was glad I wasn't 'chicken-shit' like my old man and there'd always be a job when or if I wanted to return to Rocklin. When I earned my commission as a second lieutenant, Beckett and Aggie came to my graduation. Lee and his contingent didn't."

"Not surprised."

"Lee called before I shipped out to Afghanistan the first time and wanted to know who my beneficiary was if I didn't make it back. He lost it when I told him Claire would get every cent."

"And I bet if he knew how much you invested in the real-estate firm, he'd blow a head gasket."

"Same goes for you, Tony. He tried telling me you were always a son to him."

Tony laughed. "News to me. And since Claire stays no-contact with him, I don't have to worry about it after I marry your sister."

———

Saturday morning, Claire hung out with Felix binge-watching her favorite crime drama while she broke into a box of her favorite old-fashioned, chocolate doughnuts and drank a pot of coffee. She didn't bother to shower or dress but lounged on the couch in flannel pajamas and a fleece bathrobe. *Lenny Briscoe* needed all the help and advice she could offer from her comfy position. Later, she'd go down-stairs and socialize with the residents, but this was her time. Her phone buzzed and she glanced at the text. Tony had invited her to lunch.

Claire refused nicely and asked for a rain check. She'd meet him at the Seattle office the next day. She stroked the black and white tuxedo kitten lying on top of the multi-colored blanket one of the tenants crocheted for her. "He wants to marry us and I'm not ready for that."

Felix purred in response and Claire didn't know what that answer meant. During the next stream of commercials, she dozed off and woke more than an hour later when she heard the doorbell. Pushing the cover aside, she rolled to her feet. At the door, she peered through the security window and saw Tony standing in the hall.

She yanked open the door, glaring up at him. "What part

of 'no', don't you understand? This is my lay around and do-nothing day."

He whistled softly, looking her up and down. "And I thought it'd take me longer to get you out of your clothes. Are you sure you won't accept my ring so I can carry you off to bed?"

"I've told you before, Anthony Marco Baldusi. Yes, to bed, no to the ring."

"Then, we're stuck at a stand-off, Claire Erica Rocklin. Get dressed and we'll go to your favorite restaurant for a late lunch. You need protein to make up for your junk food breakfast."

"How do you know about that?"

"Not the right question. I know everything about you."

Chapter Sixteen

While he waited for her to dress, Tony strolled into the living room where he found the kitten curled up on the couch snoozing through a *Law and Order* extravaganza. He turned off the flatscreen, folded the throw blanket and tucked it away in the antique steamer trunk. He picked up the box that still contained four chocolate doughnuts and an empty coffee cup, heading for the kitchen.

On his way out of the room, he glimpsed the photos on the plant stand. One of his mother holding Claire on her lap while he and Connor stood close by caught Tony's attention and warmed his heart. No wonder the twins stayed in contact with his mom. Lots of love there, he thought. He'd put the cup in the dishwasher and the carton of leftover doughnuts on the counter when Claire returned.

Tight, faded jeans clung to her long legs and a layered red tunic style shirt with a square neckline emphasized her slender waist and the curve of her breasts. Brilliant scarlet sequins glittered around her neck, on the long sleeves and at the bottom by her hips. Instead of wearing her usual stilettos, she'd chosen blue flats. She'd slung a navy-blue leather bomber jacket around her shoulders. "All right, let's go."

"You've got it." Laughing, he followed her into the hallway where she paused to grab her purse. "How long are you going to be snarky?"

"How long are you going to overstep my boundaries?" She glared over her shoulder at him. "I told you, 'no'. And you showed up anyway."

"You opened the door. If you seriously didn't want to spend time with me, you'd have left me outside."

That silenced her until they reached his Hummer in the parking garage. She buckled her seatbelt and demanded to know where they were going.

"I already told you. I called in our order to the *Chicken Yard*, your favorite breakfast restaurant," Tony said. "Otherwise, we'll have to wait almost an hour while they bake an omelet for you."

"You're lucky I put up with you."

'Likewise."

It was a short drive from her exclusive neighborhood over a drawbridge to the nearby community of Ballard and from there to the restaurant that specialized in breakfast and lunch. As always, a line of people waited outside the doors for a table, but thankfully reservations were honored so they didn't have to join them. They settled into a booth to enjoy coffee while Claire waited for her ham and cheese omelet, and he had a chicken salad.

After the meal, he suggested they take in a movie, but she said she'd watched enough dramas, so they ended up at the Northgate Mall. Stores were already decorated for Christmas, and she analyzed the lights, garlands, and ornaments, asking his opinion.

He put an arm around her waist and drew her closer.

"Why does it matter when we haven't celebrated Thanksgiving?"

"You have to think retail, Tony." She glanced up at him, smiling. "We need to choose appropriate holiday trimmings for the brokerages. Where do you want to have the party this year? I'll have Eileen make a reservation when I'm in the Seattle office tomorrow."

"Let's splurge and see if we can get in at the Space Needle. All the branches are turning a profit this year, and it'd make a great celebration. We haven't been able to go there in a long time because of the shut-downs during the pandemic."

"I like it." She stopped to look at a vintage display of toys in one shop window. "Connor would love that train set. Come on, Tony. We'll go shopping."

"Okay, we'll do what you want as long as I get to do what I want next."

"Works for me."

———

Her curiosity about what Tony might want faded while she talked to the salesclerk about the train set. It included fifty feet of track, an old-style steam locomotive with lights and classic train sounds, passenger cars, double container cars, tankers, a train station, pine trees, 30 sections of straight, curved and "Y" tracks and cross-section pieces. Additional completer sets had more railcars, cabooses, even more track as well as bridges and buildings to make up a town.

The elaborate model with all the fixings reminded Claire of the one their maternal grandfather had given her brother when they were children. Connor and Gramps played with it for hours while Grandma and Claire sewed extravagant, flamboyant wardrobes for her Barbie doll collection. The toys went the way of the wind after Lee married Barbara—well, actually their stepbrother and stepsister absconded with them. Since the twins lost their home within a year after the wedding, it hadn't been worth the battle to replace them.

While the clerk wrapped the gift for her brother, Claire wandered through the store aisles until she found Tony studying a collection of model horses. "What are you thinking? Who would like those?"

"Peyton is totally horse-crazy." Tony pulled out his phone and sent a quick text to his mother, along with a picture. "I bet she'd love them for Christmas."

"Who is that?" Claire tucked her hand into the crook of his elbow. "I don't recognize the name."

"You'll meet her when we're in Rocklin in two weeks." Tony stood still, obviously waiting for a response from his mother. "She's Kymm and Dex's daughter."

"What?" Fury raced through her. "I don't believe this. You actually know those people, see them when you're in freaking Rocklin. What the hell is wrong with you?"

"Not a damn thing." He caught her chin and their gazes clashed. "I don't make war on children, Claire and neither should you. Peyton didn't choose her parents and really you ought to feel sorry for the kid. Can you imagine being raised by your stepsister and an absentee father?"

"Wait just a minute! Of course, I can." Claire flung the words at him, wishing they were bricks. "Don't tell me you think Lee was any kind of a dad. He abandoned us after our mom died of breast cancer. And I'd be willing to bet he wasn't any kind of a decent husband before that. Grandma and Gramps never said he cheated on her, but I overheard them talk about him not taking her to chemo."

"Like I said, you need to feel sorry for Peyton. She doesn't have your maternal grandparents to run interference. Beckett and Aggie pay for her to take riding lessons but how much do you want to bet they offer as much emotional support to her and James' son as they did you and Connor?"

The comment made her think although she'd have preferred to remain angry with Tony. Damn it! He was right. She came from a long line of shallow people, and she'd bet they hadn't changed one iota since she was a girl. Yes, she'd visit them over Thanksgiving, but it wasn't because of anything she owed them. As Blanche pointed out, it was the right thing to do and Claire knew her strong moral code hadn't come from the Rocklins, but from her mother's side of the family.

"Okay, I can see what you're saying." Claire gestured to the *Breyer* herd of horses. "You should find the kid a barn and corral to go with those or they'll be galloping all over her bedroom. What would Jimmy Junior like? You can't get a present for Peyton unless you find one for him."

"Fair enough. He's into sports and chess so we'll check out a different store and find him something that matches his interests. He still has fond memories of you and Connor."

Claire stared at Tony, measuring the sincerity on his face. "Seriously? How does he even remember us? We haven't been to Rocklin in over twelve years."

"He told me about you taking him pony riding when he was little and then meeting Conn for ice-cream." Tony gestured to the toy stable. "Help me out here. Then, we'll go to your favorite place."

"What's that?"

"The jewelry store."

"Honestly?" She picked up the largest box containing the barn, jumps, a horse-trailer, and a play corral. "I want a diamond necklace this year."

"Of course, you do." He followed her toward the cashier. "And what idiot is going to buy you that?"

"You are, darling, because it's going to match the bracelet you gave me for my birthday last year. It will make me forgive you for hanging out with my dirtbag relatives when you're visiting your wonderful mother."

"What if I don't?"

"Careful. You won't be happy if you piss me off." Claire opted for her most innocent look. "Because then I'll date someone who will drop a couple thousand on a necklace, and you know how upset you get when I flash other guys around the office."

He captured her hand and pulled her to him. "I already told you. No more men, Claire. I don't share." His mouth captured hers in a quick, fierce kiss.

She reminded herself she was determined to keep her distance, but it didn't do any good. She surrendered anyway and kissed him back. Why was he so damned irresistible?

A short time later, they wandered into the corner jewelry store. While he waited to talk to one of the sales-clerks, she drifted over to the display case featuring several beautiful diamond necklaces. Her gaze landed on a silhou-ette pendant in a halo design. A perfectly cut round bril-liant diamond bordered by a double frame of smaller diamonds and lovely sapphires reminded her of the ring Tony carried around. Whoever created this necklace chose a white gold setting which only increased the light and airy motif.

"Did you find something you like?" He came to stand beside her. "Why am I not surprised?"

"Because you're smart." She pointed to her new favorite. "That's it."

"Nice." He caught her hand. "Come with me. I want you to try on your ring and be sure it fits."

"I told you—"

"I know. I heard you but if we need to have it sized before we go to Rocklin, now is the time."

She cast one more longing look at the diamond pendant and then focused on reality. She hesitated before she allowed him to escort her to the waiting jeweler. She nearly repeated she didn't plan to marry him but had to admit she liked the idea of using the ring to ward off the Rocklin clan. It'd lend credence to the idea that they were romantic as well as business partners.

On the way back to the parking lot, they stopped by the pet store to pick up a few more toys for Felix including a scratching post. Back at the apartment house, Tony carried her purchases up to the penthouse. He was such a gentleman in the old-fashioned sense of the word, and she enjoyed the way he treated her. Granted, he overstepped the boundaries at times, but it still made a pleasant change from the men she dated who claimed to have forgotten their wallets whenever they went somewhere.

Tony insisted on paying for her meals, opened doors, helped her on with her coat and acted the way she remembered her grandfather treating her grandmother. Claire supposed she might have a raging fit and tell him she was a grown woman who could take care of herself, but he already knew that. He'd told her more than once that he admired her work ethic even if he didn't like the fact that she dated a lot of different guys.

Of course, he probably thought dating included sleeping with them, but it wasn't on the cards. Dex Yarbro had been the first man in her bed, but she hadn't stopped there. She'd had a couple of others over the years. However, none of them were as satisfying as finding a new apartment house and remodeling it for her senior tenants so she stopped sleeping with the guys she dated and kept it casual.

No coyote dates for me! Why does Tony stir me so much with his kisses?

Chapter Seventeen

During the next four days, Claire felt as if she'd meet herself coming or going. She constantly hustled from one place to the next, the gym to the apartment office, to one of the brokerages, and to the tiny house village. In her spare time, she checked in with Logan about the remodeling, emailed Fancy about repairs at the beach house, and arranged for the shopping trip with her sorority sisters.

Wednesday evening, she sat in her office at the Seattle branch, shooting out more emails to put out even more fires. Everyone else had already left for the night and as soon as she resolved all these issues, she'd hit the road too. She glanced at the door when someone knocked. "Come in."

Perry Holmes opened the door. "I need to talk to you, Claire."

She frowned at the screen and decided the answer to Svetlana's question about a glitch on a recently listed property would have to wait. "Pull up a chair. What's on your mind?"

Perry was slender with fine facial features, fantastic

cheekbones, and a narrow chin. He had lovely blond hair tied back in a ponytail and wore a powder-blue suit that complemented his eyes. He sat down in a chair across from her. "I want a raise."

"And I want the brokerages to turn at least three million dollars in sales this year." Claire leaned back in her chair. She hoped she projected total control in the red blouse and black, knee-length, A-line skirt. "Which one of us is more likely to get it?"

"Claire, I'm serious."

"Perry, it's impossible. We're coming back after the worst pandemic in a hundred years. It was all I could do to keep everyone on the payroll during the various state shutdowns, especially when people stopped selling and buying houses. Your office is barely turning a profit. Lake Maynard makes more money, and it was totally in the toilet when Natasha sold it to me."

He leaned forward, glowering at her and trying to project fierceness. He failed. "When you promoted that old lady, she took half my wages."

"Watch yourself. There's no room for bias, or rudeness at Rocklin's." Claire counted silently to ten, striving for patience. "If you want more money, sell more properties. Your branch has tremendous potential."

He jumped to his feet and stormed toward her. "I get a raise or—"

"Or what?" Tony rumbled from the doorway, a total hunk in a white shirt and dark slacks, his jacket casually tossed over one arm. "Don't threaten us."

Perry spun around to face him. "You don't understand. She cut my share of the Designated Broker percentage at Eastside."

"You needed help, Perry, and I couldn't keep doing your

job as well as my own." Claire adopted the tone of sweet reason. "Zelda Torres is the top-selling associate in the East-side office, and she'll be a tremendous asset to you and us. When your folks are able to sell more houses and businesses, then your income will increase."

"That makes sense, doesn't it?" Dropping his coat on the visitor chair, Tony crossed the room to stand behind Claire.

She smiled up at him, appreciating the support when he placed his hand on her shoulder. "Do more work and you'll reap the benefits, Perry."

He shook his head, reached inside his jacket, and removed an envelope. "I quit."

"What?" Claire pasted on what she hoped was a shocked look. "Perry, your branch needs you and Zelda. How can you walk out on Rocklin's after all we've done for you? We paid for your real-estate classes, your license, the extra education you needed to become a broker. Where's the loyalty?"

He sniffed, stomped over to lay the envelope on the desk. "You should have thought of it before you promoted that woman. I'm leaving at the end of the week."

"Wait a minute," Claire protested. "The least you owe us is two weeks' notice."

"You're not getting it. And I want my commissions as soon as the sales close on the properties I've helped sell."

"Okay." Claire picked up the envelope, opened it and removed the letter of resignation. "Are you leaving the real estate business? What are you going to do?"

"Mike Flannagan has offered me a position managing one of his branches. I start next Monday."

"Then, you never intended to work with us?" Claire struggled to sound stunned. One more of his sneers and Perry was out her office door, slamming it behind him. She breathed a sigh of relief and relaxed in her chair. "Whoosh!"

Tony smoothed her hair, patted her shoulder. "I honestly thought he had potential. I'm sorry, sweetheart."

"Sorry for what?" She tipped her head back and stared up at him. "Did you want to keep that incompetent idiot, darling?"

He laughed, bent to kiss her. "You're an evil, manipulative woman."

"And you're just learning that? Baldusi, you're slipping. I thought you were smarter than that."

His jaw tightened and his gaze narrowed on her as he assessed the situation and came to the realization, she'd set the entire operation in motion to dispose of Perry without giving the man a dime of severance pay. She wouldn't risk the brokerages by being in violation of their employment contracts and now Perry wouldn't have a case if he claimed he'd been fired.

Before she could move, Tony spun the chair around, so she was trapped by his tall, lean body. He threaded his hand in her hair. His breath was warm on her lips when his mouth captured hers. His tongue swept inside, conquering the area. She yielded to the fierce pressure, trembling when his hand cupped her breast, thumb tormenting her nipple through the silk blouse.

She gasped for air when he lifted his head. "What was that for, Tony?"

"Just wanted to make sure you knew who I am before you try playing me like you did that moron." He unfastened the top button of her blouse, trailing kisses down her neck to the hollow of her throat. "Do you?"

"Yes." She moaned when the second button gave way and then the third. He unhooked her bra and his lips roved over her breast. He drew one nipple into his mouth and sucked, while his thumb and two fingers rubbed the other one. She squirmed in the chair, longing to get closer. She clutched at his shoulders, nails digging into his shirt. "Tony!"

He lifted his head. "What?"

"We can't do this here. What if somebody—" She stopped talking, caught her breath when he smiled down at her. "Please."

"I am, aren't I?" His hands slowly slipped down to her knees, and he pushed up her skirt. His mouth seized hers at the same moment he found his way past her black thigh-high stockings to the red open-crotch, thong panties.

She tangled her fingers in his hair, kissing him back. One kiss led to another, tongues dueling. She wanted to moan, cry out when he slid a long finger inside her. A second one joined the first, slipping in and out of her and she met the motion, rising and falling. His thumb rubbed the small bud of flesh while he continued kissing her.

She pulled her mouth free to explore his neck. To sigh, gasp, moan against his throat while he continued the motion with his hand. She arched higher and her nipples were so close to his lips. She groaned when he bent his head, sucked on one and then the other. She moved in the chair, rocking with the strokes of his skilled fingers. His lips claimed hers in one final kiss just as she convulsed on his hand, the orgasm shaking her to the core. He still waited, his hand cupping her, thumb caressing the tiny bud.

She pressed her fingers against his chest, staring into his rugged features and the smoky gray eyes. "I didn't expect—"

"What? Me to send you screaming to the rafters."

She lifted her chin. "I didn't scream."

"Not yet." He grinned, just before his finger slid back

inside her. "Bet I can make that happen if I have my mouth on you next time."

She gasped. "I don't believe you. This is a business office, Tony."

"And I locked the front door when I arrived. It would have locked again when Holmes left." Tony lowered his head. "Move for me, sweetheart."

Their lips met in a long, intoxicating kiss and she did. She moved with his hand, meeting the steady thrusts of his fingers. Dimly, she was aware that she'd never see her office the same way again. She'd always remember the night when they did this. She came even faster this time.

Then, he dropped to his knees, spread her thighs further apart and pushed her panties out of the way. He blew softly on the folds of skin between her legs. His large hands cupped her bottom. "Now, let's see how loud you scream."

Before she answered, his tongue slid across the small piece of flesh he'd tormented with his thumb. She arched against his mouth, becoming part of the intimate kiss. She twined her fingers into his hair. "Please, Tony. Oh God, please."

His tongue drove into her, repeating the same motions he'd done with his fingers such a short time ago. She lifted her hips, up and down, back, and forth as he continued, following the pattern he'd begun earlier. She was his, even if she never told him.

He switched back and forth between soft lapping kisses that barely touched and deep ones that drove her crazy. When she came, she felt him laugh against her skin. She jerked hard on his short hair. "Damn you!"

"I'm doing it over because you didn't scream." And he started again. This time it was brief, sampling kisses that roamed through the curls. Deeper ones when his tongue sank into her before he drew the nub of flesh into his mouth and sucked hard. She came apart, calling his name.

"Close enough for government work." He stood, still between her legs. His mouth claimed hers.

She tasted herself on his tongue and almost came again. When the kiss ended, she rose to her feet and pressed into him. "What's next? Is it my turn to jump you?"

He caught her wrists before she could undo his tie, unbutton his shirt, and unbuckle his belt. "Not yet. We have an appointment."

"What?" She froze for an instant. "What are you talking about?"

"Remember, we're picking up your ring tonight." He kissed her ear.

She didn't resist the temptation. She glanced down and saw the bulge in his pants. He wanted her and she shifted closer, until her body was tight against his. "I don't want to wait. Let's do it now."

"Not yet." He kissed her neck. "And if you're very, very good, I'll take you home to bed tonight."

"What if I'm very, very bad?"

He chuckled, his lips roving down her throat toward her breast. His tongue teased her nipple, and he sucked on it for a bare instant. "Then, I'll take you all night long until you beg me to stop."

She twined her fingers in his dark brown, salt and pepper hair. "Promises, promises."

Chapter Eighteen

She still ached for him on the trip to the jewelry store. She couldn't quite believe the way he'd touched and kissed her while they were in her office. She'd been so dazzled by what he'd done she'd forgotten to finish the email to the Lake Maynard broker. *I'll have to do it tomorrow.* Claire shifted in the passenger seat of the Hummer, flicking a sideways glance at him.

He looked totally calm behind the wheel, not like he'd had his fingers in her, his thumb on her, his mouth sending her spiraling through the universe less than an hour ago. If she had so many orgasms before he actually took her, what would happen when they were in bed? Then again, what would he do if she unfastened her seat belt, slid across the bench seat, and gave him the kind of pleasure he'd given her?

He stopped for a light, shot her a quick glance. "Chill out, Claire."

"How did you—"

"Because you're dancing in that seat like you did when I

had my mouth on you, sweetheart. Why do I think I'll be the first *real* man you've had?"

Heat scorched into her face. "God, I hate you."

He reached over, patted her knee and his fingers trailed under her skirt for a bare instant, teasing the inside of her thigh. "Sure, you do. Now, let me drive."

Before she answered, the red light changed to green, and his attention returned to the highway, both hands on the steering wheel.

At the mall, she deliberately waited for him to come around the vehicle to open her door. He eyed her warily and she hoped her expression didn't give away anything. As the loggers in Rocklin often said, 'Payback was hard.' She eased out of the passenger seat, stepping a little too close to him.

Although he wore his suit jacket, he hadn't buttoned it and she slid her hands over his chest, feeling his heart pound through his shirt. She rocked into him, her thighs rubbing against his legs and felt him harden. "Want me?"

"You know it." He gripped her hips, holding her still. His gaze narrowed. "I'm not having you here."

She rose on tiptoe, bit his lip until she tasted blood, then backed off. "You aren't having me anywhere."

She wrenched away and walked into the mall, leaving him behind.

A few minutes later, he caught up with her. "You're a vicious woman, aren't you?"

"And you say it like it's a bad thing." She tossed her head. "Don't start a game if you can't play, Anthony Marco Baldusi."

"Oh, I can play just fine." His arm slid around her waist, fingers caressing her hip. "Remember that when I make you beg."

She smiled sweetly at him as they headed into the jewelry store. "As long as you realize it's a two-way street, darling."

They were two of the last customers and he left her with the jeweler to fit the ring on her left hand. She saw him across the room talking to another salesclerk near a display case. She gazed at the perfectly fitting diamond and sapphire band on her finger. "It's perfect."

Tony arrived in time to hear her. He picked up her hand and kissed it. "I couldn't agree more."

Glimpsing the tenderness on his face, she trembled. "Tony, I—"

"I know." His lips brushed hers. "Come on, sweetheart. Let's grab some dinner at Petrocelli's while we're in this neck of the woods."

———

Mid-week, the Italian restaurant wasn't as busy as it was on the weekend. He opted for lasagna while she had her favorite chicken fettucine. Salads and garlic bread accompanied the pasta dishes, and they finished the meal with tiramisu, a specialty of the house. She wore the ring during the meal, and he didn't mention he had the box in his jacket pocket. Granted, she hadn't agreed to marry him yet, but she also hadn't refused again.

He sipped his coffee. "So, when did you decide to kick Perry to the curb?"

"I don't like liars." Claire forked up the last piece of her cake. "If he needed help learning to be a Designated Broker, it'd have been one thing. When he told you we were engaged, he was history."

Tony studied her calm features, noting the way her dark blue eyes didn't reveal her emotions. "He doesn't have a clue you orchestrated his departure, does he?"

"And neither does anyone else." She placed the fork neatly beside the empty dessert plate. "If you have a problem with it or me, Tony, you know where to find the door."

"Oh no." He chuckled, shaking his head. "You don't get rid of me so easily. Just remember not to treat me like a fool again."

Her eyes widened. "I didn't. I wouldn't."

He reached across the table, took her hand, squeezed it. "Yes, you did. You should have told me what you had in mind, not left me guessing and playing catch-up." He paused, recalling the wild way she responded to him in her office. "Of course, it was worth it when you showed me how well you can dance."

She blushed, red sweeping into her cheeks all the way up to her forehead. She moistened her lips with the tip of her tongue. "I won't do it again."

"Oh yes, you will." He lifted her hand to his lips, kissed her wrist, feeling her pulse skitter. Her eyes closed for an instant and she sighed softly. He smiled at her. "Come on. I'll take you home."

He didn't offer to drive her back to the office to collect her car, and she didn't mention it either. When they arrived at the apartment house, he grabbed his go-bag off the back seat and then locked the rig behind them. Hand in hand, they walked to the elevator.

In the apartment, he waited until she fed the cat. She turned around, met his gaze. "If we do this, will you agree to stick around?"

He took a step forward, framed her face and kissed her. "I'm not going anywhere without you."

"Right answer." She rested her head against his shoulder. "It's been a while for me."

"Likewise." He held her, one hand smoothing the curly black hair that flowed halfway down her back. "I've been waiting for you."

"Really?"

"You're not the only one who has issues with liars." He kissed her forehead, her eyebrows, the tip of her nose before his lips met hers. His tongue encouraged hers to play and she was breathless when he ended the kiss, lifting his head.

She clung to him, nails digging into his arms. He unfastened the top button of her blouse and buried his lips in the hollow of her throat. She gasped when he cupped her breasts, his thumbs seeking her nipples and swayed close. "Don't stop."

"I've barely started." He kissed her again, then took her hand and led her out of the kitchen, down the hallway to the bedroom. Like the rest of the apartment, it was decorated in shades of black and white. Cream walls, ceiling, and carpet. Black furniture including a king-size bed with a black and white comforter.

She pulled free and crossed the room to the nightstand and switched on the lamp. She pulled back the covers, leaving only the bottom sheet and pillows on the bed. She hesitated for a moment before she unbuttoned her blouse and peeled out of it. She stood for a moment, in her ruby red bra and black skirt. "I—"

"Keep going." He shrugged out of his suit jacket, hung it on the chair by her vanity. His tie and shirt followed. He took a moment to drop his go-bag near the nightstand so the box of condoms would be in easy reach when they wanted them. He crossed to her, his gaze roving over the full breasts down to her slender waist and curving hips. He reached behind her, unzipped the skirt and it fell to the floor. "I could wait, but I'd rather not."

"Me either." She stepped forward, leaving the skirt on the floor. Now, she only wore a brilliant red bra and matching panties, black thigh-high stockings and of course, her stilettos.

He admired the picture she made. Then, he tangled his hand in her hair and his mouth captured hers. He kissed her as if he owned her, the way he'd wanted to forever and she surrendered. Between kisses, her bra hit the floor, and he found her pink nipples, rubbing them between his thumbs and fingers.

She moaned, gasped, and wriggled closer. Her hands explored his chest. He guided her toward the bed, gently pushing her down onto it. He paused to pull off her shoes, dropping the heels on the floor. He followed her, lying beside her. He wanted her and he intended to take her, but first she needed to be as wild and panting as she'd been in her office. He lowered his head and drew her nipple into his mouth, sucking while he caressed her, worked his way down toward the nest of curls between her legs. He slowly removed the stockings, kissing his way along her legs, and then returned for the panties.

She didn't complain about the way he tossed them onto the carpet. Instead, she tormented his nipples, kissing them while her hands roamed over his chest. He slid one finger inside her. She was hot and wet and oh so wanting this. She cried out when a second finger joined the first and then his thumb rocked into her. She twisted, found his mouth with hers. He kissed her back. The first kiss led to a second, a third before he trailed butterfly kisses along her jaw to her ear, then down her neck.

He continued teasing her nipples, sucking first one and then the other. His fingers moved in and out of her while she clung to him, kissed his neck, dug her nails into his back as she rose and fell, matching the motion he started.

She convulsed around his fingers, calling his name. "Please, Tony. Do it. Have me."

"Not yet." He cupped her, stroked through the curls again. "I want you screaming."

She gasped when he slid down to lay claim to her with his mouth, his tongue driving deep inside her in a long intimate kiss. She writhed against him, moving with each intense stroke. She clutched at his hair. She came in moments, but he didn't stop. He continued lapping at her, softly, gently while she arched against him, begging for more. He gave it to her and finally took the bud of flesh into his mouth and sucked. Another orgasm swept through her.

He stood, unbuckled his belt, and removed his pants. He took a condom from his bag, sheathed himself. When she opened her eyes, he joined her on the bed, stroking her black hair. Her fingers strayed over his broad chest. She kissed the hard buttons of his nipples. He smiled, running his hands over her back to the curve of her hips. "I'm going to have you soon."

"Keep talking, Tony." She nipped his chin. "And maybe I'll believe you."

He brushed his mouth over hers. "No doubt about it."

He pulled her on top of him, and she kissed him. More touches led to more kisses as they caressed each other until she was under him again. Finally, he slid between her legs, resting his weight on his elbows. Slowly, he eased inside her. He shifted, pushed deeper. She rose against him. He lowered his head and his lips claimed hers, his tongue demanding entrance.

He pulled back, then drove into her again, a long deep stroke. She met his next thrust with her hips, then a third. She caught his mouth with hers, clawing at his back with her nails. He deepened the series of kisses, and she surrendered. Her hips met his, matching the pattern of his thrusts. Some were shallow, tiny, barely inside her. Others went deeper.

He moved faster, increasing the pace. She twisted, arching beneath him, their hips meeting as he slid in and out of her. He kept thrusting, deliberately holding back until she spasmed, wildly digging in her nails. She threw her head back against the pillows and called his name as she convulsed, tight around him.

He was still hard, buried inside her.

He waited a little longer before he started to move, one stroke after another. She rose against him and met his thrusts. Each took them farther and farther into the universe. She traveled with him on the journey. His tongue drove into her mouth as they whirled through a sensual dance among the stars. Their hips met and they climaxed together.

Afterwards, he held her close, his leg resting between hers, pressing into the nest of curls. She buried her lips against his throat, slowly licking and kissing his skin. "We're going to do it again, aren't we?"

"Soon." He kissed her forehead, his lips lazily trailing a path toward her cheek, her ear. "I'll wait until you're ready. Hot, needy, and screaming. Then, I'll have you just where I want you, Claire Rocklin. Bucking beneath me while I ride you to the moon and back."

She shuddered when his hands slid down to her hips,

and he held her still while he rocked his thigh against her core. She groaned, kissed his neck. "Tony, I —."

"Not yet." He smiled, turned his head so their lips were a whisper away. "First I'll make you come right here and right now."

Chapter Nineteen

He'd had her all night long. Thursday morning, Claire lay in the circle of his arms while he slept. She tipped back her head, studied the broad shoulders and remembered the way she'd gripped them with her hands. His muscled arms, the wide chest with its patch of hair—she liked the fact he didn't shave it, and she glanced down to where the sheet and blanket covered his long legs tangling with hers.

She rested her left hand on his side and saw the diamond and sapphire ring. She'd considered removing it at the store after it was fitted and giving it to Tony to put it in the jewelry box. The idea hadn't lingered in her mind for long. Her grandfather used to say she and her grandma were alike in their propensity to snag anything that glittered and shone. Grandma admitted if she was a bird, she'd be a raven.

It wasn't a bad legacy, Claire thought, glancing across the room at the walk-in closet where she'd moved her antique, standing jewelry armoire when she updated the bedroom. And Tony always bought her earrings or pendants or brooches for her December birthday. This was the first time he'd given her a ring, and she loved it even if she wasn't ready for a lifetime commitment.

If she awakened him, he'd take her again. And she'd enjoy it. She'd never been with anyone who saw to it that she had multiple orgasms and experienced them in a variety of ways. He knew every inch of her body. He'd seen it, touched it, kissed it from her toes to the top of her head.

She'd returned the favor, learning his just as well, but he'd been in charge. She couldn't quite believe it when he was able to make her come by rubbing his hair-roughened thigh against her clitoris. That was new and different. And the way he used his fingers and tongue on her until she was more than ready to have him inside her. When he finally took her, he measured his thrusts, from tiny to extravagant in a marathon of strokes. They continued for such a long time, she thought she'd explode. And then she did, convulsing in one orgasm after another.

He shifted beside her, opening his eyes. "If you keep panting like that, I'm going to start my day with you."

"I'm not panting." She trembled when he stroked her back, staring into his face. "Oh Gawd, Tony."

"I felt it on my skin, sweetness." He reached past her to the box of condoms on the nightstand. "Situational aware-ness. I learned it years ago in the army and you're reaping the benefit. You're breathing so hard you woke me up."

"No, I wasn't." She glowered into his rugged features, the amused gray eyes while he slipped the condom into place. "You're just a horndog with a morning hard-on."

"And this horndog is about to send you flying into the stars." He pulled her close to kiss her and she melted into his embrace. Kisses led to touches while they caressed each other. Then, his hands roved down to her hips, to her butt and finally two fingers slid inside her. She gasped, arching into the touch, rising, and falling when he slid them back and forth, thumb rocking into her.

"Tony, now. Do it now!"

"I like you wet, wild and wanting me." He rolled on top of her, resting most of his weight on his elbows. He drove into her, one long deep thrust after another starting a sensual dance. "All I'll have to do is look at you when we're in the office and you'll know what I'm going to do to you as soon as I have you to myself."

"It's hardly a secret." She bucked upward, her hips meeting his as the pattern of strokes continued, short ones mixing with longer ones. Their lips met in a series of kisses, his tongue mimicking the movements of his lower body. She came in a sudden wave of passion but knew he wasn't done. He paused for a moment before he started moving again. The kisses and various thrusts lasted until they climaxed together.

He cuddled her close, soft inside her where he'd been hard moments earlier. She sighed and kissed him. "You're such a guy."

"I know." His hand cupped her breast, gently teasing her nipple. "And now, you know what will happen when I spend the night with you."

"You're going to take me until I can't think straight." She rested her cheek against his chest, listening to his steady heartbeat, glimpsing the dark shadow of his morning beard stubble. She toyed with one of his nipples. "I didn't expect such great sex."

"Don't worry, sweetheart. I'll always make sure you enjoy it too."

Two hours later, they headed downstairs for breakfast. Without her car, Claire opted to skip the gym and join the residents for French Toast, bacon, and fresh fruit. Tony lingered at the counter waiting for one of his favorite omelets.

In hospital scrubs, Bonnie loaded up a plate and came to join Claire at a table. The older woman squealed, grabbing Claire's hand to view the ring with its two halos of diamonds and sapphires framing the round diamond center stone, set on the diamond accented band. "Is that for real? When did he pop the question? I can't believe it. What did he say? What did you say?"

Claire waited until her hand was freed and Tony came across the room. "I said I wanted more time, and he said—"

"Three years was long enough." Tony sat next to them. "I'm done waiting."

Claire focused on buttering the two slices of fried, egg-dipped bread while he and Bonnie chattered away about the upcoming wedding. He wasn't dressed for success today, but in the work clothes, a flannel shirt, and jeans he'd worn to clear fallen trees. She spotted a bruise on his neck and realized it must be the result from when she bit him during their lovemaking the previous night.

Heat warmed her face because she realized she hadn't responded to one of their comments or had it been a question. "Sorry, I was distracted."

"Bonnie wanted to know about having a reception here." Tony topped off their coffee cups from the carafe in the middle of the table. "I'm good with it. How do you feel?"

"I'll look at the calendar in my office." Claire sprinkled sugar on her French Toast, contemplating how best to change the subject. OMG, she thought. *How do I postpone this? I'm not marrying him. A party would be wonderful if people didn't decide it means more than it does. Delay, delay, delay!* "We'll have to see what works for everyone. The holiday season gets crazy."

"Which is why a Valentine's Day wedding is perfect. It will brighten up the new year when we're all tired of the rain and can't wait for spring." Bonnie beamed at them. "I'll talk to Connor about the cake. I know your favorite is white with raspberry filling and whipped cream frosting, Claire. What about you, Tony? What do you want for a groom's cake?"

Claire's fork rattled on the table when she dropped it. She shot a quick glare at Tony who simply smiled at her before he continued eating breakfast. "This is all brand new, Bonnie. Let's not rush anything."

"All right." Bonnie leaned across the table to pat Claire's hand. "I'm talking to the residents about holiday decorations today. When we finish with that, we'll discuss what we're doing for the wedding. It will be beautiful. You'll see."

"I'm sure we'll love it." Tony told her before he glanced at Claire. "Don't you think so?"

Claire forced a smile and picked up her fork again. She kicked him under the table, knowing her stiletto wouldn't make much of an impact on his work boot. She caught her breath when he edged his chair close enough to squeeze her knee, his hand lingering on her leg. She'd opted for navy slacks, a pin-striped blue and white blouse, and a navy blazer today, but it didn't mean she was immune to his touch.

When they finished eating, she stalked toward her office, fully aware he followed. Once there, she whirled to face him. "It's not real, Tony."

"What's not?" He closed the door and leaned against it,

folding his arms. His gaze swept over her. "Talk slow and I may get it."

She planted her hands on her hips. "We're not getting married, not on Valentine's Day, not ever! And what am I supposed to tell people when it all goes down the swirly? This was just to keep the Rocklins off my back."

"It won't work if you only wear the ring part-time." He paused long enough to lock the door before he advanced on her. "It has to seem natural before we go to Rocklin next week."

"That doesn't mean we plan a wedding." She lifted her chin and glared at him. "All it means is I wear the ring a while and then consider returning it when we get home after Thanksgiving weekend."

"I don't think so." His hands closed on her shoulders, and he pulled her into his arms. "You keep it on your finger, Claire Rocklin because you know you'll be *Face-Timing* Beckett and Aggie throughout the season, and we'll have to go there for Christmas. And I've never let you give jewelry back to me. I'm not starting with that ring."

She tilted her head back until their gazes met. She moistened her lips with her tongue, and he apparently took it as an invitation. His head lowered and he kissed her. She meant to push him away, but she couldn't. Instead, she gasped when his hands slid to her hips and he lifted her up, carrying her to the long worktable on the far wall. His tongue swept inside her mouth, and she surrendered.

Once she sat on the table, he pushed her legs apart so he could stand between them and kept kissing her. She tore her lips away from his, stared up into the gray eyes, saw the storm of passion rising. "Tony —."

"If you thought wearing pants would stop me from having you, it was a miscalculation."

She moaned when he unfastened the top button on her slacks, slid down the zipper, lifted her slightly so he could pull the pants to her knees. "I didn't think at all. I just wanted to get dressed after you screwed me in the shower."

"You loved it as much as I did. And I do like these crotch-less, silk panties of yours." He smiled wickedly and his hand slowly eased past the material. "You know that, don't you? It's why you wear them."

She clutched at his arms when he stroked the curls. "Tony, I have things to do."

"You certainly do, sweetness." Two fingers slid inside her, his thumb rolling against her clitoris. "And one of them is moving for me."

She found herself doing it, shifting on the table, arching against his hand, then rising, and falling with the motion of his skillful fingers. Their lips met in one kiss after another. Somehow, he managed to undo her blouse, open her bra, and find her nipples, sucking on each in turn. She gasped, sighed, and kissed her way down his throat. She came all at once, convulsing in a long orgasm. "Tony!"

"You do know who I am." He chuckled, his breath warm on her thighs.

His smile teased her senses, especially when she realized he'd brought her chair over from the desk to the table. She saw her slacks on the floor and wondered when the panties joined them. She didn't remember losing them. He sat between her legs. His large hands lifted her butt and his mouth found her, his tongue driving deep inside. It didn't come as much of a surprise he had a condom in his pocket or that they put it to good use.

Afterwards, they dressed again. He opened the windows and aired out the small room. She hadn't agreed to the wedding but decided wearing the ring for a while would be a good idea. It was a fake engagement, one destined to keep her long-lost relatives, who weren't lost enough, off her back. And the fringe benefits of screwing Tony six ways from Sunday was a definite plus. Wow, he had an amazing imagination when it came to sex.

When they arrived at the Seattle brokerage, she didn't go inside. Instead, she drove out to the tiny house village.

Blanche opened the door before Claire could knock. "Come in out of the cold. I want to see your ring."

"How do you know about it?" Claire held up her hand, diamonds catching the November sunlight. "I didn't tell you Tony's been packing it around for three years. It came as a surprise to me too."

"Bonnie called from the apartment house to let me know to save Valentine's Day to preside at your wedding." Blanche eyed the ring. "Wow, that's something. I thought you were faking it for your relatives, but that doodad sure looks real."

Chapter Twenty

After he dropped Claire at the Seattle office, he took a fast trip to his condo to shower and change into appropriate clothes for a day at the office. He made a mental note to ask if he could leave a few things at her apartment. He wouldn't mind moving into her place until he convinced her to share the house in Everett with him, but she still needed space. For now, he'd count his blessings. She wore his ring and didn't plan to remove it during the next six weeks.

Ready for work, he drove out to the office in Bellevue. It didn't come as much of a shock to learn Perry Holmes had visited only long enough to clear out his desk. Tony announced the former acting Designated Broker had left to pursue other opportunities and Zelda Torres would now be the lead broker for this branch. The associates were too professional to applaud, but Tony still saw the approval on various faces. He reminded them about the November contest before he took Zelda out for a celebratory lunch.

When he finished in Bellevue, he went back to the Everett office. He spotted Claire's distinctive red Lincoln

Navigator in the lot. The babble of the conversations ended as he walked inside. He glanced at Ingrid Swensen, the receptionist. "What's going on? Where's Claire?"

"Hiding in your office." Ingrid giggled, looking younger and far too mischievous for a woman almost forty. "We embarrassed her when George led everyone in singing, 'For she's a jolly good fellow!' since she's managed to snare you after all these years."

"Amazing." Tony looked at the prior service soldier sitting at one of the computers. "You're an asshat, Delaney. It was the other way around. I finally got her to agree."

"I know, Top." George winked at him. "But how could we hassle the boss if we told her you won the day? Ingrid and Ginny are organizing a bridal shower, so you'll want to make a list of what you two need for the new house."

"We'll keep you posted." Laughing, Tony strolled through the office accepting congratulations from the associates. He paused long enough to let Ginny know Zelda was the new Designated Broker for Eastside before he went down the hall and passed the word onto David.

Then, Tony opened the door to his office and walked inside. Claire wasn't behind the desk. Instead, she lay on the couch he told everyone he kept for visitors, sound asleep. She wore the navy slacks and pinstriped blouse he'd peeled her out of earlier that day and used her blazer as a makeshift pillow. Her shoes were on the floor. He'd worn her out last night and the memory made him smile.

He opened the bottom drawer of the file cabinet where he kept one of the multi-colored throws his mother crocheted for him. He covered Claire with it and left her to nap while he worked. She'd probably wake up before the office closed. And if she didn't, he'd take her home with him.

He removed his jacket, hung it on the coat rack in the corner. On Thursday afternoons, he checked the online real estate sites to ensure their current listings were updated and the new ones had been posted. It always took at least three to four hours to complete the various advertising tasks, so they'd be ready for potential clients to view houses over the weekend.

He'd finished answering his last email when Claire awakened. She yawned, stretched, and then sat up, pushing the throw aside. She turned to look at him. "Why on earth do you have a blanket in your office?"

"Because some nights are too long to go to the condo." He met her gaze. "Five combat tours in almost twenty years, Claire. They took their toll. P.T.S.D."

She didn't speak for a moment, sat looking at him with concerned dark blue eyes. "If it helps, you could come to my place on those nights."

"Sometimes, I already do."

She stood, walked to him, and shoved his shoulder until the chair wheeled back from the desk. She sat down on his lap, wrapped her arms around his neck and nipped his ear. "From now on, you come whenever you need me, Tony."

"I might run out of condoms." He kissed her gently. "I only have one box at your apartment."

"Buy more." She undid his tie and tossed it onto the desk. "Do you have any here?"

"No." He fisted his hand in her hair and his lips claimed hers in a fierce kiss. She yielded immediately, her tongue slashing into his mouth. She adjusted her position, rocking her pelvis into him. She intended to distract him, and it was working. He felt his body respond to the pressure, rising upward and pressing into her. She lifted her mouth from his and began to unbutton his shirt.

He caught her wrists. "Don't, sweetness. I already told you I don't have a condom."

"Then, it's lucky I grabbed a few out of your box this morning." She smiled dangerously. "However, I'm not planning to use one."

He didn't quite believe what he heard. "What if you get pregnant?"

"Not happening with what I have in mind." She pulled free from his grasp and finished yanking his shirt out of his slacks. Her hands roamed over his chest toward his belt, and she unbuckled it. "How does that saying go? Turnabout is fair play. I know how to use my mouth too."

"Claire!" Had he heard what he thought he did?

She eased off his lap, but only to unbutton and unzip his pants. Then, she was on her knees in front of him, freeing him from his underwear. His hands went to her hair. He meant to stop her, to remind her this wasn't the time or place. The door was closed, but it wasn't locked. However, all those rational thoughts fled when her tongue started to tease him.

After what had to be one of the best blowjobs he'd ever had, she left the office. He stood, tucked in his shirt, and zipped his pants. The door opened. She returned, looking as immaculate as always, carrying two cups of coffee and the last doughnut, an apple fritter. He eyed her warily. "Do I dare to ask what's next on the agenda?"

"Don't worry, darling." She flashed her sweetest smile. "You're not for a while. So, what are your plans for the weekend?"

He sat down at his desk and clicked on the file containing the designs of his new home. "I've been brainstorming about the Everett house. Bring over a chair and I'll show you."

"I don't need one." She put one of the mugs of black coffee in front of him, sat down on his lap. "Show me what you've got, big boy."

He chuckled, rested a hand on her hip. "Okay, but only if you behave yourself."

"For a while." She kissed him and he tasted minty toothpaste. Then, she drank some coffee and trailed a scarlet tipped fingernail over his cheek. "Remember, not to do anything on the place until closing. Deals have been known to flip at the last minute, and you don't want to invest more money than you can afford to lose."

He nodded, tore off a piece of the fritter and fed it to her. "I know, but I appreciate your concern for me. I want you to look at the kitchen. Don't even think about those god-awful granite countertops. I hate them."

"Polished marble surfaces are smooth and shiny—"

"They have glossy finishes but they're slippery when wet." He ran a hand across her thigh, and she squirmed a little, so he paused to kiss her. More coffee, more apple fritter until they finished both. "I don't want you falling off the counter when I'm screwing your brains out during breakfast or lunch or dinner."

"Why would I be there? I have a place of my own."

"Because I want you living with me someday." He feathered his thumb over her lips. "We could use the marble for backsplashes behind the farmhouse sink in the kitchen and also in the bathrooms."

She nipped his thumb. "Aren't you going to have me in those other rooms?"

"Definitely." He clicked the mouse and brought up pictures of the updated pantry with the washer, dryer, laundry sink and drying rack. "I'll take you anywhere I can get you."

"You've been here three years, and I didn't know how much you wanted me. Why did you keep it a secret?"

"I never did. I have no idea why you didn't pay attention." He kissed her again while he opened her pants. As she'd said, 'turnabout was fair play' and he cupped her with one hand. He scrolled to the next picture, slipping two fingers inside her. "Let me show you the living room."

She gasped when his thumb rocked against her clitoris. Her thighs clenched against his hand for a moment. "Tony!"

"That's me. Now look at what I want to do here."

"I am."

"No, sweetheart. Look at the monitor. We're talking about our new home."

She shuddered when he began to slide his fingers in and out of her. It was only a prelude to what he'd do when he had her in his bed next time, but for now, it was enough. She kissed his neck, sighed, gasped, moaned against his throat while he continued the motion with his hand.

She moved back and forth, meeting the strokes of his fingers. He didn't know how much attention either of them paid to the proposed remodeling of the house, but it truly didn't matter. How could it when he had Claire Rocklin riding his hand like a wild woman, her thoughts totally focused on him and what he did to her? Finally, she spasmed in one long orgasm, her mouth against his neck, crying his name when she convulsed in his embrace.

———

His hand was still on her, his fingers still inside her. Claire quivered when he mentioned the primary bedroom and the updates to the adjoining ensuite bathroom. How could he remain so calm when she was a shaking mass of nerves?

She forced herself to look at the computer screen. His plans for the house were brilliant, much better than hers had been. Of course, he was thinking about a home while she'd been turning it into a high-priced showplace.

His fingers started to move again, and she shifted to meet the pattern he set. Rising, falling, sliding back and forth on his lap, unable to resist the strong thrusts of those skilled fingers. Meanwhile his thumb kept tormenting her clitoris. She clung to him, arms around his neck. She hadn't thought giving him a blowjob would lead to this. She just wanted to comfort him because he'd sounded so upset when he mentioned the P.T.S.D.

She nipped his ear, kissed his throat, panted for breath as she drew closer and closer to the edge. She came in a long burst. His hands moved to her hips, and he rocked her against the bulge in his slacks. She groaned, her lips a breath away from his ear. "Tony, I—"

"You said you had condoms." He threaded a hand in her hair, pulled back her head until their gazes met. "I've fantasized for years about having Claire Rocklin in my office."

"I've been here before."

"You know what I mean." He kissed her. "Go see if we're alone. We should be by this time. It's after twenty-two hundred hours, ten at night."

"I'll be lucky if I don't have to crawl to my car. How can I walk after what you did to me?"

"Very easily, sweetheart." He lifted her off his lap and fastened her slacks. "You put one foot in front of the other. Go make sure the office doors are locked and then come back here. I don't want to tell you again."

She gaped at him, her knees shaking. Wow, she loved it when he got all macho with her, but only when they were having sex. Of course, she wasn't saying that to him.

Instead, she followed his order. She went into the main part of the office, not surprised to discover everyone had left. He wouldn't have sent her to check if he hadn't been sure they were alone. He never wanted her to take any risks.

When she returned to his office, he'd closed the window blinds. She found a full-size, double bed pulled out of the couch. Her jaw dropped. "I didn't know that was a sleeper sofa."

He walked over to the office door, closed it, and locked it. "Why do you think I said I imagined having you here? It wasn't to talk business."

"Really?" She met the amused gray eyes and trembled at his slow, sensual smile. "Then, what was it?"

"You know damned well. Quit playing with me and take off your clothes. I want you naked, begging and under me in five minutes. Move your butt, Claire. Don't make me help you."

Chapter Twenty-One

She didn't get home until two in the morning. If Felix hadn't been depending on her, she'd have spent the night with Tony at the office. It wouldn't have been the first time they'd pulled an all-nighter, but the previous ones had been work-oriented. Gawd, she'd had more sex with him in the past two days than she had in the last ten years.

Why did she think they'd be doing it even more over the weekend? *Because I'm not stupid and even though we did it three times, I wanted to do it again. I'd have jumped him if he wasn't asleep when I left.* She wasn't a nun, but she certainly hadn't thought her libido could be so high.

Her phone vibrated and she pulled it out of her pocket to see a text from him. *'Don't do that again!'*

'Do what?' Claire sent an answer with an innocent looking emoji.

'Walk out by yourself at this time of the morning. It's not safe. Let me escort you to your car next time.'

His concern warmed her from head to toe, and she responded, *'Will do! C.U. tomorrow!'*

She left her laptop bag and purse on the hallway table and went into the kitchen to feed a hungry kitten his wet food. Felix wound back and forth between her legs, doing his best to show her he hadn't been fed in years. However, his dish full of dry food belied the point as did his water bowl. So, did the partial can of kitty meat in the fridge where she also discovered one of Connor's chicken, broccoli, and fettucine Alfredo casseroles.

When her brother dropped off dinner for her, he must have also taken it upon himself to feed the cat. Of course, it'd been an eon ago according to Felix, so she gave him a little extra of his wet food. Then, she dished up a healthy portion of pasta and warmed it in the microwave. That and a glass of red wine filled her empty stomach.

A quick shower and she headed for bed, remembering to set the alarm to wake her. She needed to be in the office by nine, even if she planned to skip her usual workout at the gym. Well, how many calories did healthy bouts of sex burn? She'd have to look it up on the Internet. Laughing at the thought, she clicked off the lamp and fell asleep.

Friday morning, Claire skimmed through emails on her phone with her first cup of coffee. She responded to the one from the property manager at Tony's building, agreeing to meet the man before lunch. Logan Turner sent a highly urgent message about a delivery of flooring that wasn't the right color, and she answered she'd be there by ten a.m. She texted Fancy asking about the beach repairs. When would the woman return to Seattle and take charge of the décor at the new apartment house?

Taking her second cup of coffee with her, she went into her bedroom. As always when she had an appointment to list an expensive property, she wanted to look her best. She opted for a brilliant red, turtleneck sweater dress with tiny gold buttons on the long sleeves. It looked deceptively simple on the hanger, but once she had it on, it outlined her breasts and every curve. The thin black belt accentuated her waist.

When she opened the kitchen blinds, she'd seen frost glittering on the balcony, so she chose black stockings to go with her black suede ankle boots. She sat down at the vanity to apply cosmetics and added her favorite diamond stud earrings, a gift from Tony. She transferred the usual accoutrements into a black shoulder bag. Grabbing a short black blazer, she started out of the apartment, pausing to pick up her laptop bag on the way.

The elevator doors whisked open to reveal her brother. She tilted her head. He'd changed into sweats at the station and carried yesterday's uniform. Arriving at this hour of the morning meant he'd pulled another double-shift. "Thanks for supper last night and I don't know if Felix was appreciative or not, but I was."

"No worries. You're stylin' today, little sis. Who's on the menu? Has Tony talked when he should have listened?"

"He's fine. I'm listing his condo today and I don't want any crap from the property manager."

Conn whistled softly. "Well, he certainly shouldn't give you any." His gaze narrowed on her left hand. "Is that the ring?"

"Yes." She held up her wrist so he could see the diamonds and sapphires in all their glory. "This is temporary. We're scamming the Rocklin contingent next week and Tony thinks I should be in the habit of wearing it."

"Makes sense." Connor caught her hand and turned it to provide a better view. "Does he know you'll never give it back?"

She glared at her twin. "I'm not mercenary or greedy or immoral. I shouldn't keep it when I don't plan to marry the man."

"You shouldn't, but you have a thing for diamonds." Connor relaxed his grip. "He'd better realize it's history."

She brushed by him and stalked into the elevator. "I'm going to work. And you obviously need to hit the sack because you're headed for dementia caused by sleep deprivation."

"Yeah, right. I'm texting Tony to warn him about your propensity for snabbling anything bright and shiny."

She sniffed. "Save it. You can tell him when he's here tonight."

Connor narrowed dark blue eyes so like her own. "Why is he coming?"

"Because it will be much easier to sell his condo when he's out of it for the next three weeks until he closes on his new place in Everett." Claire hit the button for the first floor. "And he was being a macho jackass last night. Payback is mine."

"Poor guy. Like Gramps used to say, you're going to teach him to suck eggs."

"Exactly." The doors closed before she added anything else.

She was in the apartment office a few minutes before Sofia arrived. Claire draped her blazer over the back of her chair. She opened the locking cabinet on the wall and removed extra keys to her apartment and the garage. Granted, Tony generally arrived before Jerry closed the security gates, but there wasn't any point depending on that. Schedules often changed. Hers certainly did.

At the rolltop desk, she hit the power button for the computer to scan emails again. Fancy had responded to the texts, sending photos of the repairs at the beach house along with her invoice for the work. Claire debated, then added an extra charge to the bill for the emergency caused by the recent party and forwarded it to the property managing company on the coast.

The company would collect the amount due from the renters, and she also reminded the owner to blacklist the visitors. In addition, since she was a spiteful bitch, she suggested passing the word to other people who owned recreational properties so they could protect their investments. The door opened and Sofia entered, accompanied by Mrs. Nayaka, the East Indian woman who owned the cleaning company.

Smiling, Claire rose and went to hug the older woman. "I'm so glad you're home. How was the reunion? Did the kids have a good time at Disneyland? Pull up a chair and tell me all about it."

———

Tony parked behind the red Lincoln Navigator, wondering what brought Claire to the building under renovation. He'd find out soon enough. He followed the sound of voices to the first-floor apartment where the construction crew kept supplies. He found Claire and Logan Turner assessing a large stack of long, skinny boxes. One had been opened to reveal pieces of wood laminate flooring.

Tony sauntered toward the pair. Of course, Logan couldn't keep his gaze on the vinyl boards when Claire stood close by in a red dress that emphasized her undeniable assets. She'd pinned her black hair into a loose bun, and several tendrils teased her neck, shoulders and back. Diamond studs shone in her ears.

She glanced at him with a bright smile. "Hello, darling. I didn't expect you but I'm glad you're here."

"Why do I think I should be afraid, very afraid?" When he reached her, he wrapped an arm around her waist, then dropped a quick kiss on that smiling mouth. "What do you want me to do? I know you have a list, sweetheart."

"Of course, I do." She gestured toward the wanna-be wood. "Fancy will be back next week. Logan will have some of the rooms ready for her crew to paint before she does the flooring. After that, Fancy will have her people start moving in furniture."

"All right, but that doesn't tell me what's on my 'honey-do' list."

"Call and have this crap taken back and get the flooring we ordered. Logan knows the exact kind, and I hate substitutions."

Tony eyed the younger man who obviously didn't know what to think of her authoritative tone. "Works for me. What else?"

She lifted her left hand to smooth his jacket collar, the diamond ring glinting. "You told me last night you signed the listing agreement to sell your condo. Give me your key to it and the garage so I can meet with the property manager and finish putting the place up for sale. I want it to be shown this weekend. I'm meeting Mrs. Nayaka there with her crew to clean it and change the curtains to the sheer ones we use for high-priced places."

"I'm not a slob, Claire." He tightened his hold on her waist. "Are you asking—?"

"Don't be silly, Anthony Marco Baldusi. I never ask anyone anything." She held out her left hand. "I'll make copies for the secure lockbox I'm putting on the door and I'll return your keys later."

Chuckling, Tony fished out his keys and removed the two she wanted. When he handed them to her, he stared at the ones she offered in trade. "What are these?"

"Keys to my place. Feed the cat if you get there before I do." She dropped his keys into her dress pocket. "It's spaghetti night in the community room and poker afterwards. Bring lots of money for me to win."

Tony watched her stroll toward the hallway, hips swaying under the clinging red dress. He wondered what color her panties were and how soon he could find out. He glanced at Logan. "Get the info for me. I'll be right back."

The sandy-haired man in construction clothes nodded and followed directions. Tony went after his wayward fiancée. He caught up with her in the parking lot where she stood at the passenger side of the Navigator. She put her purse on the seat next to the laptop bag and a black jacket.

She closed the door before she glanced at him. "Have you already arranged for the flooring to be returned?"

"Not yet. I will." He caught her hand and pulled her into his arms. "You forgot something."

A disdainful sniff and a toss of her head. "I never forget anything."

"Want to bet?" He grinned and pinned her between him and the vehicle. When she gasped, he bent his head and took her mouth, his tongue sweeping inside.

She kissed him back, hands on his shoulders, nails digging into his back, the way he liked. He parted her legs with one of his. She moaned and tightened her hold on him when he deliberately rocked his thigh against her core. Groaning, she pressed her hands against his chest. "I can't. We shouldn't."

"We will later." He remained still for a moment longer,

his gaze locked on hers. "What color are your panties? Are they my favorite kind?"

She blushed, surprising for a woman almost thirty-five. "It's cold. They're granny pants."

"Maybe I'd better see for myself."

She squealed, grabbed his hands on her hips before he reached for the hem of her dress. "Tony, don't!"

"Answer me."

"Red. They're red."

"What else?" He kissed the spot below her ear. Her dress had hiked up and he tightened his hold on her hips. He rubbed his thigh against her again. "I'm waiting, Claire. Want to tell me or shall I find out for myself?"

She lifted her chin. "It's a thong. I don't have any granny panties, but I'm going to buy some on my next shopping trip in two weeks."

"Fair enough. I'll enjoy ripping them off you."

Two long steamy kisses later and he stepped back. He escorted her around to the driver's side and held the door for her when she slid behind the wheel. Her dress crawled up a bit, not enough to suit him. He rested his hand on her thigh and leaned in to kiss her again. She moaned into his mouth when he discovered that she was indeed wearing crotchless panties. He kept kissing her until she spasmed in a quick, violent response to the strokes of his fingers.

She opened dazed eyes, gaping at him. "I don't believe you. We're in public for heaven's sake."

"I know." He grinned at her. "Remember what I plan to do to you every time you put on your bossy britches, sweetheart."

"And you'd better realize vengeance is always mine."

He laughed. "I can't wait."

He closed the driver's door and walked back inside the building to deal with the latest catastrophe. Behind him, he heard the engine start as she drove away. He didn't doubt she'd come up with something to make his life interesting and he'd certainly find a way to return the favor tonight. What would she think of that?

Chapter Twenty-Two

She continued to tremble from the aftermath of the orgasm while she drove to his Seattle waterfront condo. Damn it! She wanted him to know she was in charge. Now, she was getting sex and playing her part in a make-believe engagement that definitely wouldn't lead to marriage. *So, why do I feel like he's the one in charge when actually I am?*

No answer came to mind when she arrived at his condo before the cleaning crew and checked in at the security desk. Her authorization was on file, so she never had any trouble visiting Tony. However, things were changing. She shared the news she was putting the condo up for sale, that other realtors would be showing the property in the next few weeks until it sold and left a copy of the listing agreement with the supervisor who agreed to forward it to the property manager. He offered to escort the cleaning crew to the appropriate condominium.

Fair enough, she thought, thanking him. Tony's place was on one of the top floors, providing a fantastic view of Elliott Bay and the ferries chugging back and forth. She opened the blinds at each window, finishing in the bedroom. She sent a quick text to Mrs. Nayaka telling her to bring white linens from the laundry at the apartment house.

After that, Claire began packing his clothes into suit-cases. She'd leave the furniture, but the personal items were out of here. He'd learn she was the boss before the night was over. Yes, they had a token engagement, but it was only for the holidays. He needed to stop overstepping her bound-aries. She refused to admit it was a two-way street. Some people called her a total bitch when they saw her *modus operandi* and she didn't care! She wanted this place *'staged'* for sale and since he wasn't here to complain, she'd do things her way.

———

While he dealt with the issue of the flooring at Claire's new investment, Tony received one text after another from the property manager of his condo building. Finally, he'd listened to enough drama. He wanted the place to sell in a timely fashion, so he sent back a note telling the man to suck it up and talk to Claire.

She was the listing agent. She'd get a hefty commission from the sale. He texted her and let her know she needed to run interference with the property manager who better let her step up and do her damn job. That stopped the chain of complaints and allowed Tony to do a walk-through with Logan where they discussed more of the changes to the Everett house as well as the ongoing renovations here.

Afterwards, he headed north to the Lake Maynard branch, making a stop for a fast-food lunch on the way. It was a long drive, but he'd already been at the other offices this week. Fridays were when he preferred to visit and make sure Svetlana Hollister was ready for a busy weekend of selling properties. While he was there, the petite brunette explained they were ahead in the running for the November contest and if the brokerage won, the associates at the branch would win extra-large year-end bonuses. They'd already agreed she should be the one to go to Cancun for the holiday weekend since most of them had family commitments and she didn't.

Tony skimmed through the recent sales contracts and listing agreements. Svetlana only needed some encouragement before she forwarded copies to the main office in Seattle and the escrow company that would make closing arrangements. He was back on the road shortly after fifteen-hundred hours, three in the afternoon. He'd hoped to miss rush-hour traffic, but no such luck. It wasn't as bad driving south as it was when he glanced at the highway heading north. As usual, the crowded lanes reminded him of a parking lot.

Claire's rig was long gone when he pulled into the garage at his condo which meant he might have to wait to get his keys from her unless she'd left them with the security guard. She hadn't, but luckily, he could open the real estate lockbox on his door with his master key. When he walked inside, he smelled bleach and other cleaners. The picture windows in the living room gleamed when he turned on the lights. No dust anywhere and the carpet had professional tracks from whoever vacuumed.

In the kitchen, the marble countertops shone. He didn't see a single dish through the glass fronted cupboard doors. No glasses either. Well, he could drink his beer straight from the bottle. When he opened the fridge, he discovered it was empty other than a box of baking soda to deodorize any smells. What had she done with his imported ale?

She hadn't thrown it away because the garbage can under the sink was empty. So was the dishwasher. Okay, what else had the woman taken? He went through the cabinets and discovered all the groceries were gone. The pantry and freezer were empty too. For a moment, anxiety rose, and he reminded himself he wasn't a boy anymore.

He could buy something for dinner on the way to her apartment. He wasn't going to starve. Leaving the eat-in kitchen, he walked through the dining room on the way to the primary suite. He used it as an office and noted only the large table remained with its eight matching chairs. The photographs of his mother and Claire weren't on the walls any longer.

It shouldn't come as a surprise that she stripped the place. She often said when she sold property, she preferred not to see any personal touches from the owners. They could stay in motels while she sold their homes, a *'bass-ackward's contingency'* to his mind. He'd always preferred having a place to go to, instead of knowing he no longer had a place to be from, and she knew that. They'd argued about it a few times in the last three years.

In his bedroom, he saw a spotless white comforter and new pillows in starched pillowcases on the king-size bed. The sterile atmosphere reminded him of a hotel. All that was missing was a Bible next to the lamp on the nightstand. The closet was empty, including the military duffel bags he kept as souvenirs of his Army days, although he didn't expect to wear his old uniforms again.

Whoever sanitized the rest of the apartment had done their magic here too. Not a speck of dust anywhere. He made a final stop in the ensuite bathroom. Nothing was left. He considered calling her but decided against it. 'Forewarned was forearmed' and she didn't deserve a 'heads-up.'

He left the condo behind, still bemused by the sudden attack. What was she thinking? She'd definitely have an excuse for her behavior, and he looked forward to hearing it. Oddly, he didn't actually mind her doing the work of removing his belongings. It saved him from packing them and would make the move to the house in Everett when he closed on the deal that much easier. Still, they were about to have a meeting of the minds, and she might not enjoy it, but he would.

It didn't take long to drive to the apartment building in the exclusive Magnolia neighborhood. He left the Hummer in the slot next to Claire's vehicle and strode to the elevator.

When the doors opened, he saw the maintenance man. Jerry Chambers nodded a greeting. "Hey, Tony. I just heard you're moving in, so I'll have a parking stall labeled for you in the next couple of days. Hope that's all right."

"It's fine. Thanks. I appreciate it." He'd keep his war with Claire to himself, and Tony waited until the older man walked away before he stepped into the elevator. He took it to the top floor and went to her penthouse.

Felix greeted him and he bent to collect the tuxedo kitten, petting it on the way to the kitchen. The food dishes were full, so obviously she'd already been here. He wondered if she still was or if he'd find her in the community room downstairs. Tony lowered the cat to the floor. He opened the refrigerator, removed one of his beers, noticing that the food from his place had already been put away. He proceeded to check out the cupboards while he drank the imported beer. His groceries and dishes commingled with

177

hers. All right. He could deal with it. The empty ale bottle went in the recycle basket under the sink.

When he glanced in the living room, he saw the photos on the plant stand were rearranged to make room for the ones from his condo. His larger studio pictures of her and his mother hung in the hall. He nodded and continued to the guestroom. Neat and tidy, but nothing that belonged to him was in the bureau, the closet, or the adjoining bathroom which guests used. He walked into her room, spotted the red dress lying on the king-size bed, her boots lying catty-wumpus beside it.

He paused to collect the dress and shoes. He carried them into the huge walk-in closet. Without it, the apartment would easily be a three-bedroom. He hung up the dress, put the boots in the empty place on the shelf next to her other shoes. Shrugging out of his jacket, it went on one of the hangers by the rest of his suits.

Removing his tie, he began unbuttoning his shirt. She'd arranged the clean, ironed ones fresh from the laundry service, by color so he could easily find one. She even had a rack for his ties. She'd stored his extra boxes of condoms on their own shelf. That would come in handy. What he considered his civvies and of course, his underwear were sorted into several drawers on the right side of the room.

Without his permission, she'd decided to move him into her place. They'd talk. He'd enjoy hearing her excuses for being such a brat.

Returning to the bedroom, he listened for a moment, hearing the shower. Then, he followed the trail of her remaining clothes into the ensuite, picking up her bra, panties, and stockings. He dropped them in the laundry hamper, then kicked off his shoes. Next came his pants, boxers, and socks. He paused long enough to grab a condom from the box on the counter and sheathe himself.

He opened the steamed-up shower door. "Hello, honey. I'm home."

Claire squawked like an indignant chicken. "What are you doing here, Tony?"

"You weren't expecting someone else, were you?" His gaze swept over her, sopping wet from her black hair to the red polish on her toenails. Her full breasts, pink nipples, and the curling black hair between her legs. *All mine*, he thought. *She's finally all mine.*

He stepped under the warm spray and reached for her. His hands closed on her waist, and he gathered her close at the same moment his mouth captured hers. He kept kissing her while the water poured over them like a warm waterfall.

Finally, she pulled slightly away. "You're early."

"I'd say I'm just in time." He kissed her neck, traced a line to her breasts and drew one of those pink nipples into his mouth and sucked.

She moaned, wriggled nearer and her hands pressed against his chest. "Tony, we'll be late for supper."

He lifted his mouth from her aching nipple. "Then, I'd better hurry up."

He slid two fingers inside her. His thumb rubbed the bud of flesh. "Dance for me, sweetheart."

She panted for breath while she moved with the motion of his hand, his fingers sliding in and out of her until she was ready. Hot and wild. He didn't wait for her to come this time. Instead, he shifted his hold to her hips, adjusted his position and drove into her. Between thrusts, he kissed her, sucked, and tormented the nipples that were so close to his mouth and kissed her again.

She wrapped her legs around him, responding to his

movements. She dug her nails into his back, moaning, gasping and finally crying out his name when she came. The next time, they climaxed together. Afterwards, he turned off the water and they stumbled out of the shower into the bathroom where they toweled each other dry.

He couldn't help it. He stood and admired her. A lovely face. Big, blue eyes and a mouth that would have tempted a saint. Black hair tumbling around her shoulders and halfway down her back while her nipples played hide and seek between the strands. The way her waist curved into those magnificent hips, the long legs, and narrow feet.

She narrowed her eyes and glowered at him. "Stop it, Tony. We're going to dinner downstairs."

"Oh, we'll get there." He reached for the box on the counter and another condom. "Eventually."

"Now!" She squealed, evaded his touch, and hurried toward the door.

He caught her in two steps, his gaze falling to her rounded backside. A moment later he had the condom in place. He drew her toward him. "Okay, we'll do it your way." And he slid inside her from behind. "Move for me, sweetheart."

———

Her knees still quivered from the orgasm when she entered the bedroom a short time later. He'd lingered in the bathroom to remove the last condom. What had she done? Claire glanced at the full-length mirror on her closet door. She hadn't considered the way he might take her decision to move his belongings into her apartment when she *'staged'* his condo for an immediate sale.

Apparently, he figured she was more than ready for a

long-term commitment when all she'd intended to do was overstep his boundaries and teach him a lesson. Most guys would have gone running down the road to the nearest hotel, screaming at her arrogance when they came home to an empty condo. World War Three should have erupted when he realized they were now full-fledged roommates. Not him. Not Tony Baldusi. He used it as an opportunity to screw her brains out. And not only once, but twice.

She was putting on a blue lace scalloped bra that matched her panties when he entered the room. His wicked grin made her tremble, but she managed to fasten the front closure anyway. Next came a bright blue tunic top decorated with silver sequins and black leggings. She slipped on ballet style flats. By the time she'd combed her damp hair and braided it, reapplied her makeup, he was ready.

He looked totally casual in jeans, cowboy boots, and a flannel shirt. Good choices, so he wouldn't be out of place when the residents saw him. He advanced on her, rested his hands on her shoulders and leaned down to kiss the side of her neck and she saw him glance at the top of her breasts in the opening of her top. She struggled not to squirm in the chair, wanting him all over again. "We have to go to dinner."

"We will." He drew back the chair, helped her to her feet. "I'll wait a while longer to send my woman screaming to the rafters."

"What does that mean?"

"Twenty-two hundred hours, Claire Rocklin and we turn into pumpkins."

She gaped at him when he guided her down the hallway. "Speak civilian."

"Ten o'clock and we're coming home to bed."

"In your dreams." She lifted her chin and glared into his

smoke gray eyes. "I haven't come home that early on a Friday night since I was a teenager."

He squeezed her hip. "Nine forty-five, sweetheart, not a moment later."

She opened the apartment door, keeping a wary eye out for the kitten. "No way, Tony."

"Nine-thirty. Want to try for twenty-hundred hours? Eight p.m., civilian time?"

Chapter Twenty-Three

After dinner, Claire helped with the clean-up before she went to the game room. Tony was already there organizing the poker game with Harry Gamack and Jerry Chambers. She counted and realized they only had enough players for one table. She left the hardcore bunch to it and went to the media room where she found Sofia setting up for a movie night.

"What are we watching?" Claire turned on the popcorn machine and waited for it to heat up before she set it in motion. "Something new and wonderful?"

Sofia giggled. "Not with Nonna and Bonnie. They told me some of the women would be offended by anything too racy so we're starting with *Princess Bride*. After that, it's *My Big Fat Greek Wedding*. Bonnie says we may get some ideas for your and Tony's ceremony on Valentine's Day."

"I don't know about that." While the popcorn started its expected racket, Claire filled cups with ice. "That might be too soon. If it has to be a holiday, St. Patrick's Day could be nice."

"Or Easter," Sofia teased. "We don't need to stop there. What about Memorial Day?"

Claire glared at the college student. "I'm serious."

"I'm not and you have to tell Nonna and Bonnie."

Despite the fact she loved the first movie filled with adventure, escape, combat, wit, and swordplay, as well as fresh popcorn and icy cola, Claire struggled to avoid looking at the clock as it grew later. She'd chosen a seat near the door, so she wouldn't disturb the others if she left before the end of the film. She glanced again at her diamond watch. Nine twenty-seven. She eased out of the chair and exited the media room.

"Great timing." Tony walked toward her, faint amusement on his face. "Glad I didn't have to remind you when we're leaving."

"What if I didn't meet you?"

"Then, I'd have found you and carried you off to bed."

"No way!" She laughed, shaking her head. "You've been watching too many old movies."

"Let me show you I can do it."

"You can't. I'm too heavy."

"Really? I'll be the judge of that." He stopped in front of her. "You're not as big as you think you are, Claire Rocklin."

She squealed when he scooped her up into his arms. Turning, he carried her down the hall in the direction of the elevator. When he pretended to drop her, she hastily laced her arms around his neck. "You're such a macho jackass. I can walk."

"The term is asshat, sweetheart." He pushed the button. "And next time I tell you what I'm planning to do, you'll believe me."

"And what's that plan?" She nipped his ear. "Or is it a secret?"

"I told you before we left." Inside the elevator, he pushed the button for the top floor. "I'm having my woman screaming to the rafters for me tonight. Call it a house-warming present."

She wriggled in his hold, desisting when his grip tightened around her knees and back. "I don't have a house."

"No, but you have one hell of a bed and if you're good, I'll wait until we're there."

She tipped her head back to look up at him. "And if I'm not?"

"Since I can't take you here without stopping the elevator and inconveniencing the residents, I'll have you up against the door of what's our new place." He kissed her quickly. "And you'll love it."

"You're a lech."

"You're right, but only with you."

When the elevator doors whisked open, he exited and walked down the hall. "Get out your key."

"What if I don't?"

"Are you always this much of a challenge?"

"Definitely." She waited to see what he'd do, and yelped when he shifted her position, until she was slung over one of his shoulders with a view of his back and tush. "Damn it, Tony. Put me down. This isn't funny."

"Then stop giggling." He proceeded to unlock the door and packed her into the hall as if she was a sack of potatoes. "And I may believe you."

In the apartment, he lifted her partway down, holding her against the front door. Their gazes met and she moistened suddenly dry lips. "Tony?"

"That's right." He lowered his head until his mouth was close to hers. "Do you know what I'm going to do now?"

"What?" She rested her hands on his broad shoulders. "I thought we were going to bed."

"Oh, we'll end up there eventually, but first I'm having you here and now."

"Are you serious?" She measured the sincerity on his face. "Number one, we still have on our clothes and number two, you don't have a condom."

"I can handle stripping off your clothes here and I learned a long time ago to be prepared for all circumstances."

She brushed her lips across his. "And the condoms are in the bedroom."

"Not the one in my pocket."

"Well, that's different." She unbuttoned his shirt and pushed it off his shoulders. "Let's see what you can do, big boy."

———

The next morning, he woke to the sound of his phone ringing. Sound asleep, Claire didn't move and neither did the kitten zonked out on her pillow. Tony reached for his jeans on the floor and removed his cell phone to see a text from Connor. *'Off today. Golf in a half hour?'*

'Make it an hour. C.U. at the elevator.' Tony put the phone back in his pocket and patted Claire's butt. "Sweetheart, where are my golf clubs?"

"The hall closet." She rolled over, opening her eyes. She propped up on an elbow, the covers sliding down to her waist, revealing her breasts. "Why?"

"Remember, Conn and I golf on Saturdays." Tony enjoyed his view of her for a moment.

She yawned, rumpled her tousled hair. "Well, have fun, boys."

"I will." He snagged the blankets and tossed them in the direction of the foot of the bed.

She yelped and grabbed for the top sheet. Disgusted by their antics, the kitten jumped down from the pillow and stalked out of the room. "You're a major horndog, Tony Baldusi. You had me three times last night when we got here. Once in the hall and twice in bed. It's a wonder I can walk."

He laughed, took a condom from the box. Opening it, he rolled it into place. "Like you say, no point in wasting my morning hard-on."

"I didn't say that." She drew the sheet higher. "Go golf with my brother so I can sleep."

Tony pulled it away and reached for her. He kissed her and despite her initial complaints, she yielded, their tongues meeting and playing. She pressed against him, their legs tangling together. His hand curved around one of her breasts, his thumb and finger rubbing her nipple. "You can sleep after I'm gone."

"Conn hates it when people are late." She groaned when his other hand explored her hip, wriggling closer. "Tony, please."

"I will." He drew her on top of him and slid into her a moment later. "Your turn to do the work. Dance, sweetheart."

———

Saturdays, she slept late even without the excuse of the last three days of sexual hijinks. He'd left her to take a shower, dress and grab his golf clubs on the way to meet her twin brother. Claire lay perfectly still in the bed. Tony definitely satisfied her a short time ago so why did she still want him? *Because I'm about to act like a total nymphomaniac. It's my turn to jump him in the shower.*

The thought propelled her into action. She was on her feet and in the bathroom, grabbing one of the condoms from the box on the vanity. She opened the packet before she stepped into the shower. His gray eyes widened when he saw her. "Your fault, Tony. You've turned me into a woman who wants her own sex-toy."

"So, that's the real reason you moved me into your place. To have sex on demand. I'm a lucky man." He chuckled, then groaned when she stroked him before slipping the condom over his hardening length. "Claire, I'll be late."

"Not if you stop wasting time." She levered up against him, wrapping her legs around his lean hips. "Quit your bitching and take me now."

He gripped her waist, adjusted her position slightly, then drove into her. "Just remember you want this."

She dug her nails into his shoulders, meeting his thrusts. "I already knew that." And she kissed him.

He said he'd be gone until early afternoon which meant she returned to bed and slept after he left. When she woke up this time, she took a leisurely shower, washed her hair, and shaved her legs. After she dressed in jeans and a comfy t-shirt, she stripped the bed and threw the sheets in the laundry. Since Mrs. Nayaka's people had cleaned the apartment yesterday, it didn't take long to tidy up after herself and Tony.

Grabbing her box of chocolate doughnuts and a huge cup of coffee, Claire headed into the living-room to watch Lenny Briscoe, and his partner solve murders for a few hours. Opening the steamer trunk, she removed her favorite handmade throw and snuggled under it on the couch. Halfway through the second case, she drifted to sleep, the kitten cuddling close.

At the sound of footsteps on the tiled hallway floor, she woke and saw Tony. "How was your golf game?"

"Good." He sauntered across the room, leaned down to kiss her. "Conn wants us to go to Pike Place Market with him. He'll be here in ten minutes."

"Have fun." She shivered when he trailed a finger over her cheekbone. "Tony, I'm happy here. It's November and probably cold outside. Go without me."

"It won't be near as much fun, lazy girl." He picked up her wrist and looked at her watch. "Come on. Move your pretty butt. It's nearly three and the market isn't open late in the winter."

Claire heaved a sigh and trembled when his gaze fell to her breasts. "What would you do if it was the same as last week and I wasn't dressed yet?"

"The same thing I plan to do tonight. Take my highly sexed fiancée to bed and ravish her for hours." He feathered a thumb over her lips. "Let's go, sweetheart. You'll need calories to keep up with me."

She sighed again and stood. "Okay, I want to brush my hair and put on makeup if I'm going out in public. Make yourself useful and straighten up in here for me."

"In a minute." He grasped her hips and pulled her tight against him. His lips teased hers for a moment. "Wear that strawberry lip gloss I like."

"Any other requests?" She threaded her fingers in his short, dark hair. "I do as I please."

He grinned down at her. "And I enjoy it when you please me."

She rocked against him, feeling the instant response as he hardened. "Likewise."

"Brat." His mouth seized hers and she surrendered to the impatient kiss.

It would have lasted even longer but there was a sudden cough and Connor's deep male voice announced his presence from the doorway. "I'd tell you two to get a room, but then we'd never have the apples, pecans, and pumpkins I need to make pies tomorrow. However, I do know where to find cold water to throw on you."

Claire escaped Tony's embrace and strolled toward her twin. Like them, Connor had opted for jeans and a sweatshirt. "Your fault. You boys should have gone to the market after your game instead of coming back to harass me."

"Blame Tony. He's the one who can't live without you."

"I can. I have. I did for too long before she agreed to have me. And it sucked." Tony picked up the crocheted throw and folded it neatly. "I'm not doing it again."

Chapter Twenty-Four

Sunday morning, they went downstairs to join the residents for breakfast. Claire finished the remaining paperwork in her office before she headed to the Seattle brokerage. She found her gaze lingering on the worktable and missing Tony when she remembered the way they'd used it to have sex this past week. She could get by without him for a while since he had plans with her brother today.

They were off on some weird, manly task this morning which would end with Tony helping Connor make pies this afternoon. That worked for Claire because she hated peeling apples, and they'd purchased several pounds the day before. After they bought the supplies Connor needed for his adventure, they enjoyed dinner in one of the restaurants at the famed Seattle icon.

More than once, Claire heard the market called, "the soul of Seattle." She wasn't sure how realistic that was, but it did make for good promotion. Established shortly after the start of the twentieth century, *The Pike Place Market* included nine historic acres in the center of downtown

Seattle where locals and tourists alike shopped, visited, ate, and discovered all sorts of handmade treasures.

Claire would have thought her brother spent enough time patrolling it when he was on duty, but it'd always been one of his favorite places. After dinner, they lingered to watch the fishmongers literally throw salmon from one side of their booth to the other. Then, they wandered through the wide aisle past the booths where Tony bought her flowers and a small slab of her favorite dark chocolate walnut fudge.

When they arrived at the apartment building last night, Connor went off to his place. She and Tony stayed at hers. Claire shifted in her chair, staring at the computer monitor. She ought to be answering emails, not remembering the way they drank wine and talked before they went to bed. Of course, they'd had sex but somehow it felt different when she recalled the way he'd said he lived without her for too long.

When had he fallen in love with her? She didn't deserve a man like him. She wasn't worthy, wasn't good enough for him. Last night, his kisses, his touch, his caresses felt more tender, more meaningful. And when he slid inside her, rocking her world seemed more important to him than ever. He was such a careful, considerate lover and he'd waited three years for her to grow up, to really see him when he came home, instead of merely being glad he was out of danger.

Tears burned and she blinked them away. *Okay, I know what to do. I'll be careful not to break his heart when I end it, and I won't let him know if he breaks mine when he gives up on us.*

Eileen had locked the Seattle office and gone to lunch by the time Claire arrived at the brokerage. She stayed in the main room until Robyn Jenkins arrived to complete her floor hours. Claire reminded the associate if there were drop-in clients to tell Eileen before leaving to show any properties.

After that, Claire headed to her own office to check the new listings on the company website. She had plenty of catch-up work to do or she wouldn't be able to show and sell properties on Monday and Tuesday. Like many other businesses, Rocklin's would be closed for a long weekend from Wednesday afternoon through the following Sunday for the Thanksgiving holiday.

———

Late Sunday afternoon, Tony parked in front of the Seattle brokerage. Since he saw her rig, he knew Claire was here, but it didn't explain why she ignored his texts. She must be dealing with some sort of emergency. He walked inside, waited for Eileen, the office manager, to finish her call. "Buzz Claire for me and tell her I'm waiting."

The older woman narrowed her gaze, irritation and concern mingling on her face. "Where are you staying? I saw Claire put your condo up for sale. And kicked you—"

"I'm fine. Don't worry." Tony grinned at her. "Didn't Claire show you the ring?"

"What ring?" Eileen's dark eyes widened. "I actually haven't seen her since last Wednesday. She was busy with the other branches and hasn't been here."

"Makes sense. We had to have it adjusted and picked it up Wednesday night." Tony reached over to the intercom on Eileen's L-shaped desk and pushed the button for Claire's office. "Sweetheart, get your butt out here or we'll be late for church."

"I didn't hear a thing." Eileen hastily reverted her gaze to the desktop computer at the sound of rapidly tapping heels on the tile floor. "You're a dead man, Tony."

"Won't be the first time I've heard that." He glanced toward the far hallway and watched Claire approach. He'd left the apartment to meet Connor before she and Felix got out of bed. Tony's gaze lingered on her. She always opted for a smart business casual look on Sunday afternoons when she didn't expect to meet clients.

Today, she wore a close-fitting, black A-line skirt with a white border, a light blue, shiny silk loose fitting blouse with a bow tie and pumps. She'd topped it off with a long dark cardigan rather than a blazer. She glared at him as she drew closer. "Some of us have work to do."

"And some of us also have to meet the minister after services if we want a February wedding."

Despite the snarky tone, she did have her purse and laptop bag, so she was ready to leave. He strolled toward her, grasped her left hand, and leaned down to kiss her quickly. "You didn't show Eileen your engagement ring and she thinks you're making me sleep under a bridge instead of us moving in together."

"Don't tempt me." Claire's frown deepened and she narrowed her eyes. "And as for getting married on Valentine's Day, I don't—"

He cupped her elbows and pulled her against him, his mouth claiming hers for a long moment. "I thought I said strawberry lip gloss."

She sniffed. "And I chose grape today. Deal with it."

"I'll get used to it." He guided her over to the office manager's desk. "Okay, Eileen. Take a quick look and then we're out of here. You'll lock up, won't you?"

"Yes, I will." Eileen admired the diamond and sapphire

ring, before eyeing him curiously. "I don't get it, Tony. Why did you and Connor bring in that couch when you and Claire are living together?"

He shrugged and took the laptop bag from Claire. "Because I prefer comfort when we have to work all night." He glimpsed a blush rising in her face and added. "Do we need to come back and finish the updates on the website?"

"I fixed most of the typos in the descriptions but it's not ready to go live yet. I'll finish it tomorrow morning."

"Okay, we can do it together later." He put an arm around her waist and guided her out the door. "It needs to be on the Internet tonight."

———

Claire waited until they were in the Hummer. "All right. Spill it, Tony. Did you buy a sleeper sofa for your office here?"

"You know it." He flashed a quick grin in her direction. "I figured you'd pitch a fit if we did it in one of my chairs, so Connor and I rearranged the furniture."

"Damn it!" Heat rose in her cheeks. "Screwing you in the Everett office last week was a one-off."

"Hmm, I can see that." He slid the key in the ignition. "We'll only be living a couple miles away, so I'll be able to take you home most times. Of course, until we are, the couch in my office will come in handy."

"Make that you'll be living in your new house," Claire corrected. "I like my place and I'm not going anywhere."

He chuckled and patted her knee quickly. "Keep thinking that. I'll change your mind before the wedding."

"In your dreams." She heaved a sigh. "I can't believe you've bluffed Blanche into thinking there's going to be a wedding when I already told her the truth. This whole thing is a con to keep the relatives off my back."

"And when they contact her, she'll be able to honestly tell them she's providing pre-marital counseling."

"They wouldn't do that, would they?"

"You should know Lee and his hangers-on better. Of course, they will." Tony drove toward the freeway. "This way we can tell them to save the date while we're there next weekend."

"This scam is getting more and more involved." Claire glanced at the traffic moving around them. "It was supposed to be super simple. What happens when I break off this fake engagement?"

The question earned her a steady, gray-eyed look when he stopped at a traffic light. "I'm not going away, Claire. You'll have to decide how you're going to handle it when I'm still there every morning and night."

She drew a ragged breath. "Tony, I've never managed to sustain a long-term relationship."

"Bullshit." The light changed and he merged into traffic flowing onto the north-bound highway. "I invested in the business ten years ago, shortly after you opened the first brokerage and we've been together ever since."

"That's not what I mean, and you know it."

"Sweetheart, it may have taken us a little while to get this far but it's always been in the cards. It may have been subconscious on your part, but why do you think you've avoided more than casual dates during the last three years?"

She stared at his rugged features, unable to come up with an answer. She hadn't really thought about the fact she found buying houses and creating homes for senior citizens much more fascinating than men who pursued her. When she wanted more male energy than occasional lunches or dinners with the associates and designated brokers, she'd hung out with Tony and her twin brother.

His question remained in her mind while they attended the evening service and then had dinner with Blanche at a local restaurant. Her sorority sister kept the conversation casual and didn't bring up the subject of an early spring wedding. Instead, they talked about the brokerage's donation for the dinner the residents of the village were preparing, the upcoming holiday season and the shopping trip after Thanksgiving.

When they returned to the brokerage, she and Tony didn't head immediately for her apartment. Tony locked the main door behind them, and they went to his office. The new blue couch was on the inside wall, and he'd kept one of the visitor chairs near his desk. The other must be in the breakroom.

Tony walked around behind his desk, sat down, and fired up the computer. "Come show me the problems on the website."

"I can do it from here on my laptop." Claire gestured to the other chair. "I don't need to—"

"Afraid?"

"Of you?" She stalked toward him, realizing too late it was a trap when he pulled her down on his lap. "Damn it!"

"Yup. Snookered you again, sweetness." He tipped up her chin and kissed her. "Let's get our work done so we can try out that sofa."

"You're such a horndog." She laced her arms around his neck and teased his lips with hers. "You're lucky I like it."

"Definitely." He slid one hand up her thigh under the skirt. "What page do I want?"

She squirmed when he cupped her and stroked the curls between her legs. "Tony!"

"Oh, I do prefer that to 'horndog'." He teased her clitoris with his thumb. "If you don't tell me what we're doing on the webpage, we'll end up on that couch sooner than you think."

She struggled to remember where she'd left off on the corrections when one of his long, skilled fingers slipped inside her, followed by a second. "Okay, it's the U-Dub house. Start there."

"I'd rather start with you." A wicked grin curved his lips.

She couldn't resist and kissed him, her tongue demanding entrance to his mouth. He responded just as fiercely and dimly, she thought they'd never get any work done for the business tonight. Did she care?

Chapter Twenty-Five

B etween showing houses, finishing up contracts before the holiday, collecting food donations from the Everett and Eastside branches and supervising operations at the Seattle office, Claire was insanely busy on Monday. She and Tony arrived home about the same time. In addition to his trips to the escrow offices and title companies, he told her about the renovations at the new building. Fancy and her crew had started painting the two apartments on the top floor. She and Logan agreed Claire could start renting it by January, so she put Sofia in charge of vetting applications.

Tuesday morning, the accountant contacted Claire and let her know the Lake Maynard brokerage won the November contest. When she picked up the airline tickets and information about the hotel reservations, Svetlana Hollister brought a large box of non-perishable groceries to add to the other contributions. Claire congratulated the young Designated Broker and sent her off for a much-deserved holiday. To smooth over any resentment from the rest of the branches, she told Eileen to put together a new contest for the two-week trip at Christmas.

"I don't understand." Eileen leaned back in her chair at the front desk. She ran a hand through her silver hair. "You always go to Mexico then."

"I know and I'm going to miss it this year." Claire heaved a sigh, swiveling in the visitor's seat by the L-shaped reception desk. "However, Tony pointed out we need to show up in Rocklin because Beckett, my paternal grandfather has health issues."

"I don't understand why you call him by his first name." Concern mounted in Eileen's dark eyes. "My kids call my dad, Grandpa."

"Beckett never liked that." Claire crossed her legs. "And his wife, Agnes preferred we call her by her first name too. So, Conn and I always have."

"Wow." Eileen's eyes widened. "Did you do it when you were little kids too?"

"Oh, it was Mr. Beckett and Mrs. Aggie or Agnes back then because we weren't allowed to be rude." Claire tilted her head to one side. "It wasn't a big deal to us. We had my mom's parents, and they were always Gramps and Grandma."

"That's awful." Eileen glanced at the door when it opened and three associates entered, ready to return to work after lunch. "Okay, I've got this, Claire. Are you dropping off the food for Blanche in the morning like usual?"

"Not this year. Tony wants to make an early start for Rocklin tomorrow, so I'm headed there in a couple hours."

"Get me your keys and I'll have the donations loaded for in the Navigator for you."

"Thanks." Claire followed directions, glad she and Eileen were back on their usual good terms. When the older woman got miffed, everyone received the silent treatment for hours.

A short time later, Claire was on the road. She'd deliberately left earlier than usual to avoid rush hour traffic. She didn't stay long at the tiny house village. Once she'd left the contributions, she headed for her place. She still needed to pack for the weekend. Luckily, Fancy had agreed to kitten-sit so Felix wouldn't be alone, and it gave the other woman somewhere to stay until she finished an apartment in the new building.

Upstairs, Claire put one of Connor's casseroles in the oven. She was setting the kitchen table when Tony strolled into the room. She put the last fork on a napkin before she sauntered to him and kissed him. "Want to open the wine while I get the salad'?"

"I can do that." He tipped up her chin. "What's the plan for tonight?"

"After we eat, I've still got to pack. What about you? Are you ready to go?"

He shrugged one of those wonderful shoulders. "Won't take long. I learned how to get ready in a hurry back in the day. Tell me you're only taking a small overnight case for the weekend."

"Don't be silly. I know how you feel about liars. I'll need at least a half-dozen outfits, plus the dress I'm wearing to dinner and shoes to go with them and makeup and —"

"Claire, we'll only be gone four days, not a year." He laughed. "Never mind. You always take enough clothes for an army when you go anywhere. Remember how cold it gets in Rocklin during the winter. Bring a heavy robe and slippers."

She was folding a gold sweater when Tony entered the bedroom after he cleaned the kitchen, Felix trailing him. He glanced at the tuxedo kitten. "Is Sofia looking after him this weekend?"

"I arranged for Fancy to do it." Claire put the sweater on top of her black leggings already in the big red suitcase. "Sofia and her grandmother are visiting their family in Spokane for the weekend. They're taking Oscar along and Bonnie will look after Isabella's cat who hates traveling."

"Sounds like you have a plan." Tony entered the closet and returned with his overnight case and a garment bag. "Want to put your dress in with my suit?"

"Works for me," Claire agreed. "Thanks, darling."

"Don't thank me yet, sweetheart." He gestured toward the radio-clock on the nightstand. "Since we're hitting the road early, we'll also want to call it a night in an hour."

"Speak for yourself. I've barely started getting ready to go. I need at least two or three more hours to finish finding everything."

"We'll compromise." He put his bag on the king-size bed. "I'll give you an hour after I'm done. Then, it's lights out."

She stopped packing for a moment and studied him. He had more than sleep in mind and both of them knew it. She felt her nipples tighten against her bra and took a ragged breath. He was tucking t-shirts around the box of condoms before he went back in the closet to fetch other clothes. Well, if he planned to jump her bones in a short time, she'd be ready. Of course, all he had to do was look at her and she was more than willing to change her plans.

———

Tony zipped his overnight bag and put it by the bedroom door. He'd placed one of the black suits he wore to the office, a second pair of slacks, a blue shirt, a pinstriped one, two ties, and a pair of shoes in the garment bag. He still had room for Claire's sexy, purple ruffle, midi-length dress with three-quarter sleeves. It had a scoop neckline that looked extremely modest on the hanger in his bag, but he'd bet it'd look different when she wore it.

She tucked extra underwear into one of the suitcase pockets. "Go watch TV while I finish instead of looming over me."

He'd promised her another hour. He could wait, especially when he thought about taking off those slacks hugging her hips and long legs, not to mention the silky blouse clinging to her breasts. The stilettos were already in the closet. He caught her hand, pulled her against him for a quick kiss. "Come find me when you want me."

"You know it." She flashed a dangerous smile. "If you fall asleep, I'll wake you."

"And why aren't I surprised?"

Bruce Willis was kicking butt in the first *Die Hard* movie when Tony saw her drift past the doorway toward the kitchen. She didn't return. At the next commercial, he followed her. "What's wrong?"

"Go watch your show." She glanced over her shoulder at him before her attention returned to the cupboard and she removed a box of crackers, studied the carton, then replaced them. "I already finished off that fudge you bought me last weekend and I have a craving for something sweet."

He nodded. "All right. What kind of ice-cream do you want?"

"I never buy that because it's too fattening."

"Good thing I do." He opened the freezer and removed two containers. "Get a couple spoons. Oh, and FYI, I gave away the diet soda and your packages of sugar-free candy to Bonnie. She said she could use it for residents with diabetes."

Claire planted her hands on her hips. "I have to watch my weight, so I never buy ice-cream or desserts. And I only get one box of chocolate doughnuts each month. I barely made the gym the past two days. Stop crossing my boundaries."

"Spoons, Claire. We're somewhat civilized. We can't eat ice-cream without them, and you always look great."

"Because I work out and never splurge on high calorie stuff." She heaved a sigh, opened a drawer, and got two teaspoons. "Never mind. You're not listening. What am I supposed to drink when I want a cola?"

"Imported *Mexican Coca-Cola*. It's better for you because it's made with real sugar and your body can process it better than the crap with high fructose corn syrup. There are several bottles of imported soda in the fridge." He handed her a pint of organic chocolate-almond ice cream and kept the butter pecan for himself. "Let's go watch TV and you can tell me why you're stressed."

"I'm not." She removed the lid, peeled off the plastic liner and tossed it in the garbage. "I'm worried."

"Okay." He took her hand and led her toward the living-room. He waited until they sat on the couch, noticing the stream of commercials continued. After a moment, the movie started again and so did the attacks on the terrorists.

On the next set of advertisements, he asked, "Why are you worried?"

"Because this weekend is going to suck." She sighed and cuddled close to him, digging into the ice-cream. "It isn't just my father and his new family. Beckett and Aggie will overstep the boundaries too, Tony. What happens if I lose it and tell any or all of them to go to hell?"

"Wait until after dinner or we'll miss out on Connor's pies." Tony scooped up a spoonful of butter pecan ice-cream, savoring a mouthful before he said, "And your brother is an amazing baker."

The movie started and he held her while more bad guys died, and the lead terrorist continued hunting for John McClane. A lot of people would switch over and stream the movie to avoid the commercials, but Tony always appreciated the opportunity to talk between segments. "The other night, you mentioned staying on the high road while Conn and I behaved inappropriately. What changed that idea?"

Claire scraped up the last of her ice-cream. She put the spoon inside the empty carton and placed it neatly on the end table, picking up Felix when he investigated the container. "I remembered the kind of things Beckett said to Dex and then to me after he ran off with Kymm. And Aggie wasn't much better. Some people think senior citizens get nice in their old age, but it's only true if they were nice to start with and Lee's parents never were."

"I'm a grown man." Tony offered her a spoonful of butter pecan ice cream and waited until she ate it. "Sweetheart, nothing they say will bother me. Don't let people who do so little for you control so much of your mind, thoughts, feelings, and emotions. You aren't the only one who went no-contact. It's a two-way street."

She gaped at him for a long moment, her mouth falling open. "I never thought of that."

"Hey, it's why I get the big money. Now, help me finish up this ice-cream so we don't have to throw it out."

A weak smile trembled into life and then she reached for her spoon. "Are you going to keep buying it for us?"

"Always."

She fell asleep before the end of the movie, and he held her close. He contemplated kicking Lee's ass when they were in Rocklin and gave up the notion. It wouldn't do any good and the older man was a credit to his parents' raising. None of those Rocklins would ever realize how much damage they'd done to Claire or her brother. And they wouldn't care. No wonder she was terrified of commitment.

He turned off the TV before the news started. He stood, took the empty ice cream cartons and spoons to the kitchen. When he returned, he lifted her in his arms and carried her into the bedroom.

She sighed softly, opening drowsy eyes. "Give me a few minutes and I'll jump you."

"In the morning." He kissed her forehead. "We'll do it then. Tonight, I just want to hold you."

Chapter Twenty-Six

By what Tony called oh-eight-hundred hours, they were on the freeway and headed north toward Rocklin. Connor dozed in the back seat and Claire wished she could do the same in the passenger one. She yawned and stretched, flicking a sideways glance at Tony behind the wheel. He looked wide awake and bushy-tailed as Gramps would have said, not as if they'd already had sex twice before they went to join the residents for breakfast in the community room.

"It's a long drive, sweetheart." He gestured to the car robe lying on the seat between them. "Get some sleep. I'll wake you when we stop for an early lunch in a few hours."

"Don't you want me to keep you company?" She covered her mouth, suppressing another yawn. "I'm okay."

"Naptime." He smiled at her. "Then, I won't feel guilty for getting you up so early."

She'd have argued longer, but he made his point when he switched on the heat for the passenger seat. The warmth felt so good, she followed directions. He was right. They wouldn't arrive in Rocklin before mid to late afternoon, especially if he planned to stop for lunch. She wasn't missing a darned thing. She pulled the handmade throw over her and drifted off to sleep.

A while later, low Christmas music from the radio woke her. She opened her eyes and noticed he'd taken the exit off the freeway to the highway that led east to Rocklin. She glanced at her watch. Almost eleven. She stretched and glanced out the window, seeing snow covering the distant mountains. "So, what's the plan?"

"Lunch. Do you want a diner or chain restaurant? I'm taking votes."

A discussion ensued and they opted for the next cafe, which was always Tony's preference. He claimed he'd eaten enough plastic food when he was in the military and Connor agreed. Claire figured she could find something healthy on the menu because the guys always wanted more carbs than she did. They'd dressed down for the trip to Rocklin in jeans, sweatshirts, and boots.

A cold, winter breeze brushed them as they climbed out of the Hummer. She shivered in the casual, V-neck, pink floral dress swirling around her knees. She'd added tan stockings and pink striped heels. Tony paused and reached back inside the rig for her long, dress coat. He held it for her, and she slid her arms in the sleeves, lingering while he adjusted it around her shoulders. "Now, I'll be too warm in the restaurant."

"You can take it off when we're inside." He wrapped an arm around her waist. "Do I want to know why you're dressed to the nines today?"

"Oh, darling. Take my word for it." She laughed, kissed his cheek. "I'm not but you do know how to make me feel special."

"And you two are so adorable it's enough to gag a

maggot," Connor teased. "Let's eat while I still can enjoy a good burger and fries before all the sweetness makes me puke."

If she were closer, she'd elbow him in the ribs, but Claire decided to wait until later. She smiled at her twin. "Lunch first and then you can mock us the rest of the way to Rocklin."

"Works for me." Connor held the glass door for them.

They pulled into downtown Rocklin three hours later. The local business owners had already started decorating the historic cedar-shingled buildings for the holidays. Claire took a ragged breath as Tony drove past the various stores, restaurants, taverns, and schools.

"I can't do this, Tony." Tears welled and she blinked hard. "Let's go home."

He signaled, moved over to the curb, and stopped the Hummer. "Talk to me. What's wrong?"

"All of this." She waved at the nearest business, a small, independent grocery. "I know I should be able to handle seeing Beckett and Aggie, but it's going to—"

"Suck." Tony leaned toward her, close enough to squeeze her shoulders. "Tell you what, sweetheart. Let's go visit my mom first. Then, if you still want to go back to Seattle, we can."

"Really?"

He nodded and his lips brushed hers. "You're stronger than you think. Any woman who builds a real estate business from nothing to something in ten years is able to kick ass and take names. Trust me."

"I always have." She heaved a sigh, determined not to look at her brother in the back seat. Connor hated to see it when she had a total meltdown and even this token one would upset him.

A few minutes later, Tony pulled into the driveway of a small rambler with a beautifully landscaped yard. He parked in front of the garage. "We're here. Let's go socialize."

The front door opened, and Maria Baldusi, a pleasantly plump woman appeared, hurrying down the walkway toward them. She wasn't as tall as Claire who wouldn't be caught dead in teal polyester pants, a matching sweatshirt, and flip-flops. Strands of gray streaked Maria's shoulder-length black hair.

"Remind me to take your mother to the nearest salon on Friday. We have to do something about her hair." Claire shuddered. "And those clothes—"

Tony chuckled. "Don't you dare. She's happy the way she is."

"No, she's not. She can't be." Claire watched as he slid out of the Hummer and went to hug his mom. Connor popped out of the back and held her door so she could join him. "I'm definitely taking her shopping. The woman needs a makeover."

Connor hugged her. "When Tony has a fit, I'm running for cover. Don't count on me to protect you from him."

"You're just a big chicken-goober." Claire walked around the front of the rig and into Maria's warm embrace. "Good heavens, Maria. You've gone small town on me. What happened?"

"Don't hassle me, *bambina*." Maria held Claire tight. "I've waited forever for you to get here. I took the day off work."

"What?" Claire shot a glare at Tony. "What's wrong with your son? He makes enough money to provide for you. Why are you working?"

"Because I like it." Maria beamed at her. "You're such a

good girl. I have coffee, espresso, and I made your favorite *biscotti*. Come tell me what a bad boy Tony is, and I'll tell you how to make him be good."

"Great ideas." Claire flashed a quick smile at Tony and Connor. "Get the luggage, guys."

"And then you take Connor's pies over to Aggie's house," Maria said, glancing at her son. "Claire and I will have a nice visit while you're gone."

"Sounds terrific." Claire frowned and picked up Maria's hand. "When was the last time you had a manicure? What have you done to your nails?"

"Nothing." Maria guided her in the direction of the house. "I've done nothing except teach math to students who don't want to learn it. In my spare time, I grade papers."

"You poor woman." Claire shook her head. "I have a hard enough time dealing with adults. I don't know why you waste yours on teenagers. And I make Tony explain proper hygiene, attire and security to our new associates. We are so going shopping on Friday."

"I know." Maria beamed, a sunshine smile. "I can't wait. I told the other Sunday School teachers we'd get presents for the kids and we're also finding ones for the day-care party."

Claire wrinkled her nose in mock disgust. "All right, but I'm still buying you at least two or three new outfits and we're sending that one to the thrift store."

———

Tony enjoyed the byplay between his two favorite women. His mother and Claire argued about clothes and the upcoming shopping trip. He carried her suitcase into the guestroom his mother still referred to as 'his' room and Connor followed with the rest of the luggage.

"We're staying, aren't we?" Connor glanced toward the kitchen where the women were. "Your mom is wonderful. How did she know Claire was freaking out? Did you text her?"

"I didn't have time." Tony boosted the large suitcase onto the queen-size bed. "Besides, it's almost impossible to get cell coverage here at the house. When I visit, I only receive Claire's texts if I'm downtown. Rocklin needs more towers."

"And your mom?" Connor put his twin's makeup case in the adjoining bathroom. "Is she psychic or what?"

"I think she's just smart. She knows how Claire feels about Rocklin. You two haven't visited in twelve years, not since the wedding brouhaha."

"Good point. I'll bring in the pies I'm leaving here and then let's go drop off the others."

"Fair enough." Tony strode out to the kitchen where he found Claire sitting at the table dunking a piece of home-made *biscotti* into her cup of strong coffee. He bent and caught her mouth with his in a quick, fierce kiss. "Unpack for us while I'm gone. Behave yourself and don't turn my mom into a fashion diva like you."

Claire smiled up at him and offered him a bite of the crunchy, double-baked cookie. "If you don't want that, you'd better get your butt back here before I convince her we need to go to the mall in Upington."

"You're a wicked woman." He kissed her again and glanced at his mother who'd turned from the counter with her own cup of freshly brewed coffee. "Did Claire show you the ring? Or tell you to save Valentine's Day for the wedding? I know how you feel about Seattle, Mom, but you'll have to come there for the ceremony. You can stay in our guestroom, or I'll volunteer Conn's."

"What?" Maria hurried to join Claire, almost pounced on her hand, and stared at the diamond and sapphire ring. "Tell me everything. Did you make Tony get on one knee in front of everyone to propose?"

Claire shot him a deadly blue-eyed look. "Oh, he was on both knees, Maria."

"And she'll undoubtedly have me there again." Tony taunted, enjoying the blush that seeped into her face.

Connor arrived with the pies and Tony opened the refrigerator door, waiting for the other man to put them inside. He crossed the room, leaned down and kissed Claire again, careful to keep it light so she couldn't bite him.

Out in the Hummer, he earned a long steady look from Connor. "Are you two seriously getting married next spring? Or is this a bullshit game for the people who live in Rocklin like she says?"

"I'm marrying her." Tony started the rig. "If everything goes well, I'm hoping for Valentine's Day. However, your sister has issues so it may be later than that."

"Well, she hasn't thrown the ring back at you yet." Connor rubbed his jaw thoughtfully. "Considering the way she loves diamonds, don't hold your breath. She probably won't return it anyway."

"I want her to have it forever." Tony glanced over his shoulder and backed out of the driveway. "The necklace I bought for her birthday matches it perfectly."

"You're toast." Connor sounded more amused than concerned. "Okay, I'm not saying a word to Beckett or Aggie about it. I'll let you and Claire break the news to them."

"That works."

The split-level house where the older Rocklins lived

wasn't far from his mother's house, but then nothing was in the small town. It didn't take long for them to reach it. Beckett's pickup and Aggie's old Cadillac, along with a new Lexus took up the driveway. Tony parked in the street in front of the house. Someone had raked up the leaves, trimmed the rhododendrons and prepared the rosebushes for winter. He'd bet it was his mother who'd undoubtedly had help from Lee's grandkids.

Connor collected the carrier with the pies while Tony gathered the bags with bottles of wine and sparkling cider. They skirted the vehicles and made their way up the walk to the front door. Tony rang the bell, and they waited.

Beckett Rocklin, sporting his usual attire of a flannel shirt, orange suspenders to hold up his whacked off jeans above laced-up boots, answered. Tall, with a shock of white hair, he looked them up and down with faded blue eyes.

"I'll be damned. You really did show up. I told Aggie you'd probably cancel at the last minute." He stepped back, gestured for them to enter. "She's in the kitchen with Barb."

Tony and Connor shared a glance before the younger man started forward. "We're so glad to be here too, Beckett," Connor said.

"Claire didn't come?"

"She's at my mother's unpacking for the weekend." Tony followed Connor through the entry, past the living-room on their right to the huge kitchen and its adjoining dining room. "We'll drop off our contributions for tomorrow and be out of your way."

Before Beckett answered, his wife, Agnes turned from the center island. A smile spread across her face, and the petite, silver-haired woman hurried toward them. "You came. I'm so glad. Maria said you were making pies, Connor. You really did."

"Of course, I did." Connor placed the carrier on the other counter away from the statuesque blonde peeling hardboiled eggs at the island. He nodded a greeting. "Hello, Barbara. It's been a long time."

"Come sit down." Agnes pulled him toward the long table at the far end of the room. "You too, Tony. Tell me about what you've been doing. Where is Claire? Don't tell me she's not visiting for the holiday."

"She's with my mom." Tony put the wine bags near the special fridge and joined the other two. "What time would you like us to be here tomorrow?"

The question hung in the air. Beckett cleared his throat. "Lee's family would prefer it's just us and Claire and Connor. I know Maria will understand."

"Claire won't." Connor kept his arm around his grandmother's shoulders for a moment longer, hugging her before he turned to face his grandfather. "If her fiancé and soon-to-be mother-in-law aren't welcome, she won't be here. If my sister's not, neither will I. You can keep the pies, the wine, and the cider. Let's go, Tony. I knew this was a bad idea."

Chapter Twenty-Seven

Tony waited until they were back in the Hummer a half hour later. "I thought you were going to let Claire and I make the announcement, Connor."

"I was until that old buzzard pissed me off. You said your mother helped take care of him last spring." Fury edged Connor's tone, and he clenched his fists. "Even before Aggie talked about the way Maria brought her students to prep the yard for winter, Beckett planned to crap on your mom. He's such a—"

"I know. And now I'm really glad Claire wasn't with us. She'd have lost it as soon as he went after me." Tony started the engine and drove toward his mother's neighborhood. "She was afraid he might. Let's keep the crapfest to ourselves, Conn. It's just one weekend."

"Only if we stop for a beer on the way to your mom's."

"That sounds great." Tony bypassed the turn-off and headed toward the nearest tavern. They weren't the only ones with the same idea. It took a moment to find a spot for the Hummer in the parking lot, next to battered pickup trucks and older cars.

When they walked inside, they found a cheerful mixed crowd of people clustering around different tables. A few more were at the stools at the bar. Three waitresses in jeans and t-shirts circulated, taking orders, and delivering drinks. Connor led the way over to the bar and ordered two beers from Dylan, a golden-skinned young man with his long hair in elaborate braids. Like the waitresses, he dressed casually but his jeans were tight and so was the muscle T-shirt.

Tony shifted onto one of the empty stools while they waited. "Thanks for speaking up, Conn."

"I was straight up with Beckett." Connor dug out his wallet to pay for their drinks. "I haven't lost anything in Rocklin, so it won't bother me to go no-contact for twelve more years."

"I can't do that when my mother still lives here."

"Maybe you can convince her to move closer."

"Won't be the first time I've tried."

The beers arrived. Connor paid, adding a tip that made Dylan genuinely smile. Tony picked up his glass and both of them drank.

Halfway through, a burly dark-haired man swayed up to the bar and demanded another pitcher. Dylan shook his head, beaded braids flying. "You're drunk, Jim. You were when you got here an hour ago and I'm still not serving you."

"Do you know who I am, you little panty-waist?" The stranger slammed a fist on the antique, wooden counter. "I'm James Rocklin. My family owns this town. Get me a pitcher, damn it!"

"I'll give you a pitcher, but I'm not putting anything in it."

James lunged across the bar, grabbing for the bartender.

It obviously wasn't the first time because Dylan quickly evaded him.

Tony and Connor exchanged a look before the younger man stood. "You heard him. You've had enough. Take off."

"Don't tell me what to do." James swung a meaty fist at Connor's face. "Mind your own business."

"I am." Connor sidestepped the punch, grabbed James' arm, and twisted it behind him, shoving him into the bar. "You're an embarrassment to us. Always have been. Always will be." He glanced at the bartender. "Call the cops."

"I already did." One of the waitresses, a buxom blonde approached but remained out of reach. "I did as soon as he knocked over a table, two chairs and sucker-punched another customer."

"Thanks." Tony glimpsed a red mark on her arm and gestured to it, glancing at the bartender. "He grabbed you, didn't he? Get her some ice."

"The owner doesn't like trouble." Scooping ice into a small plastic bag, Dylan handed it to Tony who passed it onto the woman. "He won't press charges against a Rocklin."

"He won't be." Connor continued to hold James pinned. "Unless my father adopted this worthless piece of crap and his sister, they're not *real* Rocklins. They just use our name."

"You've been gone twelve years, Conn." Tony picked up his glass and drank the rest of his beer. "How do you know he didn't?"

"Because it'd be a matter of public record and it's not."

The heavy wooden door opened to the tavern, and two law enforcement officers came across the room. The older one, a gray-haired, solidly muscled man shook his head, eyeing James Rocklin. "Raising hell again?"

"Yes." Connor gave a quick description of the situation using jargon that both cops obviously recognized, marking him one of their own. The woman guided the waitress away to take a statement while her partner handcuffed James.

The experienced police officer talked to Connor about applying for a job with the local department and surprisingly he said he'd consider it. Once the other cops left with their prisoner, Tony eyed Claire's brother. "I didn't know you planned to move back."

"Maybe someday. Not yet. Fancy has issues with my job." Connor drained his beer. "Come on. We'd better get going. If we're late for supper, we'll hear about it from your mom and my sister."

"Fair enough." Tony placed a few bills to the bar before they left, eyeing Dylan. "Share that with the waitress and send her to the doctor if she has more than a bruise."

"I will."

———

After she and Maria caught up on each other's news, Claire went into the bedroom to unpack. Tony's room wasn't as large as the one they shared at her penthouse. A queen-size bed took up most of the far wall, framed by two nightstands, each with a lamp. A long bureau with six drawers was on the right-hand wall, along with the door that opened to the bathroom. On the left wall was an old-fashioned closet — a rod and space for shoes on the floor, nothing like hers.

As for the bathroom, it was apparently shared with the rest of the house. Claire shuddered at the sight. The vanity only had one sink. A glass enclosed shower—no tub. Extra towels and other necessities were stored on a vintage wooden rack near the toilet. If or when they sold the place for Maria, it'd need a total update.

Claire debated changing to leggings and a T-shirt but didn't see the point. The pink floral dress was one of her most comfortable and so were the candy-striped heels. It hadn't taken long to put away Tony's clothes. Claire hung them in the closet as well as the purple dress for tomorrow. Shoes went underneath. He only had one pair in addition to the boots he currently wore, but she'd brought four other pairs of stilettos, running shoes, and her ankle boots. She put his empty garment bag and overnight satchel into her suitcase and slid it under the bed.

She glanced over her shoulder when the bedroom door opened, and he entered. She tucked her underwear into a bureau drawer. "How was it? Were Beckett and Aggie on their best behavior?"

"Seriously?" Tony closed the door behind him and crooked a finger. "Come here, smart-ass."

She laughed and sauntered to him. She laced her arms around his neck and teased his mouth with hers. "I thought I was your sweetheart."

"You are except when you're taunting me." He slid his hands down her back to her hips and pulled her tight against him. "If Conn and my mother weren't putting dinner on the table, I'd take off that dress, toss you on the bed and have you screaming my name."

"Not in your mother's house, darling." Claire rocked into him and felt him harden. "You'll have to wait until we're home on Sunday. I've heard abstinence makes the heart grow fonder."

"That isn't happening. You'll just have to be very good and very quiet tonight."

"Hmm. I'll think about it." She traced his lips with her

tongue. She deliberately didn't deepen the kiss. "I'd rather watch you suffer."

"Why am I not surprised?" His mouth captured hers and she yielded to the passionate demand.

Three stormy kisses later, she left him and went into the kitchen. She glanced at Connor who transferred homemade biscuits to a napkin lined basket. "I'm here. How can I help?"

"Take the butter and strawberry jam into the dining room."

She tilted her head to one side and studied him, reading the tension on his shoulders and back. "What happened?"

"I don't know what you're talking about."

Crossing to him, she poked him in the ribs with her finger. "I can tell when you're upset just like you can tell when I am. We're twins. Talk or else."

His jaw tightened. "I was going to let you and Tony share your news, but Beckett was obnoxious when we were there, so I did."

"That we're engaged? Or the rest?"

"Just the first, not the second."

Claire kissed his cheek. "Don't beat yourself up. It's my job. And Beckett is always hard to get along with so I'm sure he pushed your buttons. Now, let's eat."

A faint smile edged Connor's lips and crept into his eyes. "You got it, little sis. You got it."

She heaved a sigh. "One day you're going to have to admit you're only thirty minutes older than I am. And that's barely anything."

"It's everything," Connor retorted. "You should know that by now."

Dinner was Maria's special beef pot roast with potatoes and vegetables. Claire enjoyed every bite although she knew the gravy was high in calories, but she hadn't had a meal with her former stepmother in years. She wished Rocklin had a gym. The small town didn't, and her regular daily workouts would have to wait until next week. While they ate, they talked about the upcoming holidays, the broker-ages, Connor's job at the Seattle precinct and Maria's math classes at the high school.

Once they cleaned up after the meal, Maria pulled an old game of Monopoly out of her game cupboard and challenged them. Laughing, Claire promptly grabbed the shoe and demanded to be the banker. The others conceded and they settled around the dining-room table ready to play for a few hours. By eleven that night, Tony had cleaned up, owning most of the properties and bankrupting the rest of them.

Claire scowled at him when he took the last of her money and the deed to *Boardwalk*. "You stink. I'm sure you're cheating."

He grinned, leaned over to kiss her. "And you're a beau-tiful poor sport, sweetheart. Put away the game and I'll make Conn slice your favorite pie tonight."

"Pecan? Heated with ice-cream?"

"Definitely." Tony stood. "Come on, Conn. We're on dessert detail."

Connor rose and the two men started toward the kitchen. "Why do I think you'll be spoiling her for the rest of your life?"

"Because you're smart and it's my job."

Claire smiled after them before she collected the tokens and put them in the little bag. She glanced at Maria who'd started sorting out the play money. "Are you okay?"

"Fine." The older woman stopped helping for a moment and studied Claire. "Are you happy with my son?"

Glancing toward the kitchen, Claire lowered her voice. "It freaked me out whenever he went to war, but I've never told him that. I was safe when he wasn't. Having him here for the past three years—" She sighed and met his mother's dark gaze. "I can't imagine my life without him. He's promised he'll stay with me no matter what."

"Good." Maria gripped her hands. "I'm glad the two of you are together."

"Me too." Claire took a deep breath. The engagement might not be real, but she and Tony had something special between them. She wasn't lying about anything she'd told Maria. The woman had always been kind to her and Connor even after divorcing their father.

Although she wasn't given court-ordered visitation, she welcomed Claire and Connor when they showed up on her doorstep. Maria provided toys, meals, snacks, cookies, homemade scarves and gloves, gifts for all occasions, but more importantly, she had time for the twins when Lee and his current flavor of the month, week or day didn't.

When they entered his room a short time later, Claire turned to face Tony. "I love your mom."

"Fair enough. She loves you too." Tony closed the bedroom door. "And one day, you'll tell me that you love me too."

"Darling, of course I do." Claire walked into his arms. In her heels, she was almost as tall as he was. She kissed him. "I've loved you since we were kids, and you wanted to protect me from thunderstorms."

He framed her face with his calloused hands and their gazes met. "You're not saying you're *in love* with me, are you?"

"Do I need to?"

"Not yet." He reached behind her and unzipped the

dress, pushing it down to fall on the carpet. "You will sooner or later. For tonight, it's enough if you want me as much as I want you."

"We can't do this." She caught her breath when he trailed a line of kisses along her neck. "They'll hear us."

"Then, you have to be very, very quiet." He lifted her out of the dress and carried her to the bed. "I told you before."

He must have pulled back the comforter, blankets, and top sheet when he was here earlier.

She caught his hand and pulled him down beside her. "I'm not the only one who makes noise. You'll have to be quiet too."

Chapter Twenty-Eight

When she came out of the bathroom the next morning dressed for a run, he shifted under the covers. Claire crossed to the bed, leaned down to kiss him. "I'm going to visit my mom and grandparents. I'll be back in a while."

"Take the Hummer. My keys are on the dresser."

"I need the exercise." She brushed his beard-stubbled cheek with her lips. "We'll be eating a lot today and I didn't see a gym here."

"Went out of business a few years back during Covid." He yawned, held her hand for a moment longer. "Be careful."

"I will."

She found her brother drinking his first cup of coffee in the kitchen. He was fully dressed in jeans, a T-shirt, and a University of Washington sweatshirt. He gestured to the brewer on the counter, raising an eyebrow in a silent question.

Claire shook her head. "Not yet. I'm running down to the florist and then going to the cemetery. Want to come?"

"Sounds good." He drained the cup and put it in the sink. "I'll get my shoes."

After stretching, they headed across the yard a few minutes later at an easy jog. They often ran together when the weather was decent, but once the rainy season started in late October, Claire preferred the neighborhood gym and Connor opted for the weight-room at the local precinct.

Side by side, they made their way through a series of neighborhoods toward the downtown area. When they reached the business section of Rocklin, Claire noticed several empty buildings. The bookstore had closed. So had the hair salon, barber shop and her favorite nail place back in the day. One bank branch remained out of the three she remembered. The pizza place was closed too, permanently by the look of the boarded-up windows, not just for the holiday.

"Wow." Claire slowly turned around, jogging in place. "Mike Flannagan mentioned rumors he'd heard about Lee being in cahoots with a logging company, but nobody said the town was on the downhill slide."

"The taverns are still making money, but the café where we used to go for burgers and shakes is defunct." Connor gestured in the direction of the florist shop. "Let's get some flowers and find out what the hell is happening here."

"Okay." Claire ran across the street and slowed to a walk as she reached the sidewalk in front of the florist. The sign on the glass door said the store would open for a few hours on Thanksgiving and she led the way inside.

A redheaded woman in jeans and a sweatshirt wearing a long green apron came out of the back to greet them. "Claire? Connor? What on earth are you two doing in Rocklin?"

"Visiting Beckett and Aggie for the holiday." Claire

greeted the older woman who had a few years on her, with a quick hug. "It's good to see you in person, Yvette. How are you and Jimmy Junior?"

"He's grown like a weed. You'll see him at Beckett's." Yvette kissed Connor's cheek. "One good thing about divorcing his dad is I can stay home with a TV dinner. I don't have to show up and be nice to my ex or his family."

"Well, you don't have to worry about James being there." Connor rested his hip against the glass display case. "He talked when he should have listened last night at the bar, and I helped the cops arrest him. He's probably still in the drunk tank."

Claire flicked a quick glance toward her brother who seemed unconcerned about the meeting with their step-brother. "Yvette, what's happened to Rocklin? We haven't visited forever, but I don't recall it being so dismal."

"It's gone downhill since your dad started running it. Taxes keep getting raised and so do rents and not just on the local businesses. I was planning to email you next week."

"About what?" Claire strolled to the refrigerator that held several bouquets of brightly colored autumn arrange-ments for sale. "You have my credit card on file, and you still deliver flowers to my mom and grandparents, don't you?"

"Every two weeks. I took some over yesterday." Yvette blinked hard, her bright blue eyes filling with tears. "There were times when your orders and those from Maria and her teacher friends and the child support for Jimmy were all that kept food on the table. James has always been good about paying it even when quite a few of his jobs took him to Eastern Washington, Oregon and California during wild-fire season."

"And next week? Why were you contacting me?"

"Because I don't own the building and when my lease is renewed in January, I won't be able to make the payments." Yvette slid shaking hands into the pockets of her apron. "I'm closing at the end of the year."

"Well, that's nonsense." Claire put her arms around the other woman. "You're going to create an income and loss statement I can show to Tony, and we'll see about investing in your business. If you're not here, who will take flowers to our mom?"

"I have a friend with a mobile florist service. I was going to ask her to do it."

"We'd rather have you." Connor waved at the arrangements, digging out his wallet. "For now, we'll take three bouquets with us. Would you have time to deliver holiday flowers to Maria and to Aggie today?"

"I'll send the ones to Aggie with Jimmy Junior and take the one to Maria on my way home."

"Sounds great." Connor gave Yvette a warm sideways hug. "Doesn't Jimmy graduate soon? Maybe, you should think about following him to wherever he's going to college and opening a shop there."

Yvette laughed shakily. "Oh, I bet my son would love having his mommy stand over him when he's ready to act like a grownup. No, if Claire and Tony can figure out a way for me to stay in Rocklin for a few more years, I'll do that."

"We'll make whatever you want happen." Claire promised.

A short while later, she and Connor were on the way to the cemetery behind the church. The stone building was closed today, but a sign displayed times for services on Sunday. They entered through the side gate and strolled down cement sidewalks to the older part of the graveyard. It was in surprisingly decent shape, grass mowed, hedges clipped, markers cleaned.

Their grandparents' graves were next to each other and their mother's beside Grandma's. Claire rested a hand on the stone revealing their mom's name and the dates of her very short life. *'Erica Claire Rocklin, September 27, 1964 – October 15, 1990.'*

Connor put the assortment of brightly colored chrysanthemums, daisies, and roses against the marker. "Happy Thanksgiving, Mom."

"We miss you," Claire added. "Wish you were here with us."

Connor slid an arm around Claire's waist. "Is it freaky if I feel like she is sometimes?"

"No." Claire stepped closer to him, admiring the arrangement of various roses that Yvette must have left the day before. "I feel it too. She was younger than we are now."

"Yes, and when I have a daughter, I'll name her after Mom and Grandma."

"Me too," Claire agreed.

———

He'd hung her pink flowered dress in the closet the night before. Her undergarments and his were in the laundry bag she'd brought along and neatly stowed in her suitcase. Tony put on his jeans and a clean T-shirt. He'd change into his suit in a few hours, about the same time Claire switched to her purple dress to go to Beckett's and Aggie's for the holiday dinner. He finished tidying the room before he went into the kitchen where he found his mother stirring up pancakes.

She pointed to the brewer on the counter. "Make yourself a cup of coffee if you want and I'd love a refill, please. Where are Claire and Connor?"

"She wanted to visit their mom and grandparents, so I bet he went with her." Tony followed directions, adding water and a fresh pod to the coffee machine. "What's it going to take for you to retire, Mom and move closer to me?"

"Grandkids." Maria laughed at him. "You two are getting married. When do you plan to start a family?"

"It was hard enough getting Claire to agree to a wedding. If you mention kids, she'll run screaming out of town." Tony waited for his mug to fill. "I'm buying a house for us in Everett. She wants to do a major update and that's going to take a while especially since it doesn't have a closet to match hers in the penthouse."

"The nursery for the babies should be attached to the primary suite." Maria carried the bowl over to the stove and put the first batch of pancakes on the griddle. "Suggest that to her or I will."

"We'll both be in hot water." Tony swapped out the mugs and took a swallow of his coffee. "I'll talk her into it next year."

The back door opened, and Claire entered in time to hear him. "Talk me into what?"

"Grandkids." Maria flipped the hotcakes. "How many do I get to spoil?"

"How many do you want?" Claire flashed back. "Tony, if you're in charge of the coffee, I'd love some. The espresso stand is shut down too."

"We didn't really think they'd be open on a holiday." Connor closed the back door. "However, it looks like they went out of business last year along with a bunch of other places."

"Never expected that." Tony frowned when Claire walked over and took the coffee cup out of his hand. "What are you doing?"

"Swapping spit, darling." She took a swallow. "You don't expect me to wait around while you lollygag with the coffee, do you? Maria, how can Connor help with breakfast? I'm starving."

Tony chuckled, patted Claire's backside. "What if you jump in and help too, sweetheart?"

"Not my thing." She snuggled close to him, nipped his ear. "I don't cook. You'll need to get another woman for it."

"I'm not stupid enough to do that." Tony handed Maria's refill to her. He returned to Claire's side and added more water to the machine. "Connor, yours is next. I'll make another cup for me since mine has been absconded with by your sister."

"Hey, you're the one who wants to marry her." Connor opened the refrigerator and removed a package of thick sliced bacon. "You keep saying you can't live without her. You may change your mind if she continues stealing your coffee."

"She's worth it." Tony tipped up her chin and his lips claimed hers. When his tongue slowly explored her mouth, he tasted coffee. He caught the cup before it tipped the hot liquid on him and put it on the counter. He drew her tightly against him and continued to kiss her.

"So much for coffee." Connor rattled pans behind them. "And breakfast. Once they start necking, all we can do is find a pitcher of ice water to throw on them, Maria."

Claire wriggled free from the embrace. "We'll behave ourselves since food is in the future. I'll set the table. Those pancakes look amazing. Where do I find syrup?"

Because they were expected at her grandparents' house around noon, Claire headed for the shower while the others enjoyed watching the rest of the Macy's Day Parade on TV. She laid her purple dress on the bed but carried her stockings and black lace underwear into the bathroom with her.

She'd stripped off her workout clothes when the door opened, and Tony strolled inside. He shut and locked it behind him, then removed his T-shirt. "What are you doing?"

"I'm here to wash your back." His gaze swept over her before he unfastened her bra, dropping it on the vanity.

"You can't." She choked back a moan when he cupped her breasts, his thumbs seeking her tightening nipples. "Tony, they'll hear us."

"Not in the shower." He leisurely sought out her nipple and teased it with his tongue before he drew it into his mouth and sucked.

She arched nearer. She gasped when he pushed her panties down her legs and stepped out of them, pressing even closer. Two of his long, skilled fingers slid inside her, thumb rocking against her clitoris, and she couldn't help it. Her hips moved with the pattern he set, rising, and falling. His mouth claimed hers, his tongue mimicking the motion of his hand, muffling her soft cries. Before she came, he stopped.

"I thought —"

"I know what you think. I always know." He unbuttoned his jeans, slid out of them, and grabbed a condom from the box. "Turn on the water, Claire. Or we'll run out of time."

Chapter Twenty-Nine

When they left for the holiday dinner, Claire insisted on leaving the passenger seat for Maria and popped into the back next to Connor. On the drive to the older Rocklins' home, Claire mentioned investing in the flower-shop and asked Tony what he thought.

"Let's take time to consider the best way to do it." Tony slowed for the next turn. "An investment this far away from home would be hard to supervise, Claire."

That earned him a long look from his mother. "Do you two are constantly run around Seattle checking on your responsibilities?"

"Tony does most of that, Maria," Claire said. "I start my days at the apartment house where the three of us live, then go to the building we're rehabbing or the tiny house village or one of the brokerages, but my base is the Seattle office. Thankfully, we have a good property management company on the Washington Coast, so I don't have to go there as often."

"As I'm sure you've seen on TV, there aren't enough police officers in Seattle, so I work a lot of overtime,"

Connor added. "When I'm home, I fix meals for us and drop them off at Claire's and Tony's place."

"I'm not just on the road." Tony parked in front of Beckett and Aggie's split-level house because the driveway was full of vehicles. "I also hire staff, teach new associates, train the existing ones, handle security so our agents aren't assaulted when they show properties and—"

"He handles all advertisements." Claire unfastened her seatbelt. "Promotes our business on social media, supervises updates to the websites, acts as a liaison with the title and escrow companies. He books needed slots with the lawyers when we're ready to close on sales and handles those meetings too. Plus, he kicks ass on whoever I tell him needs it."

"Wow, I'm impressed. How on earth did you manage before Tony came home, Claire?"

"Damned if I know anymore."

Tony glanced over his shoulder before he opened the driver's door. "You used to pick my brain when we videoconferenced. It was a great distraction from what I was doing."

"Oh, good. I always felt better after we talked."

He held the rear door while she slid from the seat and paused in front of him to straighten her skirt. The purple dress emphasized her breasts and clung to all the curves he enjoyed seeing. Black stockings ending in purple stilettos made her legs longer. "I do prefer seeing you gussied up instead of in your pj's."

"Same goes. You look amazing in your suit." Claire adjusted his tie. "Now, let's go make a positive impression on these people."

"Why do I feel that you truly don't care what they think?" He caught her left hand and held it. "The high road, right?"

"That's for me." She squeezed his fingers. "You're in charge of handling the alligators in this particular swamp. Conn will help."

"You've got it, sweetheart."

———

Claire hesitated before they walked up the driveway to the front door. She didn't know how she was going to pull off the act that they were happily engaged and anticipating a spring wedding. Everything had worked out with Maria, but she wanted to believe their story.

As for children? Claire took a deep breath. She'd never thought about having them and now the idea wouldn't leave her mind. What would it be like to have a dark-haired baby with Tony's gray eyes? Magical!

Connor rang the bell and the four of them waited on the porch. A few minutes later, Beckett Rocklin opened it. He'd dressed up for the occasion, slacks, and a blue sweater over a collared shirt instead of the logging attire she remembered. He stood absolutely still for a moment, his hand shaking on the knob.

He was as nervous as she was, Claire realized. She stepped up and kissed his cheek. "Good to see you, Beckett. Happy Thanksgiving."

Her greeting broke the ice, and the rest of the group followed suit. Connor, and Tony shook hands with him and Maria hugged him. Then, they were inside, being ushered toward the living-room where they found Lee's family, at least part of it. His wife, Barbara and stepdaughter, Kymm waited, both blondes although they were twenty-five years apart.

Claire was certain Barbara's hair came out of a bottle

now since the woman had to be in her sixties and didn't have a single gray hair. She wore a pale blue sweater and slacks. No earrings and only a little makeup. Meanwhile, her daughter had on a burnt orange top, comfortable jeans, and white ankle boots.

More assessing glances from the pair and Claire was glad she made a fashionable appearance in her purple, midi-length dress with three-quarter sleeves. The scoop neckline provided a hint of cleavage, but not too much. Meanwhile, she had the two diamond tennis bracelets on her right wrist, a diamond vintage watch from her grandmother on her left, her engagement ring, and earrings for decoration. She'd pinned her black hair into a loose bun and left several tendrils down to tease her face and neck.

"Who was at the door, Beckett?" Aggie came in from the kitchen, accompanied by a young girl with golden hair. She wore slashed jeans, a red sweatshirt with a pony proclaiming it wanted Santa to bring it a child for Christmas and flipflops. The older woman gaped at Claire. "Oh, honey. I'm so glad to see you."

"Me too." Claire walked across the room and leaned down to kiss her grandmother's papery cheek, catching a whiff of a sweet, lemony perfume. A cap of curly silver white hair, wrinkles lining her smiling face and sky-blue eyes, Agnes was a tiny doll in a flowered top and pink pants.

Claire glanced at the girl again. "You must be Peyton. Tony's told me so much about you."

"He talks about you all the time. He says you're the smartest, most beautiful woman in the world." The girl's blue eyes widened as she scanned Claire. "He wanted to show me his new pictures of you, but his cell phone doesn't work here."

"Nobody's does since there are hardly any towers in

Rocklin." Claire glanced quickly at Tony. "Did you tell her about the Halloween Party?"

Fascinated, the girl looked at her, then at Tony and back again. "What was your costume?"

"Undoubtedly a saloon girl," Barbara said sweetly. "You always had a predilection for sleaze, Claire."

"I never wear anything tacky." Claire smiled at the tween who had an obvious crush on her. "I was Cat-Woman, but I couldn't get Tony to wear tights and be Batman. He insisted on being Bruce Wayne and wearing a suit."

"Like the one you have on now?" Peyton turned to Tony. "I bet you looked good for an old guy."

The blunt comment spawned laughter from her mother, grandparents, Maria, and Connor. Even Barbara managed to smile.

"He did indeed." Claire stepped back and tucked her hand in the crook of his arm. She whispered, for his ears only. "You're very sexy for an old guy."

He chuckled, put an arm around her waist and murmured. "Just remember what this old guy plans to do to you tonight, sweetheart."

Heat seeped into her face, and she narrowed her eyes. Before she could say anything, they heard footsteps on the stairs from the basement. Claire glanced toward them and saw her father accompanied by a dark-haired teen. Why had she worried so much about Lee Rocklin? During the last twelve years, he'd shrunk in size or perhaps it was her three-inch heels.

Either way, she was taller than the sandy-haired man whose wrinkled brown, sport coat didn't hide his pot belly. Tan slacks barely touched his loafers. The wrinkles on his aged features made him appear older than Beckett. Lee's polite smile didn't touch hazel eyes, and he didn't speak to her. She returned the favor and ignored him too.

Instead, Claire gaped at the boy who was almost a man. "Is that Jimmy Junior?"

"Yes, it is." Jimmy brushed past his grandfather and came toward them. He kissed Claire's cheek. "I brought the flowers for Great-Grandma and thanks again for offering to help Mom. She finally shared the news with me about the lease and losing the flower shop."

"What lease?" Beckett demanded, glowering at the boy. "She doesn't have a lease. The woman's family even if she had too much pride to accept alimony when she divorced your dad ten years ago."

"That's right," Agnes agreed. "We don't understand what you're talking about."

Before the conversation erupted into a batch of 'he says and she saids', Claire raised her hand. "Excuse me. Connor and I visited Yvette today to get flowers to take to the cemetery. She told us that she has a lease on the building, has ever since she divorced James, and the rent is being substantially increased next year so she'll have to close after Christmas."

"Which is why Claire wants to invest in the business," Tony added. "We're not adverse to doing that. I'll just want to see the facts and figures beforehand, and I'll check on the shop whenever I'm in Rocklin visiting my mother to be sure it adheres to our standards."

Beckett stiffened, fury filling his face for a moment. Then, he took a deep breath. "That isn't necessary." He turned his attention to Connor. "You're in law enforcement, right?"

"Yes, I'm on the Seattle P.D. Why?"

"Because you can take a statement from me and file it

with the police department here. Someone has been embezzling from me, and I'll bet I know who." Beckett started toward a closed door on the far side of the room. "Come on. Jimmy, too. I want you to call your mother and find out how much money has been stolen from her."

Claire hid an appreciative grin behind her hand. Apparently, her grandfather hadn't totally lost his wits. She eyed her father who looked as if he'd been sucker-punched in the guts and then her stepmother whose features paled with shock.

"Beckett, you should also ask how much child support James pays. The kid's still in high school and hasn't turned eighteen yet. If he's like Connor and Tony were back then, he probably eats like a proverbial horse."

"Oh, my word." Agnes gasped, staring after her husband, grandson, and great-grandson. "Honey, you should have told me. We'd have ordered groceries and paid for them for you and your momma. Pride doesn't fill empty stomachs."

"Hindsight is twenty-twenty. I'm sure everybody has other choices they wish they'd made." Maria advanced on Tony, patted his arm. "You go help Beckett create a quit claim on that flower shop for Yvette. Claire, you, and Kymm need to help Peyton and your grandma in the kitchen. Barb, if you and Lee don't want Connor to file that criminal complaint, I suggest you go to the study and start sucking up to Beckett."

Everyone dispersed accordingly and Claire surrendered when Maria guided her into the large kitchen. "I've already told you I don't cook."

"We have plenty of cooks today." Maria urged her toward the wine cabinet. "You and Peyton can finish setting the table and filling glasses with sparkling cider for all of us."

"Sounds like a winner." Claire followed directions.

The aroma of roasting turkey filled the air. Agnes moved to the range and began checking the contents of various pots and pans. "Connor shared your news yesterday, Claire. When is the wedding? Have you had a chance to talk to the minister yet? Did you see him when you were at the cemetery?"

Claire set three bottles of cider on the granite countertop and waited for Peyton to arrange the glasses. "Valentines' Day. We saw our spiritual advisor, Blanche LeVoie on Sunday and she's marked the date on her calendar. We'll have the ceremony in the community room at the apartment house. Connor's doing the cakes."

"Don't you want a church wedding here in Rocklin?" Kymm pasted on a super sweet smile. "You did before."

"Not this time." The diamond and sapphire ring sparkled in the glow of the overhead lights, and Claire deliberately angled her hand, so her stepsister had a better view of it. "Tony wants all of our friends to be able to attend and most of them live in Seattle, so we've agreed to have it there."

"Will your new house be ready by then?" Maria opened the large, stainless-steel refrigerator and removed plates and bowls of appetizers. "Tony says you want to do some updates."

"Oh, not just some." Claire began filling the goblets while Peyton ferried them to the table. "We're discussing it. There's absolutely no curb appeal. Blackberry bushes, scrub alder and nettles have overgrown the entire yard. The wrought iron decorator fence is more rust than metal in the front and you can't even see the back one. If Yvette wasn't determined to stay in Rocklin, I'd hire her to landscape the place."

Maria handed a dish of deviled eggs to Kymm, gesturing for her to put them on the buffet. "What does the house look like?"

"All four bedrooms are on the second floor. I'm not counting the main or primary bedroom which is way too close to the smallest. The ensuite is old. It only has one sink, no shower and a clawfoot bathtub." Claire grimaced. "There is no way I'm giving up my walk-in closet and moving to the sticks until the house has a total overhaul."

"Have you told Tony that?" Kymm inquired. "Or is it a state secret?"

"He knows." Claire hoped none of the other women saw the blush that scorched her face when she recalled the night in his office and the way he touched her. "He's already making plans for the upgrades."

Chapter Thirty

With a massive wooden desk, bookcases filled with hardcovers, a couch for naps, two upholstered chairs and an old desktop computer, the den wouldn't win a prize for fashion, but it did look comfortable. Beckett flipped the light switch and stomped across to sit in his swivel office chair behind the desk. He pointed to the land-line telephone and told Jimmy to call his mother.

Beckett's gaze fastened on Lee. "Your mother and I took time off during Covid because we're in the high-risk group. I'd have gone back to work last spring, but I trusted you to look after things."

"Not a good choice, Beckett." Connor sat down, crossing his long legs. "When Claire and I went for a run today, we noticed several downtown businesses are closed."

"Of course, they are." Barbara tried to smile but it didn't touch her eyes. "Beckett, it is what it is. Most of the stores weren't considered essential and had to close during the state shutdowns and the owners never reopened them."

"It was tough on a lot of enterprises." Tony glanced at the older man. "That's why we adjusted things during the pandemic like freezing the rents for the tenants at the apart-ment house before the eviction moratorium. Thankfully, they didn't take advantage of the situation. Some property owners weren't as lucky."

"I did the same thing. Told the Business Association, our equivalent to a Chamber of Commerce that I wouldn't be charging rent on my buildings until folks were able to re-open and get back to work." Beckett folded his arms, glaring at his son. "Didn't expect hard times to last so long, but that wasn't anybody's fault. We had to stay isolated at home for almost a year and a half, so I wasn't at the town hall three or four times a week. You took advantage."

"That's one way to say it." Connor turned his attention to his father. "And you charged your daughter-in-law rent?"

"Former," Lee said quickly. "She's too sensitive. She didn't need to divorce James."

"Yes, she did." Jimmy stood near the desk and replaced the receiver on the black, dial telephone. He shook his head. "Bad enough he had a bunch of girlfriends over the years, but when he gave her VD —"

"He is a chip off Lee's block," Connor drawled. "I can't believe Yvette shared that."

"Oh, she didn't. I overheard my dad telling her it was no big deal." Jimmy turned to his great-grandfather who looked totally disgusted. "Mom says she'll email the ledger sheet to you. The rent's been raised every year."

"My mother suggested you consider giving Yvette the shop in exchange for her payments, Beckett." Tony approached the older man. "It probably isn't enough, but Claire and I will make up the difference."

"And me," Conner added. "I'll pitch in too. Then, Yvette will be able to keep delivering flowers to my mother, Gramps, and Grandma."

"Not needful." Beckett held up his hand. "I offered to give her the shop years ago, but I was told she didn't want it." He glanced at Lee. "You lied to me about that too. I'm signing it over to her tomorrow."

"Everything happens for a reason." Barbara stepped up next to her husband. "Yvette never did have a good work ethic. Who's to say she'd have taken the business seriously if she didn't have monthly bills to pay?"

"Me," Beckett said. "My momma had to raise me alone after my dad died in the war. A single woman will do what she has to do for her children." He turned his attention to Connor. "Jimmy and Peyton call us Great-Grandpa and Great-Gramma. Always wondered why you and Claire insisted on using our first names."

Connor didn't answer right away, so Tony did. "Because from the time they could talk, they were told it's what you and Aggie preferred. I know it was well established by the time my mother married Lee. It upset her. She felt it was disrespectful, but he insisted."

"Things gotta change. No more secrets." Beckett rose to his feet. "We're gonna talk tomorrow night when Aggie, Claire and your mother are here too, Tony. Make a note of it, Connor."

"It's my business, Dad," Lee protested.

"Stopped being yours when you involved me and your momma in it, son. I should have stepped up years ago instead of always trying to respect your whims, but I didn't know I raised a liar. Thought I raised two men, you, and your older brother. Better late than never to learn I didn't."

Beckett pointed to the door. "I want back all the money, Lee, not just what you took from Yvette. Wasn't a holiday, I'd call the accountant. I'll have her, my lawyer, and the police chief meet me tomorrow morning in my old office at the town hall. Now, let's go eat."

"We're leaving." Lee grasped Barbara's arm, turning toward the door.

"Then, I'll call the police chief right now and raise a ruckus." Beckett waited behind his desk, his gaze roaming over the group. "Your choice, Lee. You go and it's the cops. You stay, act polite and treat your momma decent, I'll hold off."

Tony wasn't surprised when Lee Rocklin backed down and led the way out of the study, accompanied by Barbara. Beckett and Jimmy followed the pair back to the large kitchen and dining room.

Connor waited until they were alone. "Why do you think he wants to talk to us?"

"I'm suspicious someone else did Lee's light work." Tony frowned thoughtfully. "He doesn't have any children besides you and Claire. From the photographs I've seen, you look a lot like your mother and maternal grandparents. Maybe Lee can't have kids."

Connor whistled softly. "Wouldn't that be a wonderful Thanksgiving present?"

"We'll find out later." Side by side, the two of them walked out of the room to join the others.

————

Most of the meal was on the beautifully decorated table when the rest of the family joined them. It amazed Claire when Beckett insisted her brother and Jimmy carve the turkey at the counter and help serve it while he spoke privately to his wife in a corner of the room.

Claire carried the gravy boat over to the table. Tony

brought a large bowl of steaming mashed potatoes. She waited until they were out of earshot at the table. "What happened? Lee seems upset."

"Turns out he and Barb haven't been doing what Beckett wanted, and the ship is hitting the sand. He wants to talk to us after dinner."

"No worries. We can do that." Claire deliberately brushed her lips over Tony's as Kymm arrived with a dish of sweet potatoes. Peyton followed, a basket of homemade crescent rolls in her hands.

All of them were seated before long and after Beckett said a short prayer, Aggie started everyone passing the food around the table. She began the tradition of saying what she was thankful for—having most of the family there to share the holiday.

Jimmy went next. "I'm thankful Claire, Connor and Tony are here, and I hope they come for Christmas."

"Me too," Beckett said. "And you'll bring your mom to join us. We've been missing her."

Jimmy looked stunned but hastily agreed.

When it was Peyton's turn, she said she was thankful to share the holiday with family too. She eyed Claire. "My mom said your mother went away a long time ago, but maybe you could bring her to Christmas too."

A tear slid down Claire's cheek, followed by a second one. "I wish I could." She hastily blotted her eyes with a napkin. "My mother died when Conn and I were two, almost three years old. When we visit, we go to the cemetery to take flowers to her and our Gramps and Grandma. Jimmy's mom, your Aunt Yvette takes them the rest of the time."

"You should also take them to your *real* father," Beckett announced from his seat at the head of the table. He glanced quickly at Lee and Barbara. "I told the pair of you, no more secrets. I always figured you let the twins know Erica was engaged to your older brother, Lee. She married you to provide the kids with the Rocklin name after he died in combat. You hadn't met Barbara yet."

Silence reigned for a moment, and Aggie leaned over to pat Claire's hand. "I'm so sorry. I thought you two already knew and it was why you and Connor were so distant from us. Beckett shared the truth with me a few minutes ago."

"Wow, Tony." Connor drawled. "You hit that particular nail on the head." He lifted his wine glass in salute, glancing at Lee. "I don't know about Claire, but I'm thankful for such a wonderful Thanksgiving present. It helps to know we really are orphans."

"That's right, twin." Claire took Tony's hand. "I'm thankful to have my new, *real* family and I'll let you and Tony always be brothers, even before the wedding. Plus, I'm super thankful to have Maria for a mom."

"Such a sweetheart." Tony raised her left hand to his lips, the engagement ring glittering in the light from the chandelier. "I'm thankful to have you too and I'll keep sharing my mother with you and Connor."

"Good to know." Maria beamed at them. "And I'm so glad and thankful that you two are finally getting married. Beckett, you, and Aggie need to come with me to Seattle for the ceremony."

"We'll figure that out later." Beckett put a small serving of mashed potatoes on his plate. "I'll be even more thankful when the twins start calling me, Grandpa."

"Why wouldn't we?" Claire took a spoonful of cranberry sauce. "We didn't know who our *real* father was and now that we do, things will change."

Aggie and Beckett shared a meaningful look before she

said, "We'll tell you all about him tomorrow night when I've had a chance to get the old photo albums out of storage. Your turn, Kymm. What are you thankful for this year?"

Still reeling from the news, Claire struggled to sustain her company manners throughout the rest of dinner and to be a good guest. She suggested they delay any conversations about finances until the next evening. When they were in the Hummer a few hours later, she brought up the family soap opera. "Well, call me shocked and stunned. I never knew Lee wasn't actually our dad. Isn't his name on our birth certificates? I'm going to get copies of them next week."

"It makes more sense now that he never felt anything for us." Connor flicked a sideways glance at her. "I don't know if I can forgive him for sending me to military school, but at least now I understand why he chose James and Kymm over us. We were a reminder of the fact he came second best to his parents."

"How do you figure?" Claire gripped his fingers. "They were nicer to Lee and Barbara than I would have been if I realized how much they'd stolen from me. Beckett and Aggie never even said our *real* father's name tonight."

"They probably can't because he means so much to them even now." Connor grimaced, staring out into the night. "I've lost friends, brothers and sisters in arms. Escorted them home and I can't talk about them five years later."

"Okay." She tightened her hold on his hand. "If things change, you know where I live." She looked at the man sitting in front of her, driving the vehicle toward his mother's house. "You've lost too, haven't you, Tony?"

"Every combat soldier has." Tony's voice was soft, too soft. "It's why I took early retirement three years ago. I couldn't go back to the *sandbox* one more time, not after the last IED hit us. Three of my troops died. And I knew I'd be going again if I stayed in the Army."

"When you lose your edge, you die," Connor added. "I couldn't return either, so I resigned my commission. Streets aren't safe, but I'm pretty sure I'll make it home each night."

Their vulnerability touched her heart and when they arrived at Maria's, Claire proposed a game of *Scrabble*. She set up the board in the dining room and Tony helped arrange the tiles so they wouldn't know which letters they drew at the beginning. Meanwhile Connor made hot chocolate, and Maria went to unpack the frosted Christmas cookies Agnes sent home.

Once they finished preparing to play, Claire undid Tony's tie and unfastened the top two buttons of his shirt. When he caught her wrists, she tilted her head, smiling naughtily at him. "I'm just trying to make you comfortable, darling."

"Any more comfortable and we won't stay here for long." He shrugged out of his jacket. "Go help my mom. I'll be right back."

"Promises. Promises." She turned away and deliberately strolled in the direction of the kitchen, adding an extra sway to her hips. She smirked when he muttered something. She loved being in charge and challenging him.

She heard him walk up behind her. He caught her waist and drew her back into him. She tipped her head against his chest until their gazes met. "How much do you want to bet I make more words than you do when we start playing?"

He kissed her neck, the soft spot below her ear. "Just keep the game clean, sweetheart or it will end faster than you think."

"Sounds wonderful." She pulled free, spun around, and

slid her hands over his wide chest to those amazing shoulders. Thanks to her heels, they were nearly the same height, and she found his mouth with hers.

A long, slow kiss later and he released her. She could have stayed there longer, but he was right. If she did, they wouldn't be playing a board game. She wouldn't be sorry. Would he?

Chapter Thirty-One

F riday morning, Claire, Maria, and Agnes left early to hit the holiday sales at the mall thirty miles west of Rocklin. As soon as they arrived in Upington, Claire insisted on stopping at the first espresso stand. Once she had a skinny, double-shot mocha, she was ready to visit Maria's favorite department store.

On the way inside the huge glass doors, her cell phone vibrated in her pocket and Claire pulled it out to check messages. She glanced at the two older women. "I have to take this, so I'll catch up with you."

"Don't take too long." Taking a cart, Maria aimed it toward the toy section. "We'll start with the presents for the day-care at church. Those are the most fun."

"I know," Agnes agreed. "I always love buying them too."

Once they were happily headed on their way, Claire walked over to a table near the deli. She sat down and drank coffee while she scrolled through texts and listened to voice-mails. Then, she began returning the calls. A half-hour later, all emergencies settled for the moment, she went in search of the others. She found them perusing stuffed animals. Her phone buzzed and Claire answered the call from Dominique MacGillicudy. One from her older brother immediately followed.

Tony and Connor spent the morning helping Beckett rearrange things in his former office at the town hall. The maintenance man happily removed Lee's name from the door and reinstalled Beckett's, along with a new hours sign on the outside of the building. The secretary called various former employees and reinstated the ones who were available to return to work.

The accountant arrived for a sit-down that included removing Lee and Barb's names from all financial documents. She promised to create a statement showing what they owed Beckett and a proposed repayment plan to avoid prosecution. It'd mean the pair would have to find other jobs because they'd shown they couldn't be trusted to handle the Rocklin family endeavors and finances.

Yvette arrived after lunch. Tony ushered Jimmy's mother to a chair at the long table in the conference room. When he entered, Beckett approached cautiously and apologized for all the misunderstandings. Yvette seemed to subscribe to the theory of 'taking the high road' because she opted to be gracious, thanking him for straightening out the situation and offering to let him know whenever she had an issue with the flower shop.

By the time the secretary escorted in Wendell Frobisher, the local attorney, everyone seemed on the same page. Connor and Jimmy brought in coffee and handed around the cups. Beckett made the introductions. "Wendell, this is

Tony Baldusi, Claire's fiancé. I don't know if you'll insist on a prenuptial agreement again or not."

"That would be up to them. Claire reached her majority at twenty-five and took full control of her inheritance then." Wendell held out his hand to Tony. "Congratulations. Where is Claire today?"

"Shopping with my mom and her grandmother at the Black Friday sales." Tony shook hands with the muscular blond man in his fifties who made a three-piece suit look good. "Claire and I have been business partners for ten years, so that agreement should suffice. I'll talk to her and see what she wants."

"Business partners?" Beckett frowned, intrigued. "That's news to me. We heard Claire spent a lot of time wasting her money and traveling to Europe when she wasn't on the East Coast." He grimaced. "Never mind. That story came from Lee and his wife, so it was undoubtedly not true."

"Not in the least. She went into real estate full-time after the wedding fiasco with Dex. She opened her first office ten years ago and we've been expanding ever since." Tony reached into his jacket pocket for business cards and passed them around. "She's the Designated Broker at our four full-time real estate brokerages."

"Along with those, she's invested in another one in Baker City. She owns our apartment building," Connor said. "She's bought a second one and it's being rehabbed. When the property near the church where Blanche LaVoie is a minister went up for sale, Claire bought that, and they created a tiny home village for homeless senior citizens. She says she'll keep buying multi-plexes wherever she can."

"Impressive." Wendell beamed. "Your grandparents would be so proud of her. Does she still have their properties on the Washington Coast?"

Connor nodded. "A property management firm handles those as vacation rentals. And Claire does go on occasional trips, but not many considering how hard she works."

"Of course, she doesn't," Yvette added. "I know what it takes to operate the florist shop and that's only one business. How on earth did you ever convince her to take four days off in a row to visit us, Tony?"

"It took a lot of preparation." Tony walked over to sit down at the conference table next to Yvette, so he'd be able to advise her about the paperwork. "It helps we're incommunicado when we're here in Rocklin or she'd be getting back-to-back calls, texts and emails on her phone."

Connor laughed. "Hey, you made her leave the laptop and tablet at home or she wouldn't be socializing with any of us."

Tony glanced at Yvette who stared at him and opted to share the truth, rather than allowing the woman to believe he controlled Claire. "Actually, I've never managed to make her do anything in the last three years since we started working together full-time. It's more the other way around. Claire always has a long 'honey-do' list for me."

The wry comment sparked laughter from everyone. Then, the conversation changed to the flower shop and the neighboring businesses. Beckett wanted to see various enterprises in town reopened and Wendell agreed to help with the endeavor. It took another three hours to organize the updates in the downtown area and then they headed back to Beckett's house.

When they arrived, they found Jimmy and Peyton had returned from their skiing trip with friends. Jimmy untangled lines of Christmas lights while his younger cousin set up a Nativity scene in the front yard. Tony jumped in to help the girl with the barn and Connor opened packages of icicle lights. Meanwhile Beckett sat in one of the Adirondack chairs on the front porch to supervise and provide advice.

A short time later, Maria drove up and parked in front of the house. Agnes was the first out of the car and immediately headed to the porch to talk to her husband. Claire and Maria stood at the trunk of the car, sorting purchases. Tony went to help. Loaded with bags, he climbed the steps and greeted Agnes. "How was the shopping trip?"

"It'd have been better if Claire would have gotten off her damned phone." Agnes stomped toward the door. "Every time we turned around, she was answering it or texting someone. She didn't even put it away at the restaurant where we had lunch. Kept it on the table and it buzzed constantly."

"I'll speak to her about it." Tony paused for a moment and met Beckett's faded blue gaze when his wife entered the house, slamming the door behind her. "You have to get more cell towers in Rocklin. Otherwise, when we come for Christmas, all hell will break loose when Aggie throws away Claire's phone and she has a meltdown."

"Think that will really happen?" Amusement slipped into the wrinkled face and Beckett chuckled. "I'd sell tickets. Haven't seen Aggie with her dander up in months, not since I refused to do some of those god-awful exercises at the rehab place."

"What's going on?" Claire arrived with more parcels. "Aggie's pissed at me, and I don't know why. This isn't working, Tony. I should never have come here. I should have gone—"

He shifted the sacks, caught her chin with his fingers and met her troubled gaze. "You were thoughtless, sweetheart. She hasn't seen you in years and you made her feel like she wasn't as important as your phone calls. Was anything that urgent?"

"Well, maybe." Claire considered the question. "Bonnie called but it was just about decorating the building for Christmas. Same goes for Eileen. She's having a meeting with Ingrid and Vinnie about the decorations on the broker-ages. I told her to include Scott Jenkins because he's being assigned to Lake Maynard. Svetlana needs a receptionist, and he'll handle the holiday lights and Christmas tree there."

Tony kissed her forehead. "That could have waited until Sunday when we were on the way home. What else?"

"Robyn got an offer on your condo, but it's a crap one. And—" Claire paused, then heaved a sigh. "You're right. She knows we're out of town so you wouldn't look at the proposed deal before Sunday night or Monday."

"If you think it's crap, we'll counter then. Anything else?"

"Dominique and her brother, Nick called from Baker City. They're doing their big toy drive for veterans. They wanted to know how many boxes we needed for our donations."

"Again, it could have waited. We've done the drive the past three years." Tony brushed her lips with his, then pushed open the door. "Go apologize to your grandmother, Claire, and make amends the way only you can."

She nodded and kissed him quickly. "I'm glad you figured out what's wrong. I don't know what I'd do without you."

"You never have to worry about that." Tony allowed her to walk past him and then closed the door behind her. "We'll give them a few minutes to sort out their issues."

"What's happening?" Maria climbed the stairs and came

toward them, carrying even more purchases. "Is everything okay?"

"It'd have been better if you suggested Claire put away her phone." Beckett grinned appreciatively. "My granddaughter, the real-estate tycoon was too busy running her empire today to take shopping seriously. She's a pistol. And Aggie's having kittens. But Baldusi told Claire what to do to fix things. If he'd been around back when Aggie and I met, we wouldn't have fought as much. She'd yell, scream, and throw her engagement ring at me because she thought I worked too hard. It was a miracle we made it to the altar on our wedding day."

"That's impossible, Beckett. It'd have been years before he was born. He wasn't even a twinkle in his papa's eye back then." Maria heaved a sigh of relief. "And please tell me you didn't talk to your fiancée again like she's a buck sergeant who screwed up, Anthony Marco Baldusi."

"Say what?" Tony narrowed his gaze on his mother's face. "I don't get it."

"I've been patient for the last three days ever since you arrived, but I can't continue." Maria glanced at Beckett, then at Tony again. "When he talked to her about the phone, did he ask her to put it away or did he tell her?"

"Why, I don't know." Beckett frowned thoughtfully. "They were kissing."

"They're always kissing. That isn't as important as treating each other respectfully." Maria eyed Tony. "You do respect Claire, don't you?"

"Of course, I do. I always have even when she was a smart-mouthed kid."

"Then, treat her like it. I raised you to say, 'please' and 'thank-you'. So do it."

"And the Army taught me to give orders."

257

Maria took a step closer, grabbed his ear with her free hand and yanked. "Figure out who scares you more, Anthony Marco. Me or the Army!"

"Ouch!" Tony yelped. "Mama, they have weapons."

"Me or them?" Another yank.

"You, Mama." When she released her hold, Tony dropped some of the bags on Beckett's lap and rubbed his ear while the elderly man laughed at him. "Always you, Mama."

———

She found her grandmother brewing coffee in the kitchen. Claire put the bags of presents on the island in the middle of the room and went to hug the old woman. She stood stiff in the embrace. "I'm sorry, Aggie."

"For what, Claire?"

"I screwed up bigtime. I should have turned off my phone instead of letting it wreck the day. I got distracted by the business calls and forgot how much I looked forward to spending the day with you and Maria."

"You wanted to be with me?" Tears sparkled in Agnes Rocklin's sky-blue eyes. "Really?"

"Of course, I did." Claire hugged her again. "I was thoughtless. I hope you can forgive me."

"Certainly, I do." Agnes shifted to return the hug. "Now, get the *Irish Cream* out of the refrigerator and we'll sit down and decide what other shopping we have to do. Where's Maria?"

"That's a good question. I'll get her right after I get the booze." Claire put the bottle on the counter next to the coffee machine before she headed for the front door. She owed Tony big-time. He always knew how to finesse a situation and smooth over any hard feelings, which wasn't one of her strengths. She tended to analyze matters and decide if she had to throw money at the problem, then 'count the bawbees' as Gramps used to say, so she didn't overspend.

She opened the front door and found Tony waiting with his mother on the porch. "What are you doing? Come inside."

"Is everything all right?" Tony gathered up the bags on her grandfather's lap. "Are you okay? Is Aggie?"

"We're fine." Claire smiled at him. "Maria, we need to decide where we're shopping tomorrow. And I promise to shut off my phone. I'm sorry I was so thoughtless today. Connor would say it's because we were raised by wolves, but I really don't have that excuse. Next time, help me out. Please tell me when I'm rude."

"Oh, I don't have to, *bambina*. You just need to turn that fine brain of yours off business and onto family when you're with us."

Chapter Thirty-Two

Supper was leftovers from the holiday dinner. Afterwards, everyone helped clean up before migrating to the living-room where there was a stack of photo albums on the coffee table. Tony and Maria sat next to Beckett on one couch while Claire and Connor joined Agnes on hers. She explained her younger brother and girlfriend split up after the birth of their son, Nathan, and neither wanted the baby, so he lived with her and Beckett.

"We loved him and didn't want him going into foster care." Agnes opened the first album revealing old photos of her and Beckett when they were much younger holding a blanket wrapped infant. The series continued, eventually showing a toddler with a mop of black curls and dark blue eyes. "We asked repeatedly to adopt him, but—"

"His biological parents wanted money to sign the papers," Beckett said gruffly. "We didn't have enough to give them. Logging was in the toilet, and the Rocklin Trust was for the town's upkeep and only covered some of our expenses. There wasn't any extra for an adoption. It took a while for us to get on our feet. Didn't mean they came to get him or sent support or presents or even a birthday card."

Claire waited for Agnes to turn the pages to more pictures of the little boy playing with toys, riding a trike, and hugging a puppy. He looked so happy, especially when he was walking around in Beckett's shadow or helping Aggie make cookies.

Connor sat beside her, and Claire reached for his hand, gripping his fingers tightly. "Didn't you own most of the town back then too?"

"Yes, but it wasn't making a lot of money," Beckett said. "Every penny that came in went to restore downtown after a fire. Wendell's father was the family lawyer, and he had my back. Couldn't have pulled it together without him and the rest of my buddies."

More photographs of Nathan Rocklin growing up, starting school, and then sitting on a couch with an infant cradled in his arms. Claire passed the first album to Maria for her to share with Tony and Beckett.

Connor eyed Agnes. "Is that Lee?"

She nodded, opening the second album. "I was so thrilled to have two little boys. We wanted a houseful, but I had female problems. I could only have Lee. After a while, it didn't seem that important when he and Nate had so many friends and they were always here."

These pages held more pictures of the boys, either separately or together and with groups of their friends, often including a little girl with long dark hair. Slowly, Claire realized it was their mother. She was always beside Nathan through the candid grade school photos. Then, it was middle school, and she wore cheerleader outfits while he was in different sports gear. Again, they seemed inseparable, especially when they dressed up for school dances.

A third book held cropped high school photos of their parents in heart shapes, circles, and squares. Agnes straightened one. "Your mom helped make this album. It's why it's so cute. She was very artistic. I'm not."

"Don't say that." Claire leaned over and kissed her cheek. "I've seen the way you frost Christmas cookies. They're amazing. Of course, they never last long because Tony and Connor scarf them down before Maria and I get more than a couple."

"We'll send another batch with you tonight," Beckett said. "Otherwise, my doctor will be having conniptions about how many I eat."

"Works for us." Tony elbowed him gently. "Don't listen to Claire. She actually hogged all three Santas and Mama got the reindeer."

"Only two of them." Maria frowned thoughtfully at the book. "I don't see very many pictures of Lee."

"Oh, he has his own albums," Agnes explained. "I only got out the ones of Nate. He didn't care how many times or ways I combined the photos, but Lee started having fits about them being cousins, not brothers when he started high school. He complained constantly about following in Nate's footsteps, that the teachers and coaches compared them too often. And he was furious when we were finally able to adopt Nate on his eighteenth birthday."

"I always thought it was because Erica only had eyes for Nate from the time they were in third grade, and he used to chase her around the playground." Beckett pulled a kerchief from his flannel shirt pocket and wiped his eyes. "Danged allergies."

"So, I started making separate albums for them when they were in high school." Agnes turned to the next page. "They were in different groups and hung out with other friends. Nate was into sports and academics in that order. It was the other way around for Lee."

"We ended up going to all the events at the school. Debate and Science Fairs for Lee and all the games and chess club for Nate." Beckett smiled reminiscently. "He insisted on attending every cheerleading competition for Erica. Said he had to cheer her on because she always did it for him."

The album held candid pictures of them as teens in casual clothes or dressed up for the Prom and eventually in their caps and gowns at high school graduation, holding up their diplomas. It ended with photos of Erica in front of a college dorm at the University of Washington in Seattle, a small diamond engagement ring on her hand and Nate in different Army uniforms.

"She studied to be a teacher like Maria," Agnes said. "She and Nate planned to get married as soon as he came home from Germany. He knew he was being transferred to California but didn't have his orders yet. Only he was injured—"

"In a terrorist bombing. Died there." Beckett's features hardened. "He was here on leave a couple months before. Said he'd be back for the wedding. Only he wasn't."

Claire nodded and gazed at the photo of an American flag draped over a coffin, followed by a picture of a head-stone. It took a moment to realize it was the one beside her mother's. "They're buried next to each other."

"Yes." A tear trickled down Agnes' cheek. "She told us she was pregnant at the funeral. And Beckett talked to Wendell's dad about support from the Rocklin Trust, but she couldn't have it unless she was married to a family member."

"And Lee stepped up." Beckett stood and walked around

the room. "He loved her, but she didn't love him the way he wanted. She got breast cancer a year after you two were born—"

"She fought the good fight, but it didn't do any good. She passed and Lee was so mad when we agreed with her parents that she should be buried next to Nate. She loved him so much." Agnes turned the page. The next photo wasn't of another tombstone, but of Erica holding the newborn twins, one in each arm. "And she always loved you."

———

Claire and Connor remained quiet when they arrived at Maria's house. Tony followed his mother into the kitchen. She opened a lower drawer where she kept potatoes, onions and, oddly enough, bananas. She removed a large bottle of Canadian whisky and then opened the cupboard with the dishes. "Get some ice out of the freezer and cola from the fridge, Anthony."

After he dropped ice cubes in them, she added shots of whisky to the highball glasses. "Bring the soda. I don't know if they'll want their booze straight tonight or not. After hearing all that past history, I need a drink, and they will too."

"Are you okay, Mama?"

"No, I'm not. I want to go to Lee's house and kick his ass from here to Tacoma and back. That *figlio di*—" She stopped. "No, I won't call Aggie names. She's done her best by him, and he should have consoled her and Beckett after they lost his brother, not been determined the man wasn't related."

"I'll take you there if you want."

"You're a good son, Anthony. Let's go comfort the living. That's all we can do tonight."

In the living-room, they found Claire and Connor snuggled up together on the couch. Tony held out the bottles of cola when his mother handed over the drinks before taking a seat in her recliner. "Soda or straight?"

Claire turned slightly and he saw tears running down her cheeks when she took the glass.

"Oh, sweetheart." Tony put the sodas on the end table and sat down next to her, wrapping an arm around her too. "I'm so sorry."

"Not your fault, bro." Connor hugged his sister. "They were kids. I have to wonder if our mom would have fought harder to survive if she hadn't already lost the love of her life."

"No, don't go there." Claire sniffed, turned her face into his shoulder for a moment, then faced front again and drank some whisky. "She had us and if she could have, she'd have lived for us. I don't think she and Lee would have stayed together. No offense, Maria, but he's never been able to sustain a relationship for longer than two years."

"No offense taken, *bambina*." Maria sipped her whisky. "He couldn't get Barb to sign a pre-nup and she tolerates his cheating, so they're still together after all this time. I do wonder if she's going to stay now because Beckett demanded restitution for what they stole during Covid and this past year."

"I'll bet Lee used seeing you twins to keep her parents from telling you about your *real* dad." Tony gripped Connor's shoulder in sympathy. "Otherwise, I think they'd have shared the truth."

"Well, it does explain why they were so adamant about us inheriting from them and not giving Lee a dime." Connor finished his drink and then added another shot to all of the glasses. "So, what do you think, Claire? Beckett wanted to know why we called him and Aggie by their first names yesterday. Shall we keep giving Lee the satisfaction of creating a breach or build a connection to them?"

"Connection." Claire wiped away her tears and raised the glass to her lips. "They've lost enough. The three of us already planned to be here for Christmas so when we go shopping tomorrow, I'm adding Aggie and Beckett, Grandma and Grandpa Rocklin to my list for gifts."

"I'm picking up flowers and taking them to our dad's grave today." Connor glanced at Tony. "I'll arrange with Yvette to start delivering them to him next time she goes. Then, I think we should talk to Grandpa about adding the three of us to the board that supervises the Rocklin Trust. He needs backup whether he realizes it or not. If we're there for him, he won't let Lee weasel his way back into the financial fold."

"Works for me." Tony brushed away an errant tear on Claire's cheek. "We held distance rather than in-person meetings during the pandemic. We can do the same thing for the board here."

"I like it." She heaved a sigh. "I'm so lucky to have both of you. Now, if you don't want me getting stinking drunk, let's watch a sappy holiday show."

Connor groaned and Tony saw his mother manage to smile. She picked up the remote, turned on the television and found a *Hallmark* movie that fit Claire's requirements.

She fell asleep halfway through the second feature. Tony stood, gathered her into his arms and whispered. "See you in the morning."

Connor and Maria both nodded. He signaled that he'd help her clean up after their drinking bout. Tony nodded and carried Claire into his bedroom. She sighed against his chest but didn't awaken.

He lowered her onto the queen-size bed. He went through the dresser and found a white nightshirt with a loose neckline, long full embroidered sleeves, and a ruffled, shirttail hem. When he turned around, he saw her grasping one of the pillows, but still asleep.

He returned to the bed, removed the ankle boots and socks before he unbuttoned her leggings and slid them off. He left her panties, a lacy blue thong this time. He switched out her tunic T-shirt and bra for the nightgown, then tucked her under the covers. Another deep sigh before she burrowed into the pillows.

He hung her top and pants in the closet when he put away the boots. Her bra went with the rest of the laundry she kept in her suitcase. After he undressed, he hit the lights and slid into bed beside her.

Pulling her into his arms, he felt her soft breaths change as she drowsily opened her eyes. He kissed her forehead. "Sleep, sweetheart."

"A night without sex?" She yawned. "We've already had one of those. Are you sure?"

"Yes, and we'll undoubtedly have other times when all we want is sleep." He chuckled, kissed the tip of her nose. "Sleep now and we'll have wild sex in the morning."

"Promises, promises." She sighed, draped her arm across his chest and closed her eyes. "Your mom and I are going shopping. I told you before we left Seattle. Abstinence makes the heart grow fonder."

Chapter Thirty-Three

Early Saturday afternoon, Claire followed the winding cement walkway to the gazebo in her grandparents' back yard. She wasn't the only one seeking solitude. She discovered Peyton huddling on the bench, softly sobbing. She'd obviously been to the riding stable today since she still wore black breeches, a cream turtleneck sweater, and low-heeled, black ankle boots.

Claire sat down beside her, removed a blue stiletto, shook out a pebble, and then replaced the shoe. "Want to share?" She patted the girl's back. "What's wrong?"

"My lesson horse is for sale." Peyton cried harder. "Grandma promised to buy him for me and now she won't. And my teacher says he'll be gone by Christmas. Somebody else will get Summer Solstice for a present."

"Well, that sucks." Claire put her arms around the tween. "I'm sorry. What does your Great-Grandma Aggie say? Tony told me she and your great-grandpa pay for riding lessons."

"Mom says I can't talk to them about it because she's gotta ask 'em about reopening the bookstore and she's going

268

to see if she can get back part of the rent so she can restock it. And she says we haveta move into it and share a bedroom and not be in our house anymore, 'cause she can't rent both places and—"

Grateful she hadn't worn one of her silk blouses, Claire let the girl cry into her blue sweater. She'd never thought she'd feel sorry for her stepsister, but she did. Poor Kymm had a tough row to hoe if she had to give up her house for a business to support herself and her daughter. Wait a minute! Why the hell was the woman paying rent on two places when her mother was married to Claire's fake father, and he'd been managing the town while Beckett was unavailable? Had Lee really ripped off his stepdaughter too?

I've got to do some research. Either that or I need to put Connor and Tony on the case. When Peyton's tears began to subside, Claire shifted on the bench. "I'd love to see pictures of *your* horse. Do you have them on your phone?"

Peyton shook her head and wiped her cheeks. "I don't have a phone. Mom says she can barely pay for hers. And it's not like we have good cell service here."

"Okay." Claire stood. "Come on. Let's go."

"Where?"

"When life is tough, the tough go shopping." Claire beckoned to the twelve-year-old. "Move it."

"How can I shop when we're broke?"

"You're broke, but I'm not. It's a benefit of working six days a week, at least sixteen hours each day." Claire grasped the girl's hand and towed her in the direction of the back door, heels clicking on the sidewalk, blue sweater pencil skirt swishing around her knees.

When they entered the kitchen, they discovered Agnes making coffee. Claire flashed a smile at her grandmother. "Peyton and I are going shopping. Where's her mom?"

"Talking to Tony in the living room while she waits for your grandpa, Connor, and Jimmy to return with a tree. Maria went along with them to make sure it's a pretty one that doesn't have any bare spots. Tony's untangling the Christmas lights. You'll be back in time to help decorate it, won't you?"

"Definitely." Claire gave Peyton a gentle push in the direction of the half-bath. "Go wash up and fix your makeup while I get Tony's keys."

"I don't wear it."

"Really?" Claire caught the girl's chin and studied her features for a moment. "Damn, I wish I'd had those long lashes when I was your age. They're fantastic. Are you telling me that peaches and cream complexion is natural? Wow, you're so lucky."

A smile slowly trickled into life and Peyton hustled away.

Claire glanced at Agnes. "Did you know Kymm is in financial trouble? She's been paying rent on her house and the bookstore all this time. She'll freak if I try to help her."

"Not your job, Claire." Agnes scowled, anger rising in her eyes. "Lee always claimed he thought of her as a daughter. I guess I shouldn't be surprised he 'double-dipped' on her when he was skinning Yvette alive. We'll handle it."

"Thank you, Grandma." Claire hugged the woman quickly and then sauntered into the living room. Tony sat on the couch, a jumble of multi-colored bulbs at his feet and on the cushions beside him. Kymm was curled up on the thick carpet nearby, switching the burned-out ones for fresh holiday lights.

"Hey there." Claire smiled sweetly at the duo. "Kymm, are you cool if I take your kiddo shopping? I won't spoil her too much, but I'd love to get her a mani, pedi, a new hair-style and some makeup."

Kymm gaped at her. "Why would you do that?"

"Umm, because I like kids and yours is a cutie, and you should learn to share." Claire strolled over to the back of the couch, leaning close enough to kiss Tony's cheek. "Give me your keys, darling. We don't want to walk to the mall."

"Especially not in those shoes." Tony chuckled, dug in his jeans' pocket, and pulled out the ring of keys. "Sweet-heart, get some flip-flops while you're there and give your legs a rest. You forgot to bring your slippers this weekend."

"Not happening. I never wear those." Claire shuddered dramatically. "I have my standards. And I definitely don't do flip-flops."

"Thanks for offering, Claire, but funds are a bit tight." Kymm focused on the bulbs again.

"Not for me." Claire rested her chin on Tony's shoulder. "I made several big sales this month."

"You make at least one big sale every week." Tony turned his head to look at her, gray eyes amused. "And you've got an offer pending on that condo you listed a few days ago."

"Yeah, but it's a crap offer. They're going to have to come up with a lot more moolah if they really want it and pay more than market price." Claire glanced at Kymm again. "My treat. I won't go hog-wild as Gramps used to say."

That earned a snort of disbelief from Tony and Claire dug her nails into his arm. "Stop being a jerk. I want the kid, and Kymm has too much pride to let me blow major bucks on her."

"Ouch." Tony grabbed her wrist, prying her fingers away

from his skin. "Kymm, give up your daughter before I have a shitload more battle scars."

Kymm laughed as Peyton entered the room. "Okay, you two win. Peyton, mind your aunt, wear your seatbelt, and don't let her spend too much money on you for Christmas."

"All right." Peyton hugged her mother before she hustled toward the front door. "Thanks, Mom. We'll be back to help with the tree."

"Sounds great." When the girl was gone, Kymm added. "I didn't expect this, Claire. My mother says you're still jealous of me because I took Dex away from you."

"Bullshit." Claire kissed Tony's cheek again. "Next time you see her, tell your mom I'm never jealous when I see one of my exes with someone else because she's the one who taught me to give my toys to the less fortunate."

"O.M.G., Claire." It took a moment and then Kymm laughed instead of taking offense. "She will totally whizz herself when she hears you think I'm needy."

"Making Barb do that would totally brighten my day." Claire smiled. "Maybe, I better buy her some adult diapers for Christmas."

Kymm laughed harder and Tony grasped Claire's hand. "Stop being snarky. Behave yourself. Go have a good time with your niece."

"I will." Since he was issuing orders, crossing boundaries again and it annoyed her, Claire bent closer. She didn't want Kymm to hear the whispered taunt. "I had to hurry this morning. Didn't want to keep your mom waiting."

"What does that mean?" He glanced over his shoulder at her.

Claire blew softly into his ear before nipping it. "I forgot to put on my panties." She straightened and walked out the door, adding an extra sway to her hips. Now, he'd have something to think about while she was gone!

———

His hands shook for a moment while he tried to untangle the next set of cords. Tony glowered at the lights. He'd nearly gone after her and taken her to his mother's house for a *quickie*. Claire knew how to torment him. Hell, she'd been doing it for longer than the past week and a half. Well, payback was hard and now so was he!

"I wish I'd gotten to really know Claire before this weekend." Kymm twisted a blue bulb into place. "Now, I feel even more horrible for going after Dex that summer."

"Please don't." Tony glanced at the curvaceous blonde in a sky-blue top and jeans. "If you two hadn't gotten together, I wouldn't have Claire now. After seeing the way Lee traded in one wife after another, it's no surprise she doesn't believe in divorce. Dex would have a life sentence with her."

"I don't think so. She'd have kicked him to the curb faster than I did." Kymm swapped out another light, a red one this time. "He'd cheated on me twice before and I forgave him. He and our nanny were together several times before I found them in our bedroom."

"Lucky for him that Connor and I were in the *sandbox* then because Claire would have wanted us to kill him if she didn't do it herself." Tony passed the string of lights to Kymm. "This one's ready for you to test it."

"I appreciate Claire spending time with Peyton. She's really upset because my mother told her there won't be a horse under the tree this year." Kymm paused. "I didn't share this is something she does every year. She makes and breaks promises all the time. I've always managed to pick up the slack, but I can't afford to buy and keep an expensive animal."

Carrying a tray with cups of coffee and a plate of holiday cookies, Agnes entered the room in time to hear Kymm. "What makes a woman do such a wicked thing?"

"Power play." Tony took one of the mugs. "Thanks, Aggie. I remember my mom telling me that Barb said it was time to put down Claire's dog a few days after Connor was shipped off to military school."

"Now, that was just mean." Agnes put the plate of cookies on the table and a cup of coffee near one end of the other couch. She pulled out a bright skein of red yarn and began to knit. "Fonzie was barely thirteen. Erica's parents gave him to her when she was going through chemo as a way to boost morale. He didn't live with the twins until your mom married Lee, Tony."

"I remember Claire used to take him with them when she and Connor went to their maternal grandparents' house."

"He had a good, long life. He passed away naturally in his sleep when Claire was a sophomore in high school." Agnes tilted her head to one side. "Does she have a dog now, Tony?"

"Oh, that might make a good Christmas present." Tony sipped coffee. "I'll have to ask her what she thinks. I know her cat wouldn't mind. Felix is a rescue and his doggie friend lives in a different apartment now."

"Do you have a picture of him?" Agnes lowered her knitting for a moment. "I'd love to see it."

"I'll show you if you join us for breakfast tomorrow morning before church. I don't get the Internet here."

"That's a wonderful idea." Agnes chose a star-shaped cookie. "We'll be there."

Their shopping trip started at the mall with manicures, pedicures and then a quick visit to the hair salon. Peyton refused artificial nails saying they wouldn't hold up at the barn, but she loved the bright Christmas designs the technician helped her choose instead. Claire went for a touch-up on her acrylic nails, opting for a new red glitter color. It looked so festive.

At the hair salon, Peyton wound up with a minimal trim of her long blonde hair, before the stylist created waves with a curling tong, then brushed them out for a softer look. She parted the hair ear-to-ear and left aside the hair in front. Then, she backcombed the crown area and used a textured spray on the curls to create volume. Finally, she gathered that hair into a low ponytail. The front sections of the hair were wrapped around the ponytail one after another.

Peyton stared into the large mirror. "I can do this at home, and I bet my helmet would fit over it when I'm going to the barn."

"Definitely." Claire tipped the stylist at her station before leading the way to the front of the salon. "It's called a textured wrap ponytail, very suitable for somebody your age. Let's get some decent shampoo and conditioner before we leave."

Next was the cosmetics store where they also found adorable earrings. Then, it was a cell phone store where Claire purchased one with a reasonable calling plan for the girl. Afterwards, it was Peyton's turn to take Claire to a shop specializing in equestrian attire. They had terrific clothes, and she found a perfectly fitted wool blazer that Peyton said was appropriate for the show ring.

Claire told the girl not to be silly. Horses were big and

smelly and sooo not her thing. She planned to wear the blazer with a silk blouse and her wool, tweed slacks to the office, finishing off the outfit with her black stilettos.

Meantime, since they were talking about horse-shows, Peyton required suitable garments. The tween explained she didn't actually take her lesson horse, Solly to shows. It cost enough for classes twice a week. Claire listened and then signaled for a salesclerk, requesting the woman find appropriate attire for her niece.

Hauling several bags toward the Hummer, Peyton eyed her warily. "I have a question, Aunt Claire."

"And I probably have an answer or two. What is it?"

"What are you going to tell my mom about all this stuff?"

"That it's her fault, of course." Claire unlocked the back of the rig and waited for Peyton to load the purchases. "What else?"

"How is it her fault when she's not here and she said not to let you spend lots of money?"

"Because I'm sure your grandmother has told you I was engaged to your father when your parents met and if Barb hasn't yet, she undoubtedly will." Claire waved toward the front of the Hummer. "Since I'm not lucky enough to have you for a daughter, Kymm will just have to suck it up and share. She has to deal with it when I spoil you rotten and you're a total brat like me."

"You're toast." Peyton giggled. "She'll never let us go anywhere alone again."

"Then, we just have to make the best of it." Claire slid the key into the ignition. "All right. Let's go get pics of your horse. It's not too late to visit the stable, is it?"

"Not yet." Peyton looked at her watch. "It's barely four-thirty. They'll still be doing classes, and the horses won't have dinner for three more hours. We should stop and get carrots on the way."

"We will." Claire drove out of the parking garage into the dark afternoon. Truth was the first casualty when she was determined to charm someone, and her new niece was an easy target. "Now, tell me all about this creature. I hate meeting strangers, even four-legged ones. I thought you said his name was Summer Solstice."

"It is, but I call him Solly for short."

"Okay, now dish the dirt about his current owner."

Chapter Thirty-Four

It was after six at night when the Hummer pulled back into the driveway of Agnes and Beckett's house. Tony walked out to greet the missing pair. Peyton popped out of the passenger seat, happily waving at him. He reached the driver's door and opened it before Claire could. "Where have you two been? I was about to call out Search and Rescue."

"Shopping, darling. It's my life." She slid out of the seat into his embrace, calling over her shoulder. "Do you need help getting the bags with dinner, Peyton?"

"No, I've got them, Aunt Claire." Burdened with several bags, the tween headed toward the front porch. "I guess it's tradition to have Chinese food while we decorate the tree. I didn't know that, but I like it."

"Me too." Claire handed Tony his keys. "I couldn't look at one more turkey sandwich, so I called Grandma and told her not to cook. We were bringing supper."

After he put his keys in his pocket, Tony rested his hands on the doorframe, leaning close to her. "You're a wicked woman and I have plans for you."

"Of course, you do." She slid her arms around his neck, her lips a breath away. "Too bad you were sleeping like a log this morning, or I'd have jumped you."

"I need to find out if you've really lost your underwear. We'd be leaving now if it was up to me."

"You wish." She kissed him, a quick teasing taste.

He could have left it light, but he wanted her too badly, and his mouth seized hers. The memory of what she'd said earlier about going commando today still haunted him. He wanted to urge her back in the rig and go straight to his mother's house where they'd have privacy and he'd be able to see if she really was only wearing thigh-high stockings under that skirt. Not a possibility, not yet.

"Supper's waiting!" Connor called from the porch. "And there won't be any sweet and sour pork left if you two keep necking out there."

Tony lifted his mouth from hers. "You'll get what you deserve later."

"Be nice, darling." She rocked against him, and he felt himself harden in response. "Or we'll simply have to stay so late, Grandpa will chuck us outside unless Grandma offers a place to sleep."

"You're such a brat." He kissed her again before stepping back and pushing her in the direction of the porch. "And we're out of here by twenty-two hundred hours, Claire."

"Maybe." She sauntered away. "Maybe not."

He stared after her, waiting for his reaction to subside in the chilly winter night. Stars glittered in the ebony sky. Gawd, he wanted her. He always wanted her and always would. What kind of fool did that make him? A lucky one, he thought. If he didn't initiate sex tonight, she definitely could if she had the opportunity.

When he reached the house, he found cartons of

Chinese food on the kitchen island. Before he loaded up his favorites on one of the empty dishes, Claire signaled from the table. He saw a full plate next to hers and went to join the rest of the group. Peyton chattered eagerly about the shopping trip, her new smart phone, and the pictures she'd taken of her lesson horse.

At a brief pause in the conversation, Kymm eyeballed Claire. "Didn't you say you wouldn't go crazy at the mall?"

"I love shopping." Claire forked up fried rice. "And my credit limit just got raised on my new card. If you wanted me to stop, you should have come along."

"Grandpa and I needed to talk about the bookstore." Kymm heaved a dramatic sigh while her daughter laughed at the byplay. "Oh, why do I even bother? Claire never listens."

"Yes, I do when it's something I want to hear." Claire flicked a sideways glance at Tony. "Don't I always pay attention to you, darling?"

He chuckled, caught her wrist before she nabbed another piece of his almond-fried chicken with her fork. "I'll plead the *Fifth Amendment* on that, sweetheart. Now, eat your own dinner and leave mine alone." He saw the warning look from his mother and recalled what she'd said about his manners and lack of them, so he squeezed Claire's knee before he deliberately drawled, "Please."

———

Claire trembled at Tony's slow smile and the teasing touch of his hand on her leg. It only lasted a moment, then he returned to eating supper. She was having a surprisingly good visit with the extended family over the holiday weekend. She'd expected it to be an endurance contest, not an occasion where she learned the truth about her parentage. Now, she had even more justification for remaining 'no contact' with Lee Rocklin and his wife.

It doesn't mean I have to sever the ties with the rest of the family. While Kymm might never be as close as one of her sorority sisters, they didn't have to be strangers. While they ate, the other woman shared her plans for reopening the bookstore by the first of the year. Peyton whooped with delight when Kymm announced they wouldn't be moving into the tiny studio apartment on the second floor but remain in their small two-bedroom house.

Prior to the Covid shutdowns, the store manager had lived there as partial payment of her salary and Kymm intended to see if the former employee would be able to return before Christmas. Agnes promised to call around town and reorganize the book clubs that used to meet there. Yvette had joined them for the tree decorating party. She volunteered her and Jimmy's services to help clean, paint and organize the bookstore, saying she didn't want to wait until the new year to load up on her favorite authors.

Jimmy said he'd bring along his friends from high school too and they'd finish the renovations in record time. Kymm should be able to re-open before Christmas. He brought the rest of them up to date on the sports car, a black Trans-Am he'd seen advertised online, one he could afford to buy. He admitted he didn't want to wait for Barbara and Lee to come through on their assurance to get him a car for Christmas since they'd broken so many previous promises. When Beckett and Connor inspected it that afternoon, Connor suggested taking Jimmy to the next police auction for seized vehicles instead.

"What's the issue?" Claire asked her brother. "It sounds like you have one."

"The tires are shot, and I could tell the transmission needs work when we took it for a test drive." Connor came back from refilling his plate and sat down at the table again. "What did you think of the body, Jimmy?"

"It has a few dents," Jimmy admitted. "And the pedal went all the way to the floor when I stepped on the brake. Good thing there wasn't any traffic in the parking lot, and I hadn't taken it on the road yet, or I could have hit something or someone."

"Add in the cracked windshield and the vehicle's going to suck up more money than Jimmy's saved." Beckett took a fortune cookie from the bowl on the table. "He's a good driver but that car won't stay on the road in the snow. It's a wreck looking for a place to happen. When he and the rest of the emergency responders get the call that Jimmy's injured, it will break James' heart."

"If I'd realized he was a firefighter, I wouldn't have talked to the other cops when he was drunk and raising hell at the bar on Wednesday night," Connor said. "We, first responders stick together."

"Best thing for him to face the consequences." Agnes reached over to pat Connor's hand. "The fire chief told him if he got in trouble again, it'd be thirty meetings in thirty days, or he'd lose his job."

"Dad loves the fire department." Jimmy took one of the cookies. "He has a rough time after Labor Day weekend when they've spent three nights scraping want-to-be racers and drunk tourists off the rocks after they've rolled their vehicles."

Although he didn't say he agreed, Claire saw Connor's faint nod. It sounded like their stepbrother had grown up a lot too. Suddenly, she remembered him sending a condolence card when her maternal grandparents died and volunteering to be a pallbearer at their funeral. Why had she forgotten Yvette saying Jimmy wanted both his sisters, Kymm, and Claire to be two of her bridesmaids?

Because I was a snarky sixteen-year-old who hated his mother! Gawd, I can be such a bitch on high heels! Even if Barb was a great teacher, I didn't have to buy into her program!

When they finished eating, Claire jumped in and helped Kymm with the cleanup. Peyton left with the others to move furniture in the living-room. Then they'd place the fir tree in front of the picture windows.

Once they were alone, Claire lowered her voice to ensure they couldn't be overheard. "Peyton shared Barb's Christmas crapfest with me. It's been more than twenty years. I can't believe she still does the same stunt to Peyton and Jimmy that she did to us."

"James, Yvette and I've called her out on it time and again." Kymm sorted the silverware into the basket in the dishwasher. "It doesn't make any difference. She just tells us we can't take a joke, and I've taught Peyton to be too sensitive."

"Hurting your kids is mean, not a joke. It wasn't funny when Barb did it back in the day and it isn't now." Claire spooned the last of the fried rice into a storage container. "I talked to the owner of the barn about the horse. He's a real looker, bright red, four white socks and a blaze. She says Solly's a registered Arabian and perfect show horse."

"Tell me you didn't buy him for Peyton. I can't afford what it'd cost to keep him."

"I didn't buy him." Claire put away the remainder of the beef and broccoli. "I couldn't with your kid standing there. I wouldn't without talking it over with you. What I did do was sign her up for what's called a 'Pre-Owner Package' in addition to the lessons Beckett and Agnes already give her."

"What's that?" Kymm finished loading the dishwasher and started it. "I've never heard of such a thing."

"Well, like the instructor and I discussed, your kiddo can throw fourteen fits, Kymm, but she's really not ready to have a horse of her own. She doesn't know anything about taking care of one. She doesn't even prep Solly for lessons. She just rides him. I had more responsibility with my mom's dog when I was her age than she has with that big carrot-munching monster who nearly took off one of my new nails."

"I never realized that." Kymm wiped down the center island. "You're right, Claire. I've seen one of the staff bring the horse into the ring quite a few times and then put it away after Peyton rides. But—"

"Not anymore." Claire closed up the refrigerator and turned. "From now on, things will be different. Peyton will go to the barn all day on Saturdays and Sunday afternoons after church. She'll groom, saddle, muck stalls, feed, water and learn about hoof and vet care. It's unlimited lessons, trail-riding, gaming, showing here and at outside barns. She'll not only take total responsibility for her horse, but she'll also help care for the other horses. Plus, she has to tack up for weekday lessons."

"She'll either love it or hate it," Kymm said slowly. "You're brilliant, Claire. I never thought of getting her more hours at the stable."

"Not done yet. The owner told me when Peyton comes to horse camp in the summer, she just has a good time socializing and riding with the rest of the students. Her peers help teach beginners, but she doesn't. Peyton and I talked. If she wants me to believe she's serious about having a horse of her own, she has to attend the leadership program at spring break, then be a camp counselor from June through August."

"Nice!" Kymm whistled softly. "I don't care if you like it or not, but I'm going to hug you."

Before Claire could fend off her older stepsister, Kymm nearly strangled her in a fierce embrace. "And you've saved my life. Before Covid, I'd be trying to run the bookstore in the summer and dealing with Peyton's tantrums about not liking any of the budget camp programs I could afford. And if it wasn't for Aggie and Beckett, she wouldn't be in horse camp at all. Wendell does his best to get money from Dex, but the guy works under the table and avoids paying for child support."

"It doesn't mean Peyton will actually like any of this, Kymm, or follow through on it."

"No, it doesn't, but it gives me a way to go."

"Well, I figure Grandpa Beckett and Grandma Agnes will also like it because Peyton's lessons and camps won't cost as much since she's doing more of what Tony calls, 'the grunt work' and receives a hefty discount because the staff won't be waiting on her. It'll make up for having to drive her over there when you're working."

"Good point and it takes Mom and Lee out of the picture. If they ask, I can say Peyton has to build up her horsy knowledge until she's ready to own one."

"Makes sense," Claire agreed.

Before the conversation continued, Peyton rushed into the room. "Great-Gramma wants the ball of string out of the junk drawer. As soon as they tie up the tree so it can't fall down, we're ready to decorate. Are you coming?"

"Definitely." Claire hooked her arm through Kymm's.

"Let's go give them the benefit of our advice since I'm sure Peyton can get the string without us."

"Of course, I can. I'm twelve!"

"There you go." Glad the conversation with her step-sister went so smoothly, Claire strolled with her into the living-room. She didn't add she'd put a deposit on Summer Solstice, the horse of Peyton's dreams. If everything went well, he'd belong to her niece next Christmas. Claire negotiated a deal that if Peyton didn't keep her part of the bargain, then the horse would remain with its current owner.

No harm, no foul, Claire thought. And as Tony said, sometimes a person didn't have a 'need to know' certain details. She'd wait a while to tell Kymm the rest of the story. In the living-room, she found Tony stringing lights on the tree and went to help.

He handed her one line of brightly colored bulbs. "I already shared the word that we'll take off in an hour and a half, at twenty-hundred hours, sweetheart. We don't want to make a late night of it when we have a long drive home tomorrow."

Chapter Thirty-Five

When they finished decorating the tree, there was still time for pie. Claire took requests and helped her grandmother serve everyone their favorite. Her grandfather had turned on the flatscreen over the mantel so they could listen to holiday music. It'd been a very pleasant evening, she thought, taking a seat on one of the couches next to Tony.

Maria waited until there was a lull in the conversation before turning her attention to Claire. "We've spent so much time talking about the holidays and shopping for them that we haven't really discussed your wedding."

"We told you when it was." Claire smiled sweetly, hoping she didn't look as desperate as she felt. "Save the date. More shall be revealed when Valentines' Day is closer."

"Good point." Connor rocked in the recliner. "Tony may have been packing that ring around forever—"

"Three years, but it took a while for Claire to realize I'd stick and stay." Tony finished his pie and leaned forward to place his empty dessert plate and fork on the coffee table. "At Christmas, we'll have more plans to share."

Claire appreciated his support, but it didn't seem to make a great impression. Yvette and Kymm immediately began discussing the kinds of flowers that would be available in February for decoration, boutonnieres for the guys, and Claire's bouquet.

Maria and Agnes talked about taking Claire shopping to find a dress when she visited at Christmas and Peyton wanted to go along. She said she'd researched it online and could be either a flower girl or a bridesmaid. A wedding dress would be first and foremost, but perhaps they could also look for an appropriate one for her.

"It's good to be men." Connor glanced at Jimmy and Beckett. "All we have to do is rent tuxes for the big day and make sure Tony's there on time."

Finished hearing the conversation about the upcoming ceremony, Claire stood and gathered up some of the empty plates and silverware. She gestured toward the clock. "Tony wants to turn into a pumpkin early, so we're ready to hit the road. Peyton, would you and Jimmy help Conn move your bags into your mother's car?"

"Sure." The girl jumped to her feet. "Come on, Jimmy. Wait until you see my new riding boots. They're awesome."

Claire glanced over her shoulder when Tony entered the kitchen a few minutes later, her dress coat in his hands. "Let's get out of here."

"I'm not arguing." He held up the coat so she could slide her arms in the sleeves, then lifted it onto her shoulders. "I told Connor to ride with my mom because you'd want to discuss wedding plans with me."

She jabbed her elbow backwards, but he caught it before she made contact. "You're dreaming."

He laughed, pulled her around and into his arms. "I'm not the only one."

She glared at him. When she heard footsteps coming toward them, she slid her hands up his chest to his neck, and her lips met his. The kiss only lasted a moment before he cupped her elbow and guided her toward the front door. She called out her farewells and promised to meet everyone for breakfast and would be happy to hear their ideas.

"You've got a long way to go before you're a bridezilla, Claire," Kymm told her. "Don't worry. Yvette will give you lessons since I can't because Dex and I eloped."

"I'll look forward to it." Claire breathed a sigh of relief once they were outside and headed for the Hummer.

Bright holiday lights framed the windows, doors, and the eaves of the split-level house. The crèche in the front yard was outlined with more strings of red, yellow, green, and blue bulbs. A plywood Santa along with Mrs. Claus stood near the flowerbeds.

"Get me out of here before it starts snowing and the carolers show up, Tony. I'm about ready to help the Grinch."

"No worries, sweetheart." He hit the key fob and unlocked the passenger door. "We're moseying."

It didn't take long to reach his mother's house. Claire didn't wait for him to escort her inside. She reached the porch before he did. "I thought it'd be enough to let them think we were engaged, and a wedding was on the horizon. I didn't expect all the hoopla, and I don't know if I like it."

"You definitely aren't a bridezilla." He unlocked the door. "And I'm glad."

"Shut up, Tony." She shrugged out of her coat, went to hang it in the hall closet. "I told you this wasn't real. How am I supposed to end things in January if we buy a stupid dress at Christmas?"

"That's your problem." He swung her up in his arms and walked toward the guestroom. "Mine is seeing if you really did leave your panties behind this morning."

"What?" She gaped up at him, reading the intent in his gray eyes. "Weren't you the one who told my brother we were going to talk about the wedding?"

"I didn't say when." In the bedroom, he managed to hit the light switch with one hand and then kick the door closed. "It can wait until I've had you screaming my name a few times."

She began to unbutton his flannel shirt. "Didn't you say I had to be quiet the other night?"

"We weren't alone then." He lowered her to stand near the bed. "We are now."

She kicked off her shoes, caught the hem of her sweater, lifted it over her head. He took it from her, tossed it in the direction of the bureau. It didn't make the top of the dresser, and she laughed. She caught her breath when he unfastened her bra, and it followed her top. "Tony!"

"That's me." He cupped her breasts, thumbs seeking her nipples. He lowered his head, his lips a breath away from hers. "Say, please."

"What?"

"Ask me to take you."

"I never ask for what I want." She unbuttoned his jeans, pushed them down his legs. His boxers went right after them. "I'm the woman who tells you what to do and when to do it."

"That's not what I remember."

She surrendered to his kiss, barely aware he unzipped her skirt, and it fell to the floor followed by her stockings.

He lifted his mouth a bare inch away. "You did skip your panties. I'm glad."

"I told you." She cried out when his hand found her, two long fingers sliding inside, her hips moving and meeting the strong thrusts. His thumb rocked against the waiting, eager bud of flesh and she moaned his name. "Now, do it now. Please, Tony. Please."

"I will, and you already know it." He sought out the nipple so close to his mouth. "And I was right. You did say, 'please'."

———

Afterwards, she lay in his arms, fingers toying with the hair on his chest, their legs tangled together. "What are we going to tell them tomorrow morning?"

"Nothing, sweetheart." He kissed her forehead, her nose and her cheek, soft butterfly touches. "We'll listen and you'll take notes on your phone since you left your laptop at home."

"What do I tell Peyton about being a flower girl? She's a kid. I don't want to hurt her."

"Tell her to find dresses she likes and send you pictures." He ran a hand along the curve of Claire's back. She trembled when he stroked her hip. "You didn't buy her a horse, did you?"

"Not yet." She reached across him to the nightstand and the half-full box of condoms, snagging one. "I put down a deposit. Do you think Kymm will let us use a picture of Peyton riding her horse when we want to advertise farms for sale?"

"We only get those up by Lake Maynard." Tony threaded his hands in the shoulder-length black hair framing Claire's lovely face and brought her near enough to take her mouth in a fierce kiss. She yielded and his tongue invited hers to play. When the kiss ended, he met her gaze. "We'll talk about it later."

"What's wrong with now?" She smiled, taunting him. "Or do you have something else in mind?"

"Indeed, I do." He caught her wrist and removed the packet in her hand. "And this time, you're going to have to be quiet since I heard my mother and Conn arrive home."

"I will if you are."

———

They overslept the next morning. They showered and dressed quickly. Claire opted for leggings, a T-shirt and sweatshirt plus her ankle boots for the trip home. Tony wore jeans and one of his favorite flannel shirts. While he stripped the bed, made it with fresh sheets, dusted and vacuumed, she packed their clothes. The team effort paid off, providing enough time for Claire to have a cup of coffee before they had to leave for breakfast at a downtown café. In the kitchen, Connor shared Yvette planned to bring bouquets of flowers for them to take to the cemetery on the way out of town despite the fact they'd done it a few days earlier.

Claire propped a hip against the counter, eyeing her twin. "You told her four bunches, right?"

He nodded. "Yes, and when I asked her to start putting them on our father's grave because we're not here to do it all the time, she said she would."

"Perfect. I know you said you intended to ask and I'm glad she agreed." Claire nodded a greeting to Maria when she entered. "Good morning. Tony's loading our luggage in the Hummer, and we were good guests. He said he *G.I.'d* the room. I guess that's Army speak for cleaning it."

"That's right." Connor started the coffee machine brewing a cup for Maria. "What did you do while he was working, twin?"

"Packed." She finished her coffee, rinsed the cup, and put it in the dishwasher. "I'm not a total waste of space, bro."

"Never said you were." He glanced at Maria. "And I tidied the living-room too. Tony told me where to find fresh linens for the sleeper sofa. Now, I'll be able to stay because we're coming here for Christmas."

"You're always welcome." Maria kissed his cheek when he handed her a mug of freshly brewed coffee. "I've missed you two."

"You're not the only one who gets lonely," Claire told her. "You should visit us more often in Seattle. I still need to get the gifts I bought yesterday out of your car, but I told Tony to nab the ones we stored in the garage."

"We'll do it before we go." Maria paused. "Claire, I want you to ride with me to the café and we'll let the guys go together."

"Why? I've been good."

"Because I want to talk to you in private. We've barely been alone together the last couple of days."

"All right," Claire agreed. "But only if we get to go shopping together, just the two of us, when we come for Christmas. You and I never did get to the hair salon on Friday or Saturday when we were shopping with Aggie, and I do want to take you for a mani and pedicure."

"Sounds like a winner. I'll mark it on my calendar."

It was her turn to make a cup of coffee for Tony when she heard him in the hallway. Claire handed him the mug of strong black java. "Guess we're dividing up by gender to go to the restaurant. Your mom wants a chat."

She pressed against his side, when Tony put an arm around her waist before he eyed Maria warily. "What's bugging you?"

"She'll probably ask you about wedding plans." He took a swallow of his coffee. "Tuxes, yes. Don't volunteer me for anything else." A long look from his mother and Tony added, "Please."

"You've got it."

A short time later, Claire waited for Maria to back onto the street and follow Tony's Hummer toward downtown Rocklin. "What's on your mind?"

"I'm concerned about the two of you." Maria focused on the frost-covered street. "I spoke to Tony earlier. He needs to remember he's a civilian now, not an Army Master Sergeant and you're not one of his non-coms."

"Good luck with that." Despite the attempt at humor, warmth flooded through Claire at the concern. "Maria, we're fine. We understand each other. I think we always have. He's bossy, but he looks after me."

"And do you take care of him?" Maria coasted to a stop at the next light. "It has to be reciprocal, Claire, or your relationship won't work."

"We argue about the way he crosses boundaries, but he knows he can count on me no matter what."

"I see." The car rolled forward when the light turned green. "Do you respect my son?"

"Definitely."

"Do you like him?"

"That's a weird question. Shouldn't you be asking if I'm in love with him?"

"No. Loving is easy, but liking is hard. If you like and respect each other, you'll do better in the future. You'll be together like Beckett and Aggie are, no matter what."

Claire frowned. "Did you like and respect Lee?"

"Not at all. I was in love with him but discovered it wasn't enough when push came to shove. Same goes for Tony's dad. I saw a counselor who taught me a lot after Lee and I divorced. I probably won't be around in fifty years. With luck, you and Tony will still be married to each other then."

"Undoubtedly. What else?"

Maria pulled into the parking lot at the restaurant and found a spot next to his rig. "To stay together, you need to talk to each other as if you're friends. Courtesy, Claire. You use it with your clients and staff, don't you?"

"Of course, but Tony is different."

"Use it with him too, honey. It will help in the long haul."

Chapter Thirty-Six

At breakfast with the extended family, there'd been a few attempts to talk about the upcoming wedding. However, Claire, Tony and Connor managed to redirect the topic to holiday plans. Since they closed the brokerages the week before Christmas and didn't reopen the offices until after New Year's Day, they'd be in Rocklin most of that time, which delighted everyone. Connor had almost a month of vacation that he hadn't used yet, so he wouldn't have any trouble joining them. He said it meant he and Jimmy could visit various car lots as well as nearby auto auctions.

After a quick trip to the cemetery, they were on the road to Seattle before ten that morning. Claire relaxed in the passenger seat going through the texts, messages, and emails on her phone. She sent off responses to various questions, none of which appeared urgent.

"How is everything?" Tony's attention remained on the highway. "Any emergencies?"

Claire lifted her gaze from the screen and glanced at him. Why was he so attractive in down-home work clothes? No answer came to mind. She took a moment to admire his rugged features. "Everything seems fine. Let's swing by the Seattle office and pick up the paperwork for the offer on the condo. You can read through it tonight and tell me what you think."

"I thought you already decided it's crap."

"It is, but you're the owner. You should make the final decision. All I ought to do is advise you what to do with the property."

He chuckled, flicked a quick sideways glance at her and then returned his attention to the road. "When it comes to you and me, I don't recall you ever doing what you 'ought' to do, sweetness. I want your honest opinion."

"Okay, I think if you hold off, you'll get more offers. You won't have to settle for bargain hunters. The right person will be willing to pay more than the list price and have cash. It will give you the funds you need to rehab the house you're buying in Everett."

"It might take a while longer to sell the condo." Connor pointed out from the back seat. "Are you okay with that?"

"I only listed it a little over a week ago." Claire shifted to eye her brother. "We have a couple weeks before Tony closes on the house."

"And I have enough in the bank to meet those costs. I'm not desperate."

"There you go." Claire's attention reverted to the smart-phone again. The next time she looked up, she glimpsed tiny snowflakes landing on the windshield. "When did the weather change?"

"About ten minutes ago." Tony frowned thoughtfully. "Think we'll skip lunch until we're out of the foothills and back on the interstate heading south, closer to the larger cities because they're in lower elevations. Then, we can see if the weather improves."

"It may for a couple days," Connor said, "but according to the forecasters, the temperature's going to drop this week, and we'll be lambasted with snow. Claire, let's do a test run on the new generator and make sure we'll have power for the entire apartment building. Text Bonnie and tell her to go to Costco and stock up for the next week or so."

"I hate snow." Claire glowered out the window at the increasing snow. "Plus, this week my sorority sisters and I are doing our annual holiday shopping trip. We're staying at a hotel and partying for three days."

"You may have to put that off if we get a ton of snow." Tony turned the wipers to a faster rhythm as the snow's intensity increased. "The entire city shuts down and so does the airport."

"Well, if we get crappy weather, I won't be happy." Claire sent off appropriate texts to Bonnie and the receptionists at the brokerages. "We'll also have to remind the associates that we won't be open if we have a heavy-duty winter storm. None of them need to risk their lives to sell a house."

"That's my girl."

"Don't push your luck, Baldusi. I haven't been a girl in years. I'm a woman."

He grinned appreciatively. "You'll always be my girl and my woman."

"Lucky for you that you're gorgeous." Claire heaved a dramatic sigh. "Or your macho attitude would get you in trouble."

———

The snow cleared off, changing to a cold winter rain with occasional bursts of sleet when they drew closer to Seattle.

Purple-gray clouds still piled up on the horizon. The storm Connor had told them about was coming. He suggested pushing on to the city and stopping closer to home for an early supper. It made sense, Tony thought, especially when Claire agreed.

He pulled into the brokerage parking lot a little after four. While she hurried inside, he called in a reservation at their favorite Italian restaurant in the Magnolia neighborhood, close to the apartment house.

She returned a few minutes later with a sheaf of papers in a file folder and promptly collapsed into the heated passenger seat. "It's freezing outside."

"It doesn't look like anyone is in the office now." He drove toward the main street that wound toward the Ballard bridge and eventually the turn-off to their home. "Did anybody work today?"

"I don't think so. Eileen's desk was cleared off." Claire smoothed damp hair with her free hand. "It seemed super quiet, but we should have a full crew tomorrow. Eileen wants to have holiday lights on the building before lunch."

"Fair enough." It was only a short distance to Petrocelli's Pizza and Pasta Palace. Because it was early for supper, there were plenty of places to park in the lot. He reached for Claire's dress coat on the back seat. "Let's find some food."

"I'm okay." She slid out of her seat when he came around the back of the Hummer and opened her door. "We'll be inside in a few minutes."

"It doesn't mean I want to listen to you pitch a fit." He draped the coat around her shoulders. "Good thing you opted for sensible shoes this morning instead of those damned stilettos."

"And it's a good thing you're buying." She tucked her hand in the crook of his arm, stepped closer to him and waited for her brother to join them. "Otherwise, I'd tell you what to do with your lecture." She sighed. "Okay, so much for listening to your mom's sermon about being nice to you. I've already failed."

He chuckled. "Did she really tell you to be nice to me?"

"She said, courteous. It amounts to the same thing."

"It definitely does." He brought her nearer. "She told me the same thing."

"What? That I ought to be nicer to you?"

"No, that I shouldn't issue orders to you like you're a buck sergeant who just screwed up."

She laughed, pressed her head against his shoulder. "Well, you don't tell her when I have, and I'll return the favor."

"And how much will you pay me not to rat out the pair of you?" Connor asked, obviously amused. "I'm sure Maria will offer me a bonus."

"Be careful," Claire told him. "The road runs both ways and we'll let her know how often you think you're large and in charge."

"Now, I'm really scared," Connor teased.

"You should be." Tony escorted Claire inside and the hostess promptly guided them to their booth. Once they were seated, he ordered *vin brule*, hot mulled wine with fruit. While they waited for their drinks, they studied the menus.

————

When they reached the apartment house, the three of them unloaded the Hummer. Upstairs, Claire cuddled the kitten on her way to the kitchen to top off his food dishes. Fancy had cleaned the litterbox before she left. Claire started the washer running and then headed into the bedroom to begin unpacking. She found Tony doing the same thing, hanging up his suit and putting his shirt in a laundry bag with a few others.

Claire eyed him. "I only have a couple loads to do. There's plenty of soap. You can use the washer tonight."

"I will when you're done, but I'll keep dropping off my shirts and suits at the cleaners on the way to the office."

"That costs too much."

He chuckled. "And it takes too long to wash, dry and iron my office clothes, so I'll keep doing what I do, and you keep doing what you like to do, Ms. Penny-Pincher."

Since she wasn't about to offer to iron his business attire, Claire ignored his teasing while she sorted her panties and stockings into mesh bags. She always washed her bras by hand, but they needed to soak for about a half-hour first. It'd give her time to put away everything else and review the holiday purchases she'd stored in the guestroom for now. She could start wrapping gifts tomorrow night after she packed for the shopping extravaganza with her friends. She'd meet them at the hotel on Tuesday evening in time for dinner.

When she joined Tony in the living-room, he sat on the couch studying the contract she'd picked up earlier that afternoon. She lingered in the doorway and watched him. Felix curled on the back of the sofa, occasionally batting at the pages.

"What do you think? Are you going to accept it or reject the offer?"

"Counter it." He glanced at her. "Come take a look. If they increase the downpayment and obtain a bank loan for the balance—"

"Didn't they want you to carry the contract?" Claire

301

crossed to him, holding out her hand for the appropriate pages. "Unless they have excellent credit, waiting for them to make monthly payments is risky. It takes too long to evict potential buyers when they stop paying and, in the meantime, the property is trashed."

"Very good ideas." He drew her down beside him and passed her the first three pages. "Let's go through this line by line and then we'll reward ourselves with ice-cream."

"Sounds like a winner." She opened the little drawer of the end table and removed her reading glasses. She didn't need them most of the time, but they came in handy when she read legalese and didn't want to miss key points. She realized he was staring at her and lifted her chin. "What now?"

"I never can decide when you're the most alluring. Right now, you look like a sexy librarian or very strict school-teacher."

She pushed the glasses further up her nose. "And you look like a rough, tough lumberjack from old time Seattle. Stop leering at me and let's get some work done."

"Only if this logger gets to jump you later. Wear those glasses to bed, Claire."

"Don't be silly. If I did that, I couldn't find them next time I want them."

He leaned close enough to kiss her. "If you wear them and nothing else, I'll return them for you."

"Maybe I will." She brushed her lips over his. "If you're very good and finish your homework without dillydallying."

"Oh, I do enjoy taking my time on certain activities." The sensual note in his deep voice made it clear what those were and so did the way he gazed at her for a long moment. Then, his attention reverted to the paperwork. "I can wait and so will you."

She removed the contract from his grasp and put it on the coffee table. She eased onto his lap, deliberately sitting upright on him. She shifted and unbuttoned his flannel shirt. "What if I don't feel like waiting after all?"

"You're a very bad influence on me." He groaned when she opened the shirt and slowly explored his chest, teasing the hard buttons of his nipples. "I did have good intentions."

"Oh, I know what they are." She adjusted her position slightly, rocking against him and feeling his response. She kissed him, her tongue exploring his mouth.

A few kisses and caresses later, he lifted her off him. He stood and picked her up, carrying her out of the room. Claire laced her arms around his neck, nipped his ear. "I thought you said something about ice-cream."

"Later. Much later. First, I'm taking my sexy librarian to bed and cataloging all her important parts."

Chapter Thirty-Seven

O ver breakfast, they discussed the offer on the condo and created a counter proposal that Claire promised to deliver to Robyn Jenkins later that morning. Then, Tony suggested they 'divide and conquer'. He went off to check in with Logan Turner on the upgrades at the apartment house. Determined to return to her usual routine, Claire headed for the local gym, stopping by her favorite espresso stand on the way back to the apartment house.

Since she'd already had scrambled eggs, toast, and fruit, she skipped the muffin top and just had a small, skinny orange mocha. She didn't go straight to her office but opted to find Bonnie in the kitchen off the community room. It was obviously her day off because she wore jeans and a sweatshirt instead of blue hospital scrubs.

Bonnie greeted Claire with a warm smile and continued inventorying the cupboards. "I'm headed to Costco this morning. Did you want me to pick up anything special? I already have Tony's and Connor's grocery lists."

"Better get me two boxes of chocolate doughnuts in case we get Conn's snowstorm. If we don't, I can always freeze one." Claire perched on a counter stool. "Talk to me. How was Thanksgiving? Black Friday? I saw Jerry starting to hang holiday lights. Are we getting a live tree this year or an artificial one?"

"I'll bring you up to date if you share the deets about your visit home." Bonnie moved to the next cupboard. "How was it? You always go to Mexico and Connor works overtime so I know you have issues. Leo Tolstoy wrote, "All happy families are alike; each unhappy family is unhappy in its own way." Was there drama?"

"Definitely, but it was surprisingly good." Claire eyed her engagement ring, recalling the way it served its purpose of protecting her from all slights, real and imagined. "My paternal grandparents made amends and told us about our biological father. He died before we were born and since our mother passed when we were small, she didn't have the opportunity to share anything about him."

Bonnie turned, concern mounting in her golden features. "I heard neither of you got along with your dad—"

"That was part of the drama." Claire shook her head. "He was our mom's husband but never acted as a father to us. And now, we'll continue to go no-contact with him and his current wife and not feel guilty about it. So, it's your turn. How were things here?"

After catching up on the gossip and agreeing to join the residents for dinner, she headed to her office where she found Sofia answering emails and happily drinking the mocha Claire had left her. Her spaniel, Oscar, snoozed under the college student's desk. Claire turned on her desktop computer and listened to the twenty-something's chatter about the weekend at home in Spokane with her family. When Sofia finally asked about the visit to Rocklin,

Claire provided a surface answer, not sharing any of the details she'd given Bonnie.

Sofia frowned thoughtfully, staring at the screen. "Claire, there's emails from two real estate agents I don't know how to answer."

"What are they?"

"Questions about showing Tony's condo. They want to know if it's really off the market with a pending offer."

"No, of course not. He did get one but it's not what he wants." Claire pulled out her phone and sent a quick text to Eileen, telling the office manager to make sure that nobody posted any signs on the condo. It was still on the market. "I'll show it this week to potential buyers."

"Sounds good. I'll let these two know and they can pass the word to other interested parties." A few minutes later, Sofia finished the emails. "Are you ready to talk about the applications for the new apartments?"

"Certainly. What did you find out about the applicants?"

For the next hour and a half, they reviewed the paperwork. Claire approved the selections Sofia made and added a few more of her own. The younger woman agreed to start checking references the next day, then left to go walk dogs with Fletcher. Claire locked up the office and headed to the garage.

When she drove out of the building, she grimaced. Frost still covered the grass on the front lawn. Purple-gray clouds hunkered on the horizon, what Gramps always called a 'snow sky' and he was never wrong. Of course, how could he be when Rocklin was in the foothills of the Cascades.

"If we get hammered by that winter storm Connor mentioned, I'm thumping him," Claire murmured. "I hate snow."

Despite slowing down and driving for the conditions, it

didn't take long to reach the Seattle brokerage. When she entered, Eileen was on the phone, so Claire waited to speak to her. Instead, she crossed to Robyn Jenkin's desk, handing her the counter-proposal for the condo. "Tony didn't accept your client's offer. Let them know."

"It was a good deal."

"Not good enough." Claire walked away. If the woman hadn't pushed the proverbial envelope and tried to take the condo off the market, Claire knew she'd have discussed the options with the associate. Now, she could read them for herself.

Eileen gave her an unobtrusive 'thumbs-up' as Claire approached. The older woman had dressed for the colder weather in black slacks, and a white sweater with a geometric design. "I've made three appointments back-to-back for you to show Tony's condo this afternoon. I sent emails to the associates that until there are signed acceptances on offers, no sales are "pending," and I told the other office managers to pass the word to their Designated Brokers."

"Great. I can always count on you, Eileen." Claire wheeled a chair close to the older woman's L-shaped reception area. "Bring me up to speed on what else happened this weekend. Then, I'll head to my office and get some work done before I go to Tony's old place."

—————

Tony walked through the new apartment building, amazed at how quickly Logan Turner completed different parts of the renovations. Even with a holiday weekend, the construction crew finished hanging drywall on the third floor and were hard at work doing it in bedrooms on the second floor. He followed the sound of tapping and discovered a crew laying strips of vinyl wood-looking planks in an apartment on the top floor.

A petite redhead in a U-Dub sweatshirt, loose fitting jeans, and work boots was obviously in charge. Tony recognized her as Fancy Flannagan, Connor's girlfriend, and nodded a greeting. "It's coming together. What's next? How can I help?"

"The insulated drapes Claire ordered haven't arrived." Adjusting the toolbelt around her waist, Fancy narrowed her brown eyes. "Did Logan talk to you about the heating system? The old HVAC needs to be replaced. It's not going to hold up to what the new tenants will need."

"I'll check in with him before I go. Let's do a walk-through and you can tell me what else you need."

Fancy led the way out of the bedroom. "My crew is painting on the fourth floor. We'll skip that for now." She gestured to the cream walls in the living-room. "We opted for neutral colors, alternating white, beige and earth tones in each apartment. We're switching them around so the apartments don't look identical, but the tenants will be able to add individual touches the way that they've done at Claire's other places."

"Makes sense." They walked down the hall to the kitchen, and she pointed out where the appliances would be placed when they arrived. Tony began taking notes on his phone while she spoke to follow up on various deliveries. He hoped his surprise didn't show when Fancy said she'd be moving out of Logan's construction trailer where she currently stayed into the two-bedroom apartment for the maintenance person as soon as it was ready.

When they finished their tour, he tracked down Logan to get the details about a new heating system. They agreed the initial purchase would be expensive, but it'd save money in the long run. The parking lot was due to be repaved next week, but it might have to wait if the weather turned against them. Logan didn't have a problem with Fancy camping in the construction trailer on-site, but her safety concerned him since the new decorative cyclone fence around the property wasn't installed yet.

Tony promised to call the fencing company too. It'd taken longer than he'd expected to check on progress at the building, so he didn't stop for lunch, opting for a drive-through burger on the way to the Eastside brokerage. It didn't take long to reach the office in a Bellevue strip mall. Bright holiday lights blinked around the doors and windows. Several of the associates helped Vincent Wong, the office manager, arrange holiday decorations around the room, including the snow-flocked, artificial tree.

Clusters of plants separated the three long tables providing an aura of privacy. A comfortable conversation area took up the center of the room. Tony scanned the area. "Now, all we need is Santa and his sleigh."

"Zelda told us to forget that because the reindeer aren't housebroken." Vincent grinned at him. "We're going to win the toy drive this year. Dominique is bringing the boxes tomorrow."

"Sounds amazing." Amused, Tony sauntered toward the back offices. "Let me check in with her and make sure we're on the same page about the closings. We want everyone to have a great holiday, and I'll be sending along the info to the accountant for December bonuses."

The news prompted a round of applause which brightened Tony's day even more. He found Zelda Torres at her desk frowning at the computer screen. "Hi there. What's happening and how can I help?"

———

Showing the condo to three sets of potential buyers took up the afternoon. Shortly after five p.m., when Claire left the waterfront building, she knew a bidding war was in the offing, welcome news for any real estate broker. She found herself singing along with the carols on the radio. Instead of returning to the office, she headed for the apartment house in Magnolia. She sent a quick text to Eileen to close when the last associate finished sales floor hours.

Holiday lights blinked bright red, green, blue, and gold when she pulled into the underground garage. She preferred the white, elegant gleam of icicle lights but the residents always chose more traditional ones, and Claire wanted them to be happy. She parked, gathered her coat, purse, and laptop bag before locking the Navigator. Before she reached the elevator, Tony arrived, and she waited for him to join her.

He greeted her with a kiss. "Lots of news to share. How was your day?"

"Busy." Claire let him take the laptop bag from her. "We're having dinner downstairs so we can share everything we know about the business later."

"Sounds like a winner."

In the apartment, he put her laptop and purse in the study while she fed the kitten. A few minutes later, they were on the way back downstairs. As soon as they reached the dining room, she smelled butternut macaroni and cheese, one of her favorite comfort foods on a cold winter night. She was so ready for it even if she'd have to do extra time at the gym the next day.

When they returned upstairs, she listened to his update about the renovations at the new apartment house. He promised to check prices on a new HVAC system to heat the place and to follow up on deliveries as well as kicking butt on the fence company. She told him about giving the counteroffer to Robyn and then showing the condo to other people.

"There may be a bidding war in the offing," Claire said. "We'll find out in the next few days. I had to drop a note to Eileen to run interference when Robyn thought she could short-circuit other offers on the place."

"She's certainly pushing the wrong person." Tony put an arm around Claire's shoulders. "Should I be afraid you're going to orchestrate her departure too?"

"Not yet. She's actually a very good associate when she remembers who is in charge and she's not. Eileen will straighten her out before Christmas and Svetlana dropped me an email to say Scott has already decorated the Lake Maynard office for the holidays."

"I'll look forward to seeing it on Friday."

"And you can tell me about it when I get home that night." She leaned forward, picked up the remote and turned on the flatscreen, before cuddling closer to Tony. "I'll watch a couple episodes of *Law and Order* with you before I pack to go to the hotel tomorrow afternoon."

Halfway through the first episode, Felix woke up from his nap in the recliner. The tuxedo kitten strolled across the room, jumped onto the couch, and snuggled onto Claire's lap. She petted his long, black fur which prompted him to begin purring. It was a lovely night at home. Despite her best intentions, she dozed off during a long bout of commercials.

When she woke, she discovered Tony had switched over to the news. The forecaster blathered constantly, providing a winter storm warning. He predicted several inches of snow in the Seattle area for the next week.

Claire glared at the screen. "Did you tell that fool I have plans and to keep his damned snow in the mountains where it belongs?"

"I'll let you know if that works, sweetheart." He kissed her forehead. "Meantime, you should probably put off your shopping extravaganza for a week if he's right about the weather."

Chapter Thirty-Eight

F rost covered the grass, and she knew there would be black ice on the road when she drove to the gym. Tony had loaded her suitcase in the Navigator for her. He'd told her to reconsider the shopping trip if the weather changed and she promised she would. Meantime, Claire followed her usual routine, ignoring the occasional snow flurries because the flakes melted before they reached the ground. It wasn't quite cold enough for them to stick or accumulate.

She headed out to the tiny house village when she finished her shift at the apartment house, arriving in time for lunch, tomato soup and grilled cheese sandwiches. She brought Blanche up to speed on the Rocklin family soap opera. "I didn't have a clue Lee wasn't our biological father—"

"If he was married to your mom when you and Connor were born, then he's your legal one according to Washington State law. I've heard enough to know that when I do marriage counseling. You'd have to get a DNA test to prove otherwise and I'm not sure how you go about that when your bio-dad is deceased." Blanche rose and went after the coffee pot to refill their cups. "What are you going to do about it?"

"Continue to go no-contact with Lee and his wife." Claire dunked her sandwich in the cup of soup. "I am staying in touch with his parents. Connor and I agreed to call them Grandpa and Grandma. We're also reconnecting with our step-sibs. They've grown into human beings, and their kids are great."

"Does that mean you're going to Rocklin for Christmas?"

Claire nodded. "I'm giving away my trip to Mexico to which ever Designated Broker has the most sales this month. Svetlana sent pictures of her holiday in Cancun to her cousin, Natasha. She and Ryan emailed funny but slightly snarky comments to me because their agents are saying that my brokerages are better than the Hollister ones."

Blanche laughed. "You'll undoubtedly hear more about it this week. When is Natasha arriving from Spokane?"

"I'm not sure." Claire drew out her phone to check emails. "I told her I'd pick her up at the airport. O.M.G., this sucks."

"What?"

"Natasha cancelled because of the upcoming blizzard. It hasn't even hit over there yet, but her husband is having kittens about her flying out because she won't be able to get home on Friday."

"Cut the guy some slack, Claire. Tasha is our age and in her first trimester. No wonder she's being cautious." Blanche stopped and stared out the window. "Then again, maybe she has the right idea."

"What are you saying?" Claire swiveled in the chair and followed her friend's gaze. Huge white snowflakes drifted by, and the intensity increased as they watched. "Well, this sucks. I guess I'd better head for home too."

"Do that. Drive safe. I'll email the sisters to say that we'll meet up next week. Drop a note to the hotel to change the reservations."

"Great idea." Claire stood and hugged Blanche. "Thanks. I'll call when I get there."

"Please do."

A half inch of snow already covered the ground when Claire walked out to her vehicle. She wasn't super excited about driving miles in the snow, but she'd paid extra to have four-wheel-drive when she bought the Navigator. That meant it was safer in bad weather than many other SUVs. Before she started her rig, she contacted the hotel. Accustomed to plans changing with the western Washington weather, the desk clerk was surprisingly cooperative about moving the reservation for the shopping party to a later date.

Her phone buzzed, and Claire saw a text from Tony. He'd already let the office managers know to close early and wanted to know if she was okay. She answered she was heading out and would meet him at the apartment.

Needle sized snowflakes filtered across the parking lot, landing on the ornamental shrubs, and beginning to cover the pavement. Tony glanced at the sky and the gray clouds piling up on the horizon. As a boy, he'd learned how to judge the weather conditions in the winter, and things would get a lot worse before they were better. Luckily, Claire had decided to opt to play it safe, and he didn't have to raise hell and put props under it as her grandfather used to say. She'd have a serious meltdown if he insisted she cancel her nonsensical shopping trip for the duration of the snowstorm.

On his way to the Hummer, he received a text from Logan Turner telling him they had a power outage at the new apartment building and Fancy still intended to camp in the construction trailer. She was a grown woman, Tony thought, and could make her own choices. He called the younger man. "Got your text. What's the issue?"

"She doesn't admit it, but I've got three kids, and I know she needs help even if she won't admit it." Concern mounted in Logan's voice. "You gotta fix this. She can't be here alone."

"Talk slow, Turner. I don't understand."

"I think she's pregnant and I don't want her up to her ass in snow. What if she falls? What do I do?"

"Why do you think she is?" Tony listened while the construction supervisor described what he'd witnessed during the last week from Fancy refusing to lift anything heavy, avoiding painting, and then he'd seen her throwing up when she smelled coffee in the break area. "All right. We'll agree something is happening and I'll take her home with me. Be prepared for a shitstorm when your crew gets back to work."

"I don't care about that. Fancy and I've teamed up on several projects and I'd hate to see anything happen to her."

"Thanks for looking out for her." Tony put away his phone and flagged down George Delaney when he came out of the brokerage. "Need your help."

"You got it, Top. What do you want?"

Tony provided what he still considered a quick sitrep. "So, I'm taking her home with me."

"Is that a smart thing to do? Won't the boss have a fit

when she gets there and finds another woman in the apartment? We could take this Fancy to a motel."

"No guarantee we'd find one with a vacancy on the way to our place. Follow me."

"You got it," George repeated, but he still looked wary as he strode toward his Ford pickup. "You have a lot to learn about women, Top, but I'll watch your six although I won't stop the boss from kicking your ass."

Because of the snow covering the road and beginning to pile up in drifts, it took longer than usual to drive to the apartment house in the north end of Seattle. Buildings around it were still dark which meant the power wasn't restored yet. Tony wasn't surprised to see Fancy sitting in her van, running the engine to get warm. He took a moment to swap out his dress shoes for the old combat boots he kept with his go-bag in the back of the Hummer.

Then, he walked across to tap on the driver's window. When she opened it, he scanned her. "Got your gear in there? Let's roll."

"What are you talking about?" She shot a brown-eyed glare at him. "I'm fine. I told you I stay in the construction trailer."

"Not tonight. Not in a winter storm that's packing feet of snow." Tony planted his hands on the window-frame. "You have a choice. Either you follow me to Claire's place, or I call Connor. I'll tell him what's up with you and where you are."

"What's up?" She sputtered for a moment. "I don't know what you're—"

"Don't *Bravo, Sierra* me, little girl. I've served with a lot of women, and I know what a pregnant one looks like with or without a baby bump." He looked past her at the empty passenger seat. He turned, waved at George. When the former Army Ranger joined them, Tony gestured toward the trailer. "Get her stuff."

"I don't believe this." Fury mounted on her face. "Who the hell do you think you are?"

"Your future brother-in-law and my niece or nephew isn't freezing to death."

Tears welled up in her eyes. "You really suck."

"I know." He'd lived long enough to know a lot of women cried when they were upset or frustrated or angry, so Tony patted her shoulder. "We'll go to Claire's, and I won't say a word to Conn. You can tell him in your own time."

"And Claire? She never keeps secrets from him."

"I'll tell her to keep this one."

George came back with a carry-all and a sleeping bag. He opened the passenger door and put them inside on the seat. "Is this it? I didn't see anything else that looked personal."

Fancy wiped her nose on the sleeve of her work shirt. "That's it. Logan and his crew chief are in and out all the time, so I didn't make a mess. I have to lock the trailer."

"Give me your key and Delaney will."

In a few minutes, she was following his Hummer to the street and George brought up the rear in his pickup. The snow worsened as Tony drove further south into the city, increasing to almost two inches on the ground. He was glad he lived with Claire closer to the north end, rather than still being in his waterfront condo downtown.

The roads would be a sheet of ice before long if they weren't already and because the storm was coming from the south, the Army base close to Tacoma was undoubtedly in the thick of the onslaught. Luckily, the plows were already out, clearing and sanding the streets.

When they reached the apartment building, he stopped on the street and allowed Fancy's van to enter the underground garage first. Tony switched off the Hummer's engine and went to check in with George. "Thanks for the help. You okay driving home?"

"No worries, Top. I only live a few blocks from here. I'll hunker down for the next couple of days."

"Us too." Tony watched the other veteran pull away and then returned to the Hummer. Fancy had parked her van in Connor's extra slot and waited near it. Claire's red Navigator was already in her assigned spot and Tony drew up beside it. Before he joined Fancy, he touched the hood and discovered it was still warm. So, she hadn't been here that long.

Collecting his briefcase and laptop, he locked up the Hummer before he took Fancy's carry-all from her. "I think we must be having dinner upstairs because Bonnie said breakfast was the community meal today. Let's go see what we can find."

"I don't know about this." Fancy glanced anxiously around the garage. "Did you text Claire and let her know I was coming?"

"Not when I was driving in that crappy weather. She won't mind."

"I hope you're right."

———

When she arrived home, Claire changed into jeans and a white turtleneck sweater, trading her stilettos for ballet flats. Since the shopping trip was on hold, she unpacked her suitcase and considered sending a volley of texts to Tony to learn where he was but decided to wait. She didn't want to distract him while he was driving. Instead, she took care of the cat.

Checking out the refrigerator, she discovered an oblong cake pan filled with Pedro Ramirez's fabulous chicken enchiladas. She put them in the oven to bake for an hour. Obviously, Mrs. Nayaka's crew had come to clean before the weather changed and Claire was one of the beneficiaries of their efforts since they'd also delivered dinner.

She heard the door open and left the kitchen to greet him, Felix an eager escort. Everyone needed a watch cat, she decided, amused. Claire stopped, surprised to see Fancy in front of Tony. "Well, hello there. How are you?"

"Imposing." Fancy jerked her head toward Tony. "I was fine staying in the construction trailer. He insisted I come here."

"Yes, I did." Putting down his briefcase and laptop bag, Tony gestured toward the kitchen. "Go make yourself some tea and warm up."

The younger woman reluctantly followed his directions, stomping down the hall with Felix chasing her bootlace.

When they were alone, Claire took a deep breath. He'd overstepped the boundaries again, bringing an overnight guest without so much as consulting her but she wouldn't throw a fit. Not now, not yet, not in the hallway, not when her brother's ex could overhear. She and Tony didn't argue in front of other people. It started with the associates and other staff at the brokerages three years ago and now he seemed to think it included her brother's ex-girlfriend.

Claire gestured toward the guestroom. "Obviously, we need to talk. Let's do it in private."

He nodded and followed her. In the bedroom, he put the satchel on the queen-size bed next to several bags from her shopping trip in Rocklin. "Okay, say it."

Claire studied his rugged features, trying to analyze his emotions. "Why did you bring Fancy here?"

"Power's out at the new apartment building. It's locked up and so is Turner's trailer." Tony folded his arms across his broad chest. "Logan called me. He was worried about her, and I said I'd take care of it."

"And you certainly did." Claire walked toward him, reading the tension in his stiff shoulders and tight jaw. The decision hadn't been easy on him, but he'd stepped up to do what he considered the right thing. "Thank you. I agree she needed someone, but I don't know if it had to be us. Still, I appreciate you looking after her. What else?"

He hesitated, shifting the canvas carry-all from one hand to the other. "We're guessing, but she might be expecting."

"What?" Claire froze, her thoughts spinning when she recalled Fancy claiming she and Connor had a fight and split up earlier that month. Her brother had said she was pissed about something but didn't admit what. He was a grown man. They'd be thirty-five in less than three weeks. Why hadn't he practiced safe sex? And if he had, what happened?

"Connor." Claire hissed his name in a bare whisper. "I'm killing him."

"Not yet." Tony kissed her. "Let Fancy do the honors. I promised we wouldn't tell him."

"All right." Claire stepped into his embrace. "If it's real, I'm killing him. Since he won't be home from the cop shop before morning at the earliest because of the snow emergency, he's got a temporary reprieve. After that—"

"You're killing him." Tony kissed her again. "I'll help."

Chapter Thirty-Nine

A fter Tony left the carry-all in the guestroom, he went to the kitchen to finish preparing dinner. Claire moved the presents she'd already bought, along with the wrapping paper, brightly colored tissue, and holiday bags into her study. Thanks to Mrs. Nayaka's crew, the guestroom was ready for company and so was the bathroom next door once Claire moved her dry lingerie to the drawers in her walk-in closet.

It only needed a few more things to make Fancy comfortable and Claire quickly added those before she returned to the kitchen. She found Fancy setting the table for the three of them while Tony added the final touches to the green salad.

"What do the two of you want to drink?" Claire poured water into the brewer on the counter. "I'm having coffee."

"Sounds good." Tony carried the large bowl over to the table, then returned to the refrigerator for dressing. "I'll have a cup too."

"Another decaf peppermint tea, please." Fancy gestured

toward the window. "There's two more inches of snow already. The roads are going to be a mess by morning."

"The entire west side of the state shuts down when the weather goes gunny bag." Claire added a dash of Irish cream to her mug. She held up the bottle and Tony nodded, so she put a shot in his too. "I'm glad you both arrived before it got worse."

"And your shopping trip with the sorority sisters?" Tony opened the oven and removed the casserole dish. "What did you decide about that, sweetheart?"

"Next week. I moved the reservation at the hotel and Blanche contacted the rest of our crew. Safety first."

"Good choice."

His comment earned a scathing glare from Fancy. "I'm amazed you didn't order Claire to cancel her plans."

"He didn't need to." Claire carried a ceramic trivet over and put it in the center of the table, waiting for Tony to follow with the chicken and cheese enchiladas. "We grew up in a logging town in the foothills, Fancy. When winter storms hit, we head for shelter. That's why I beat the two of you here."

"And had time to start supper." Tony brought over their drinks. "Let's eat."

Claire sat down and began filling their plates. When she passed one to Fancy, the younger woman stared at the engagement ring. "I didn't know you two were—"

"Tony decided three years was long enough to carry around my ring and finally handed it over." Claire passed the next plate to him. "And since I'm selling his condo, it was my turn to be the boss. I decided he's living with me until the deal closes on the house he's buying in Everett. Has Logan talked to you about that project yet?"

"No." Fancy sipped her tea. "We've been so busy with the current one."

"Tony will show you the plans after dinner while I do dishes." Claire took the salad bowl from him. "If I don't have a decent closet, I'm staying here."

He chuckled, leaned over to kiss her. "It's on the list, sweetie, right next to the nursery Mom says we need."

Claire heaved a sigh, piling spinach leaves on her plate. "I love your mother, but the woman has 'grandma' dreams and schemes."

"And I've told her it will take a year or two before we're ready." Tony winked at Fancy. "We'll let you and Conn do the honors first."

Fancy frowned, baffled. "I don't understand. She's your mom, not his or Claire's."

"She was our stepmother for two years until she dumped our legal dad on his butt after he cheated on her too many times." Claire passed the bowl of salad to Fancy. "Hasn't Conn ever told you about our dysfunctional family?"

Fancy shook her head, focusing on adding salad to her plate. "Not much. He said he went to military school when he was a kid. Stayed there through high school, then went to college on a scholarship."

"He was in ROTC, reserve officer training." Tony cut into his enchilada. "When he graduated, he entered the Army as a second lieutenant. He served eight years and was a senior Captain when he resigned his commission. We both were tired of going to war."

"Tony was only seventeen when he enlisted in the Army. He took early retirement three years ago and came to work with me." Claire added a spoonful of ranch dressing to the salad on her plate. "We'll be snowed in for a few days. I'll tell you what you need to know about Conn's and my childhood. It will give you a clearer picture of what you can expect when you meet the rest of the Rocklin contingent at Christmas."

"Okay, but don't expect me to return the favor. I grew up in foster care, aged out when I was eighteen and started doing construction work. When I had enough money, I tracked down my older brother, Mike here in Washington state," Fancy said. "So, I was always good with Connor not divulging much of his baggage."

"Sounds fair." Claire deliberately changed the subject to the progress on the new apartment building. Soon she had Fancy describing the plans she had for the two-bedroom suite she'd have as the maintenance person. She'd handle the general upkeep of the place for the residents.

Her duties would include supervising Mrs. Nayaka's cleaning crew when they took care of the communal areas in addition to the various apartments. Fancy would handle any ad-hoc painting, electrical, plumbing, and small carpentry repairs. She'd also resolve the tenants' concerns whenever possible, taking care of clogged drains, showers, and toilets, changing locks, replacing keys, and acting as a liaison with Claire and Tony.

—————

Three hours later, Tony stood at the picture window in the living room watching the neighborhood fill up with even more snow. The area had grown quiet because most people knew enough to head for home and stay off the icy streets. Holiday lights on different houses shone. Almost six inches of thick white snow on roofs, trees and lawns reminded him of winter Christmas cards. He heard soft footsteps and glanced over his shoulder to see Claire. "How is our guest?"

"Asleep." She came across the room and stood next to him. "Usually, Fancy never complains but I don't think she was sleeping well in that trailer, so she was a bit snarky tonight."

"I texted Logan and told him to move her new apartment to the top of the list as soon as the crew gets back to work once the snow melts." Tony put an arm around Claire's waist. "You're being the soul of patience tonight, but I know when I've screwed up, sweetheart."

"You? The man who prides himself on being totally in charge of the world as we know it?" She heaved a sigh and rested her head against his shoulder. "Okay, spill it. I'm still hung up on having an unexpected house guest. What else have you done? What am I supposed to do about it?"

"You already did." He held her closer. "Delaney and Fancy both wanted to know if I asked you about bringing her here and I didn't. I just decided and followed through like I was still in the Army."

"Wasn't this one of those occasions that Connor talks about? He says sometimes it's better to ask forgiveness than permission."

"I didn't consult you and it's your apartment."

"Yours too for the duration." She nipped his ear. "What would you have done if you called and I said, 'no'? Would you have respected my decision or—?"

"No." He shook his head, then met Claire's dark blue gaze. "I'd have figured there'd be consequences, but I still would have brought Fancy here so we could look after her. Even if she and Conn aren't together, she's family and I couldn't turn my back on her. I'm a grown man. You didn't chew me out."

"That doesn't mean I won't when I've had time to think about it." She remained in the circle of his arm, but he felt her stiffening and caught the note of censure in her voice. "You dissed me tonight, Tony. Other people shouldn't have had to give you a heads-up that I deserved respect and consideration. You had time to call or text me, but—"

"I didn't." He tipped up her chin. "What happens now? Are you kicking me out?"

"Don't be silly." She kissed him. "You screwed up big-time and I don't know what the end result will be, but I think you'd better take me to bed and beg forgiveness."

He traced her mouth with his thumb. "I can do that."

"And you're not getting back this ring." She waved her left hand, providing a solid view of the diamonds and sapphires. "You always do what you think is right. Yes, it's irritating when you overstep the boundaries, but I want to be with a man who has a moral code rather than one who bends like a willow."

"Anybody in particular?"

"Mike Flannagan's a good guy when it comes to business, but apparently, he has crappy taste in women. His latest girlfriend told Fancy that she'd 'overstayed her welcome' when she was at Mike's house for a few days after she got back from Ocean Shores. It's why she was camping at the construction trailer. She felt guilty for visiting her brother."

"Why do I think you're going to intervene, sweetness?"

"Somebody has to." Claire lifted her chin. "If I was between a rock and a hard place, Connor would insist on me moving in with him for weeks, months or even years. What about you? If we weren't together, would you allow a girlfriend to kick me, your once-upon-a-time, stepsister to the curb?"

"Never." Tony kissed her. "And I wouldn't be with someone that shallow or petty for long. Conn says you measure the men you've dated against me and find them wanting. It's a two-way street. No other woman holds a candle to you. I love you, Claire Rocklin. And someday, you'll admit you're in love with me."

"I wish it were that easy."

"It's not as hard as you're making it."

———

Wednesday morning, she was the first one out of bed. Claire drew on a blue fleece robe over her nightgown and headed for the kitchen to brew a large cup of coffee. Felix joined her and she fed him. With her weekend box of doughnuts in hand, she went to see what was on TV at this hour. She put her mug and the carton on the coffee table and crossed to the picture windows to open the drapes.

Snow covered the streets, houses, lawns, bushes, and trees. Silence reigned, not much of a surprise because everything closed when Seattle was blasted with a big winter storm. After she grabbed her favorite crocheted throw, she sank down on the couch, picked up the remote. She turned on the news and listened to the talking heads announce school closures including the colleges and the University of Washington. Roads, especially those with steep hills, were shut down too. So were some stores and other businesses, not just their brokerages.

Felix cuddled up with her. She stroked the kitten's long black fur while she contemplated her future. She admired and respected Tony Baldusi, but she had a feeling it wasn't reciprocal. Yes, he rocked her world in the bedroom and anywhere else they had fantastic sex. And how long could she be with a man who gave her multiple orgasms and nothing else?

Okay, so that wasn't quite true. He supported whatever she decided to do with the brokerages and understood when she wanted to rehab housing for seniors. He also had wonderful taste in jewelry – the engagement ring was another sign of that. He'd undoubtedly come up with something spectacular for her thirty-fifth birthday in three weeks.

Granted, she liked the fact that he did what he said he was going to do and said what he was going to do. How would she live with him for the next fifty years when he thought that made him the boss of everything and forgot to consult her?

She still hadn't decided when he arrived an hour later, looking incredibly sexy in faded blue jeans and a gray T-shirt that clung to his broad chest, wide shoulders, and muscled arms. Holding a cup of freshly brewed coffee, he sat down next to her. "So, what does the city look like?"

"A winter wonderland." Claire held out the box of chocolate doughnuts and he snagged one. "We're home until it warms up and the snow melts."

"And both of us are going to be bored out of our minds." He sipped coffee. "I'll appoint you recreational director and ask what the plans are."

"I'm not sure who is making lunch today, so I guess we'll hit the community room and find out. After that we can talk to Bonnie about helping with holiday decorations. We always put up a Christmas tree downstairs and start collecting donations for the Baker City toy drive. Sofia and I will process applicants for the new apartment building."

"And me? What's your plan for me?"

"Oh, I'm sure you'll need to update online listings and

organize the advertisements for the upcoming monthly brochure. Which listings do you want to feature?"

While they watched the news and drank coffee, they discussed the real estate business. When the newscasters began to repeat their stories, Claire turned off the TV. Tony went to make waffles for breakfast with Felix's help, and she returned to the bedroom. She took a leisurely shower, shampooing her hair, shaving her armpits and legs. No rush today, she thought. And she didn't have to dress up for work, so she opted for blue jeans and an old U-Dub sweatshirt over a T-shirt.

Claire found Fancy and Tony sitting at the kitchen table, reviewing his plans for the Everett house. He stood and went to make a waffle for her. Meantime, Fancy continued scrolling through the slides, making notes.

Taking a fresh cup of coffee with her, Claire sat down next to the younger woman. "Have you touched base with Logan about timeframes yet?"

"No, but I will." Narrowing her golden-brown eyes, Fancy studied the picture of the primary suite. "I'm not sure how he plans to include a walk-in closet like the one you have here. What if we divided the small bedroom next to it? Use half of it for the new closet and the other half to expand the ensuite?"

"Where do you plan to put the nursery?" Tony asked. "If we don't have one when my mother visits, she'll lecture us six ways from Sunday."

"Easy. It goes on the other side of the main. For now, we put in an archway and create a sitting room until you start having babies." Fancy drew a quick sketch in her notebook. "What do you think, Claire?"

"I'm barely considering living with Tony in the boonies. I'm not even thinking about kids yet." It wasn't quite true, but she didn't want to share her fantasies of a happy-ever-after future with him. Heat rose in her cheeks when he measured her with one of his long, steady looks. "Damn it, Tony. I'm serious."

"Of course, you are, sweetheart." He brought over a plate with a steaming waffle, two rashers of bacon on the side. "Syrup's on the table. Drink your orange juice. Eat your breakfast while I contemplate ways to change your mind. I'd love a little girl just like you."

Chapter Forty

The weather remained cold and intermittent snow fell. When they went to the community room in the early afternoon, Claire discovered Harry Gamack had purchased a live evergreen. It stood by the windows in the large dining room, and the residents had already begun bringing in lights, garlands, and decorations for their *real* tree.

Concern over Claire's feelings melted when she asked if she could borrow the artificial, flocked, white one from storage and Bonnie promptly agreed. She sent it to Claire's apartment with her husband while Fancy inventoried the tote-boxes in the supply closet, looking for appropriately colored ornaments to create a fashion statement.

Tony claimed to be bored before dinner, so Claire gave him a shopping list and sent him to the large hardware store two miles away. Jerry, the maintenance man went with him because Bonnie wanted fried chicken from the local fast-food place if it was open and from the gas station-grocery deli if it wasn't. Slogging through the snow would definitely provide entertainment for the two combat veterans.

Upstairs, Claire stationed the white, snow-flocked, pre-lit Christmas tree in front of the picture window in the living room. Fancy twined a red tinsel garland through the branches while Felix sat on the arm of the couch and provided supervision. He jumped down when Claire began to hang the red bird-shaped ornaments she'd inherited from her maternal grandmother on the branches. He pounced on one and dragged it halfway across the carpet.

Laughing, Fancy went to retrieve the decoration from the half-grown kitten and brought it back. "I can't believe Tony and Jerry want to hike for miles through the snow, dragging a plastic toboggan while they hunt for stores that are open regardless of the weather. What's up with that?"

"PTSD." Claire placed another cardinal on a branch. "Tony and I usually work six days a week, twelve to sixteen hours each day. I like to rest up on Saturday mornings when he plays golf with Conn. We spend afternoons together."

"And today?"

"Hey, after helping Jerry clean the media and game rooms, plus scrubbing down the big group kitchen, shoveling snow off the walkways and then taking the dogs to Discovery Park with Fletcher, Tony and Jerry were freaking out. Bonnie is coming up with a long list of chores for them to do during the next week until the weather clears. She says the other guys may be ready to help them tomorrow."

"Connor doesn't have that issue." Fancy started to hang red glass bulbs on the fir tree. "He never talks about his military service."

"He volunteers to work extra shifts at the cop shop all the time." Claire kept her tone even as they continued decorating the tree. "When he's home, he cooks meals for us and desserts for the residents. On his days off, he—"

"Always has a million things to do." Fancy stopped and turned to stare at Claire. "When we lived together, he either wanted to help organize donations at the food bank or planned to play basketball with the kids at the neighborhood court or inspected and cleaned the apartment even if Mrs. Nayaka's people already had."

"Exactly. He's like Tony. They both have to stay busy, so they don't remember being in combat." It was Claire's turn to rescue a tiny red and white classic metal Santa figurine from the kitten and bring it back to the tree. "What did you want to do when you lived with my brother?"

"Be with him." Fancy shrugged. "It wasn't a big deal to go to the food bank or the gym, but I hated cleaning a place that already was immaculate. It reminded me of some of the crapfests I went through in foster care, so I'd leave him to it and take in a movie or go get groceries, although he always bitched when I didn't buy name-brand items and got generic things close to their expiration dates."

"Was that a residue from your past?"

"Sure. I lived on the street for a while and did my share of dumpster diving. I'll eat just about anything as long as it's not moldy or rotten and stale food doesn't bother me." Fancy tilted her head to one side, as she paused to consider that. "I'll have to get my shit together because there's no way my kid is going to suffer what I did. If something happens to me, I don't want my baby to end up in the system. Will you look after—?"

"Always." Claire started toward the other woman to hug her and then stopped, seeing Fancy's clenched fists and tight jaw. "Tony and I will always have your six. When the snow melts off, we'll visit my lawyer and put it in writing."

A tear trickled down Fancy's cheek and she blinked hard, more tears still swimming in the large brown eyes. "He said you'd let me be the one to tell Conn, but I didn't believe Tony."

"It's your business and my brother's, not mine. I'll just do whatever you want me to do."

"Thank you."

"No worries." Claire hung the last cardinal in place and stepped back to look at the dozen bright red birds. According to Grandma, cardinals were seen as loved ones visiting from Heaven. Every Christmas, she'd reminded the family that the birds were spiritual messengers and protectors, showing up just when they were needed most.

I thought she was talking about our mom. I didn't know she included our biological father. And now, I'll expect them as well as Gramps and Grandma when I need help.

———

Snow crunched under their boots as they walked through the neighborhood toward the various businesses. The moon shone overhead creating even more light. Pulling the large sled he'd borrowed behind him, Tony relaxed as he breathed in the cold night air. "I could have driven the Hummer, but I needed more exercise."

"Not a problem." Jerry sauntered beside him. "Sitting around and watching people hang ornaments on that tree was making me nuts."

"Preaching to the proverbial choir." They kept walking. "Claire wants us to buy more pet-safe ice melting stuff for the walkways. I don't know if we'll be able to find it or not at the hardware store or have to go to a bigger outlet tomorrow."

"If we don't, we'll get it later this week." Jerry chuckled. "The big deal is finding fried chicken at the deli. No guarantees the grocery is even open tonight."

Josie Malone

"We'll find out soon," Tony said, spotting lights from the strip mall in the distance.

A short time later, they walked through the plowed parking lot toward the hardware store. Tony recognized the truck in front of it. "Looks like Conn is already here."

"Let's catch a ride home with him."

"Works for me." Tony put the sled in the back of the rig, and they paused on the sidewalk to stomp snow off their boots. When they entered, he spotted Connor at the register. "I know what your sister wants, so what are you buying?"

Connor turned toward them. In jeans, boots, and a heavy jacket over his sweatshirt, as usual, he'd changed at the cop shop when he finished work. "Figured we'd be low on de-icer and Claire always worries someone might fall after we get hammered with snow, especially when the sidewalks freeze around the building. Thought I'd stop and pick up more because extra weight helps give my pickup traction. What are you guys up to?"

"Going stir-crazy at the apartment house," Jerry admitted. "If she can't get to the hospital tomorrow, Bonnie will have a mile-long, 'honey-do' list for me."

"If I don't get called in to work, I'll help." Connor gestured to the cart filled with several plastic buckets. "What else do we need?"

Tony pulled the note from his coat pocket and began reading. Items ranged from various sizes of batteries to clothesline to removeable hooks for hanging pictures to several bags of kitty litter. "She only has one kitten so why does he need so much and why does it have to be the old-fashioned, clay kind?"

The cashier, an older, silver-haired woman in a flannel shirt and jeans grinned appreciatively. "It works for traction, honey. Put it under your tires and you can get back on

336

the road. Plus, it doesn't hurt puppy paws like some of the commercial de-icers do. What else?"

"Silver, red and gold Christmas garlands to decorate the apartment. No other colors." Tony grimaced. "She under-lined that and used exclamation points. What is she thinking?"

"She's a fashionista." Connor shrugged. "And it's your fault. You're the one who said she has to visit family for the holidays instead of lying on a tropical beach in Mexico. Be afraid, bro, be very afraid. This is your first real Christmas together. It's going to get worse."

"That's right." Jerry slapped Tony on the back. "Wait until after the wedding next spring. Your life is over as you know it. Claire is nearly as high-maintenance as my wife."

"She's worse than Bonnie ever thought of being." Connor glanced toward the front door. "Better get started. It's snowing again."

The trip home would have been a winter adventure except Connor had already installed chains on the truck's tires. He also drove for the conditions which meant it took almost an hour to reach the apartment house, slightly less time than it had to walk to the stores. Jerry had bought out the fried chicken along with the usual fixings from the deli at the gas station – grocery. He told them if it took any longer to reach the building, he'd break open the provisions, so they didn't starve.

When they arrived at the underground garage, Connor pulled into the spot next to Fancy's van. Relief swept across his handsome features. "I'm glad she's home. I was worried she was stuck somewhere at a construction site."

"You're still on her shit list." Tony opened the passenger door. "She's staying with Claire and me."

"That's fine. It's a lot closer than wherever else she's

been." Connor switched off the engine. "When she's pissed, she doesn't answer my phone calls, and she blocks my emails."

"Wow." Jerry looked him up and down. "What did you do?"

"Kept my job. I'm a cop. Fancy believes the crap she sees on the TV news and worries too much about it."

And you don't worry enough, Tony thought, but he didn't say that. He'd spent sufficient time in war zones. He didn't need to risk his life on city streets trying to rescue people in bad situations. He'd much rather help Claire operate real estate brokerages. It was less 'life and death' and more everyday living when he helped find new homes for their clients.

———

When they finished decorating the tree, Claire pulled out pints of ice-cream, leaving Tony's favorite butter-pecan in the freezer. They settled into the living-room to watch Lenny Briscoe solve a murder or two before they figured out what to fix for supper. As Tony's mother, Maria often quoted, "Life is short, eat dessert first!"

After Claire muted the first long stream of commercials, she heard Tony call out a greeting from the entry hall. Leaving her mint chocolate chip ice-cream on the coffee table, she went to meet him. "How was the snow excursion?"

"Good." He passed her two bags. "One of those is from Jerry and Bonnie. She said if we ate some of the chicken, it wouldn't blow her diet."

"Sounds reasonable." Claire waited while he unfastened his wet jacket and peeled out of it. Next came the stocking cap and his gloves. "Put that stuff in the laundry to dry. Do you want coffee to warm up? I'll make you a cup."

He headed for the kitchen and the room close by. "You're wonderful."

"I keep telling you that." She followed him. "Glad you're listening!"

One of the sacks contained the new Christmas decorations she wanted so she put it on the counter to keep Felix from kitten destruction. The other held a box of fried chicken, a container of baked beans, another of macaroni and cheese, plenty for the three of them. After she started the coffee machine brewing a cup for him, she grabbed plates from the cupboard and began dishing up the food.

Tony arrived in time to remove the mug and turn off the coffee maker. "We ran into Conn at the strip mall. The de-icer and cat litter are in the storage area near the garage. Jerry said that was the best place for them because it'd be handy to use them tomorrow."

"Works for me." Claire looked him up and down.

Despite the protection from his hat, his salt and pepper brown hair was damp, but not soaked. He'd taken off his boots and left them in the butler's pantry adjacent to the laundry. Although he'd tucked his jeans into the lace-up, combat boots, the pants were still wet from the knees to his calves.

She gestured toward the hall. "Go change and dinner will be up when you return. Is Connor coming over?"

"Not tonight. He's worked straight through from yesterday afternoon, so he was exhausted. He has Thursday off so he may join us for lunch."

Chapter Forty-One

Snow showers continued throughout most of Thursday. When the residents finished decorating the community rooms for the holidays, Connor organized them to make treats for the upcoming Christmas party including brownies, date bars and fudge before they started on various kinds of cookies. By the time, Isabella DiFalco commandeered the kitchen to make supper late that afternoon, his crew had started frosting old-fashioned sugar cookies.

Desperate for what she thought of as 'alone' time, Claire slipped away to her office. She still hadn't decided what she intended to do about her relationship with Tony, and she debated visiting or calling Blanche and asking for romantic advice. *I'm a good snow driver*, Claire thought, *but there are too many nuts on the road for me to drive out to Edmonds. She didn't answer my emails or texts so she's probably dealing with Tony's alligators and has a lot to do at the tiny home village. The weather needs to warm up soon or I'll be absolutely bonkers.*

No wonder Tony had left with Fletcher and Harry for the last dog walk of the day. If she still had knee-high winter boots, she'd have escaped too but she'd stopped buying them years ago when she moved to the big city and she hated trudging through snow in her running shoes because her feet always got sopping wet. And she definitely wasn't wearing heels or her ankle boots because neither had good traction in crappy weather. She didn't intend to break bones when, not if she took a tumble.

Seattle rarely had these kind of long-lasting snow events. However, she needed to update her wardrobe to counter the effects of climate change. Decision made, she turned on the desktop computer. She didn't feel like driving through the foot of snow and the icy streets to the brick-and-mortar stores that might not even be open, so she'd do some online shopping instead. After she ordered the boots and other winter clothing she wanted, she decided to be responsible and check business emails.

Sure enough, agents for the three potential buyers she'd shown the condo had sent emails. All of them intended to bring their offers to her when the weather cleared. She always enjoyed a bidding war for a piece of property since it meant a bigger sales commission for her. She scrolled through the rest of her inbox, deleting requests for political donations. Amazing they still showed up when the election was weeks ago.

She forwarded the ones from schools and charities to Tony. He could skim through those and decide which deserved contributions. Store advertisements were always fun to peruse so she kept those for later reference. A note from Robyn Jenkins caught Claire's attention. Her clients wanted to increase their offer on the condo.

Claire responded politely, saying she welcomed them to the upcoming negotiations. Hopefully, they'd start the following Monday when everyone returned to life as usual.

Next on the list was a message from Mike Flannagan asking for an update on what happened in Rocklin. Claire debated the best way to deal with the situation, then opted for the truth.

She told him that she, Connor, and Tony would be joining the Rocklin Board of Directors to help her paternal grandfather run the town. She didn't know what the final result would be but expected her father and stepmother would eventually leave since he'd lost his job. Claire added Fancy was staying with her because the power was erratic in the construction trailer where she'd been camping at the job site. *When he gets back to me, I'll throw his girlfriend to the wolves. I'll bet he doesn't know she kicked his younger sister to the curb.*

The office door opened, and Tony entered. Claire nodded a greeting and sent off the last email. "How was your adventure with the pups?"

"Cold, wet and we have over a foot of snow in most places, higher where it's been plowed off the streets." He walked across the room and leaned down to drop a kiss on her hair. "Dinner will be up in five minutes. Spaghetti with either marinara beef or chicken alfredo sauce or an all-veggie alternative. Isabella already sent Sofia to the apartment with a serving for Fancy. What's that about?"

"You're not the only one who knows what's up with her. Most of the women who live here had children." Claire leaned back in the chair, toying with her engagement ring. "Those who don't are aunts or friends of those who did. Because her pregnancy hasn't been confirmed, they won't mention it to Conn."

"Makes sense." He glanced at the screen. "Have you heard from your grandparents?"

"No, but I thought I'd try a video chat tonight. Want to

join me?" Claire eyed him. "You can keep them talking about the weather and we'll avoid discussing the wedding. After that, let's check in with your mom."

"Works for me. I've texted her a few times and she says they don't have as much snow as we do because the storm came from the south."

"If it doesn't warm up, conditions could change in the mountains and Rocklin will get hammered by snow. Believe me, I'm willing to share our weather. Let's go eat."

———

Visiting online with Beckett and Aggie Rocklin along with his mother before they returned to the game room to join the residents made for an enjoyable evening. Claire seemed quieter than usual, but nobody else seemed to notice, not even Connor. When they went upstairs, she said she needed privacy to wrap presents and retreated to her study. She had something else on her mind, and he'd wait for her to share it. Eventually, she would. She always had.

Tony snagged one of his imported beers and headed for the living-room where he found Fancy watching a sappy holiday movie on TV and dangling a feathered string cat toy for Felix to attack.

She glanced at him. "Is Claire coming to join us?"

"After she does her Santa thing." Tony drank some beer. "Have you talked to Conn yet?"

She shook her head, red braid bouncing against her back. "The doctor only confirmed it two weeks ago and I'm not sure what to say. We took precautions, but stuff happens. What if he doesn't believe it's his baby?"

"Could you explain the "stuff" and is it believable?"

Tony turned the bottle and eyed her. "You didn't cheat on him."

"I never would." Her attention remained on the kitten leaping and pouncing on the toy. "It doesn't mean he'll understand."

"He can't if you don't talk to him," Tony said gently.

That was good advice, he thought. Maybe he should take it and try talking to Claire. Would she share what was on her mind or continue to keep it to herself? When her grandmother, Aggie brought up the subject of the wedding invitations tonight, Claire insisted on dealing with what she referred to as the 'hoo-rah' about Christmas first.

She agreed to consider ordering "*Save the Date*" cards for the reception, claiming the community room wasn't large enough to hold more than sixty people at the wedding. However, they'd have to make a reservation at a local restaurant for the party and there wasn't any guarantee the reception could immediately follow the wedding. She'd asked Aggie to start a list of potential guests.

Nothing changed during the next two days. More snow accumulated around the neighborhood. The plows attempted to clear and sand the streets, but the pavement still had several inches of snow and ice. So did the sidewalks. They stayed home, socializing with the residents. In the apartment each night, Claire often retreated to her study to continue wrapping gifts and to organize her lists for the upcoming shopping trip.

In an hour or two, she'd join him and Fancy in the living room to watch TV. She was still thinking about something. If it'd been a business issue, he'd have heard about it by now, so it had to be personal. He grew tired of waiting but confronting her wasn't going to resolve the problem. Obviously, she wanted to work it on her own.

Whatever it was, it didn't stop her from jumping his bones when they went to bed or passionately responding if he initiated sex. On Friday morning when he was called into the cop shop for an extra shift, Connor borrowed Tony's Hummer because it had better traction than his pickup. He returned home after lunch on Saturday.

By then, it'd warmed up and snow slowly began melting. Tony helped Jerry clear the piles of snow and ice covering the storm drains so the walkways wouldn't flood around the apartment house. Claire was thrilled when a delivery driver showed up with her new boots and eagerly went off to walk dogs with Fletcher, Harry, and Sofia.

"What's going on with Claire?" Jerry scraped ice from a street grate. "She usually has a lot to say about everything. She's been real quiet for the past few days, keeping to herself in the office."

"She has something on her mind and when she's finished thinking it halfway to death, she'll share." Tony headed further down the sidewalk. "Learned a long time ago to hurry up and wait."

"Isn't that the truth?"

When he entered the apartment a few hours later, he found Claire placing more brightly wrapped packages under the tree. Felix supervised from his perch on the back of the couch. So far, he'd left the tinsel garlands around the arched doorway and the large red stockings on the mantel alone. Fancy reminded them that poinsettias were very toxic to cats and dogs, and Claire had said it was why they didn't have any of the plants in the building.

"Did you finish wrapping everything?" Tony lingered to watch her. "Or do you have more to do tonight?"

"It's done for now." She sauntered toward him. "Did you know you're standing under the mistletoe?"

"That's new." He glanced overhead and saw the seasonal plant in the middle of a tinsel ornament. "You just hung it today, didn't you?"

"I'm in a holiday mood." She smiled mischievously. "And that's not all."

He drew her into his arms and kissed her. "You've had something on your mind for days. Ready to share?"

"Getting there." She rested her head against his shoulder. "Aggie emailed a humongous list of pretty much everyone who lives in Rocklin. She wants to invite them to a wedding reception at the church there."

"What did you say?" Tony rested his chin on top of Claire's head. "I'm good with whatever you want. We can put it off until—"

"I told her I'd talk to you about it, and when we came up with a date sometime in March or April, we'd let her know."

He froze, his arms tightening around her. "What? It sounds like a commitment, Claire."

"It is." She shifted slightly, and their gazes met. "But that's not all. Your mom's right."

"What?"

"We should treat each other with more respect. So, I'm going to consult you before I make a decision that affects us, and I want you to consult me. We do it at the office. I want us to do it at home each and every time. Will you?"

He stared into her blue eyes and managed to nod. "I can do that."

"I know you can, Anthony Marco, but will you?"

"Yes, I will."

"Good." She kissed him. "Fancy's making supper. Let's go eat."

———

Fancy had created a deep-dish hamburger and potato puff casserole that included water chestnuts and frozen vegetables topping it with cheese. Green salad and garlic bread accompanied it. When Tony complimented her on the entree, she admitted it was one of Conn's favorites. "It's like stew, even better when you warm it up the next day."

"Good to know." Tony forked up another mouthful. "I'll remember that."

"All right, you two. I'm still doing the usual and taking him a plate." As usual, Claire chose the chair next to his. She added more dressing to her salad. "So, let's be sure to leave some casserole for him."

She'd used these snow days to contemplate their relationship. Tony loved her and he wasn't leaving her. He'd made that plain more than once. She was the one who'd been afraid, bringing so much of the baggage from the past with her. And why was she allowing Lee Rocklin to control her life now when she'd left his house at the age of twelve? It didn't make sense, and she wasn't stupid.

I keep saying I'm not giving up Tony. Why didn't I realize what that really meant?

He looked at her, concern rising on his rugged features and landing in the smoke-gray eyes. "What is it, sweetheart? What are you thinking?"

"About the wedding on Valentines' Day." She sat next to him and leaned close enough to kiss his beard-stubbled cheek. "And how much I love you."

He turned his head, and their lips met in a long kiss. Afterwards, he smiled at her. "Say it again."

"Like you haven't always known." But it was her turn to smile. "I love you, Tony Baldusi and you love me."

"Always have, always will. Glad you realize it." His mouth claimed hers.

THE END

Don't miss
Rainy Day Retreat
Seattle Lost Lovers #2
coming soon!